EXCEPT A SEED

DEBORAH HOFFMAN

EDITED BY
ABIGAIL TURNER

DESIGNED BY
ABIGAIL TURNER

PipStones

EXCEPT A SEED

PipStones Publishing
P.O. Box 4507
Fort Walton Beach, FL 32549

Author: Deborah Hoffman
Editor & Designer: Abigail Turner

Except A Seed - **PipStones, LLC.**
Library of Congress Catalog Number: 202393377
ISBN-13: 978-1-7328594-3-2, Paperback
ISBN-13: 978-1-7328594-4-9, Ebook

For Wordlwide Distribution.
Printed in the United States of America.

TABLE OF CONTENTS

DEDICATION

Jan,

You were wrong. It would be impossible to ever forget a character like you! You have touched and changed so many lives. Our journey together is complete. What an experience of a lifetime! Now, you live in "The Forever" and are deeply missed. Thank you for the comforting last words you spoke to me... Revelation 3:20.

DEAR READER

Enjoy The Journey!

Here are some clues for you:

When the symbol above is within the text, a time-lapse or a room change within the same general area is indicated. Often, the same people are present from the previous section.

When the symbol above is within the text, a complete scene change is indicated, and they are often titled. We refer to these titled sections as interludes.

Italicized sentences are the character's thoughts.

I

ONLY A WHISPER

The proverbial phone call came, but not in the anticipated wee hours of the morning. Oh no, the ringing came at two o'clock on a beautiful and crisp October day. The sun shining through the window had interrupted a desired, and I thought, a well-deserved sleep. I almost didn't answer the phone. I wished I hadn't! *How could I have been sleeping while she screamed?*

Past the point of my aunt sobbing out those horrifying words, I couldn't hear anything but screams, pounding, and yelling. They told me they broke the door down. The screams must have blocked out the noise. I later found they weren't Adlin's screams, they were mine.

I had missed the funeral, flowers, and all. The screams had been replaced with a small, tender whisper. Adlin saying, *"Help me, Dee Dee."*

❧

"You need some time off, and the department has approved a mandatory leave with pay. This comes with the strong recommendation that you spend some time with your aunt."

"I agree, Ben. I do need time to get my head together. I so appreciate the department and you for always providing and watching out for all of us. I won't argue with you." A little cartoon pops into my head. That is what I said, but this is what I meant to say... *"Thank you for the time to not have to quit my job, and hunt for this devil and get paid while I do it. Remember the movie,* The Hunt for Red October? *Well, this is the name I gave this devil— Red October. Oh, and I am sorry, but I will disobey the order to stay away from the case."* Thank goodness Ben didn't make me promise. I hate broken promises.

It's May now, but last October was indeed Red. I started with a list of good things— ever so pure, to think on these:

1. *My parents didn't have to grieve through this.*

2. *My Aunt Linda is still with me.* Her faith keeps her sane and gives her strength. Adlin was her namesake. Mom just rearranged the letters. *Aunt Linda is my closest link to Adlin.*

3. *I am back, and the screams have stopped.*

4. *I have paid leave.*

5. *Ben has given me time to find Red October.*

6. *I'm a policewoman, so I have access to investigate and the time to help Adlin.*

I call Linda and tell her I'm coming to visit. I think I'll spend a few days with her. Then, I'll begin my hunt for Red October.

Ben drove me to the airport. The flight was smooth. I slept. In fact, I also snoozed all the way from the airport to Aunt Linda's. Her friend, Dot, sent her driver to pick me up. *Classy.* That sweet man driving let me sleep.

Arriving at the house, I tell Linda how much I love her. Tears begin.

"Dee Dee, have the screams stopped?"

"Yes, it's just a whisper. 'Dee Dee, help me.'"

"Then, that's what we need to do... help Adlin."

My aunt is a sharp lady and a stand-up kind of person. One might call her tough.

"I've been praying, and the Lord gave me a scripture. '...when good men do nothing, evil abounds...' I know we cannot just sit here and do nothing. That monster is out there and may hurt someone else. That's why we need to help Adlin. She would not want anyone else to scream."

"I call him or her, it, whatever— Red October... Let's have dinner."

Grace is a beautiful experience, and we feel the presence of comfort come over the room. As Linda prays for Him to give us wisdom and clarity of thought, for the Lord to heal us both, I feel all the rage dissolve into resolve. *We will find the truth.*

You'd have to know my Aunt Linda and how great it is when she talks to God. It's a gift.

Dinner is so special; in fact, we lovingly call it "the last supper." We dine, with Adlin and my parents weaving through our conversations. We agree that we would not speak of Red October until tomorrow, just great times and precious memories for tonight.

Dishes? Not tonight! We stack them and spend the evening looking at myriads of photos. Tears and laughter.

Linda tucks me in. I hadn't been kissed on my forehead since I was a child, and my dad had said prayers with me. *Now I lay me down to sleep… Adlin, tomorrow's a new day.*

❧

The sunlight, once again, interrupts my sleep, but this time the screams don't start. The rage had been replaced with a small stone, like a pendant hanging on my heart. One day, I'll lay it down as an unseen marker at the feet of Adlin after we find Red October.

Coffee and breakfast. This was the first time I had tasted anything that went into my mouth in months. Not only is my Aunt Linda a great prayer, but a great cook as well. Linda believes that what the enemy means for evil, the Lord turns for good to those who love Him. She has lived through much tragedy, so I know she is qualified to believe that.

"Linda, what do you know about Adlin's case?"

"I know that the police have come up with nothing."

"Nothing?"

"Nothing."

"Was she beautiful at the service?"

"It was a closed casket. It was horrible what Red October had done. We surrounded her with her favorite blanket, the one she named Bebie when she was little. She had beautiful taste, so we picked a lovely white dress.

You know how much your dad liked to see her in white. Her feet were not damaged, so we put on those slippers you gave her the Christmas before."

"You keep saying we, but there's only us left."

"My church family and the ladies who have been my friends through everything came and helped me make decisions. The service was beautiful, and the church was packed. Many of Adlin's friends traveled here for the services. I had her brought home so you could visit. She loved you. She would've wanted to come home."

"Did you have a registry at the church?"

"I knew you would ask that. Yes! Also, I should tell you that my friends were all assigned to… should we say, work the crowd? They're great visitors, and you know that it's an art to be a talker and listen and remember what people say. They each have a journal started with conversations of everyone who was friends with Adlin. We took pictures. Lots and lots of pictures of the church inside, outside, at the cemetery, and at the reception. It was lovely. While you were away, we were putting everything together for you. I guess I've either been around you and police stuff or have watched too many detective shows."

"You *are* the good aunt!"

"I'm your only aunt! That narrows the competition. Listen, seriously and prayerfully, these women stand ready to help. You must let them. They feel the Lord has called them to help. Ones that could be there, as well as other women and their families, are ready to help. It looks like a lot of people have received Adlin's Whisper."

Tears. God refuses to let that alone feeling come back. "Do any of them have a confidant or friend involved with the police department in Oak City?"

"I don't know. Let me make a few phone calls and see. First, I think you should see all the pictures and journals. Carolyn wants to have a luncheon at her home and invite the ladies. The pastor will be invited, but neither pastor Don nor his wife, Cherie, knows anything about this, nor do other women of the church. It will appear like a bunch of old ladies trying to reach out. Invitations will be given to you to stop by certain ladies' houses, or go to coffee, or other places. That's where you'll get your "gifts." Accept the invitations but tell them you'll have to call them as to when it will be convenient. I so wish you had lived closer so you would've already known them. The 10 plus 2— hunt for Red October. Oh! How funny, that makes twelve, and then as always— Jesus. Dee Dee, these women are the ones who kept me together when you, well... you know. I don't want to go there right now. Shall I call Carolyn?"

"Yes."

"Tomorrow at 12:00, okay?"

"Yes."

I suppose the phrase, luncheon at Carolyn's house, evoked a mental image of a large house. *It will be formal and boring.*

2

THE INVITATION

Carolyn's house was nothing like that image. It was a small, three-bedroom, one-bath ranch, but wow, the backyard was quite the calling card. You could feel that truly the gift of hospitality had been manifested in this house and well-practiced. Forty-five people showed up on short notice. After being with Carolyn for five minutes, I knew why. What an honor to be invited to be with her. I thought Linda was a great cook, but she may have met her match with Carolyn.

✽

Not one of the Big 10 batted an eye. They all could be stars. I can't figure out who the 10 are. They all asked nice questions and chatted and hugged me and cried. They talked about Adlin and their memories of her. Adlin had come home more often, stayed longer than I did, and had gone to church when she visited. I wish I had, too.

As the luncheon progresses, invitations started coming. The first invitations were from Lareece and Dinah. They had been talking to Dot. Apparently, Dot wants to meet me, but she doesn't get out much.

"I'd love to, but I have to check with Aunt Linda. I'll call you."

"Hey, Kiddo. I was thinking that since you haven't been here much, you'd like to take a ride and have a look at the ranch. It's about a forty-minute ride, so we'll have to plan."

Peaches looks the part— silver and turquoise. *What a striking woman!* "What is that fragrance you're wearing?"

"Annie Oakley, of course!"

Seems appropriately perfect. "I'll give you a call, and I'll look forward to that ride out there." *The count is 4. Those were the only invitations. Where's the rest?*

It's after 3:00. Everyone cleans up. Linda says she has an errand to run. She asks Jan to drive me home. *Did I mind? No, not at all. She's number 5.*

Now, Jan, she was a book all in itself. We hop in the beamer with the top down. *The warmth of the sun and the open air are so relaxing. This ride is going to be great!*

"You know, Dee Dee, I used to be an officer myself."

Oh, that explains the tiny golden handcuffs on the chain around her neck.

"Sometimes in life, you feel you've been prepared for a purpose and a place. I feel this is my moment in time. I was gone when Adlin came home. I couldn't be there for the service. I just know there's a constant voice in my head, heart, whatever, to help. I would consider it a fulfillment of a lifetime to catch this monster."

"The name's Red October. This devil's name is Red October. Jan, I need you to help me pore over the journals and pics."

"Oh! Absolutely, but I want to do more than that. I want to catch Red October if it's the last thing I do. Can you keep a secret? Dee Dee, I am in a losing battle with my body. I have cancer, and I really need to win this one. So, when I said if it's the last thing I do, I meant it. I'm not where all the others are with God. I've seen so much, and I always wondered where He was. Evil, now that's another story. I know that exists everywhere."

Maybe the little golden chain with the handcuffs speaks. I notice that the little handcuffs have a partner, a small, golden Star of David. *How did I miss that before? I'm not going to ask the question.* I know that I like this woman. She is an enigma, a definite contrast to the other ladies. The lady driving the red roadster might just become my best ally. She already feels like a friend. I know she is a loyal soul. A plan is developing. Jan's connections to information will be of great value.

"We have to keep a very benign and harmless profile; also, an awareness of the need to protect these women."

Besides Adlin's Whisper, a new and constant tapping at the door of my conscience has begun. *There's more! I can feel it. It's a knowing, but what is it that I know?* Like Bubba, one of my street friends always says, "You don't know whatcha know until you know it, but keep your eyes open and your guard up. This piece of advice will keep ya alive." So far, that advice has proven true.

Linda meets me halfway down the sidewalk with kisses and hugs. She signals Jan to park and come in.

"Madelyn called, and she had a dream last night, something about a little green car. You know she's very prophetic. You really need to meet Madelyn. Her memory is sometimes not good. She loses things, but her mind is fine. I suppose others would blow this off, but I know that many times the Lord tells her things in dreams. The day before Adlin was extinguished, Madelyn called and asked about her. She said she had seen Adlin in a dream reading a book in the library. I had forgotten about it until she called today.

The look on Jan's face causes me to laugh. *Well, here we go with the great outdoors of the unseen hand moving.*

"I used to blow this stuff off, but over the years, many kooky things turned out to be accurate."

Jan gets a notepad out of the desk. She's apparently been a guest at the house many times.

Jan writes:

> The Dreams:
> Little Green Car—May 15
> The night before—May 14—Dream—MP
> Library—Oct 21
> Library Dream—Oct 20—MP

Standing up and turning to look me right in the eyes, Jan makes a chill go down my spine. "I keep having the feeling that there is much, much more!"

Her words are like a cold blast of water hitting me. Either she's a mind reader, or there is so much more! "Me, too."

Adlin's Whisper comes again... *"Much more."*

"Jan, we'll meet tomorrow." Linda heads out to run errands and Jan decides she's got to go.

❊

The clock ticks on, syncopating the dragging time until Linda returns. One hour, then two.

A thumping at the door. As I open it, there's Linda buried under packages and sacks. "Good grief, Linda!"

"All I could do was kick the door with my foot. I had too much in my hands to keep the umbrella up and open the door."

As Linda inches her way into the entry, the plastic bags begin to tear, and a cascade of office supplies spills onto the floor.

"Here, let me help you. Mmm, something smells good. You bought Chinese!"

"I don't know why we never put an attached garage on this house. The errand I ran was to see Benny. He repairs copy machines and always knows someone who is trading them in. I told him it was a present. I made it clear to Benny that this was a surprise, a secret. He assured me that he would "keep the lid on." Benny was a young man when your Uncle died. He has continued to be as good of a friend as he was an employee. God bless Benny. All that Special Ed stuff. As I think back then, only your Uncle and I saw how special he was, precious to God."

"I loved Benny when I was a kid. I remember him."

"Let me dry off, and then we'll eat."

The fragrance of the Szechuan and sweet and sour pork takes us back to the days when my dad would pick up Chinese on Christmas Eve. The whole family gathered to eat and sing carols afterward. He loved that movie, *A Christmas Story*, where the family ends up eating Chinese for Christmas. We would all sing "Deck the Halls" in total joy, just like the scene at the Asian restaurant! Linda and I burst out laughing. Good times. Great memories. No dishes. We stack the boxes in the fridge and wash the chopsticks. That was the rule; everyone ate with chopsticks. Memories of Adlin trying to master the rice. We both choke up. Sadness still remains— the stone pendant.

We decided that the living room is too high profile to work on the case, so the back bedroom, Allen's old room, would be appropriate. No one has gone in there in all these years other than his mom to clean. Allen, full of jokes and laughter, would love having his room used to answer Adlin's Whisper. He was always a great helper. It seems to give Aunt Linda pleasure to think of her house as "Grand Central." The tender smile on her face as she shows me the room makes me cry. Allen, Adlin, all of them. Aunt Linda says this is the first time in all these years she has shared Allen with anyone.

"Let's move this stuff around so when Benny comes, he'll be able to set up the copier. Benny remembers Allen. He'll get a kick out of being back in his room. I'm going to let him pick something out of Allen's room. Allen was his hero."

I wonder where Adlin's stuff is, and who's moving it around.

The furniture and the amount of rearranging didn't even show on Linda as we close up for the night.

"We'll make the calls about the "invitations" in the morning."

Tucked in and kissed and prayed over once again.

"Your mother would expect me to love on you. I understand your pain. She was my little sister, just like Adlin was yours."

Click! It comes to me that, in fact, she does understand. *My Mom and Adlin together.* Tears again. *Goodnight, Mom. Goodnight, Adlin.*

At what time I woke up, I don't know, but I know I heard voices in my dreams. Whispers. Several whispers... *"Dee Dee."*

Coffee and breakfast again. The comfort of home. A knock on the kitchen door. It's Jan, with notebook in hand.

"Let's hear about the dreams! Oh, listen, I took my car in for an oil change, and they loaned me a car. Can't be too careful. I parked in the back drive. This rain is something else! It would've been closer to the front, but you seemed to have blocked the sidewalk and the drive. It looks like you abandoned the car and ran. Okay, lay those dreams on me."

"The dreams, well...

> Madelyn was in the library searching for a history book. When she moved through the aisles, she ended up going in the wrong direction and got confused. As she turned the corner, she spotted Adlin at a table reading a book. Adlin took something out of the book, had a troubled look on her face, stood up, and rushed out of the library before Madelyn could catch her. The library was closing. As Madelyn hurried out the door, she saw Adlin get in her car and drive away. As Madelyn stood at the top of the steps, the air was filled with the scent of cherries. Then, she woke up.

"When she called me later, she said she could still smell that scent.

"In the dream about the small, green car...

> Madelyn said everything was gray at night, but a light was shining down on the car so she could see what color it was. She said she woke up with the distinct feeling that it had something to do with Adlin."

"Wait a minute, I'm confused. Why do you believe these dreams?"

"Dee Dee, Madelyn is not one of the 10. She knows nothing about the journals. In fact, she wasn't well at the time of the funeral, so she knows nothing about any of this, at least in the natural. She knew something about Adlin that no one could have known. In the first dream, it took her a moment to realize it was Adlin because her hair color was different with highlights. Since it was a closed casket, no one but me, the police, the coroner, the funeral director, and of course, Red October, ever saw her hair. There was no way Madelyn could have known that. That's why I give credence to the dreams.

"Adlin and I had talked about two times a week. That's how I knew she had a hair appointment at 3:00 on the day she died. Madelyn was so upset that she wasn't able to avert the tragedy. She can't understand why God didn't tell her so that she could have helped Adlin. I told her she is helping Adlin now."

For a split second, I feel a twinge of anger. *Why hadn't He told Madelyn and saved my little sister?* Linda sees that look in my eyes. I guess she must see it in Jan's, too.

"Listen, girls, we can't change the past, and for some reason, God didn't disclose everything to Madelyn. We must keep moving forward and not question the whys. The issue before us is how do we help Adlin now? We can't afford to get tangled up in things too great for us to understand. Okay?"

"Okay," we utter in unison. Jan and I stand corrected.

At least the timeline is beginning to develop. We know she had made the hair appointment for 3:00 and left the library at closing time if Madelyn's dream was accurate.

Jan writes:

> 3:00-Oct 21-Hair Appt.
> Where? What shop?
> Library before closing-Adlin Reading
> What book was she reading?
> What did she take out of the book?
> Was the history section significant?
> Is the wrong turn significant?
> Is there meaning to the wrong turn?
> What was making the cherry scent?
> Green Car?
> Night light overhead?
> What kind of car? Make or model?

Linda calls Lareece and asks her when we should come over. Lareece says she and Dinah want to take food over to Dot's for all of us to have lunch. They will call Dot and see if it will work for her. If it does, they will come by at 12:00 to be at Dot's by 12:30. Jan says she is going to get online from her house and get a list of salons and beauty shops in Adlin's area, the whole state if she has to. Out the back, she goes.

Dinah calls back and says lunch is on, and no, we don't need to bring anything. She says Dot has a little remembrance gift for us. My heart starts to pound. *It's only lunch with some older gals. Can't wait to get the gift.* I feel like a kid the night before Christmas. I keep telling myself, *there's probably nothing there.*

Twelve o'clock couldn't come fast enough, but Benny calls. He is going to pick up a unit under a maintenance contract, and he got it for one hundred dollars. He says it's miraculous. He'll be at the house by 11:00. We'd rather wait until the afternoon, but he sounds so excited. He assures Linda that no one will know.

�֍

Sure enough, he shows up at 11:00 in an appliance van, with a dolly and a quilted cover. "Here's your replacement washer!" Benny has a big, folded-up box underneath the copier with the words WASHER.

After placing the copier in Allen's room and running it to make sure that all was in working order, he pops the box together, covers it with the quilt, wheels it out the door, and back into the van.

He comes back in smiling and says, "It's all taken care of."

Linda tells him to get anything he wants from Allen's room, and lets him go in there alone.

"Anything?"

"Anything."

After about fifteen minutes, Benny reappears with a smile on his face. We could tell he had been crying.

"A baseball? An old baseball? That's what you want?"

"Yep. Allen was the only person that ever played ball with me. I know he would want me to have this. I sure miss him."

Now, we are crying.

"I have always known how special you are. I am proud of you. This just confirms how important you are and why God sent you to our family so long ago."

"Yep! Jesus is really something. He knows how to make something out of nothing. Look at me. Love changes everything. If you need anything, Miss Linda, let me know. When you are ready to move this to Miss Kay's, I'll be there. I'll always love you!"

With a big bear hug, Benny disappears down the driveway to the appliance van, tosses that old ball up, and catches it all the way. A toot of the horn, and he's gone.

More tears.

3

GIFTS

Dinah shows up in the nick of time so Linda doesn't travel down the wrong road of memories today. Lareece is tucked snuggly in the back seat, with hot-covered casseroles in the middle and a large, glass salad bowl perched on her legs. "Dee Dee, ride in the front with Dinah so you know the way next time. Linda and I will guard lunch back here."

The thirty-minute drive flies by. The gals are like carbon copies of Linda. Linda and I decide not to share the dreams at this point. We all stay focused on their journals and photos. The conversation is bubbly and full of laughter (whatsoever is good). The light-hearted drive does not set the stage for the luncheon at Dot's.

As we move up the drive, I can feel my heart pounding again. Wow! Dot's! Dot's house is the exact image I had in my head of Carolyn's. They tell me the house had been in the family for over 130 years. What a house it is! The making of a movie house. *Was Christmas coming?*

❃

Dot had household help, Margaret and Louis, whom she lovingly referred to as her family. She had given them the afternoon off, so we got our own place settings and napkins. Dot turns out to be sweeter than sweet and really down-home. She is the perfect lady of the house.

Dot's prayer over our lunch was magnificent. The beauty of her humble words to God causes me to tear up... and then that stone pendant shows up again. At the exact moment she asks God to join us and bring His light to the situation, rays of sun shoot between the clouds and stream through the large arched window directly behind her. She's illuminated. We all are. It's breathtaking. *Is this a sign?* It is so reverent. Dot simply whispers, "Help us, Lord, in your Son's name."

The feeling of awe remains throughout lunch, with no one wanting to ruin it by talking too much. Lunch is almost silent. It is as though He set the format for this meeting. I knew it was "Christmas."

Dinah and Lareece had actually wrapped all the journals and pictures to present to me— gifts for me and for Adlin.

They had made a copy for me and for themselves and the others. I'm informed that Dot had always been the one everyone went to for sense and information. She had been a reporter, and that's how she met her husband. As she put it, "The only man in the world." They had owned a newspaper. Dot thought perhaps they still had connections to get information. She was still a major stockholder in a syndicated news system— TV, paper, and radio. As she referred to it, "No garbage, just good reporting."

"I made some observations in what the other gals documented. Well, you'll see, I'm sure. Let's go into my office. Dee Dee, Peaches made sure we all had cameras with zoom. She's our tech girl. She took us all through a quickie lesson in photography. I think you'll be shocked at how well all the girls did."

Dot's office is a definite police department's dream. A long conference table dominated the center of the room. We all choose a seat. Dot scoots to the head of the table. Linda and I remove the wrapping and trimmings from our gifts. Everyone else has their folders. Dot says the pictures had been loaded into the "little" viewing system. She and Matthew, her one and only, had it designed for the office.

Hard photos were stacked in order in front of the viewer. Only Dinah and Lareece's materials were being reviewed. We begin narrowing the field. There were shots of the areas all around the church— a full panorama on video with the timer running. Lareece had driven there days before and filmed the area. Then, each lady was assigned an area to record with film or still shots. Dot had made a complete list of all 134 attendees.

"Let's run Dinah and Lareece's films. Dinah's first."

The church, trees, flowers, the ride, and the entrance to the west end. Nothing too significant. Guests beginning to arrive. Peaches and Carolyn positioned at the corner of the church greeting those who parked in the west lot, and directing them to the front entrance. The rear entrance had deliberately been blocked off to siphon everyone toward the front and the registry.

Adlin certainly had friends whose tastes in clothes were equal to hers. It was touching to see the number of people who had flown in to say goodbye. Friends hugging and talking, then quietly moving up the front steps to the church. Peaches disappearing around the back of the church. Carolyn walking with what appears to be the last mourner (who then gets a phone call) and motions Carolyn to go into the building. The woman continues to hold the phone to her ear, but the zoom from the video camera indicates that she is not speaking past the hello.

I begin writing on a 5x4 card. Approximately 130 pounds, beautifully dressed in a soft gray and black suit with very expensive black alligator shoes and clutch. A slightly overstated black hat with a gray band and draping brim. Hard to see her hair, blonde or streaked, perhaps. A very significant-looking bracelet with tiny pearls around it and a pearl necklace. Impossible to see her eyes behind the sunglasses as she talks to Carolyn.

"Carolyn, what color are her eyes?"

"Dee Dee, you'll find a complete description under number eighty in my gift. They were green, but I think she had contacts. She was the last person I saw before I went into the church. As you noticed, she had sunglasses on, but I found her in the church, and I made a point of speaking with her after the glasses were off."

Opening my gift from Carolyn, I find a small notebook labeled:

"In Loving Memory, From Carolyn."

A little poem, a recipe that she had given Adlin after a luncheon at her house, pictures of Adlin when she had visited Linda, thank you cards from Adlin, and the journal entries. All the names of the guests she had greeted. *How in the world did they remember all those names?* Come to find out, they were wired with a recorder in their jacket pockets when they greeted everyone. *Duh!* We all laugh.

Carolyn thoroughly enjoys telling me, "Tapes are in the little gift box tied to the bow."

Silly me, why hadn't I thought of that? It pleases them that they were more clever than me, the "Lady in Blue," the police officer.

"Another thing... everyone else Peaches and I greeted gave us their names and spoke about Adlin. You know how people feel the need to share their history. Pretty much they gave us a connection of church, work, college friends, or otherwise. Not this one. She simply said how grieved she was at the loss of someone so young. It didn't seem like she really knew Adlin. I could hardly get my eyes off that bracelet. You know how I like jewelry. It was no cheap bauble! It looked antique to me." Carolyn was emphatic about the importance of this person.

Peaches labeled her gift:

"Lasting Impressions, For Adlin."

Pictures of Adlin at the ranch. *I didn't even know Adlin could ride.* Sadness over how much I had missed out on. Adlin always bugged me to come and meet her at Aunt Linda's. It always seemed too hard to travel home; my selfishness and the hoarding of old feelings wouldn't let me. How I wish I were in the pictures with Adlin at the ranch.

Tucked inside the journal was a present that Adlin had made Peaches. A flat, silver chain with a turquoise bead and a little feather attached stretched the length of the page. One tiny pearl was attached to the other end of the chain. Peaches explains, "Adlin had found it on the seat of her car. No one claimed it, so she used it for this bookmarker."

Peaches included some still shots of the back of the church. I look up and see the tiredness on Dot's face. Almost four hours had passed. "Time to go."

"But I hadn't even shown you what my observations were." Dot reverts to reporter mode.

"Dot, I'm exhausted. If it won't offend you, can we get together later?"

"Offend me! Of course not, darling. I'll share with you later, but remember, you've only got five weeks of that paid leave left. So get rested, and then let's get moving. I know you'll need time to solve this."

✼

The drive back is quiet. The tape must be playing in everyone's mind. The experience of grace, the light, the illumination, the loving efforts of those who are acquainted with Him and with sorrow. The unselfish generosity of these women leaves me reflecting on my lack of true empathy.

Linda closes the reverent silence. "Thanks so much for today. Only Jesus knows how grateful I am to have His friends as mine. Lord, we bless you today. Bless Dinah, Lareece, and Dot with your loving favor. Protect each one of them and all the others. We thank you for Dee Dee, and we thank you for the opportunity to help Adlin by finding the truth."

Must be wonderful to flow in whatever it is they all flow in. Life beyond themselves seems so natural for them.

Linda closes with, "In His name, Amen."

"Dinah and Lareece, I thought Linda and Carolyn were great cooks, but now there's you two. Maybe we should have the Big 10 Cook-Off!" They all giggle.

"Well, you might not want Peaches or Jan included in that! Dot doesn't cook anymore, but she did have her day. So it would be the Big 7 Cook-Off!" Lareece raises her eyebrow.

Does a close relationship with God enhance a witty sense of humor?

✼

As Linda and I walk into the house, the phone rings. It's Jan.

"I've got the salon list ready for our trip. Can I come over?"

"Trip?"

Linda smiles.

About ten minutes later, a soggy mess drips through the door. It's Jan. "I walked. I was looking for a green car or anything interesting. Who knew it would start raining again? Good I wore a hoodie."

"You look like you're about twelve."

"Great, that was the idea! But anyway, I didn't see anything out there."

"Get in there and put on a robe and some socks. I'm making some coffee. We have work to do. When you've changed, take a look at Allen's room. Tell us how you like it."

"I've never been in there."

"Well, it's a new day, and there's always a first for everything."

❋

Jan is quite impressed with the boards and the copier with fax capability. "Kay is going to love this when she gets it." They can barely contain their sneaky chuckles.

The coffee and the remaining slices of Mr. Berry's pound cake were exactly what we needed to loosen up and get motivated.

Jan keeps going over the still shots that Peaches had taken. We keep trying to get her to focus on the Lady in Gray that Lareece had filmed and was in Carolyn's notes. Jan pins all the pictures of the back of the church and the alley up. While we yack, she intently studies them. The shot of the alley going east seems to, as she puts it, speak to her.

"Give me one of those magnifiers. There it is! Dee Dee, stick this photo in the copier and blow it up so we can really get a look."

The large bushes on the eastern side of the church almost blocked it out. A tiny bit of a car was visible. A small, green car! The bushes precluded us from identifying a make or model, but it was a green car. *Just a coincidence? Maybe?*

Jan says, "Do you think we could get Madelyn to dream about a dealership so we know what kind it is?" Laughter. "Tomorrow, I'm going to drive over there and see if there is any street parking on that side. I can't remember if there is. I also have a friend in Parking and Ticketing. It's worth a stab to see if any tickets were issued there. Listen, if it's okay, we'll cover more of this in the morning. I'm half blind from searching phone lists for salons and beauty shops. I promise I'll listen to you both about Carolyn's journal and her film tomorrow. We still have other invitations, which will take up another day. Time's ticking... Where am I sleeping?"

"I made out the bed in the den while the coffee was brewing."

After Jan had been properly hugged, Linda does our nightly ritual—prayer, hugs, and a kiss to the forehead.

"I've been thinking about Julia all day. Your mom never got to know these ladies. She would've loved them all. You remind me so much of her. Since Julia was gone, you were my point of contact with her. It's so wonderful to have you here. It's like being with my little sister again. Thanks for coming. Sleep tight. Sweet dreams."

How can I tell you that what you prayed for is actually happening? I feel old wounds closing. Adlin, goodnight. I know you're smiling far away from the horror of Red October. Today was "Christmas." Gifts from the heart. Whatsoever is pure, whatsoever is... Now I lay me...

The Odd Couple

"Now, what are we going to do? I didn't find anything out of order there. All those people were so nice, and it was a lovely service. She must have been a wonderful person. What were we thinking going there? It made me feel that all over again. You know that's the first time we've been in church since—"

"Please don't start. I've cried for the last time. I feel like we've been abandoned. No one cares to hear our story. It's like they're deaf. I know He hasn't left us, but sometimes it feels like He's also turned a deaf ear. Do you keep wondering if that family is looking, too? Do they feel like we do?"

"I don't even see how the girl is connected. Why do you keep poring over the clippings of her death? It's been months."

"I don't know, but I feel like God is reaching out. I think this was special. It all means something. I almost panicked when that woman looked me right in the eyes. I felt so exposed. Do you think she knows anything? I spoke to her outside the church."

"Yes, she knows. She knows you're beautiful." He chuckles.

Claps of thunder bolt me from my sleep! *Goodness, it's raining again. What time is it? 5:00?* The smell of coffee. Somewhere in the house, I hear voices.

Jan and Linda are sitting in the den, curled up, talking. *I think they were discussing me.* "What about me?"

"We were wondering if you're ready to make a trip."

"What trip?"

"The trip to Oak City."

A cold numbness floats over my body— *the hunt for Red October*. I'm paralyzed, and the sweetness of the last two days disappears. The rage starts to come.

Linda announces, "See, I told you she's not ready. Dee Dee, stop it, darling. It's okay. You'll be ready when this is all gone."

Linda hugs me, and the clean, sweet smell of her skin brings me back. She smells like mom used to.

Jan offers to get coffee. "Do you want anything in it?" Her voice has a raspy tenderness.

"No, just black. Wait, a little sugar never hurts." They laugh.

"See, she's getting there."

"Actually, I think I'm going to lie down for a couple of hours and skip the coffee until later. Thanks for being here. If you want to look at the pictures and journals, just put down some good notes for me."

❋

I haven't been taken care of in a long, long time. This all seems so outside of the life I've created. I am really trying to be nice. While I was gone, they were all working, preparing, and praying. How can I be laughing and walking around with this "Christmas" feeling?...

> *Am I asleep? I don't remember falling asleep. I'm in the library. I'm with Madelyn. I can't see her, but I know it's Madelyn to my left. I start towards the history section but turn the wrong way, exactly like Madelyn did. Madelyn is saying, "Can you see her?" I can see Adlin. What is she reading? Adlin! Panic! I've got to wake up. I'm shaking. Too Close! Too Close! Wake up! Dee Dee! Wake up!*

Linda's voice is coming from a millennium away. "Dee Dee, wake up!"

"I'm okay. Thanks for waking me. I was suffocating. Everything was too close." The shaking was Jan trying to wake me up. *I can't start screaming again.*

"I came in to make sure you were okay. Good thing Jan and I both came. I was ready to call 911. You frightened me and kept yelling, 'Wake up! Wake up!' Who were you yelling at?"

"I don't know. I guess, myself. I was panicked. Madelyn was there. Adlin was there. We were in the library. I knew exactly what the library looked like. I've got to see Madelyn. Linda, call her."

"Dee Dee, it's only 6:30. She doesn't get up until 8:30 or 9. She won't even hear the phone."

"Okay! Okay! Let me get my head clear. I need to lay here a minute. My heart is pounding." *This doesn't feel like Christmas. I feel sick. I was there with Adlin, and all I wanted to do was wake up. How could I have panicked like that?*

I try to close my eyes and go back to the library, but sleep doesn't come. *If I had just walked over and looked to see what Adlin was reading... If I had spoken to her, done something.*

The shower has become a refuge. The pounding of the water overrides the throbbing of my heart. The panic. The fear. The shame and guilt of screaming to wake up. *Linda is praying. I know she is. All things are made new. Whatsoever is pure... Whatsoever is... I can do this, but this isn't only for Adlin. It's for me.* I am grateful for the water. I start to cry. Way beyond crying, mourning, moaning, deep waves of grief washing down the drain, running off me. Almost like someone else is grieving for me. If there wasn't a drain, I'd be drowned. Crumpled at the bottom of the shower, I hear Adlin's Whisper, *"Help me, Dee Dee."*

I get up and out of the shower. *I... we... can do this.*

"Where's that coffee, and unless I'm not alone, where's that sugar?" Linda hugs me, and then there's Mom again.

Jan has her back turned, looking out into the backyard. "Dee Dee, I think we should not go on that trip. We've all tried to stay focused on finding truth and Adlin so much, that in trying to help, we are pushing you to a dangerous place. You are as important as Adlin, and I'd like to keep you in-tact. Life is so short. We can all keep going to lunch and hire others to do this for us." Her voice is a raspy quiver.

"Jan, I have to go there if it's the last thing I do! I'd like to do this with you and the others. I need to talk to Madelyn first. I'll be okay, and anyway, Linda's praying.

"Linda, it's 8:45. Please call Madelyn."

"Madelyn, oh good, you're up... I waited to call... You've been up since 5:00? That's not like you... Oh, the thunder woke you up, and you've been up since then?... Yes, Dee Dee is here. You want her to come over?... Okay, what time?... We'll have to get dressed and drive over. Jan is here. Is it okay for all of us to come?... All right, let me ask.

"Breakfast at Madelyn's?"

"Yes!"

"Jan?"

"Count me in."

"We'll be over in about an hour. Call it brunch... Okay, I'll stop and get some. See you then. Love you... Bye.

"Well, I guess you heard. It's like Madelyn has been expecting the call. Let's get moving. I've got to stop and get some milk for her. Jan, you won't have time to go home, but I dried your clothes last night. Or get in my closet and find something in short. Everything I have will be too long."

"I only need a top, and I'll wear the short jeans I came in. Thanks!" Laughter.

I just realized how short Jan is. Some people live bigger and taller than their size. "Thank goodness you guys are not primpers. I'm starving. Is appetite a good sign?" They all grin and nod. Linda briefs me with the news that Madelyn will want to have a lovely breakfast and a tour of her home.

"Don't start asking her questions about dreams. She'll get around to that."

"Okay, mom!" Jan pulls the hoodie over her head, and we dash to the car, umbrellas, and all.

"Oh, my gosh! I forgot to turn the coffee pot off." Linda sprints back to the house with the keys in her hand.

Tic, tic, tic.

"Oh, you two. I left you out here with only one umbrella in this drizzle. I'm sorry. When I went in, Peaches was calling. If the rain stops, she wants you to take a ride to the ranch. We'll call her when we get back."

❋

I follow Linda's lead and don't bring up the dreams. The tour of the house and a wonderful trip through its history and Madelyn's life was first. Actually, she's right. The history of a person tells you a lot about who they are. She's a gem. A lovely breakfast. Great conversation. Bringing up all "the news." As spry and spunky as she is, she still doesn't like to go out much. Loves company, though.

"Linda, why don't you show Jan some of my photograph albums and magazines? I want to visit with Dee Dee."

The "Christmas" pounding starts again.

We go into the soft, pink living room and sit on the brocade couch at the opposite end of the room from the baby grand, right under the solid, silver chandelier. Madelyn snugs herself onto the couch.

"Dee Dee, something happened. Tell me what. I couldn't sleep. I knew the Lord was showing you something. What is it?"

I tell her of the dream, the library, the panic, all of it, even the part about the shower.

"Dee Dee, He was revealing to you how weak you are. The word says His power is made great in weakness. You can't do this without Him. He loves you. All of this, even the horrible, is being woven into His plan for your life. Remember, you weren't alone in the library. I was with you. I was only there in your dream to tell you... you are not alone. He always sends someone.

"I have been so sad and so guilty that He didn't let me save Adlin, but there is so much more. I had to turn those feelings over to Him. Do you need to let go of something so you can see the truth and find this evil person?"

"I call him Red October."

"That gives me chills."

"Me, too."

"When I called Linda about the little car, I didn't mention the pearl that was in my first dream. Does a small pearl mean anything to you? I had forgotten that as I was hurrying to catch Adlin in my dream, one of the people at the counter picked something up off the floor. It was a tiny pearl. I thought maybe it was 'The Pearl of Great Price.'"

"Oh, Madelyn, I think it is significant, but I can't explain why. You really are something. I promise I'll be back to see you soon. If you get anything else, write it down. Thanks for dreaming well, Madelyn."

Madelyn is beaming. "Can I pray for you?"

"Yes."

Madelyn begins to pray. "Lord, I ask that you keep Dee Dee in all her ways. May she think on whatsoever is pure, and whatsoever is good."

Goosebumps spring up all over my body. *Those words. Was God telling me something?*

"Keep Dee Dee's mind stayed on you so you can keep her in perfect peace."

Perfect Peace? "Oh, Madelyn, how can I thank you?"

As I hug her, she whispers, "You just have. Dee Dee, please come back to visit. I so enjoyed Adlin, and she has a very good older sister. I know you'll be able to help her."

Tingles again. Tingles. "Let's go. Madelyn has made my day. Thanks, Madelyn. I love you."

✽

"Linda, Jan, please don't ask me any questions. I need to think." Linda and Jan don't say a word; we ride in silence.

The rain has stopped; the heavens aren't weeping. *Looks like I'll be enjoying an afternoon at the ranch.*

4

THE RANCH

"Peaches, how did you get your name?"

"My maiden name is Patricia Chess, P. Chess. You know, kids in school. I guess it just stuck. Certainly, more distinct than Patty. Maybe a little exotic sounding. That has caused teasing in itself, but I liked it. Too bad I didn't marry someone named Cream. I could've been Peaches and Cream." We laugh.

"Were, or are you married?"

"Yes and no. Danny was killed in a car wreck about eight years ago. He was a wonderful person but was a heavy drinker. He was out with his buddies, and on the way home, he rolled down an embankment. That's when Jesus found me and loved me back out of despair. Fortunately, Danny was a good businessman, so financially I was okay. He had purchased the ranch to retire on but didn't get to retire. I sold everything, bought a smaller house in town, and kept Danny's special place. It's called Cream Creek Ranch. I got Peaches and Cream, after all. It's an inside joke with God and me. Most people never knew, so let's keep it secret. I live as Patricia M. Marko, but I'm really Peaches and Cream."

Well, looky-looky, here we are. Cream Creek Ranch. What a beautiful drive. I can see why Adlin kept asking me to visit Aunt Linda's and meet Peaches. It looks like we had arrived at The Ponderosa. I expected Hoss and Little Joe or Adam to come riding up. My dad loved Bonanza, re-runs, and all.

"Do you like to ride?"

"I don't know. I've never been on a horse, except once at a carnival, where you go in a circle."

"Well, we'll fix that. If you take a test drive and like it, we'll take a longer ride, weather permitting."

"Did you bring my gift?"

"Let's go in and take a look at it. I'm itching to know if the pictures or anything in there will be helpful."

A slender, gray-haired guy comes from the house and greets Peaches. "Joe, this is Dee Dee. Dee Dee, meet Joe. He's my best man." Joe laughs, and Peaches asks him to saddle up a couple of horses in about an hour. "Make Dee Dee's a gentle one. She's not used to riding."

"Okay, Peachie. Nice to meet you, Miss Dee Dee. Welcome to Cream Creek. I'll bring Lucy and Sky around in about an hour."

I wonder and ask if they have Diamonds, too. Peaches and Joe both laugh.

❉

Peaches pours us each a glass of tea. She hands me one and moves through the back door to the porch. "We better enjoy the break in the rain. Do you mind sitting outside here on the porch?"

Mind? It's heavenly to be outside. I haven't been outside since the luncheon at Carolyn's, unless one calls dashing to cars and the house in the rain an outdoor experience. "Bring me up to date. First of all, that was some gift you ladies gave me." I tell her about seeing Larcece and Dinah's films and point out that the "gray lady" appeared to be waiting for someone. "Your shots of the alley were really something. Dot told me you showed everyone how to use the cameras. How do you know so much about photography?"

"Do you want me to languish in suspense or what? Never mind how or why I take good pictures. Tell me what was in the shots I took."

"Well, at the end of the alley, you caught the tail-end of a car on the street." Peaches looks puzzled. "Oh, you don't know about the dreams. Do you?"

"Let me guess, Madelyn's been dreaming?"

"Yep! And may I say, she is a great dreamer."

I tell her about the dreams and my meeting with Madelyn. Well, not the part about the shower and the drain, but the library, Adlin, the cherry scent, the car, and the pearl.

"Hold it! Back up. Tell me about the part with the cherry scent. Why cherries?"

"I don't know yet."

"Show me the shot of the car. I have a full set. Let's go inside."

We string the photos out on the big butcher block in the kitchen.

"There it is."

"Why didn't I have my lens on zoom?"

"Doesn't matter. We blew it up on the copier. Do you know Jan?"

"Only by reputation and from the luncheon at Carolyn's the other day. Why?"

"I think you would be good friends."

"I know if Linda loves her, so would I."

Right then, Joe strolls in. "Ready to ride?"

"Let's go." Peaches had told me to wear jeans, and I was ready. She gives me a soft jacket and ties a couple of rain ponchos on her saddle.

Joe helps me up and says, "Lucy wouldn't hurt a fly." I ask if she would hurt people. He's tickled, and his eyes crinkle. He chuckles, "Touché."

Off we go. It was relaxing riding with Peaches. She talked and talked about Adlin. It was so comforting picturing Adlin smiling and riding Lucy.

Peaches says with a softness, "Adlin always rode Lucy."

Adlin, why didn't I meet you here at least once?

Peaches explains about her gift. It was a bookmark that Adlin had made her. *Peaches wore Western jewelry, so Adlin used the silver chain, a feather, and a pearl—*

"Oh, my gosh! The pearl! Adlin had found the pearl in her car and had no idea where it came from but thought it a nice touch, 'The Pearl of Great

Price.' Dee Dee! Madelyn's dream! Where did the pearl come from, and who did it belong to?"

Drops begin to fall— little May showers. Peaches tosses me a poncho. Perfect for our ride. The horses seem to not mind the rain.

"We'll have to take the long way home. Following the creek bed will be easier on the horses. The canyon's shorter, but way too slick if this rain lasts. The ride takes about thirty more minutes."

I'm not sure I'm cut out for this ranch life. The rain drowns out the conversation. We ride in silence. I keep patting Lucy. There's something ethereal about the fact that Adlin used to ride where I am now. *Does Lucy know that I'm part of Adlin? Thank goodness for the soft jacket that Peaches gave me.* Lucy and the jacket are keeping me warm. The poncho keeps repelling the rain from drenching me. The last little bit of day has flickered out of sight.

Peaches lets me know it's okay. "Lucy and Sky can see fine."

A tiny light is somewhere out in front, gleaming like the beacon from a lighthouse. Peaches points and gives Sky a nudge. Lucy follows the lead and begins to run. The storm engulfs us, and my heart is pounding as an unsettled feeling comes over me. *Where are we going?*

The cold savagery of the storm is suffocating me. I'm struggling to breathe. Jagged rips of lightning pierce the dark rain. I can feel Lucy's muscles quiver. I turn my head down and to the right to catch my breath. The frequency of the wicked strikes increase until I can see the rugged terrain.

On the rise to the right, standing on a large boulder, is a tall figure. I can see the reflective blasts of light off the figure's hooded slicker. Thinking it might be Joe, I yell out his name. *Who else would be out here in this storm?* The figure extends his hand out towards me. I catch a quick glimmer of something silver. A heavy burst of rain hits my face, and when I open my eyes, the figure has vanished into the darkness. I can feel the charge still in the air zinging around me. I'm paralyzed.

Lucy snorts and turns her head to look at me. I must have tightened the reins. She is almost at a stop. *Am I asleep? Wake up!* I know the water is rising and beginning to churn. Lucy whinnies. Sky is coming back. Peaches grabs my reins.

"Let's go!" She pries my hands off the reins and loops them over the saddle horn. We're moving again. I close my eyes.

Peaches is dragging me off of Lucy. A blinding light from somewhere is shining in my eyes. A flashlight. Warmth. A blanket coming toward me.

Peaches apologizing. "Baby, I'm so sorry. What is wrong?"

"I don't know. When it got darker, and the rain was pounding..." I stop mid-sentence. Two other faces are looking at me.

"This is Clayton. Clayton Barons and his wife, Pam. Clayton, Pam, this is Dee Dee; at least what's left of her."

"Dee Dee, the famous Dee Dee. Welcome to our home. We, unlike Peaches, try not to drown our company." Laughter.

"Dee Dee, I'm so sorry. What in the world, girl? I wouldn't have started out if I had—"

"Stop apologizing. I'm fine. Something came over me. The worst feeling, like something awful was happening."

Clayton starts praying. Pam and Peaches are too. "... in His name."

I feel that peace coming. Pam and Peaches look relieved. Clayton is putting on a poncho and heading out the door.

"I'm putting your horses up for the night. Jenny's spending the night in town with a friend. You gals are spending the night with us. Pam, call Joe and tell him they are okay."

Pam dials and hands Peaches the phone. "Yes, we're fine. It got a little worse than I expected. The water from the creek was running over the trail. I let the horses have their heads, and they got us here... Call Linda and tell her we're fine... Oh, she's already called?... Okay, I'll tell Dee Dee... Tell Linda I'll take good care of her baby."

Pam tells me she has been wanting to invite me over. *The count is 8.*

"I'm sorry, I couldn't come to Carolyn's for lunch. Jenny had a play at school. It's the end of the year, and you know how crazy things are before summer break.

"I've got dinner ready so when Clay gets in we'll eat. Peaches loves Mexican food, and there isn't a decent restaurant that knows anything about enchiladas or green chilis in this part of the world. Hope you like it, Dee Dee."

It turns out that Pam had grown up in New Mexico, and the flavor of her food and their home is tastefully Southwestern. Clayton is, as Pam refers to him, a "reformed town kid." Their home isn't *The Ponderosa,* but is absolutely charming. Clayton is also a great host and makes me feel comfortable. He's like a western version of my dad.

Clayton looks me deliberately in the eyes. "You know, Dee Dee, all these women seem to think that guys are dense, but I know you are all up to something. If I can help, please let me know. I'm so sorry about Adlin. She was a great person. We so enjoyed her visits. Peaches used to have Jenny come over when Adlin was visiting. Jenny was devastated. Adlin was her most admired person. She'll be mad that you came, and she wasn't there. She thought of Adlin as an older sister. Jenny's a tailender, and her brothers have been out on their own for a while. I think Royce was in college when we met Adlin, and Jacob was already married. We're older than dirt and still have one in high school.

"I'm going to slip off to bed so you girls can keep doing whatever it is you've been cooking up. Remember, I don't need to know everything, but if I can help "cook," let me know."

"Thanks for everything and especially the prayer. Goodnight, Clay."

"Pam, make sure Dee Dee gets that gift." Pam and Peaches don't make a sound. "Night, love. See you in the morning."

Pam is shaking her head. Both ladies suggest that we open the gift after Clay leaves the house in the morning.

❀

Sleeping in the loft was like being lifted higher, free suspended. I'm floating. I'm away from everyone and everything...

"Adlin, you're being so quiet." Adlin smiling. Adlin reading on a park bench. It's spring. I can smell the grass.

I'm jolted back to reality by the phone. I see Pam pacing back and forth across the living room downstairs. I can't see her face, but I can feel the tension as I peer over the rail. I put on my jeans. Something is wrong, and Pam is agitated.

I hear Pam speaking, "What was she doing out there?... I'll be right in to get her."

"Jenny? Is she all right?"

"She fell. Those crazy girls slipped out of the house and went climbing. They don't know if her leg is broken. At least they were smart enough to take a cellphone. I've got to go. Clay has already left for the horse show. You and Peaches make yourselves at home. Eat whatever. The house will be empty, so open your gift if you want to. I'll be back, but it will be a while. I'll make coffee before I go."

Pam rushes around dressing and leaves the coffee on for us.

"Pam, thanks for everything. We'll pray for Jenny." I think I said that as a courtesy, not because it's a reality for me.

Pam's on a dead run to the car. At least it's not raining. The quiet is almost surreal— peace in the house. Peaches is still sleeping. I'm convicted of the shallowness of my promise about prayer. It shocks me at how much I've been sucking up the prayers of others. Time to give back and mean it. "Heal precious Jenny. Let nothing harm her. Work your wonders, Lord. Give comfort and blessings to everyone who's been praying for me. Forgive me for being so selfish. Teach me to live a life of beauty as I see in these people. You are so real in their lives. I want to..." Peaches is up. "Talk to you later, God." I open my eyes.

"You've been praying." Peaches is glowing. She shuts her eyes. "Lord, whatever Dee Dee was praying, I say, me too."

You can't get anything past these people.

5

OAK CITY

The calls from Miss Summers's aunt in Meadow Brook were like clockwork. The last few days, though, had been silent. *Did she give up on me? What's going on? Great, one more person to worry about.*

"Tanner, Lieutenant Tanner. Calling, Lieutenant Tanner. Where are you?"

I didn't realize I had been engrossed in thought, watching the replay in my head. Libby was trying to make dinner conversation, and I didn't even hear her. She's intensely looking at me with that pursed expression on her lips. That tiny line has etched itself above her left eyebrow, the one that shows up when Lib is concerned. *She's beautiful.*

"I'm here!" No apology. No, I'm sorry. I just sit here drifting with her looking at me.

"Is there someone else, Tanner?"

"No." No explanation. Again, no apology.

"You won't even look me in the eye. You've been so distant lately. I can't stand it. You barely even speak. I don't know what's going through your head. I'm going home. I drove, so you'll have to walk. Call me if you ever feel like telling me the truth. I can feel you're thinking about someone else." Libby gracefully lays her napkin down, rises, slings her wrap over one shoulder, and walks away. About ten steps away from the table, she returns. "Don't forget to tip the waiter."

She's always impeccable, and she knows I always forget... tipping, that is. I'm left with the waiter looking at me. I'm embarrassed. "Check, please!" At least one person is smiling.

"Sir, that is very generous. Thank you so much. Can I call a cab for you?"

"Nope." *For that kind of tip, he should drive me home.* The huge tip is an apology for the look in Libby's eyes.

❧

The evening is cool, and the air feels good. It's good to be outside in the dark. I'm such a jerk. I couldn't bring myself to tell her about Adlin. How do you tell someone like Libby that another woman doesn't exist anymore, that I can't stop seeing the memory of that pulverized young woman? Telling Libby that stuff seems like it would defile our relationship. The stench of evil. Looking for a devil. I start to feel rage at that monster, but mostly at myself for not seeing well enough to figure it out and catch the evil.

Winston, my old friend and mentor's words keep hounding me. "Look for the holes. Find the holes. Once you find the holes, you can find what's missing. You can begin to fill in the puzzle."

Winston, the problem here is that the whole thing is one big hole: no evidence, no motive, no witness, no nothing. I feel like nothing. I so want to help this young woman by finding the killer. The term killer doesn't even fit this one. I'm at a loss for a word for this kind of evil.

The thought of a restless night doesn't hold much appeal. I turn right and head to my office. *At least there will be other officers up, and the lights never go off.*

I check in for messages, and to my surprise, my phone rings. The man on the line identifies himself as Ben Garcia.

"I'm interested in the Adlin Summers case, Officer Tanner. Would you send me copies of what you have in the case file?"

He sounds legit, but one never knows, so I ask if I can call him back. I tell him I'm working on something else right now.

I get his information, check him out, and call him back after poring over the files, photos, and my personal notebook.

"Chief Garcia, this is DJ Tanner... Okay, Ben. Why are you interested in this case? You're halfway across the country from here. Is there a similar case back there?"

"May I call you DJ?"

"No, call me, Tanner."

"Look, DJ, I mean, Tanner, this involves one of my officers."

"A dirty cop?"

"No, but rather a desire to help. Do you have anything? Leads? Anything?"

"No. It's a hole. There isn't even one shred of anything. No prints. No fibers. None of that CSI stuff. Just one of the worst visuals, ever. I'll fax you some pictures while we're talking. Wait until you see them. This is the evilest thing I've ever encountered."

"Umm, I'm looking at the pictures now. It must have been horrifying. Dear God, is this what you walked in on?"

"Yes, the pictures don't even do the gore justice. The topper was that the monster took the time to clean up the blood spatters off the fan and the lights. The place was so tidy, we couldn't find anything. There were fresh flowers in a vase on the table and soft music playing when we arrived. What kind of an evil sicko are we dealing with? He spent hours in there cleaning up. He vacuumed, took the bag out, and even cleaned the vacuum. Her fingernails were cleaned underneath. Nothing in her mouth, or what was left of it. You wouldn't know if there had been a struggle. All the rags or whatever used to clean up must have been bagged and carried out, too. Cleaning products were gone as well.

"I'll send the files sealed if you promise not to share them with your staff or other officers. On second thought, if you want more, you need to come and see them in person. Her townhouse is empty. I mean... empty! He cleaned out the fridge and the freezer, and all the other garbage was gone, too. The only thing we found was one crummy sticky note on the fridge that read, 'It's not nice to fool others.' The reason I want you to come out is that I don't trust anyone at this point. There were officers who began to throw up. It was beyond shocking."

"It will take me a couple of days to get it together here. I'll be back to you. Do you have a cellphone?"

I surrender my private cell number to him. I don't know why, but I feel he is like Winston. I need a Winston to talk to. "I'll be waiting to hear from you. I need to make sure we don't end up with everyone here looking over our shoulders.

"Thanks. Maybe I can help fill in the holes."

I knew it! Ben is like Winston! Holes! Thank God! Someone with some instinct. Everyone else around here, other than Travis, thinks I'm losing it talking about evil and the devil.

The mile walk home seems to have cleared my head, and the key slips right into the latch. I hesitate to open the door. I don't think I'll ever get over walking into "that room." The poor girl who found Adlin Summers is still not okay. That monster left the door slightly open so someone could walk in. *Oh, my God! Were they watching to see or hear the reaction from whoever found her? Oh, God! Libby! I let her go home alone... Emily is there, though. What a jerk I am. So self-absorbed.* Frantically, I dial Libby. She doesn't answer. I call Emily, her roommate. Actually, she's Libby's younger sister.

"Emily, is everything okay over there?... Good. I'm sorry Libby's not up. I'll call back tomorrow. Lock your door. You both have the cellphones I bought you by your beds, right? Remember, punch the key number, and they will all ring to mine. Emily, don't be stupid, be careful... Okay... I'll be in touch in the morning. I'm glad Libby isn't there alone. I'm glad you're there. Goodnight, beautiful! Tell Libby I'm sorry." *That does it! Tomorrow, I'll be hiring someone to watch the girls. I wonder if Travis... Well, I'll talk to him about it tomorrow.*

❦

"Emily, what did Tanner want?"

"He was being his usual officer self, making sure we're being careful. He said he would call tomorrow. Lib, I don't think your feelings about someone else are right. Tanner's a good guy. Dumb emotionally sometimes and not exactly Don Juan, but he's a good guy. Something else is going on. Stop crying and believe in him a little."

"I'm glad you're here."

"Thanks! That's what Tanner said... Nice to see you laugh. I've done Tanner's drill— doors, phones, and all. I have to tell you this drill has made me a little nervous. How about if you sleep in my room with me tonight? It'll be like when we were kids before we had to grow up."

"I'm in. I'm nervous, too. Tanner, with his 'Be careful,' is making me look at everything with a suspicious eye. Are you sure you locked both latches?" Laughter.

❧

"Peaches, let's open my gift from Pam." I'm almost trembling as I open the journal. Pictures of Adlin and Jenny together. Joe, Peaches, Pam, and Clay. Adlin smiling. *God bless all of you.* There's a note Adlin had written to Clay. A pressed wildflower with a little-braided string. Another note saying Adlin had taken Jenny to town with her. While they were at the park, they braided string and pressed the wildflowers. Jenny was in eighth grade. Here's a picture of Adlin reading at the park. Jenny took it. Tingles... *My dream. Adlin smiling and reading. These people are rubbing off on me.* "I dreamed this last night."

Peaches is sobbing. "I dreamed about Danny last night. I haven't dreamed about him in all these years. I guess Madelyn's rubbing off on me, too. I was so mad at him, but I don't know why. He kept repeating, 'Don't be mad. You'll see. It wasn't like that.'"

"What? What does that mean?"

Peaches is really crying. Her head in her hands. "I don't know. He was so real. I could feel his presence when I woke up."

"Peaches, we're all together in this."

"I know, I know."

I hug Peaches and kiss her on the forehead. *Good Lord. How could I do that?* I guess she looked like a little girl at the moment.

"Dee Dee! Danny used to do that every night. I was his "baby." How come you did that?"

"I don't know; it seemed like the natural thing to do at the moment."

"It was. Thanks. God always knows, doesn't He?"

Kind of weird to think that God was using Dee Dee Summers, selfish me, to show His tender care to someone else.

Peaches clutches the journal tightly to her chest. "Let's see what Pam has to say. Focus, Dee Dee."

Pam was as meticulous with her writing as she was with cooking and decorating. A collection of many segments about each person she met as she greeted the arriving guests at the service. Number three stands out.

Pam had written:

3. The old guy with the limp, named Leon, said he had met Adlin at the library. He also said he had read about her death and what a tragedy it was. He said he had relatives in the area, so he came to the funeral. He was hard to understand because he mumbled. I helped him up the steps. The whole thing seemed odd.

4. The man who called himself James seemed to be slightly impatient about getting into the church. Perhaps he was anxious to get in, but then why did he hesitate at the bottom of the steps? He glanced slightly to his left and then went up. He didn't make any comment about Adlin, either. He mumbled it was tragic. He was going in when a white car came down the street and slammed on its brakes. I couldn't see what had happened because of those big bushes along the south side. Hope I didn't screw up and miss something by being distracted.

Love, Pam.

P.S. I hope this helps you.

Pam, how could you think you missed anything? She hasn't called. I wonder if Jenny is okay. Wow! I actually have concern for someone else. "Peaches, do you have a cellphone number for Pam?"

"It's on the fridge. You should know by now how organized she is. Call her."

Maybe I'm not quite as unself-focused as I think. I hadn't even filled Peaches in about Jenny. As I look for the number, I give Peaches a full rundown about Jenny's accident.

"Pam, is Jenny okay?... Listen, you're terrific, and tell Jenny thanks for the pictures of Adlin and the flower and the string... How long is she going to be in the hospital?... Do we need to call someone, or is there anything we can do for you?... You have really outdone yourself with the journal. Take care of Jenny and call us when you know more... No. I don't think we'll be here when Clay gets back... We've got to see the films Lareece took. We'll fill you in tonight... I love you, too. Thanks...

"Peaches, Pam wants to talk to you."

Peaches begins to pray on the phone, and I bow my head. *Maybe someday someone will hand me the phone, and the other person will want me to pray.* These women are heart-to-heart as Peaches prays for Jenny, Pam's child.

"Do you need to be with Pam, 'cause it's okay if you do?"

"No, Pam's mom is headed to the hospital with her, and so is her sister. Clay is also on his way. He's leaving his horses at the show, so I'm going to call Joe to come and get us with the trailer. He'll take Sky and Lucy back to the ranch.

"Joe, would you bring the horse trailer?... Put a hustle on it; if you're doing something else, drop it and get here ASAP, please...

"Dee Dee, Joe will be here in less than an hour. Get moving. He's going to have to fetch the truck and horse trailer to take care of all the horses."

We straighten up the beds, turn the coffee pot off, and pack up the gift. After checking the doors, we head to get Sky and Lucy from the barn. "We'll bridle them and lay the saddles on them until Joe gets here. No sense in saddling up."

The horses are delighted to be out of the barn, and I'm sure, to see that it's not raining. Lucy nudges me as I'm leading her and runs her head under my arm with a gentle nuzzle. *I guess she's forgiven me for last night. I can see why little girls are drawn to horses. They are so comforting, strong, and very wise.* I pat her nose and tell her thanks for carrying me to safety and for carrying my little sister so many times. Lucy nods her head up and down. *I wish I could package Lucy up and take her everywhere with me. Maybe I could become a Mounty and ride Lucy. I think I'm becoming addicted like Adlin was — a big Lucy fan.*

Peaches kisses Sky's neck and softly says, "You're my guy." He nuzzles Peaches's neck.

"I'm surprised they didn't kiss you on the forehead." As we're laughing, both Sky and Lucy lift their heads and do a horsey chortle. *It's gonna be a great day. Here comes Peaches's best man.* I wonder if she really ever notices Joe. He's kind and handsome.

"Hi, Miss Dee Dee. I heard you had quite a ride last night.

"Peachie, thanks for calling me. I was getting ready to saddle Ruby and head out. I knew you'd follow the creek. I was worried. That storm was something."

No diamonds, just Lucy, Sky, and Ruby.

"Let's get movin'. I've got a bunch of things to do.

"Joe, table whatever you're doing today. Jenny's been hurt. She's okay, but they're keeping her in the hospital. She took quite a fall. Her leg might be broken, and her ankles and shins are really bruised up. They're keeping her because she also has a concussion. Clay needs you to take his truck to get the trailer. Someone else is showing his horses today. He's heading to the hospital."

"Peachie, not Jenny. She's my Little Partner. If anything ever happened... well, you know."

"Joe, she's going to be fine."

Peaches kisses Joe on the cheek and gives him a hug. "You're such a tender heart. You're my best man, as always."

I have the impression that Joe would've liked to kiss "Peachie," but not on the cheek. The hug Joe gave her slightly resembled an embrace. "Peachie" didn't seem to notice, though, but I did. I pat Joe on the back, and he winks at me. *Mind reader.* He knew what I was thinking. *Hello, Peaches. Open your eyes. Maybe I should rephrase that to, open your heart.*

✤

Joe deposits all of us at the ranch and heads out to the horse show.

"Call me and let me know how my Little Partner is."

"Okay, Joe. She'll be fine. God's going to take care of her. You be safe, and I'll call you when we know more. Thanks. I know Clay and Pam really appreciate it. We'll go to see Jenny and have dinner tonight in town."

I hear Joe whistle as he drives off. It's a good sign. *Dinner together. In town.*

We hit the door of the ranch house on the run. "I'll call Linda. Do whatever you need to do and take something nice for your dinner with Joe. You can change at Linda's later. I'm going to shower and change at home." *Home. How funny that sounds. Home is where the heart is. Am I finding my heart? I was beginning to wonder if I had one. Probably the only person that knows I have one is Ben. Dear Lord, Ben! I must call him! He's probably worried. Maybe he's even mad that I haven't called. Don't let that dark thought in. Not today, Dee Dee. Whatsoever is pure. Whatsoever is...* I realize I'm humming.

Peaches emerges, looking like she's been to the salon. She is a striking woman. I imagine Danny is smiling. *Peaches M. Marko. Peaches and Cream.* I notice she has a tote bag and something in a hanging clothes bag. And what? A pair of heels? Looks like it will be dinner somewhere nice. She flashes a smile.

"Let's go. Tell Lucy goodbye and Sky too."

One more pat out in the yard, and we're flying down the road.

"Call Linda and tell her we're going to Dot's, if Dot is free to meet."

"Linda, we're okay. I'll tell you everything when we get there. Please call Dot and see if she's free and up for watching Lareece's film. Ask her to invite Dinah and Lareece, too, if it's okay. It's going to be a great day. I'm almost ready to take a trip... Yep. Call Jan, too... Really? She's already called? What's up?... Okay, we'll be there in about thirty minutes, but I have to shower and change. Don't set it too close. Tell her I'll make a phone call when I get there...Maybe around lunch. We could pick up something for lunch. Be there soon.

"Peaches, Linda is setting it up. Looks like you're going to get to meet Jan, reputation, and all. Peaches, did Joe know Danny?"

"Yes, Joe was the best man at our wedding, and he still is. When Danny died, Joe came to live at the ranch. He was Danny's best friend but wasn't in the crowd of drinking buddies. Joe's the one who introduced me to Jesus. He's a very good man."

"Yes, he is, and very good-looking, too." Peaches nods. She seems to be deep in thought, so I ride the rest of the way to Linda's, keeping my thoughts to myself.

"I'm going to sit here for a while. Go ahead and get ready."

Her head is turned to the window. *Is she crying?*

❊

"Where's Peaches?"

"She'll be coming in a minute. I think she's making a phone call or something. Did you call Dot?"

Dee Dee places a phone call. "Hi, Jan... Yeah... Peaches is excited to meet you. She's heard a lot about you." Laughter.

I step into the shower. *The water is pounding again, but this time, it's like April showers, refreshing and invigorating. It's a new day. Happy times.* I realize I'm humming again.

Find something soft to wear. I look in the closet. Linda mentioned that Adlin had left clothes in there. *There it is, that beautiful lavender top that she had on in a picture.* I pull it over my head. I can smell Adlin. *Help is on its way, Adlin.*

"Oh, Dee Dee, you look so beautiful, and your hair is so pretty pulled back like that. It's as though Julia walked in. Peaches and Jan are chatting away in the den. I think they're going to be very good friends. Dot said she's got Margaret fixing some lunch, and then she has Louis and Margaret running errands all afternoon so we can have some privacy. Dinah and Lareece will be with us, too. Are you girls ready for lunch and a movie?" We all laugh.

6

ADLIN'S PROJECT

No stopping and no visiting during the drive to Dot's. Peaches and Jan talk quietly in the back. Linda keeps the music on. I find myself humming yet again.

Louis greets us at the door and escorts us to the dining room, where Margaret has laid out a real spread. "Miss Dot will be in shortly. Please have a seat."

Margaret begins to pour lemonade or tea, whichever we prefer. "I hope you ladies enjoy lunch. The others will be joining us soon."

I hear Dot's sweet, little chuckle. She appears arm in arm with Carolyn and Lareece.

"Dinah couldn't come today, but we have an additional guest. Claire is going to join us. She has a "gift" for you, and I thought this would be a great time for her to meet you."

A tiny blonde-haired lady, about fifty, steps into the room. She has a beautiful package grasped in both hands.

"Claire, this is our Dee Dee."

"Oh, Dee Dee, how lovely to meet you. I've been gone for the last few days. I wanted to have you over, but He knows how to work things out. Bryce, my husband, has been on vacation, so we have been off enjoying the family. I feel guilty that all of you have been working lunches." They all laugh.

"Claire, it's so nice to meet you. I'll open it after lunch."

❃

Dot stands at the head of the table and says grace, but no heavenly sunbeams this time, just great company, laughter, and some tears. Peaches is filling everyone in about Jenny. When the last spoonful of crème brule disappears, Dot taps the side of her water glass and calls the meeting to order.

"Ladies, adjourn to the office, and let's get busy." The big conference table was lined once again with pads and pens. "Lareece, you're on. Let's see what you've got."

The video that Lareece had taken begins to run. It's a film like a flip-flop of Dinah's. Lareece had filmed from the front of the church with a view of the East parking lot. Friends are arriving. Pam and a lady I didn't know, greeting and inviting guests. Zooms of faces or friends. Groups chatting.

What a good job the women are doing, maneuvering people toward the front in a manner to be able to get good shots of each individual. The old man with the limp and a cane, Pam helping him part way up the steps. Dot explains that the lady with Pam is Gloria. Gloria is writing, shaking hands, and patting people. The film shows the distinguished, well-dressed man, pausing, and glancing to the left, and going upstairs. Gloria is moving toward the church, looking behind her at the parking lot. She walks into the church, slightly behind the "gray lady" whom Dinah had also filmed.

Pam is starting up the steps and turns as a white car slams on its brakes, careens to the right, and turns down the other street. *It was the same as Pam's journal entry.* The video runs for another couple of minutes. It's 2:00 on the video time log. The service is beginning.

My cellphone rings. "It's Ben! Lord, I forgot to call him...

"Yes, I'm okay. I'm having lunch with some of Aunt Linda's friends. We're watching some videos of the service... Yes, I'm really okay." *Maybe more so than any other time in my life.* "I don't know what you mean... I don't know if that's a good idea. I... Okay! Okay! I'll call you when I get back to Aunt Linda's. Ben, I'm sorry I haven't called... Good, I knew you'd understand. Thanks for being you, and for being there for me. I'll call ya back later."

The ladies are dead silent. "Ben Garcia, my boss, wants to come here and make sure I'm okay. He has something he wants to tell me." *I think he wants to be sure I'm not working the case.*

"Let's pray. Dearest Lord, the timing of this call seems so odd, but it seems like it's right on cue. There are no coincidences, and so we join together, believing that you have everything under your watchful care. We thank you that Mr. Garcia has a watchful heart over Dee Dee. Show Dee Dee if he is supposed to come here. Give us all your insight. We ask for your wisdom, which surpasses our understanding. We commit all of this to you, and may you protect over all of us and Mr. Garcia. In the name of Jesus— the way, the truth, and the life. Amen."

The room stays quiet for another couple of minutes. Claire is smiling as she slides her gift towards me. Inside the wrapping is a small journal with the registry from the church service.

Claire's journal cover reads:

"Given to Dee Dee as a token of faith of the one who brings truth, who is the truth. Love, Claire."

Claire had been in charge of the registry. She had made sure that everyone signed in. She had a recording. Her tape was tucked inside the envelope with the gift. Dot pops the tape into the player.

"The entries all seemed pretty normal, except the old man, Leon Dolan. Look at his signature. Bold and firm, not at all that of an old person. Seemed to be in a hurry to get in. Slightly disgruntled about having to sign the register. He mumbled.

"The "gray lady" is Alicia Parsons. She was the last to sign and seated herself on the left.

"James, the well-dressed gentleman, was next to last. Seems nice, but I could feel deep sadness surrounding him. He paused at the door to the sanctuary before going in and held his eyes closed for a moment. He seated himself on the right.

"I felt like they knew each other. I took my chair and sat by the door after I closed it. The other doors had been closed to siphon everyone through the left side. From where I sat, I could see a quick glance they made towards each other. It was a quick flicker but a confirmation of my feelings.

"Others making their way to the front, passing by the casket. Linda greeting them with Pastor Don by her side. The old man with the cane is at the front. He has his jacket over his arm. He leans over the casket for a minute. It looks like he whispers something. Linda and Pastor Don are at the other end. He seems to take a long time up there.

"The door opens, and I'm distracted. I see Lareece and Dinah coming in, and they sit down."

"Where's Leon, the old guy?... He's sitting up front, about five rows up. He has his jacket back on. That seems odd to me.

"Dee Dee, from that point on, I guess I wasn't a very good observer. The service was so touching, and I was crying. Adlin was so precious. How could this have happened to someone so special?

"As the pallbearers went out, I noticed that a couple of flowers were hanging down, so I followed them out, and tucked them back up as best I could. People were filing out. I really couldn't track much after that.

"The police escort was lining up the vehicles. Linda had arranged for us to be in limos, so I got in. I couldn't see anything past that point. I hope this helps Adlin and you. We might appear to be a bunch of "silly" women, but we needed to help Linda, you, Adlin, and ourselves. May God help us all to find the truth. Yours in Christ, Claire." The recording ended.

"Claire, thank you so much. Your gift was wonderful."

Dot brings us all back. "Get your pens out, and let's take notes. Dee Dee, the floor is yours. Fill us in. I was going to share my observations, but that will come later."

"First of all, in the words of Tiny Tim, 'May God bless us one and all.'" Everyone laughs. "No, seriously, may the tender care you gave Adlin and the loving gifts that you have given me be returned to you all many times over. I would like Jan to give you a run-down of her notes." Jan looks surprised but pulls out her little notebook and starts.

"Though I am not as close to God as all of you, through my friendship with Linda, I have learned to not discount the unseen component." Everyone smiles and nods. "I want to back up to the beginning, Madelyn's dreams. If you don't know about the dreams, you will. Ask questions later. October 20, Madelyn has a dream. October 21, she calls Linda."

Jan reads a full description of the first dream. The library, the history aisle, the wrong turn, Adlin reading something in the book, Adlin's puzzled expression, the cherry scent, Adlin's hair— the whole dream. The morning of October 21, Adlin's call to Linda, filling her in about the hair appointment and that she'd send a picture if it turned out well. "This is significant! It brings an element to Madelyn's dream that convinced me that it was more than a random dream. She couldn't have known about Adlin's hair."

The women have surprised looks. None of them ever knew about any of this. Linda didn't allow them to see the body. *Something about the wrong turn in the library, but I can't put my finger on it. What does history have to do with it? I can't get a hold of that either.*

"Madelyn's second dream with the green car..." Jan gives a visual of what Madelyn told us about the car and the light shining on it. Pens are flying. Everyone is writing. Jan backs up to the pearl.

Claire gasped, "Oh, I forgot to put that in my journal. The lady in the gray suit had the most beautiful pearl and silver bracelet on." I make an insert in Claire's registry by Alicia Parson's name. "I'm sorry, Jan, please continue." Claire looks like a schoolgirl who is about to be reprimanded.

"It's okay, that's an important observation. Anyone else on the pearl?"

Peaches pops in, "Adlin found a pearl in her car. It's attached to the bookmarker. Dee Dee has it. It was in her gift." More writing. They're all writing.

"Anyone else?" Jan moves back to the green car. "The green car in the second dream... we have a picture of that. Peaches took that shot behind the church. The tail end of a green car is at the end of the alley. This ties to, I believe, the white car, which distracted Pam. It would've been coming towards the green car."

Carolyn pipes up, "What kind of car?"

"We don't know. I asked if Madelyn could dream about a dealership so we would know what it was. No results so far." Laughter.

The world of women. Laughing, crying, praying. Sometimes, all at the same time. I used to want to be a boy, but I'm starting to think that girls are pretty special. Jan is beaming. Jan looks like she's five-foot-eight. She's in her element. I feel a twinge. Unless God rats her out, no one in this room knows how important this is to Jan. As she weaves on through the information, I see how pleased the women are to see the pieces coming together— the Big 10 Conference. Dot is intensely looking at Jan. *Wonder what she's thinking? Where is Gloria, and who's number 10?*

Jan tells the ladies that each one will have their own complete file but that she feels it's not good to have them everywhere. "Pick a house where two or three of you can meet without bringing attention to the gathering. Maybe I'm paranoid, but you can't be too careful. We have access to copies and faxes at Linda's. Can you decide which houses and groups by tomorrow?" Every head nods in agreement.

Dot interjects. "Initially, as you know, I'm usually the spearhead over projects, but I feel the Lord has been touching my heart that Jan needs to put this all together for us. She is the one that God has chosen to drive this one, not me. Not this time. I see His tender hand over Jan. All those in favor of Jan being our girl of the day, head of the Adlin Project, say aye and raise your hand." It was unanimous.

"Jan, do you accept this assignment?" Jan is crying and nodding yes.

"Carolyn, will you lead us in prayer for God to anoint Jan to do His will?" Dot moves towards Jan and all the others stand up. They gather by Jan. Gentle hands reaching and touching her.

Carolyn prays, "Oh, Lord, Father, Giver of Wisdom..."

I am motionless. It's like watching a movie. I have never seen anything like this. Eyes closed. Lips moving. The room is heavy. A magnificent presence. I haven't ever felt anything like this before. I can't move. I feel like I'm being pushed to my knees. I surrender to whatever, whoever is in this room.

"Amen." As Carolyn finishes, everyone is silent, still bowed, and lips moving. I can't even describe the look on Jan's face.

I hear her soft, raspy voice say, "Wowww!" Laughter. Every hand goes up, and the women begin to sing and worship. *Adlin, you never told me about any of this. No wonder you always sounded so great after a trip to Aunt Linda's.* Hugs and kisses, Dot gently speaking to Jan and hugging her. *I wonder what she's saying.* Dot embraces Jan as she lays her head on Dot's shoulder in the curve of her neck. Dot, patting Jan. A final kiss to the forehead. *I wonder what a kiss to the forehead means to God.*

Jan gives instructions to the women. "Pick a house. Get together. We'll have complete files for you. One last thing. Lareece? Your filming was superb. You haven't said anything all day." Carolyn is leaning towards Lareece, repeating face-to-face. Lareece is smiling, beaming. Jan didn't know, and for that matter, neither did I, that Lareece was born almost completely deaf.

Dot tells Jan, "Nothing could have been done back then, and too much time has passed. Hearing aids don't help."

Jan walks over to Lareece and signs, "Great job. I love you. Thanks."

Lareece signs back, "You're welcome. I like your jewelry." She gently touches Jan's Star of David and the miniature golden handcuffs.

The whole group is touched. There's always more to Jan than that which you can see. *I wonder how many more surprises this short, stocky person contains. Aah, now it makes sense why Dinah and Lareece always travel in a pair.*

❦

On the way home, Linda explains that what we experienced was called the anointing and the presence of God. Peaches and Linda seemed like it was normal, but truthfully, Jan and I feel slightly overwhelmed by the responsibility. I could see it in her eyes when I turned towards the back seat. "Are you okay, Jan?"

"Yes, just a tad humbled by it all. How about you?"

"Ditto."

Peaches and Linda smile, that knowing smile I keep seeing. "It was really something, Jan, for Dot to do this. She walks with God in authority. I could see her looking at you, and I knew something was up. By the way, Dot said to tell you she will fund whatever it is you need. She feels that it will be her contribution to Adlin's Project. She's going to open a card for you tomorrow. If you need a car, pick one out. She thought your little sports car was a bit too high profile."

As they pull into the drive, Jan's speechless. No joking this time. She doesn't want to come in. "Got to get home. I'll call you this evening. I need to put a plan together."

She starts to back out and hollers, "Dee Dee, call your boss!"

I don't want to. He has an uncanny knack for smelling news.

7

HELP IS ON ITS WAY

I'm relieved he doesn't answer. I'm in luck; I hear a cheerful message. While I'm heading to Allen's room, my luck disappears. Ben is dialing in.

"Dee Dee, did you have a nice time with your aunt and your friends? I'm coming to check up on you. I need to share something with you. I'm going to be on vacation and will be traveling right through there. I'll be there day after tomorrow." I try to squeeze out of it. "I'm not taking no for an answer. Ask your aunt Linda if that will work for her." Linda nods yes, and Peaches offers her house too.

"Okay, let me know if I can pick you up... Oh, you'll have your own car?... Okay, but do you know when you're coming here?... Ben, thanks. I'll look forward to seeing you... You, too."

Good grief, that man is a bulldog. An endearing bulldog, but a bulldog nonetheless. "He's going to be here day after tomorrow. Thanks. Great news! Now, all that stuff in Allen's room, the women, everything. He'll know. I'm telling you he'll know."

"Maybe that's not so bad; maybe he needs to know." Peaches explains that it gives her peace to know that he is coming.

Linda nods in agreement. "We'll play it by ear and rely on Jan's plan."

"Peaches, you've got a date. You haven't even talked to Pam or Clay."

"No, but Carolyn has. She told me what was going on. I guess Joe couldn't stand it and had to talk to Clay at the hospital. Joe's coming here at 6:00 to pick me up."

Great, it's 5:00 now. Peaches heads off to put on her heels.

"Gloria called; she left a message for you. Dee Dee, come listen."

"I'm sorry. I couldn't have lunch today, but I have a small gift for you. I was wondering if I could stop by about 8:00. Hope that's not too late. Carolyn told me about Jenny, so I wanted to go to the hospital first. Pastor Don and Cherie are picking me up and we're having prayer with the family. You and Linda are welcome to join us. Please give me a call. We're leaving at 6:00."

I should feel strange calling someone I've never met. Linda dials the phone and hands it to me. Gloria picks up on the first ring. I hear a voice that sounds like something out of *Gone with the Wind,* saying, "Hellooo."

"Hi, this is Dee Dee."

"Dee Dee darling."

Man, Gone with the Wind. I am so entranced with the voice I don't know if what I said made sense.

"I am pleased you had time to return my call so promptly. I do apologize for my absence today. You know that I am the church secretary?"

Actually, I didn't know that, but Gloria keeps on speaking, so the question requires no answer.

"Well, anyway, I was with the pastor, and you know that he isn't informed over some of the issues at hand. I felt I should not leave. You understand, don't you?"

"Yes. That's perfectly okay. I do understand. I think 8:00 would be fine, and give the Barons' family our blessing." *I can't believe I said that. This all is rubbing off on me.* "See you at 8:00. I look forward to meeting you."

Linda is smiling. "We're on!"

"Linda, are we going to give Gloria the full load when she gets here?"

"I don't know. I think we should have Jan come over. Call her and see if she can come back."

Peaches emerges from the bedroom looking like a dream. The dress is soft and flowing. Tiny beads of turquoise dangle on the edge of the skirt, and the top draping down is banded at the waist with a silver chain belt and matching turquoise concho. Against her olive-colored skin, the white and turquoise outfit is stunning. Beautiful silver bracelets and those shoes, pale gray leather matching the gray shawl over her arm, finish the effect. She is beautiful.

"Do I look okay?"

"Goodness, couldn't you tell by Linda's and my mouth dropping open? Stunning! Stunning! Oh, you look more than okay." They all laugh.

The doorbell rings. Peaches's face turns slightly pink. "It's probably Joe."

"Indeed it is, *and* a very good-looking and tailored Joe."

"Hi, Miss Linda. Is Peachie ready?"

"Well, I think so."

Joe takes off his silver-bellied cowboy hat and steps in, hat in hand. The look on his face when Peaches comes into the room is worth a million words.

"Well, you look really fine this evening, Peachie. Peachie keen!" We all laugh.

"You do too, Joe." Peaches is blushing pink again. "You do indeed."

Joe takes her arm, and out the door, they go. I noticed he drove a Lexus instead of the truck. *Nice touch, Joseph. Nice touch. Thank goodness it isn't raining.* I find myself humming again (*This is the night with the heavenly light...*). The scent of Joe's cologne is mingled with Peaches's. *Annie Oakley. Lovely, lovely.*

"Jan's coming over at 7:00. She thinks we need to include Gloria in working on duplicating the stuff for the others. I had told her how efficient Gloria was, and one thing led to another. Are you hungry?"

"No, but I bet Jan will be. She told me she never cooks."

"I'll see what we can get together. Follow me."

Linda, always the caretaker, begins to fix the salad, pops open a frozen container on the counter in the kitchen, and hands me a knife. "Chop these green onions, would you?"

A sudden knock at the back door jumps us both out of our skin. A kind of bumping sound.

"Who is it?"

"It's me," says a raspy voice from the other side of the door. "Let me in."

Jan has arrived. There she is, struggling to get her shoelace out of the chain. "I about killed myself. I don't remember the last time I rode a bicycle."

One more surprise from Jan. We free the dangling shoe from the chain. This explains the bumping against the back of the house. The shoelace was destroyed in the process.

"Run water over the container and then dump the soup in that big glass bowl." A big frozen chunk of something slides into the bowl. Put the microwave on defrost. I'm headed to straighten up in Allen's room. Jan, would you work on the salad?"

Jan looks at me expectantly. "Having soup, are we?"

Staring at the chunk, I slide the bowl into the microwave and set it on Soup. After dicing tomatoes, Jan begins to construct the salad, which looks like an advertisement. "Thought you weren't a cook, Jan."

"Oh, it's something I learned from an old friend. Presentation is everything." Laughter.

"I'm impressed. Any other surprises?"

"Peaches said she was going to dinner. Have they already left?... Too bad! I wanted to see her. You know, that's the second time I've met her. She is a neat, neat person. I would like to know her better. What did you think about today at Dot's?"

"Well, I think they made a great choice, or did you mean all the other stuff?"

"Listen, I'm pretty new at all this, but these people are not flakes. At first, it all kind of shocked me, but now I'm going with the flow. I feel better than I have in years."

"Better inside? In your head?"

"Yes, in my head and my heart."

"Me too, but the pain still goes on."

"Dee Dee, the secret war is raging. You haven't told anyone, have you?"

"No." I wonder if God has, but I don't say it.

"We have to get moving. We must hunt. We have to finish Adlin's Project."

I don't get to answer. My phone is ringing. "Ben, it's only been a couple of hours since we talked... You're coming tomorrow instead?... What happened?... Okay, I'll tell Linda. Do you want me to make reservations?... Okay."

Jan's got one eyebrow raised. "What's going on? I don't—"

"He had to change his plans and wants to come tomorrow."

"Looks like it's going to be a short night."

"I'll get Linda."

The microwave dings and Jan pushes the green mush around with a spoon. "Linda will let us know what to do with that."

"Perfect!" Linda takes the mush and beats it with a whisk and pours the mush into a pan on the stove. The salad comes out of the fridge. "Okay if we eat here in the kitchen?"

The green mush turns out to be a lovely cream of broccoli soup, and the whole dinner is casual. It feels good to slump in a chair in the kitchen. This is what I am used to. Up to this point, everything had been pretty formal— meeting people, luncheons as a guest. *Home. This feels like home.*

Jan beams. "Don't you love it here. This reminds me of an old friend's house, other than there's no notes or clutter on the counters."

Jan is a woman after my own heart. *Do you have a home, or simply a place you live, Jan?* I don't ask the question. We inform Linda that Ben is coming tomorrow.

"Where are we going to put him? Maybe in the den. At least we'll ask him to stay here. Maybe he won't want to." Linda is on the phone asking Dot if she can borrow Margaret and Louis for tomorrow. "... Great, I need them to get this place in shape for our dinner... Thanks, Dot... I'll see them about 8:30."

"Get the place in shape? You could have lunch in the bathtub and never get a germ." Jan and I giggle.

Linda looks baffled at us. "I'll clean up the dishes while you girls get busy putting files together. I've got to make some lists, food, and all, you know."

We sit in Allen's room, surrounded by the boards, photos, and all the other stuff. Jan's been busy the last few days. She was making copies of the lists of beauty shops she had found. She wanted each woman to have part of the list to call and see if we could find the one Adlin had visited that last day. Nine lists plus two. Eleven lists. She presses the copier. Eleven. She had completely typed out Madelyn's dreams word for word and her conversations with Linda.

She tosses me a copy to read and make corrections. I am amazed at how detailed she is. She includes the part about the pearl and where it went in the sequence of Madelyn's calls and our visit with her.

It's perfect.

"Dee Dee, grab these file folders and a marker. Label one for each lady. Peaches, Carolyn, Dinah, Lareece, Pam and Gloria. I'm number 7. Oh, we have Claire and Dot, too, but who's the other one? Number 10."

"Linda, who's number 10?"

"Marty, of course."

"Who?"

"She and Oliver work at the church. They have a janitorial business, but they clean the church as a service to the congregation and God. They have really struggled financially. I can't wait to see her journals, but I don't read Russian. Her real name is Martina. I hadn't heard from her recently, but she already told me she'd write it all down. You know she has a hard time writing in English, so they will tell you her story."

"From Russia, With Love." Jan has the same humor as I do. Laughter.

The phone rings again. Pam updates us on Jenny. The news is that she has no concussion and no brain injury. Her ankle is broken, but they've finished casting, and no pins are necessary. She has a hairline fracture in one finger. *She's okay.* Miraculous, considering falling down about twenty feet of rock. Pam tells us all to read Psalms 91. The pastor and Cherie are there with Gloria, and that's the scripture Gloria got for Jenny. They're keeping Jenny under observation for two days. They hadn't seen Joe or Peaches yet, but they were so grateful for help with the horses. They figure they got tied up somewhere. *I hope they're dancing cheek to cheek.* I'm humming again. Dad used to do that. A tune for every occasion. That's what he used to say. I can see Dad and Mom dancing.

Another hour passes, but no Gloria! Jan and I continue to work on the folders, numbering photos, and narrowing the field of players. "The old guy, Leon, is a prime area of question. Don't forget the "gray lady," Alicia Parsons, and the other man, James. We don't want to take any wrong turns. Remember, it all starts in the library. Who's linked to the library? The old man told Gloria that he met Adlin in the library and that they were history buffs. Adlin must have really made an impression for him to travel almost nine hundred miles for this service. Could there be another reason—"

The doorbell rings and stops Jan mid-sentence. We hear that "Scarlet" voice. *Gloria must be here.* Her beautiful drawl seems quite agitated. A sweet-faced woman who looks more like Miss Melanie than Scarlet moves in and fills the room with her presence.

"Quick! Oh, you must be Dee Dee. Hello. Jan, how are you? Quick, open my gift. Open it! Open it!" She shoves a lovely package my way. Gloria tells us that she thought she would never get here. "The pastor and his wife wanted to randomly visit a few patients. It was lovely. I had to try and stay calm, though. Then, they wanted to go for ice cream. It was a real job of acting. If I told them I wasn't feeling well, they would nurture, so I told them the truth; that I was supposed to meet you, Dee Dee. The truth, not necessarily the whole truth, is the best route. They bought it. They thought it was a wonderful gesture on my part, and they could see the gift I had with me. I told them I had gotten the gift for you and the one for Jenny mixed up at the hospital, so this was working out well anyway. I thought I would see Peaches at the hospital and have her drop this off before I got here so you could open it up and be reading. No Peaches? Is she okay?"

Linda answers, "Mmmm, we're sure she's fine. Do you want coffee?"

"Darling Lin, I'm already too wired."

While Gloria tells us the story, Jan and I keep reading— flamboyant and elegant details about everything from their watches and jewelry down to their shoes. You could even smell the colognes and perfumes that the guests were wearing. Her details were impeccable. They really shouldn't have worn that style, and the reason why. The only two that she considered totally tasteful were the "gray lady" (other than too much dye on her hair), and James.

"I can't figure out why the old man, Leon, would have such trendy slacks. Usually, someone of that age picks something more... well, you know, old people style. More unusual were his shoes, not the kind old guys wear." We all laugh. Gloria doesn't. "Come on, think super-thin, hard soles and too slick to put on old feet. I don't think so. Thin socks in October? If you walk slow, you would wear thicker socks."

Jan begins to belly laugh. "What a visual! We can't contain ourselves!"

Gloria begins to chuckle. "I know, I can't help it. I do love that movie, *The Devil Wore Prada*. Maybe the devil wore Gucci in October. That man gave me the creeps. Anyway, he mumbled everything he said. Oh, and my dears, he didn't even wear old people's cologne. It was Obsession. Not exactly on the shopping list for the elderly. He had on gloves, so I couldn't see his hands. Not one other person had gloves. Thin socks and gloves. It doesn't make sense. I'll bet they weren't old people hands. Another thing, someone elderly who limps usually knows how to use a cane. He didn't even hold his other arm like someone does when they are afraid of falling." Gloria demonstrates. "When Pam helped him up the steps, I noticed he didn't lead with the same foot each time like a truly crippled person does. I had a broken leg one time, and after it healed, I had to learn to use one foot out and then the other." She demonstrates again.

"By Jove, I think she's got it! Gloria, you are a hoot. A very tasteful hoot. I think your observation only confirms that this guy does not line up." Jan hands her a copy of Claire's and Pam's notes.

Gloria's eyes are squinting. "Another thing, I tried to catch up with him after the service, and he was gone. He must be a very fast limper." Laughter. "The lady in the beautiful gray suit was gone, and that other well-dressed guy looked like they should've been together by the clothes they had on. Here he is, James. They didn't hurry, but they didn't linger either. I don't know what she drove, but I saw him walk to the parking lot alone. I couldn't see her, though, because I got in the limo."

I hand Gloria a folder. "This is your copy." Gloria reads as we fill in the details of the project and the meeting at Dot's. She keeps reading and nodding. She closes her folder, folds her hands on top of it, and shuts her eyes. We sit and wait.

Gloria takes a deep breath. "Dear ones, I understand we have no film of the processional of the church, but I have license plates of people pulling into the lots. If we don't know who owns the cars, we should take some of the photos to the rental places, the airport, and hotels to see if anyone matches the descriptions. Jan, divide up the beauty salons. Maybe we'll come up with something. I see copies of everyone's journals but not Marty's. Shouldn't we have hers too?"

"Yes, but she wants to do almost what you are doing. She wants to tell her story. She wrote in Russian. Can't always find the right words in English. See, some of us are more verbal. That's okay, isn't it?"

"Yes, darlin', it is."

Gloria is a real steel magnolia and smart. "Are you married, Gloria?" *I can't believe I blurted that out.*

"Yes, dear, I am, but Timothy's gone all the time, so it's like being a part-time wife. He's a very busy man, so I shop. It's kind of, well, you know, like a hobby. Some people plant flowers. I shop, sample colognes, and sit in restaurants and watch people. Even when I used to travel with Tim, I was alone. When the babies began arriving, I stayed home. At least I wasn't alone then. Now that they're all living their own lives, I fill the void with the people at the church, the job at the church, and Pastor Don and Cherie. It's perfect. I'm so excited about Tim coming in tomorrow. That's why I had to see you tonight."

Tim ought to stay home more. Wonder if he knows or cares how much it means to have someone excited that you're coming home.

"I'm leaving my folder here, but I will do whatever you want me to. When Tim leaves, well, I'll be available. Tell Marty I want her to be in the group with me. We're always doing stuff for the church, so it won't seem odd if we're together a lot. We're used to praying together." Kisses and hugs. "Dee Dee darling? Don't think of me as a material girl. That has nothing to do with it. It's one of the many things I do to pass the time. I hope I can help Adlin. By the way, that top is one that she and I had shopped for. You look beautiful in lavender. Your hair is gorgeous. I approve." We all laugh.

"I do, too," Linda adds. She is beaming. She gives Gloria a hug and walks her to the door, hand in hand.

"Jan, it's been a long time since I had met anyone who drives a Sportster. I approve of that, too. I didn't see it out here, though. It's so cute. Work on that shoelace. I think it's died. It's been a pleasure, and as I said, give an order, Jan, and I'll do it. Will someone drive me home?" We had all forgotten that Gloria had been dropped off. "I have been deposited here by Pastor Don and Cherie. Listen to my tape. It's glued in the journal inside the packet in the back. Maybe Mr. Trendy is in there. Mr. Mumbly. What a creepy person. Oh, Lin, you're going to drive me?"

"You be safe, Gloria. Enjoy your time with Tim. I will bury the shoelace and work on the groups.

"Dee Dee, you're a million miles away."

"I'm picturing the evening with Peaches and Joe."

8

BELLA NOTTÉ

Anthony interrupts with menus. He quietly lays them beside each of the people at table twelve and walks away without asking the usual questions about drinks. Back in the kitchen, the staff whispers, "Mr. Joe and Miss Peaches have come in here bunches of times, and never have we seen them act like this."

"Peachie, I don't know what is going on with you and the girls, but the other night when you and Dee Dee were out in that storm, well, I was worried. Way beyond worried. I realized it was time to speak my mind."

"Joseph, don't start. It was foolish. I should've been—"

He's smiling. "Always the first one to take the blow. Quick to forgive and quick to ask forgiveness. You know, that's one of the things I always loved about you. What I was going to say is, well, what I know is that I was really praying for God to help you through that storm. Praying to let you and Dee Dee be okay. I was panicked. Fear was setting in. Right then, I knew I had to tell you the truth. Patricia M. Marko, I have always and will always love you. You're my girl. After all this time, you still make me tingle. I decided that even if you were totally disgusted and never wanted to speak to me again, I can't keep it in anymore. He told me that He would bring you through safely, that love is the greatest, and it never fails. I knew He was talking about you and me.

"Up until He spoke that to me, I felt like, well, that somehow, I would be between Danny and you. He was my best friend, and I loved him like Jonathan and David. I wished I had died instead of him." Joe has tears in his soft, gentle eyes.

"Joseph, don't. You always tell me Jesus knows best. I'm sorry Danny is gone. You're right; he's still alive to me, even though he's not here. I'm also glad you didn't die and that you weren't in that car. Danny would've never gotten over it if he had lost you. You were the person that made him the wonderful human he was. He told me that many times. I know about when you were kids and how you brought him out of the streets and into life. Your relationship with God saved Danny. It gave him life here. God used you to bring Danny and me to Him, eternal life. Danny's alive with God. It was drinking that killed Danny."

"What? Peachie, Danny didn't have a drinking problem. It was a cover. Something he used to get information and join some parties. You know, business."

Anthony reappears. "Can I make some suggestions for this evening's entrees? But first, may I get you something to drink? Miss Peaches, the usual iced tea for both of you?"

"Yes, Anthony, tea for both of us."

Joe nods. "You know, Anthony, the same that we always have."

"Good enough. Thank you, Mr. Joe."

Anthony pours water and scoots away. The whole staff is looking at him. "What's going on? Usually, Mr. Joe and Miss Peaches are full of laughter. The whole atmosphere is different tonight. They're not even sitting where they usually do. They never sit in the corner."

Anthony mouths, "Don't ask," and waves them all back to their tasks.

"What do you mean Danny didn't have a drinking problem? Joseph, you know—"

"No, Peachie, it's like I told you, it was a cover. The business Danny and I had was also a cover for our real jobs. We were undercover for years. Coming off the streets with the last names we had made it so easy to fit in. The Feds approached us years before you met Danny. Peaches, my last name isn't Landry, it's Lanero."

"Oh, Joe, it's my dream!" Peaches tells Joe about what Danny said in the dream. "This is what he meant."

"Do you hate me now? I always felt trashy for not telling you. But it was for your safety—"

"You're explaining so much. One time, I saw Danny dumping a little bottle of liquor in a shot glass that he got from the back of the cabinet. He stuck his fingers in that shot glass and put some on his tongue and behind his ears like a cologne. He poured some in his pocket on his handkerchief. I never asked him about it. I look back now at some of the things I thought of as a drinker's behavior. There were so many little things that didn't make sense. Oh, Joseph, peace, and truth at last."

Out of the corner of his eye, Joe sees Anthony bringing dinner. He shakes his head and gives Anthony an upraised hand to stop. Anthony quietly retreats. "Peachie, I want to go back to my story. Remember what I said earlier about Jonathan and David?"

"Yes."

"David got to be king, and I didn't die like Jonathan, but I felt like I had. I was at the coronation when Danny was seated on the throne— the throne of your heart. I felt like I was dying that day when you and Danny were married."

"Oh, Joe, no—"

"But, let me finish while I have my nerve up. Danny was God to you. I—"

"Now, you wait a second!... You're right. Danny was God to me. He used to tell me, 'I'm not God; I'm only a man.' He loved Jesus and always told me I needed Him, too. I would laugh and say, 'Why do I need him? I have you.' I know it was disappointing to him, but I never could figure out, if he loved God so much, why didn't he quit drinking? I was so stupid."

"You were young. What I started to say, was, well, Peachie, I love you, and I'm giving this my last effort. Will you, well, will you—"

Peaches reaches across the table and takes his hand in hers. "I think you're trying to ask the wrong question. Here's the right one. Do I love you?"

"Peachie, I'm sorry."

"Well, in fact, I do. I thought about it all last night and today. Now, what about the next proper question?"

Joe is speechless for a second. "Will you marry me? If you need some time, it's okay."

"Joseph Landry, or Joseph Lanero, whomever you are. When did you ever know me to be indecisive? I have a surprise... Yes, you'll have to decide what my last name will be."

"Let's do this properly." Joe motions for Anthony.

"Did you get the beverages?"

"Yes, Mr. Joe, and it's chilled." His wife, and the kitchen staff, and the other waiters all emerge with glasses of champagne. Anthony's wife is standing beside him. He motions to everyone to put down their silverware. "I've got an announcement." He pulls his wife close to his side. "We, the owners, and the staff at Antonio's, and Mr. Joe and Miss Peaches, our guests, are here for a very special occasion." Each guest has a glass of champagne. "Mr. Joe, you're on. Please, folks, be quiet."

He takes Peaches's hand and leads her away from the table. Anthony turns the chair so everyone can see them. Joe seats Peachie, kisses her on the cheek, and drops to one knee. "Patricia M. Marko, Peaches, may I have your hand and all the rest of you as my wife? I promise I will still be your best man."

Peaches blushes and laughs as she whispers, "Yes, Joseph, you will always be my best man." She answers so everyone can hear, "Yes, I would be honored to be Mrs. Joseph Landry." Peaches winks.

Anthony says, "Please toast the soon-to-be Mr. and Mrs. Joe!" Anthony pulls his wife close to his side as they begin to sing, "This is the night, with the heavenly light..." The restaurant goes wild, with Joseph and Peaches dancing to the old couple singing. Other couples kiss and toast and dance tenderly close. It looks like a whole family hugging and kissing. Very Italian.

Peaches whispers, "Joe, Danny's smiling."

Joe whispers back, "I know. Let's go home."

"Anthony, send the check to me."

"No, Mr. Joe., Mama and me want to do what we can for you. This is what we can do for Miss Peaches and for Mr. Danny. He was a great friend. We'll mark it up on his tab. We both love you."

"We can't let you do that."

Mama shakes her finger and kisses both Peaches and Joe on the forehead. "Yes. We can. This was paid for a long time ago. I have your dinners already in your car and three bottles of champagne. Go, go, go."

The Scarpelinis watch as Joe tenderly covers Peaches's shoulders with her soft wrap and kisses her on the back of her neck. Anthony softly kisses Mama— still his baby after fifty years.

Amoré.

9

ASSIGNMENTS

"Can I come in?" Travis looks like a little boy peeking around the door, trying to hide the fact that he is in his underwear.

"Sure, but what's the deal? It's 6 a.m. It must be important. Shut the door behind you."

Travis makes a one-eighty and disappears into his bedroom. Hopping on one leg, he's pulling his jeans on as he comes back out. "Tanner, what is going on? Have a seat. You look like garbage. Let me guess, you've been up all night again. Man, if you don't stop this—"

"Travis, would you consider doing a little side work for me?"

"Is it lawn work?"

"No, it's more along the lines of security. I need someone I can trust who isn't going to blab it around."

He trusts me. Wowww. "I'm interested; what do you need?"

"Well, as you know, this case of Adlin Summers really has me bugged. I know that evil is still out there. It hasn't moved on. Libby and Emily live about six blocks from where that happened. I want you to take care of them. It may turn out that we might be getting some help, but I don't want to be worrying about Libby constantly. What do you think? Can you handle it?"

"You know I can. What do you mean you might get some help?"

"Better that you don't know for now. These jerks around here think I've lost it. You know what they think. It makes me not trust 'em. They think it was random. They're idiots with the instincts of a gnat."

"I don't think you're crazy... yet. There's not one clue. Nothing. All I know is that if you're losing it, so am I. It keeps trying to run in my head."

"You, too?"

"Yep."

"So, you'll take care of the girls for me?"

"Yep. When do I start?"

"I want you to meet with Libby and me. We'll develop a plan. I've decided to tell her, well, not everything, but how serious I think this is. I want you to stay there, but I don't know how that will work with school and everything. You really don't want to attract any attention. We'll make it work. I'm going to need to stay focused. I've got three cases going. What are you doing about 8:00 tonight?"

"Nothing. Why?"

There is no reason to tell Travis about Ben Garcia. This is on a need-to-know basis. "Hold that thought a minute." Tanner dials his phone.

"Libby, I know it's early, but I wanted to apologize for last night... No, don't hang up. Can we have dinner this evening?... I'll pick you up. Bring a jacket. Dress casually, and we can go for a drive afterward... Thanks, Lib. I'll see you at 7:00. Libby, it's truth time.

"Okay, Travis, we're on. I'm going to dinner with Libby, but I want to meet you at the Wilderness Walk marker between 8 and 8:30 tonight. May have someone for you to pick up and bring out there."

"Who?"

"I don't know if they can make it, but I'll get back to you. Don't get too far away today. Okay?... Okay, thanks, Travis." He looks shocked as I hug him. It seemed an appropriate gesture of deep gratitude. *Give Libby an hour to go to work and then call Emily.*

&

At the office, I work through calls and a list for the day, pretty much mundane. I use my cellphone. "Emily? Don't give me your usual twenty questions. I'll explain later. Are you free around 7:30?... Great. Do you suppose you could leave your car in the garage today? Take the bus, and I'll have someone pick you up from work. I want to meet with you. Lib's going to dinner with me... Yes, Emily, I apologized... I'm glad you are pleased, but seriously, don't tell anyone anything, not even Lib. Well, I don't know if you call it romantic, that's not the issue. Will you do it?... I'll send a young guy. I'll give him a greeting for you so you know it's him. Don't get in with anyone else. Don't go near any cars. Okay... Oh, stop it, just do it. The code word is Sugar Plum... Stop it. Be serious. I'll call ya later... Take the phone I gave you and be careful. Don't say anything to Libby about this conversation. Promise?... Thanks."

Considering the life that she had once, Emily is really an overcomer. Don't know how, but she did it. She has a great mind and a good sense of humor. She is a sugar plum. Is that her calling back? Oh, no! It's Ben Garcia.

"Chief... Okay, Ben... You are? Why so soon?... No, I'm glad, but I thought it would be around a week. Do I need to make some arrangements for you?... Okay... Yes, I'm cleaning up some concerns I have personally, and I'll be waiting for your arrival... How long do you have?" *Wasn't that convenient? Great timing.* "Let me know when you'll be here so I can clear my work calendar; taking a vacation, I guess. Thanks, Ben... It will be an honor to meet you. See ya soon."

I really wish he could have met Winston. Stop it. I don't have time for the replay. Thinking of Winston, his wife has called again.

"Hello, Mrs. Carter... Yes, I remember the Chief. He's often in my thoughts. He was a great man. What can I do for you today?... You're reporting about a book?... A book left where?... Laying in your flowerbed?... You opened it to see whom it belonged to?... Whom did it belong to?... There's a note in the book?... What does it say?... Mrs. Carter, I'll be right over... Yes, ma'am." *I've been there so many times I could drive it blindfolded.*

There she is, waiting on the step, waving me in. "Tanner, do you know why I always call you? Well, you'll always come. That's the reason. Also, because Aaron always said you were the only one with any smarts."

"I'm honored."

The Chief was a smart and savvy man. The Chief spoke kindly to older people and took time with them. "Kid, you'll be there someday, too." He was not only smart but a true gentleman.

"The second I found the book, this little bell went off. Aaron always told me to listen to my instincts. I went in and got my gloves, just like he taught me. There's no I.D. in the book, just a library card. I would've returned the book to the library, but I started to read the back because I thought my bell was going off. Many things in my life are off since I got old. I have to really think through everything." She chuckles.

"So do I. I know what you mean."

"I was walking along by the lovely plants and flowers, and there it was. One of those little notes, you know, that sticks to things. The oddest feeling went over me."

"What does it say?"

"Roses are red. Violets are Blue. I'm looking forward to meeting you." She looks shaken. I know it sounds like a sweet thing, but I heard that bell again. You know, not really a bell, just that little gut feeling. I never liked the word gut, so I called it my bell."

Mrs. Carter looks at me, waiting to be assured that it is nothing like all the other times. "Oh, Mrs. Carter, the Chief would be so proud of you. This could really be something. Where's the book?"

"Tanner, the second I saw that note, I shut the book, and it's here in the brown bag." She gets up and opens the bottom door to the china cabinet. "Come and get it, I don't want it. I don't want to touch it again."

As I take out the brown bag, I notice she is expectantly looking at me, like a little puppy waiting for a loving pat. I hug her and kind of lift her up. She's so tiny. It was an instantaneous reaction. "Thank you. Thank you."

Constance looks ten years younger. "You mean I've contributed something? Tanner, you know I was Aaron's best confidant. Don't you tell anyone, but back before all the technology came, I used to help him with cases. I didn't really interview people; I would visit with people and get information— what he called, you know, undercover. We never had any children, so I helped Aaron help other people. I think we did some fine work."

"You did indeed. Everyone used to wonder what kind of snitch he had. It was you, the great agent, Mrs. Carter—"

"Call me Constance."

"Constance, I can't share details with you right now, but this could turn out to be very important. Please don't tell anyone about this."

"Oh, I would never, never. I'm sure I've worn you out with various trivia over the years. It's hard to let go of the life I had with Aaron. I'm always looking and praying for something to put me back in the loop." I laugh. Constance laughs and hugs me. "Be careful, and do let me know if it helps. Be careful!"

Someone's telling me to be careful? That's a switch. "I promise. I'll be careful. Constance, give me a few days and we'll have lunch, and talk about old times with the Chief."

"You're on. Call me. Tanner, Aaron was right about you. You do have smarts and a lot more. He said you had very good instincts and a whole choir of bells."

I'm still laughing as I drive away. Looking at such a much younger version of Mrs. Carter, Constance, waving goodbye from her porch.

Chief, you really are a dog. What a life you had. What a great lady. Instantly, I feel guilty for all the times I felt like she was an inconvenience. I can hear the Chief telling me, *"Son, I told you about old people. Be nice and take time with them. You'll be there someday."* He was right. A wave of homesickness comes over me. Homesickness to see the Chief, to see Winston. *I should've asked Constance why she always called him Aaron.*

❧

Back at the station, I pretended that the brown bag contains lunch and not the mysterious book. "Travis, are you in the building?... Would you come to my office and bring me an evidence bag? But I don't want anyone to know what you're doing."

Travis shows up with a big "lunch," too. I marked the evidence bag May 30 11:55 a.m. and the location where it was found. He peeks in the bag. Travis doesn't say anything other than, "You got tuna! I didn't even know you liked tuna!" We slip the evidence bag inside the other brown bag.

"Yep, it's tuna. Let's go outside and eat. It's stifling in here." *I always have a feeling someone could be listening— another little tidbit from the Chief.* Ever since I saw that apartment cleaned up like that, I wondered if it wasn't someone from the forensics or connected with the department in some manner. The thought that it could be an officer never left my mind as a possibility. Travis and I head out the door with our "lunches." We're making a side trip to an old friend. We hop in the car and drive about two blocks. We keep making chit-chat the whole time. We turn left six blocks down and double back towards the park. "Call Irene at the University. Tell her to bring a brown bag lunch and meet us at the park."

I pull over, and Travis uses my cellphone outside. He nods that she's coming. He told her it was me and it was a case. Irene has such a marvelous research lab at the University. We both go back to the days when Winston was the head of forensics. He was her boss. I can see him smiling.

✻

As always, punctual. With every hair in place, no one would ever suspect Irene is my mad scientist. She's better than my forensic team. Irene does exactly as Winston had taught us. The code words in our conversation tells her that it's a little secret operation. Irene sits at another table, pretending that she doesn't see us. I holler, "Irene!"

"Well, DJ Tanner. Hi, Travis. Is he getting you into table trouble? It's been a while. Haven't heard from you in months. What are you having for lunch?" She peeks in the bag. "Oh, I hope it's not too dry." We all laugh. Smart girl, she slips me a sandwich and a bag of chips under the park table. I pretend that I'm eating.

"Irene, this could be the first break in the Summers case. I haven't even read it. You get to be the first to peek."

Irene goes from shock to, "You really haven't seen it?"

"Nope, I wanted you to have at it first. Pay special attention to the little something sticking inside."

Irene's face turns white. "You mean like on the fridge?"

"Could be. Give me an opinion. I trust your instincts and look for everything you can find. It was found in a flower bed, so there may be evidence on it, or not, but test it all."

"Tanner, I didn't call, but I wanted to tell you it's like I have an instant replay of that case. I can't let it go. Maybe we can put that girl to rest. Maybe this is the break you need."

To make it look like an old friend lunch, we keep chatting, and Travis plays right along. He pretends he gets a phone call and says he has to go. Irene says she'll clean up, and we walk away.

As we drive off, I see Irene depositing her "half-eaten lunch" in her tote and throwing the trash away. Once again, clever girl. She switched the bags.

We drive to the station and hop out. I tell Travis before we go in that the date is on and to pick Emily up at 7:30. I tell him to give her the code Sugar Plum and pretend it's a date. Maybe a little peck on the cheek.

Travis laughs. "Yeah, just like in the movies. Don't worry, I'll be there. But where?"

"I'll call Emily and arrange where she should be picked up.

"The University library?" I'm paralyzed. "Are you going to a lecture?..." *Dear God.* I try not to sound panicked. "Emily, is it an open lecture?... Great. Change of plan. Your date will be attending, too... What time does it start?... 6:00?" I glance at Travis. He nods. "We're on. Act excited and Sugar Plum, by the way, what are you wearing?... He'll be there... Yes, I guess he's cute... He'll be there.

"She'll be wearing tan slacks and a black and tan knit top. She also has a black jacket. Her hair is almost black, and she has great, big brown eyes. Remember, she's a Sugar Plum."

"Knock it off; you act like I'm a complete twit. I've gone on dates before, believe it or not. Tanner, you treat me like I'm twelve."

"All right. I know. I'm trusting you, Travis." *I suddenly feel very old. At forty-one, I feel like I've lived three lifetimes.*

"See you later. I've got a class this afternoon."

This internship program is producing at least one good product. He reminds me of someone the Chief used to know.

Back to the mundane, I'm working on my list for the day in my head. Bernice, my secretary, says, "Did you have a nice lunch?" and she winks.

That woman, she's sharper than all the rest of them. I wonder why she's a secretary.

"Yeah, it was good to be out of the building." *I've really got to be more considerate of Bernice. She is a good person. At least, I think she is, but she's new. She only came about three months ago.* My phone distracts me from thinking about Bernice. *The list. I have to be at the District Attorney's office for a meeting with the mayor. Remember 2:00. Better get moving on the rest of the list. Seaview Apartments. Something about a car. That's Traffic.*

I buzz Bernice. "Bernice, I know you didn't know this, but that car stuff goes to Traffic."

"Sir, it was Traffic that called. They want you to call Seaview Apartments. Talk to Erica. They wouldn't tell me anymore. Would you like me to get them on the line for you?"

"Yes, please. I'm reading the reports from yesterday. Blah, blah, blah, blah, blah." Bernice buzzes me.

"Sir, I have Erica from Seaview on the line, and by the way, please call me Beanie."

"Okay, put her through.

"Miss, this is Lieutenant Tanner here." Before I can speak, she starts rattling. "Wait! Wait! Erica, may I call you Erica?... Hold on." I motion for Beanie to come in and take shorthand. I put the phone on speaker. "Now, slow down and give us your last name."

"Erica. Erica Long. She's gone! She's gone! She has long, dark hair and green eyes, and she's gone. Anne. Anne Johnson."

"Erica, I thought this was about a car."

"Yes, Anne's car. I was out of town visiting my family in Georgia. It was my little sister's graduation. When I got back, I ran over to see Anne. Her car was in the lot, but she wasn't home. At first, I thought, okay, she's out on a date, or someone picked her up. She still wasn't home that evening, so I thought she had gone camping or something. When the weekend was over, no Anne. I got worried. Anne's my only friend here. I didn't know who to call. The numbers we have for references don't answer or are wrong numbers. You know, college students and cellphones."

Beanie's writing, and I can't get a word in edgewise.

"I'm really worried. Can you help? I think she would, well, you know, need her car. It's out in the lot. It's like it's staring at me. I'm afraid. Should I be afraid?"

"Erica, calm down. Are you working right now?"

"Yes. I'm standing in the office right now."

"And do you have help?... Do you have keys to the apartment?"

"Yes, we have a master key. My boss wouldn't use it. He told me, 'These college kids are all a bunch of kooks.' Not Anne, she's a great person. Can you come? You sound nice."

"Erica, it's going to be all right. I can't come, but I'll send help. In fact, my secretary is sending someone as we speak." Beanie heads out and is on the phone. She is back, giving me the okay sign. "I have a meeting, but I will see you later today. Give me another number I can reach you on... I see. I'll stop by your apartment, or you can come with the officer down here. I'll be back, and we'll talk."

"I want to come there. I'm afraid and don't want to be in my apartment. I know something happened to Anne."

"Erica, the officer will be there shortly. Let him into Anne's apartment and show him the car. I'm sending someone else to be with you."

"Okay, okay, but I'm waiting on the front step for them."

"That's good. Don't be afraid. Help is on the way. I'll see you later. We'll find Anne."

"Thanks."

"Who are you sending? This kid is terrified. You know what jerks some officers are."

"I guess I'm sending you. Take notes and bring Erica back here. Take care of her, Beanie, until I can get back. I've got to make that meeting at two. It's 1:20, and it's a thirty-minute drive in traffic. Do you know where Seaview is?"

"I have GPS. I'll get there, but who will take your calls?"

"Forward them to Sheryl in Traffic. Tell her you have to run an errand for me."

"Okay, Sir, thanks for trusting me."

"Get scootin'." Strangely, I trust her, and I can't really say why. I don't really know her.

§

The traffic was horrible. It's almost 2:00. I take the stairs to the second floor instead of waiting for the elevator. The secretary smiles and directs me into the DA's office. There's the mayor, looking very official and concerned.

"Tanner." He shakes my hand, but I feel like I'm being called into the principal's office. "There's a situation that has developed. At first, I thought he was on vacation. Then, I got a call from an old friend who lives out of state. He told me his friend who runs a business here is missing. I told my friend I'd look into it. The shop has a going out of business sign on it. His apartment is empty. His car is missing, and there's no sign of him. It's like he has vanished. His cards haven't been used. He's vanished into thin air."

So much for the mundane morning. "What kind of business did he have?"

"A bookstore. You know, Kaplan's Bookstore."

A chill goes over me as a bell goes off. Loud, clanging, in fact.

"I need you to look into this quietly. You know, all that stuff in the papers about the Summers case? It's an election year. Doesn't bode well if we have another high-profile case. My friend is really putting pressure on me."

Good God, this man is so self-serving. "Sir, I'll be back to do what I can. That's my job. I'll be discreet." I can see Garrett, the DA, sitting behind his desk. His eyes are closed, and he's shaking his head in disbelief at the shallowness.

"Good. I know you and Garrett can handle this. I need something this weekend to tell my friend. Report only to me with what you come up with. Garrett has the additional information. I've got to get back to my office— late lunch with my wife. Good PR, you know. Oh, and thanks, Tanner. Thanks, Garrett. You guys give the taxpayers a bang for their buck."

Garrett and I stare at each other for a moment. "Woww. That was a brief briefing." We don't laugh. Mr. Kaplan was a nice man. I had met him a long time ago. The Chief and he were friends.

Garrett rolls his eyes and slides a large folder my way. "Here's what I have so far. He used a private detective to keep this out of the public eye. The mayor's friend hired him. You'll see that Mr. Kaplan ran a little ad that thanked all his customers. He was closing his business due to health issues. It was called in, and a courier delivered cash to the paper. My question is, where is Mr. Kaplan, and who ran the ad? Read the file and get back to me tomorrow. We've got to do something for him, Kaplan, that is."

"Okay, I'll see what I can come up with." *Ben Garcia's coming in. Oh, my God, my date with Libby, and Erica Long, and Beanie.* "I'll be back." Garrett shakes my hand. "What, no hug?" We laugh. *Well, this day is turning out to be anything but mundane.* Garrett grins and motions me out. Unlike most DAs, Garrett Wilson is a real person with a heart and a brain. *Mr. Kaplan. Where are you? Adlin Summers, dinner, monsters.*

The traffic was worse. It's nearly 3:00, and everything seems like slow motion. I'd like to take a spin past Kaplan's Bookstore, but that kid Erica is waiting, I'm sure. It gives me a sense of relief that Beanie will be with her. *Thank you, Beanie.*

Finally, the traffic cleared enough for me to keep south and come in the back way past University Park. *Irene, I wonder if she's on it. Of course, she is. She's the most "on it" person I know.*

Arriving at my office, I noticed Beanie was still not at her desk. No one's seen her. *What now?* I call Sheryl and tell her to let my calls through.

"I hope it's okay; I sent some officers out on these calls."

"Absolutely, you always know what to do."

I tell her thanks for being a team player and I appreciate her for being a friend. She's a little bossy but a good woman, nonetheless. I know she was disappointed when I didn't hire her as my secretary. When Tessa got married and moved, I couldn't tell her that it was her bossiness. I took her to lunch and explained that I needed a well-trained person familiar with everyone to keep traffic running smoothly. I didn't tell her that she was getting a service award and a raise. She deserved it. She says, "Look for the fax of your calls. I'm sending it right now."

I turn the slats on the blinds to see Beanie the second she comes in. I stick the folder from Garrett in my briefcase and try to work through my list for the day. I call Jim and ask him to bring me the fax from Sheryl. Jim's not a bad sort, but kind of the office jokester. He's not the most astute and wants to be out there so badly on the streets, but he doesn't have any instincts or street smarts, so he'll have to remain here in the office.

Aah, a tap.

"Sir?"

"Come on in, Jim. Have a seat. I need you to take care of a few items on my list. I'm putting you in charge of these calls and need my list done by 5:00." I can see him straighten in his chair as I say the words in charge. Everyone needs to feel needed and to be in charge sometimes. "Also, be sure everyone from the shift turns in their reports." I hand him Sheryl's fax back and say, "Save this for tomorrow. Work through as many of these as you can."

"Yes, Sir. I'll get it done, and those reports will be on your desk before I leave."

"Thanks, Jim; I always know I can depend on you. Unless it's important, skip whatever you were doing and finish my list, please. Provide me with some good notes."

"Thanks, Sir. I will."

I catch a glimpse of Beanie coming in. *Thank God.* "See you tomorrow, Jim."

Beanie is with a slightly chunky but very pretty redhead about twenty or twenty-one years old, maybe younger. Beanie buzzes me.

"Sir! If you have time now, Miss Erica Long is here to see you. Will you need my assistance further?"

"Yes. Please show Miss Long in and bring your notebook." I rise. Beanie introduces me to Erica. The kid grabs my hand like it's a lifeline.

"Call me Erica."

I walk from behind my desk and pull up a chair with my back towards the door like friends chatting. "Okay, tell me again what happened."

"You tell him, Miss Orr. You are better at this than I am."

Beanie gives me the timeline and a short rundown about the call. "Nothing was disturbed in Miss Johnson's apartment. Art was sent on the call and didn't take off until forensics could get there. Everything was extremely neat and clean. That bothered Art, so he was having it checked out. Usually, college students aren't that tidy. The car was locked, and Art ran the plates. It's registered in Anne's name. The car seemed to be fine, but Art was having it towed and checked out also." Beanie suggested it would be a good idea if Erica told me what she had dreamed of.

"Dreamed?" Beanie gives me a stiff glance, one that says, don't blow this off.

"Well, it's like the car is trying to tell me something. Every night, I've looked out that window, and there it sat, in the corner of the lot, with that light shining on it. Gives me the creeps. Anne never parked there. Well, anyway, I had this dream…

> Anne is trying to hide. She keeps stumbling like she's drunk. Anne doesn't drink. She has her boots on, and she's carrying a notebook. She keeps stopping and mumbling, 'What are these?' She keeps pulling something from her tote and sticking it to the pages of the notebook. She pushes the notebook pages together hard. She looks lost or disoriented. She's shivering. I wake up.

"Where is she?"

"I don't know, but we'll find her. Do you know where she likes to hike? Does she normally take a notebook with her?"

"No, she doesn't carry a notebook, at least when I've gone with her. I've only been two times. I'm not much of a hiker. More of a TV and snacks person. Anne was getting me out so maybe I could slim down a little bit."

"Where did you go with her?"

"One time, we walked across the wooden bridge at the crossing. We spent some time walking in the woods. Once, we even went to Wilderness Walk. That didn't last long because it started to rain, and it was late in the day. I know she used to go with some other people, but I don't know who. I think some guy named Myron, but I never met him. Like I told Miss Orr, I'm new here, and I work at Seaview a lot. Anne wasn't really friends with this bunch. They're more the party types, not hikers."

"Okay, you have been most helpful. I'll have an officer drive by and keep an eye on you. I'm going to have Art have a little chat with your boss."

"Don't get me in trouble; I need this job. He's a... Well, you know, a grouch."

"Don't worry. We're going to let your boss know how important you are to Lieutenant Tanner and to watch out for you. He'll get the message, if you know what I mean. Beanie, will you get that directive out to Art? Have him get it across to Erica's boss. Have Art escort Erica home and check her apartment and the area. Here's my card, Erica."

Beanie stops my hand. "I've already given her my information, and since we've spent this time together, I told her she can call me. Okay, Sir?"

"Okay, but I want Art to drive Erica home in a squad car and visit with her boss. Tell him it's important." Erica is ecstatic. Here comes the hug. I pat her as she hugs me. "We'll find Anne. It will be okay."

Beanie hugs Erica and escorts her to her desk. I see her make a call and speak to someone, probably Art.

"Sir?"

"Come in, Beanie."

"I hope I didn't overstep my boundaries. I thought she needed a mom right now. If I had a daughter in that situation, I—"

"Beanie, it's okay. I agree. Did you get Art?"

"Yes, Sir, I'll type up my notes tonight at home and—"

"No, you won't."

"Really, it's okay. I'm free this evening."

"All right, but put the time down. When Art gets here, tell him all this is not to go anywhere. Not anything about you being there. Nothing. He's a very decent person, strictly by the book. Tell him the Lieutenant is asking him to keep it under wraps. Oh, and tell him to come in about 8:30 tomorrow. Tell Erica not to say a word to anyone. Not anyone."

I see Erica nodding yes, and she looks right at me and blows me a kiss. Beanie laughs and hugs her. Art pats the kid on the back, and away they go, but not until I see Beanie whisper something in Erica's ear and squeeze her hand. Erica kisses Beanie on the cheek and walks away with Art. Everyone else is so busy filling out their shift reports they don't notice. *Good.*

Phones are ringing; it seems like people always wait until the end of the day to have a crisis. It's 4:45. "Beanie, I'm leaving early." I write my private calls down, grab my briefcase, and walk past her desk. I tell her, "No one else ever gets wind of this."

"I understand."

"Call me if you need me."

"Goodnight, Sir."

"Goodnight, Beanie. Wrap it up and get outta here." She smiles.

Dinner with Libby. It seems like it's okay to tell her the truth. I can smell her perfume already. Yes, dinner is going to be good.

IO
MUCH TO DO

"Hurry up and finish those folders! I'm going to put the boards in the closet because Louis and Margaret will be here at 8:30 in the morning. Good grief. I've got to get a hold of Marty. Dee Dee, you'll have to get her gift before Ben Garcia gets here." Linda seems almost flustered, school girlish.

"Aunt Linda, you really don't need to go out of your way, Ben is just—"

"Just your boss!! Dee Dee, I want him to feel welcome. I know how good he's been to you. I felt safe knowing you were far away but with someone trustworthy who could watch over you. Call it returning the hospitality."

Ooh, I'm seeing a side of Linda I've never seen before, bossy!

"I'm doing laundry this evening, and I've got clean sheets laid out for the morning. We'll all be up at 6 a.m. and have the beds changed and washed by the time Margaret and Louis arrive."

Linda is setting cleaning products out and writing notes. "Jan, you'll have to take Dee Dee to meet Marty. Make sure you have a folder for her."

Linda's dialing her phone. "Marty, I'm sorry to call so late. Are you at the church tomorrow? Dee Dee wanted to stop by... No, I have a, I mean Dee Dee and I have a guest coming. I have a lot to do. They're arriving earlier than expected, so I have to shop. Do you remember Jan's still coming along? Dee Dee will share with you about her visit here. I know you had mentioned you have a gift for her, so don't forget to bring it... I know I sound rushed, but it's a very important guest. It's Dee Dee's boss from California... Yes, I knew you'd understand... God bless... They'll see you in the morning. Give Gloria my love. Be blessed. Tell Oliver hello and give him a hug for me."

"Marty will be at the church at 10:00 in the morning. She'll bring the gift. She is excited to meet you, Jan. She thought this would be a good time to get to know you better." We keep working on the folders and snickering.

Linda is on another planet. "Do you like rosemary potatoes, Jan? Do you, Dee Dee?"

"Yes," we answer in unison.

"I can hardly wait. Kind of like Ben is being fattened for the kill." Jan bursts out laughing.

"What are you two laughing about?"

"Nothing. We're getting silly from being up too long."

Jan crosses her eyes and sticks her tongue out. "I missed out on the slumber parties when I was a kid. So this is what happens when everyone gets crazy."

"Are you staying tonight? It's okay if you want to. You rode that bike, and I'm too exhausted to take you home." Linda is talking loudly from the kitchen.

Jan looks down at her mutilated shoelace and drags one leg like, yes, Master. "Linda, thanks. I'd appreciate not riding my bike in the dark. You're a doll."

"Anyway, you can help Dee Dee and me in the morning." Jan bites her knuckle and crosses her eyes.

I do love this woman. In a short time, she has wormed her way past my crust and into my heart. She's becoming a friend. "Jan, I can't stand this anymore. I'd rather get up early and work on these in the morning."

She signs, "Me, too."

Even I can read that, and I can't read sign language. Linda is engrossed in her list. As Jan sneaks up behind her and covers her eyes, Linda jumps but begins to laugh. "Earth to Linda? Come in."

"I'm sorry, I'm kind of not here. I haven't had a real male guest in the house in a long time." Now, that sets us off laughing again. Linda is red and embarrassed. "You know what I mean."

Jan promises she won't tell any of the guys that they're not real males. "Just kidding." Jan can't quit laughing, and neither can I. We hug Linda and snicker.

"See you at 6 in the morning, Dee Dee."

"It looks like we've got our day planned out for us," and we giggle again. Linda ignores us and heads off to bed.

I close my eyes. The last thing I remember is Linda tiptoeing into my room and tucking me in. A gentle prayer and a kiss to the forehead. "Goodnight, Dee Dee." I smile, but I'm too far gone to answer.

It's not even light when I'm awakened to the smell of coffee. Looking at the clock, it's 5. *These women.* I turn over and boom, on my mind, is Ben. I sit on the edge of the bed and then head to the shower. There's a funny smell in the bathroom. *Oh, dear Lord, the toilet's plugged! There goes the shower!* "Aunt Linda!"

"Dee Dee." Linda pops her head around the door. "I've already called the plumber. Jan's dressed. You're going to her house to shower. If you need to tinkle, do so, but don't flush. Do me a favor and strip the sheets while you're up."

Boy, she doesn't miss a beat. I pull the embroidered pillowcases off and the sheets and the regular pillowcases, too.

"Towels, too, please."

I scoop up the pile at the end of the bed and walk towards the laundry room. Linda holds up a hand, "Don't go in there. You don't want to see it. That's how I knew we had a problem. I got up and started the washer."

Oh, boy!

Linda's look is somewhere between crazy and the agony of defeat. "I can't believe this."

"Linda, it'll be okay." *Easy for me to say. What do I know?* "Jan, have you stripped too?" Even Linda laughs. Jan points to the pile of bed linens and towels on the kitchen floor.

"Dee Dee, bag your clothes up, we're going to my house. We're under strict orders to get out." Linda hands Jan the keys to her car.

"I feel like we're abandoning the sinking ship." Linda tosses me a large garbage sack. I put the laundry in it and lug it to the front door. As we go down the drive dragging the sack, a Roto-Rooter truck pulls up.

The driver gives us a cheery but tired, "Hi, ladies. Benny called me. This gal must be special."

We chime, "She is. Be nice to her." Jan tells him there's a bonus in it if he can fix it before 7:30. He tells us his name is Tubbs, and he'll do his best. Now, he looks like he's on a mission from God. Maybe he is, but Jan seems to have given him some extra drive with the bonus.

We are still laughing as we drag the bag through the front door of Jan's house. "I should have brought my suitcase."

"There's the washer. You're smart; get a load started. I'm making coffee." Jan's back is heading away from me. More surprises. Not many people have a pink pig, a bear, a Monopoly game, and an Emmet Kelly picture in their laundry room. At least not many people that are fifty-two. I start a load. I quickly sort the clothes into piles. I noticed Jan already had her piles sorted, lots of piles. I wander towards the sound of coffee being made. "Jan, how about it if I throw your stuff in?"

"You're kidding, right?"

"No, do you want me to put your stuff in too? It's not that hard. Yes or no? Payback for your smart comment."

Jan laughs. "Touché."

Boy, she's quick.

"Yes, if you want to. I haven't had help in a long time."

I head back. *Some of the most interesting and whimsical things I've ever seen an adult own.* I match Jan's clothes up with my loads and start with the whites. *Success!* The first load is churning away.

"Coffee's ground and ready!"

"Jan, you make great coffee."

"It's an Ethiopian blend. It's my favorite. Do you want a piece of toast? I make great toast." Laughter. Jan pushes the button, and the bread goes down. "See, I can cook."

After the meal is down, I get the tour of Jan's train set and all the other fun stuff. Not quite the same tour as at Madelyn's, but equally as interesting. Kind of like Disneyland. A place where James Christensen meets Salvador Dali.

"Do you like it?"

"Jan, who wouldn't? It's wonderful. Even your pink bathtub and pink kitchen counters. Have you ever had any of the women over?"

"No. Look at their houses. They look like something out of House Beautiful. They'd think I was crazy."

"Here's a newsflash for ya: we already know you're crazy. They would love your house. It's the expression of Once Upon A Time when we were kids. Jan, you have great taste."

Ding! "Next load." From the time the first load went into the dryer, I started another one. Jan got in the shower, and I read magazines while I waited.

"You're turn, Dee Dee."

"Well, there's a little problem. In all the rush, I didn't bring anything to wear for today. Eeh, this is what I had on yesterday."

"Not to worry." Jan came out with a beautiful, white, thick, terry-cloth robe. "Compliments of the Venetian in Las Vegas." *Another surprise.*

The shower feels great, and so does the gorgeous robe. The washer's dinging, but the first load is barely dry. I take it out and toss the items loosely over the furniture in the den. Switching out the loads, I find an inhaler in a pocket. "Jan, do you have asthma?"

"Yeah, kind of. Don't ask."

I hear the great Peter, Paul, and Mary music, Joan Baez, Phil Collins, and on and on: music and laundry.

Linda calls. "You'll never believe it. The guy was done by 7:25. I've already got most of the nasty stuff disinfected and cleaned up. He used a machine to suck up the water in the laundry room. He just left. He waited until I ran that load, though. I tried to pay him, but he said he owed Benny a favor. I gave him a fifty-dollar tip, but he wouldn't take it. He said he was getting a bonus. Isn't that wonderful? Finish your laundry. Louis and Margaret will be here in about ten minutes. I was working on Allen's room while the plumber was here. The stuff is almost all in the closet. I have the folders in a tub in the closet. Got to call Kay. Remember, you're going to church by 10:00." Click and she was gone.

Jan shrugs her shoulders. "What?"

"Looks like Tubbs will be looking for you." Laughter. "Linda's on a tear. She said she was calling Kay. She's getting flowers. I'll bet she's even getting her hair and nails done."

"What are you doing?"

"I'm looking for some mood music. I'll take more CD's over. I feel like I'm out in left field."

"What's going on?"

Jan answers her phone. "Peaches, thank God! What in the world?... Okay, no questions. Glad to hear your voice. How is Jenny?... That's such good news... Yes, Dee Dee's here. There's been a change in plans. Her boss is coming in this morning. Yes... Linda is going bonkers. Wait until you hear that story... Oh, she'll tell ya... Yes, it's been quite the day, and it's only 8:30... I'll tell Dee Dee. Someone has a gift for her, so we'll call you after lunch... Thanks. I enjoyed our visit too. Tell Joe, 'hi.'

"Peaches wants you to know she had a very nice dinner. Jenny's okay, and she's anxious to see you. Dee Dee, something else has come up, but she'll tell you later."

A movie and laundry. We've had such a great time. Jan put all her clothes away, and I put mine in an extra suitcase she had. Jan takes the Beamer, and I drive Linda's car with no license and no identification. *I hope I don't get pulled over.*

"Good grief. I forgot you had my car. I've got ten minutes to make it to the beauty shop." Linda grabs the keys, and out the door she goes. Louis is outside mowing and getting the flowerbeds and everything pristine. Margaret already has the living room and dining room sparkling. She said she didn't understand, but the laundry room was sparkling clean. Cleaning supplies in hand, she heads to the bedrooms. We both head up to help her make beds, or at least we can contribute something to the building of Rome. Rome in a day.

Louis is yelling to Margaret. He's out of gas. Jan to the rescue! She grabs the gas can and heads to the station. Louis stares in surprise. Beamer and a gas can in the front seat. *That's Jan.* He blows her a kiss and begins to weed the flower beds. With all that rain, Linda's yard was starting to resemble a jungle.

Margaret has Linda's bed made and is dusting. She heads to the bathroom. I expect a shriek. I see Margaret kneeling and cleaning out the tub. Linda must've been flying to get that mess cleaned up. I tell Margaret to do my room last. I have to get dressed. I make the bed. I pick a red suede jacket and realize I had left my suitcase in the car.

Louis apparently saw it on the back seat, and as I'm headed out the door, he bumps into me. "Do you want me to carry the case?"

"Yes, please." *I'm not used to this.* He smiles, gets the case, and carries it for me.

"Miss Dee Dee, Margaret and I want you to know how sorry we are. Miss Adlin was one good person, for sure. If you need us, you can count on us. We want to help you find that "thing!" Okay?"

"Okay, Louis. We'll find the one that did it."

Louis hesitates and sighs. I hug him. "Margaret and I pray you won't be so sad. God loves you. He will take care of it."

"I believe he will, Louis."

Jan is back with gas. Louis talks to her about what a great lady she is. Jan heads to Allen's room to dig in the closet to find her folder. While she's filtering through the bin, I get dressed. The beautiful, moss-green silk top is in the closet, hanging way in the back. *I gave this to Adlin last spring.* She told me she wore it on a date when she went to a lecture at the University. *Sounds like barrels of fun, Adlin.* I slip into it and button the front. It's snug but not too tight. I like it. It makes me feel warm. *Adlin, you must have looked great with your soft green eyes changing color with whatever you wore.* I laugh as I remember Adlin when we were kids asking if purple eyes are rarer than other colors. *"How come eyes weren't red sometimes?"* I didn't know the answer, so I told her it was a dumb question. I feel the tug of that little stone pendant on my heart.

Interrupted in my thoughts, Jan asks if I'm ready to go. I throw the suede jacket over my shoulder. Jan tells me I look like Christmas. "I don't care. It feels good with my jeans. I feel great today. Let's go learn Russian."

❧

My reaction to the church was different than I anticipated. I had avoided coming here. Maybe the videos and the photos had made me more comfortable. There's Gloria talking to Pastor Don. They greet us, and Pastor Don gives me a hug. That's not surprising; he is such a decent person. Looks like somebody's brother. The kindness on his face is touching. *Kind eyes.*

"Welcome, Dee Dee. I was hoping to see you. Cherie and I have always prayed for you. This is horrible. Is there any promising news of an arrest?"

An arrest? I had thought of eradication, like exterminating a bug, but never an arrest. It sort of shocks me. I'd never thought of Red October just sitting in jail. "No, nothing promising." I can barely get the words out. Suddenly, I feel like I want to hide. I hope he can't read my mind. Jan is staring at me but quickly looks away as Pastor Don introduces himself. Gloria tells him we're going on a tour of the church and for him not to forget his 10:30 counseling session. Pastor Don smiles and excuses himself. Jan is quiet, glancing at me from the corner of her eye as Gloria chats on. She thinks Marty will be in the upper balcony area.

"They clean the church in three sections. We thought it would be, well, private up there."

The church is beautiful, but I feel exposed. As we reach the balcony, Gloria directs us through the doors to the back. In the hallway is a gorgeous, slender woman, about forty, and an equally attractive man.

"Dee Dee darling and Jan, meet Marty and Oliver."

They were not the square-built, Russian cleaning couple I had envisioned. *So much for stereotyping.* I quickly pull myself together. "It's a pleasure to meet you." I know Jan is thinking the same thing.

She says, "It's so nice to see you." Their accents are light. They speak very good English. "Dee Dee, I must tell you, because of our background, Oliver knows what I'm doing. We don't keep secrets with each other. I know I was not supposed to speak outside our group, but it's a long story. I'm sorry, forgive me."

One look at Oliver, and I know it's okay. "No forgiveness necessary." Oliver kisses my hand.

"I will never say anything to anyone, but if you need me, I'm very good at handling things. I have other skills besides cleaning churches. God has mysterious ways of working."

"Thank you, Oliver. I will let you know if I need anything."

He tells Marty he will finish and for her not to hurry. At least, that's how Marty translated it. He kisses Jan's hand, too, and disappears down the hall.

I whisper, "Wow. From Russia, with love."

We sit in one of the Sunday school rooms, and Jan hands Marty a folder. I open the small package from Marty.

On the cover, it reads:

"From Russia, With Love."

Marty hands Gloria a notebook and a pen. "Please write as I read this. My written English is horrible." All the guests were in her book, too, but it was a view from the upper balcony. She gives Gloria more details to write by names on Jan's list. She had noticed the strange little man and couldn't see what he did at the front. When he put his jacket back on, she noticed there was a little flower in his lapel. It wasn't there before. Gloria gasps and tells her about the flowers. She didn't notice anything about the "gray lady" or the gentleman named James, except that the lady kept crying. Jan makes a note by Alicia's name. Odd because she had seemed like she barely knew Adlin, according to Carolyn's recording and notes.

Marty pops up and says, "There was no evil in the church during Adlin's service."

Jan and I gasp. "What?"

"There was no evil in the church. Oliver told me; he's very instinctive. It's in my journal right here." She shows me in Russian big letters.

"I can't believe that. What about the little man?"

"Read the notes: the flowers, the woman in gray, and the gentlemen. I don't know how he knows; he just does. I thought the little man was creepy. Oliver said he was pretending and did so very well." She had read Gloria's notes. "See, he's right. Oliver says he's a clue. A connection to the evil."

"Now I'm really confused. Marty, isn't Oliver ever wrong?"

"Never, especially with this sort of thing. Like I told you, he is always very on the mark."

Jan diverts me. She tells Marty about the dreams. Marty seems really interested.

"Oliver and I were reading about Joseph. We both know that God is revealing the truth to keep this from happening again. The loss of Adlin is not in vain. There is much more. God is sending someone. He is working in many people. I wrote this in my journal. Our gift to you should not disappoint you, Dee Dee. I can see that you're disappointed, as I tell you." She reaches over, places her hand on my chest, and begins to quietly pray. "Dee Dee, don't let that little stone grow and make your heart hard. You must deliver it to its proper place, to Adlin, and to the foot of the Cross. That's in my journal, too."

I'm dumbfounded and confused. *How did she know?* Jan and Gloria look blank. Gloria's writing. Marty smiles and says that she must get going, but to call. Jan tells her what Gloria had said about being in her group.

"I will call her then. May I keep this folder? I know Oliver will want to see it. May I share this with him?"

"Yes."

"Dee Dee, it's been a great pleasure. I wanted so badly to meet you. I am sorry if you find my gift displeasing, but I... we... Oliver and I can only give that which we believe is true. Blessings on you, and may God give you speed on your journey to truth. We want to help."

Jan and Gloria hug Marty. Not a word as she leaves. We all stare at each other. Speechless. *I feel sick.* A tug from the pendant is painful. I touch my chest. My heart is pounding...

✱

Jan and Gloria are shaking me. "Dee Dee, are you okay?" I open my eyes to a very white and frightened pair looking down at me.

Gloria tells Jan to call 911. I grab Jan's hand. "Don't. I'm okay."

Jan's lip is trembling. "Dee Dee, are you sure?"

Gloria's putting some kind of oil on my head and is praying.

"Let me lie here for a minute."

Jan's phone is ringing. I hear her say, "We'll be there shortly. Let's go."

The squeezing around my heart is subsiding. Gloria is rebuking something... *I don't know what she is saying.* They help me up. Gloria is laying her hand on my head. I feel like something is letting go of my brain. A relief, a relief. "I'm okay."

"No, you're not. We're going to the hospital. Gloria, help me."

I feel almost euphoric. Jan and Gloria are fading in and out of my vision.

"Take the elevator." Jan's voice is panicked.

Gloria has a confused look. "I don't understand what happened. I saw the light dim, and the next thing I knew, Dee Dee was on the floor."

✱

Jan is driving like a crazy person. Gloria had to stay at the church to pretend that nothing happened, avoiding questions.

At the tiny local clinic, the doctor assures Jan that I am fine. Everything checks out normal. It could've been a drop in blood sugar. "Oh, Dee Dee, all you had was coffee and toast. I'm sorry."

"Jan, what do you mean? I'm used to having coffee and *no* toast. I'm not Martha Stewart, and you, of all people, know how a police officer lives."

Jan seems relieved. "Dee Dee, something happened after Marty touched your chest. Did she do something to you?"

"No, Jan, she didn't." *That wasn't quite true, but not how Jan was thinking.* "I think I was overwhelmed by being inside the church where they had Adlin's funeral." *Once a cop, always a cop.* I can see Jan's mind whirling through the events. *Linda will be worried. She's already called me twice. I didn't tell her. Gloria knows not to say a word.*

Linda is frantic, "Where have you been? It's almost 2:00, and we must plan Ben's arrival." She has that look again, almost like a girl getting ready for a first date.

"The lawn and the house are beautiful, and so are you. Your hair looks great."

Linda is glowing. "Do you like it? How about you, Jan? I thought I needed something a bit more up-to-date." Soft layers frame her face. It takes several years off Linda. Jan nods in approval and gives her a thumbs-up. "I've had lunch delivered, some salads from the deli."

I move to the kitchen, and sure enough, there's food. *I'm starved.* Linda doesn't want to do dishes, so we eat out of the plastic boxes they came in.

"Now, this is what I call my kind of dining. Isn't it perfect, Dee Dee? I'll bet this is your favorite pattern of dishes." I laugh at Jan's comment.

The humor seems to go unnoticed as Linda looks at her watch. "Tell me how the visit went with Marty."

"It was good. She's reviewing the file, and after that, we'll all get together. I met Oliver." I tell Linda how shocked I was at how different they were than what I had imagined. "It was a very interesting visit."

Jan is nodding in agreement. Linda is barely listening. She's moving through the day in her mind.

II
CAT AND MOUSE

"Stuart, where have you been? I've just finished the lecture. I needed you to pass out fliers and information. I turned around, and poof, you were gone!"

"I've been in the restroom. I'm not feeling well. It seemed like everything was going fine." Actually, Stuart hadn't been in the men's room. He had gone upstairs to take pictures of what was going on below in the lecture. He especially watched to see the roster and zoomed in on it. He made sure it was set in a very visible place where it would be easy to shoot. "Do you want me to keep the rosters and the sign-in sheet?"

"Not tonight. I'm almost packed up."

"I'm sorry, Professor Jacob."

"Aah, call it a day. Things happen. You couldn't help it. See you in the morning. Call me if you still aren't well."

"Okay, goodnight, sir."

I've got to get to my car and watch. Who knew the Professor could have adoring fans? There's that girl and her date. Almost everyone else is out. My count is thirty-eight. Where's the last one? He's handing her a card. Great. One more groupie. The Professor is so charming.

The librarian is out. The Professor is getting in his car. I'm going to follow her.

The Professor is right behind her. What's he up to? That's not the way to his house.

Stuart changes his mind and follows the Professor. *Stay back, don't get close.*

When Stuart stops at the light, he pulls over like he's parking. *Keep your eyes on the taillights.* Up ahead, the car turns left. *Where is he going? He's pulling over. Looks like he's reading something. Wait. Stay back. Okay, he's moving again, weaving his way through the city. I've been driving for forty-five minutes. He's parking. Oh, my God. There's that girl's car. We're only about fifteen minutes from the library. Is he on to me? Hide, quick!*

Stuart pulls into the alley. *Don't panic. Drive through the alley and come around to the corner of the building.* There's the Professor casually walking down the street. It's like he's studying the building. He's writing in a little notebook.

Dear God, he's coming back. Get outta here! Back down the street and go the other way. Whew, that was close. I better be careful. The Professor is definitely not stupid. He's almost uncanny with his instincts.

The young man feels a shiver go down his spine. His hands are sweating. Glad to be at his apartment, getting the keys out. Stuart hears his phone ringing. Running, he answers.

"Where were you, Stuart? I thought your machine was going to come on."

"I had to stop at the pharmacy to get something for my stomach... Yes, I bought all-natural, herbal. I am headed to the bathroom right now. I'm in trouble... Yes, I'll see you or call you in the morning. Thanks for checking in on me." *I feel more like he was checking up on me. I've really got to be more careful.*

Stuart double locks his door and heads to the shower, but having such a wild night makes him decide to skip the shower. He tucks the camera from his tote into the cut-out place under his mattress.

I've got to come up with another plan. I'll look at the list tomorrow to see if that girl is on it. At least I know where she lives, and I wonder what other girls were on that list.

§

Professor Jacobs sits by the phone. A puzzled look on his face. "Is Stuart really sick? He looked fine to me. I wonder where he was. Maybe he did go to the pharmacy. What do you think, Roscoe?"

"I don't like him; I always feel funny when he's around. He's too nice. That's always weird. Thanks for making sure my visits are short when he's around."

"You know, Rose liked him. He started as her assistant. I just kind of inherited him."

"I don't like it when you talk about Rose. It makes you sad. Always seems to distract you from your work when you start traveling down memory lane. I know she was a wonderful woman, but all these projects we have started have been for her. Now, haven't they? In memory of Rose."

"Yes, Roscoe, as always, you're right. Stuart must be okay if Rose liked him."

"Huh?"

"Thanks for helping me, Roscoe. I haven't been nearly as lonely as I was after Rose died."

"No problem. It's not easy to find someone who will be as open to a guest as you have been. Everyone who knows me is so excited about your research. It's an honor to be in your life, and that I can work on projects with you. Maybe you should make me your full-time research assistant instead of Stuart."

"Well, I don't think that will happen. The University holds Stuart up as one of their best grad students. Rose brought huge amounts of money into the coffers through donations from the food industry, perfume companies, and, well, you know all that. Her studies in plant medicines were astounding. The pharmaceutical houses practically funded the entire science wing, the forensics department, my lab, Rose's garden, her lab, and, of course, the chapel."

"That's almost a joke, something so grafting and greedy, and... building, and funding a chapel."

The Professor seems oblivious to the disdain in Roscoe's voice. "Rose felt it was perhaps their biggest contribution to humanity."

Roscoe is laughing. "Like penance?"

"Yes, I guess, sort of. I've got to go to bed. I hope you have a restful night."

"Goodnight, Professor. Get some rest." *If I know the Professor, and I do, he's going to be really busy. I'll make sure he stays focused. That Stuart. I was so glad he was gone for a few days. The Professor seemed right on track. What's Stuart up to?*

12

THE LOST IS FOUND

The door opens, and there she is, Libby. "Gosh, Lib, you look like you could be, well, in college again. I haven't seen you in jeans. It's been a long time." She looks like the first time I met her. My hands are sweating. "Libby, I'm so sorry. I have a lot to tell you. Let's go to Hush Puppies."

"Okay, that'll be a trip back in time."

"It was magic then, wasn't it?"

"Tanner, I miss us. You know, like we were then."

"So do I, Lib. Maybe tonight will bring us back closer." *Or completely ruin us.*

"Let's go. I've been on needles and pins all day. Let's take my car with the top down. You drive." Libby tosses me the keys and smiles.

Yeah, Libby with her hair flowing free. Maybe I'll soft-peddle the truth. I don't want her to feel as old as I do, carrying the weight of the world.

Malts and fries, and of course, hush puppies. Jalapeno hush puppies. The restaurant has eight kinds. I can feel the heartburn coming. Speaking of heart, I better get down to it. It's 7:30. Emily and Travis will be waiting.

I tell Libby about the Adlin Summers case and that she's the one who has been distracting me. I find myself telling her everything— the condensed version, of course. Libby is totally shaken up. I can see the fear in her eyes. She turns pale. *Great, I've ruined us.*

"Tanner, are you in danger?"

"What?"

"Are you in danger? I'm frightened for you. I feel the evil. This is like a scary movie. You've got to get away from this. Tanner, there's a monster out there, and you are hunting for it, aren't you?"

"Yes, and I can't run." I'm shocked that Lib's whole concern is for me. She's amazing, selfless. "Libby, I have to catch this "thing." I've been afraid for you and Emily."

"That's why you've been so crazy with the 'Be Careful,' the phones and locks. Oh, Tanner, how could I have been so stupid? I've been joking around about it. How sick I must've made you with all the other woman stuff. Emily's right; you are a really good guy. I love you, Tanner. DJ Tanner, I know you can't run, but I'm not going to run either. I'm in. Don't give me that look! Either I'm in, or I'm out! I mean it, Tanner, Dereck Jason Tanner! We used to do everything together, plotting and planning. We've got to help this girl. We've got to stop this thing."

I stand up and give Libby a long, hard kiss. The diners all applaud. I throw money on the table. "We've got to meet Emily and Travis." Libby's eyes shoot me a look. "I'll tell you all about it on the way."

❖

The drive to Wilderness Walk is cool and refreshing. Libby's hair is loose and beautiful. Her hair is shining in the moonlight. A huge burden is lifted. Libby's chatting away. We both avoid the discussion of anything bad.

As we come around the last curve, Emily and Travis appear in the headlights. Travis has his gun out, down at his side.

I quickly park and am out of the car, running with Libby right at my side.

"We heard something somewhere out there." Travis is pointing up the dirt path to the right.

"Do we have a flashlight?" *Oh, why didn't we drive my car? How stupid. How could I have endangered us by being unprepared?*

"I have one." Emily reaches into her purse and brings out a little flashlight.

Libby follows suit. "So do I. See, we've been following orders."

"Okay, you girls wait here, or take one of the cars and go."

"Tanner, remember? I said, I'm in or out." Libby is adamant.

Emily places her palm on my chest. "We're going. It's way too creepy being left here."

"It's probably an animal." My bell is dinging. I can tell Travis hears one, too.

"I'll go first with the girls in between us. You bring up the rear, Tanner. If you girls feel like screaming, don't. If it's an animal, we'll all be sorry. Promise to stifle it."

Libby and Emily grab each other's hands. I hear them say, "Protect us, oh Lord." Amazingly, the little flashlights illuminate the path. Travis motions us to stop, cups his ear, and points further up the path. We go about twenty yards and stop. Nothing. We stand motionless in the night. Travis signals to turn off the lights. *Why couldn't it be a full moon, at least?* I feel Libby's arm tapping me. Her flashlight is on but under her jacket. I see something move to the left. Emily taps Travis. There's a faint sound, like a mumble. The lights go on, and we're running up the path. A small clump of brush is to the left, and out of it, something is moving towards us. Travis is already down on one knee, ready to take the shot. I've got the upper shot. I grab Libby and Emily and shove them behind me.

Libby whispers to Emily, "Get ready to run."

Smart, Libby. The girls are crouched low to the ground. The bushes keep rustling as the sound is moving onto the path.

Travis yells, "Stop!" but it keeps coming. We can see someone weaving back and forth. "Stand where you are, don't move!" Travis shouts, "Don't!" Whoever it is keeps wobbling around in circles.

I motion to Travis that I'm going in below to get behind whoever, or whatever it is. I hear a low growl. *Maybe I was wrong.* It's an animal, maybe a bear. Libby's flashlight is shining right into the brush. I see a mountain lion cut across our path and disappear into the darkness.

It must've been stalking a deer. That's why the deer stopped moving. It was caught between us and the lion. Libby is ahead of me, now moving her light back and forth. She shakes my arm off when I try to pull it back.

There, a figure is standing at the end of the ravine, and a quick glimpse of the steep drop is visible in the beam of the flashlight. Travis and Emily are coming on the run. We hear them crashing through the sticks. Libby is getting close to the edge, trying to reach out. The dirt starts to slip. I can't see it, but I can hear it. I grab her arm; it's a long drop. Whoever it is seems to be oblivious that we're even there. Travis holds the flashlight to his face and signals that he's going to grab them. He lies face down, wriggles along the ground, and grabs the figure, pulling it over backward. Emily shines the light directly over the figure. It's a young, blonde-haired girl covered with dirt and scratches. She is mumbling something. Libby leans close.

"I've lost them. I've lost them. Oh, I've lost them."

We get her up. Travis has to restrain her from walking back to the ravine.

The girl looks up, and Emily grabs her arm. "Hey, look, I think they're over here." Libby gets the girl's other arm. "Let's go find them."

Emily, smart Emily. I'm impressed.

The girls talk all the way back down to the car. We can't take her in Libby's convertible. Travis opens his rear car door. Emily starts to put her notebook from the lecture onto the front seat, but the girl grabs it. She presses it to her chest and gets in the back seat. Emily hops in beside her.

"Travis, you drive. I'm going to get in the back with Emily." As I start to get in, the girl goes ballistic. She freaks out, clinging to Emily. Libby pushes me aside and slides in. Instantly, the girl calms down. "Libby, I don't think—"

"Tanner, bring my car. We're going to the hospital." Libby begins to sing. Travis and Emily do it, too. The girl also starts to sing "Amazing Grace."

Amazing, women are amazing. As I turn Libby's car around in the lot, I see a quick movement, and then it disappears. Might have been the big cat, but it looked more like a person. My mind is whirling. *Ding, ding, ding, what if someone else is there looking for this girl?*

The conversation with Erica Long is running like a tape. *Hiking at

Wilderness Walk. By some miracle, could this be Anne? Maybe she hit her head. We'll soon know. Where is Beanie's number? Oh, no, it's in my briefcase.

I call the station. "Angela, this is Tanner. Where is Beanie's phone number?... Call her and tell her to get back to me. She has my number..." *Come on. Come on...There she is.*

"Beanie, I'm sorry it's so late. I need a big favor. Call Art and get Erica Long to meet us at Memorial Hospital... Beanie, calm down! ... I don't know if it's her or not. Call Art... Great. You have all their numbers at home? Call me back... Don't go there alone!... Beanie, it's not okay, wait for Art. Get him on the phone."

We're almost at the hospital. My phone is ringing. "Travis, go straight to the front. Don't go to the side emergency entrance. I'm right behind you."

Libby and Emily are still singing as they walk the girl clutching the notebook through the front door. Travis remains behind, with his gun under his jacket. I catch up, and we walk into the hospital together.

I speak with security, showing them my badge. "Take a cigarette break. If you don't smoke, pretend like you do. Send someone out the other entrances. Tell them to keep their eyes and ears open. I'll need the reports when we get done."

The lady at the front looks confused. She was getting ready to shut the switchboard down. She informs us that we should have gone into the Emergency Room. Flashing my badge changes her demeanor.

"I'll call someone immediately."

"I want a doctor to see her now. Find us a room. No Emergency Room."

The singing is softer but still going on. The attendant rushes the girls into the office behind the desk.

My phone rings. It's Beanie. She's with Art and Erica, headed to the hospital. "Come to the front. We are not in Emergency. I'll tell security. I didn't want to use the Emergency. Too easy for someone to find us. Too easy for reporters, too."

"Hi. I'm Doctor Lovett... Oh, my gosh! Tanner, Travis, what a surprise!" It freaks the Doc a little that we have our guns out.

"Take a peek at her, but not a word to anyone. I have a feeling someone else might be looking for her."

"Tanner, I have got to have testing supplies. All I have is a stethoscope on me."

"Okay, get a gurney. We are going to pretend it's a trip to the coroner.

"Libby, put your jacket on her and pull the hood up. When the gurney comes, you get on it. Pull the sheet up over you.

"Travis, you and Emily make sure you keep the back of her blocked from view. Lib, hold her hand so it looks like she is walking beside the gurney."

Doc calls for a gurney from the basement. Libby puts the jacket on the girl and zips it up with the notebook tucked tightly under her arm inside the coat and the other arm through the sleeve. She kisses her on the forehead and pulls the hood over her hair, and ties the drawstring. The gurney arrives, and Libby climbs on. Doc covers her up, and Libby pulls the girl's hand up tight to the gurney with hers from under the sheet.

"Doc, wait until the cart gets here. Give it some time. Whatever would be normal and pronounce her dead." The code is blue, and the team is rushing to the front. I head to security. I tell the guy at the front to have everyone stay in position. I tell them that an officer and two ladies will be arriving. As I turn back into the entrance, I see the cart disappearing back into the hall. *Good. She's dead.*

Doc has someone wheeling the gurney to the elevator directly behind the office and then to the basement. Travis walks away from the desk, calls Beanie, and quickly lays out the plan.

Beanie shows up really shaken and tells Erica to start crying when the officer at the front gives her the news.

When I tell him the girl has died, the security officer says, "I'm sorry."

"Me, too. Thanks, buddy. Tell the guys, but don't move out of position. I'll be back. Okay? Be on the lookout." *Where's Beanie?*

As I head to the elevator, the front door opens, and there's Art, Beanie, and Erica. Miss Long is sobbing. Beanie is comforting her as they walk into the back office. "Is this the end? Oh, my God, it's Anne!" Anne stares at her blankly.

Erica whispers, "What's wrong with Anne? What happened to her hair? It's blonde!"

"We don't know yet. We are ready to run some tests. Libby, can you or Emily get her to pee? I think the pan is in the toilet, so we can catch some."

"Let's go to the bathroom." Travis walks to the door and shuts the door behind them.

"Tanner, I'm not sure how she's going to react to blood draws. I'll get the nurse."

"No, you won't. You do it."

Doc starts to set up the tray and waits.

"Success! That wasn't hard at all; she did it!" Emily sees the tray. "Oh, boy. This part might not be so easy."

The Doc says, "I don't want to sedate her because she may have a head injury."

Emily says, "She probably won't even notice it if I can distract her. She's almost catatonic. Something's changed."

Logical Emily.

"Okay, show me your book." Anne begins to turn pages and mumble to Emily.

Libby starts rubbing her arm.

Now, Erica is crying for real. "What could have happened to her? She's like a child."

"Everything will be all right. I told you we'd find her. Let's be thankful she's alive."

"The girl doesn't even seem to notice." Doc is confused. "She didn't even flinch. She's really banged up, and I wouldn't be surprised if her knee is broken. I think she has a sprained ankle, but it's like she doesn't have any pain."

He sends the blood to the forensics lab down the hall. "I'm going to tell them we were having blood drawn when she went code blue, in case they notice it's not from a dead person. I'm unsure what we're looking for, so I have practically drained her. Just kidding. But I drew a lot so that we can run the whole gambit."

"Where are we going to put her?"

"Tanner, we will put her in the special trauma ward. Kind of a mini-psyche ward but more nurturing. They can take X-rays and other diagnostic tests. It's a locked facility, so no one gets in. They'll get her cleaned up and find out what's broken. I'll make sure samples of everything are taken and preserved."

"Put her down as Beth Adams. That's my mother's maiden name. No one and I mean no one, other than you and I and others we approve, visit her!"

"Yes, Sir."

"Thanks, I'll brief ya later. Art, you're spending the night with Beanie and Erica. Will your wife mind?"

Art hadn't said a word this whole time. "On one condition... that you brief me in the morning."

"Erica, are you okay with that? You're staying at Ms. Orr's."

"You already know how afraid I am."

Art reaches out and grabs Erica and holds her like a big teddy bear. "The kid's gotten to me, okay? Beanie, I guess you got run over by the Tanner truck."

"Beanie, is it okay if they spend the night?"

"You know it is, Sir. It's an honor that you trust me and that you care about Erica. Art and I will take good care of her." I hug Beanie and Erica.

Erica caresses Anne's hair and says, "I'm so thankful to see you. Anne, I love you. You're my only friend. Well, other than these guys. God Bless."

A Voice From Somewhere Else

"How's your end of the little project going?... You couldn't get her?... What happened?... Someone keeps interfering with the program?... What do you mean?... Several someones? How dangerous is this?... That has nothing to do with keeping that seed nurtured and growing. Speed up the growth and make some progress."

13
INSTANT REPLAY

Stuart is up early. He plugs the chip from his camera into the computer. He locates the shot of the roster and enlarges the images. "Yep. My count was right. Thirty-nine people." As he sends the enhanced images from the computer to his printer, he looks for the girl from last night's lecture. Though he had practically memorized the list, he was double-checking his memory. He mentally reviews who signed in and his conversations with the attendees.

He hops into the shower, and immediately, thoughts replay the drive from last night. *How do I make contact with her without the Professor knowing? Why did he follow her? Why did he walk past her apartment building? He's so strange anymore. So different.* The simple thoughts about the Professor trigger an instant replay of the trip to the island. Stuart stands perfectly still as he is caught deep in his thoughts. It's like a movie playing in his mind, and he's standing outside watching it.

The Professor had taken Stuart with him on a University-funded research project. Jacob had told Stuart it would be like a working vacation. *That trip was no working vacation. Some vacation. The plantation, way out in the jungle, was depressing.* He had barely seen the Professor, and Stuart definitely wasn't allowed to participate in the research. The little guy, Robert, and his sister, Corina, were the only people, at least normal-acting people he saw.

As the "movie" plays...

Stuart sees Robert pulling him by the hand. "Mr. Stu, come see."

Corina is cutting flowers and hands Stuart some. "Mr. Stu, please act like you're interested. Get down and look at these, please. It's important. Don't put your eyes anywhere else. Smile and talk to me."

Stuart can see himself kneeling and acting interested as Corina is smiling and chatting. "Mr. Stu, last night I see Professor Jacob leaving with Desmond. Mr. Stu, Desmond is the Big Man on the island."

The blank look in Stuart's eyes causes her to lean over and whisper, pretending to point something out. "You know, Big Man, dark powers. You don't tell no one I tell you this. This is bad. You be careful, you and the Professor. I'm scared for you, Mr. Stu. It's your last day here, and I will miss you."

Stuart shudders in the shower as he remembers his thoughts. *Oh, my God, she was telling me Voodoo!*

"Promise me you not tell. People go away all the time. They never come back." Corina is pleading. Stuart sees himself smiling and nodding. Stuart assures her that he won't say a word. He puts the cut flowers in a basket and takes the plants she up-rooted for him. He thanks her and walks her back to the house carrying the basket, acting like he's really studying them and thanking her the entire time.

Stuart smiles at the memory of Robert and Corina. His smile fades as he replays his interactions with Desmond and Professor Jacob.

Desmond had picked us up at the airport the night we arrived. When he asked the Professor who he was, Stuart was led to believe that Desmond was their security, sort of a guide and bodyguard. "You know, we're not in our element, Stuart. Desmond knows things we don't."

❋

"Stuart, we've almost been here a month. I have learned so much." Stuart had barely seen him. Jacob had slept until 1:00 every day and disappeared right after dark each evening; meetings, he said, with locals who know about natural medicine.

"My notebooks are crammed with information. I have pictures and interviews with all the people I met. I have some good recordings too, necessary information for my new project. Really excited to get home."

"Professor, are you okay? Your voice sounds like you've caught a cold or something." He sounded different. When the Professor quit speaking, Stuart asked him what he knows about Desmond.

The Professor seems to stiffen and never moves from his journal. Stuart feels like his eyes are narrowing. "What are you asking me?" Stuart doesn't mention Voodoo. He knows not to. "Why are you asking me? I don't like your tone. Desmond is a very respectable, almost revered in his profession. His assistance has been of immeasurable importance. I felt honored that he has guided me through this foundational trip. This could be revolutionary to the world of plant medicine. You will never bring this, whatever it is, up again. Do you hear me? Never!" That throaty rasp lets Stuart know not to go down that road again.

"I didn't mean to interfere."

The Professor loosens up. "Let's get these final samples and flowers you've got from Corina prepared for shipping. Let's get moving."

Stuart smiles, "Yes, Sir. I gathered them this morning right out back. They are packed and ready. The kids helped me. I have so enjoyed Corina and Robert."

The Professor is hurrying. "Desmond will handle the shipping of everything. He will take care of customs, cutting the red tape, you know, and counting the crates. Done. Let's have some lemonade on the porch until Desmond comes."

"Corina, lemonade, please." Corina serves Stuart. He thanks her, taking both of her hands and pressing a one-hundred-dollar bill into her palm. *Extra vacation spending money. But since there was no vacation, it could help her and Robert.* Robert runs up the steps, hugs Stuart, and politely says goodbye to the Professor. Stuart winks at Corina. "You have been very helpful. Thank you. Be safe."

She smiles. As Desmond drives up, the smile fades. "Remember me, Mr. Stu. You take care." She takes Robert by the hand, and they scurry quickly into the house.

Desmond and the Proffessor sit in the front. He tells us the crates will be sent by ship later. The Professor tells him not to break the seals. Desmond laughs and says, "For sure." They both laugh.

Stuart is looking blank. *What's funny about that?*

On the drive to the airport, Desmond looks into the rearview mirror as his eyes narrow. "How about you? Did you enjoy your stay? Anything you want to know about?"

"I've had a wonderful time… And in answer to your question, I guess the Professor will have much to tell me about your travels together. I am very excited about the plants and the research I did. Thank you for your courtesy."

"You're welcome. Come again, and I will show you more. When you are ready to come, don't worry. I will be here."

That's an invitation that will never be accepted. "Thank you." Stuart can't wait to get on the plane and return to the good old USA.

The trip through customs was a breeze. Desmond just waved his hand, and the officials stamped our passports, and not one suitcase was opened.

Seated on the plane, the Professor seems engrossed in listening to a cassette with his earphones. He closes his eyes, and so does Stuart's. Stuart suddenly gets up and goes to the lavatory and washes his hands. He can feel Desmond's handshake still on his skin. Returning to his seat, he falls asleep. His last thought is of Dorothy clicking her ruby slippers together, saying, "I want to go home. There's no place like home."

Stuart steps out of the shower, shaken by the visual replay of the trip to the island. *What in the world was that? Pull yourself together.* Stuart vigorously rubs away the "movie experience" with his towel. *Get going, don't be late.*

Running up the back stairs of the University Lab, Stuart meets the Professor.

"Stuart, you look well today. Did you sleep all night?"

"Yep, like a baby. How about you? You look tired."

"Well, Roscoe had a restless night and kept me up. I finally had to go for a walk. Don't even know what time it was when I finally rested. I had an exhausting dream. Let's get busy. I need you to organize everything from the lecture. Get the addresses and all personal information into the database. I re-typed the list so you could enter it." He hands Stuart the folders and goes down the stairs.

Stuart quickly enters the office and begins reading the file. *Exactly the same as my count. Whew! He doesn't know I followed him last night.* Stuart makes a copy anyway and stuffs it into his pocket. He puts his thoughts from the shower out of his mind and begins entering the list.

Irene is at the door. "Stuart? I need to borrow a book on plants from the Professor."

"I'm sorry, the Professor has taken almost every one of them home. Actually, they were his personal materials. He uses his own money to buy them. He is entering most of the information into a huge file he's creating."

"Thanks anyway. Is he sure that's a good idea? Suppose someone broke into his home?"

Stuart laughs. "The chances of that happening is like successfully breaking into Fort Knox. The Professor tells me Roscoe is there 24/7. He's pretty rugged."

Irene looks puzzled. "Stuart, are you all right?"

"Yes, it's different since Rose passed away."

Irene nods her head in agreement. "I know. We all miss her, and you're right, it is different. I'll see Jacob later. No need to mention I was here."

Irene pulls the door shut and pauses for a minute. *Odd what Stuart said about Fort Knox and Roscoe.* She walks quickly to the end of the building.

14

WHERE ARE YOU?

Mr. Kaplan, where are you? Tanner arrives at his desk looking like he's been out on the town all night. Beanie, with a cup of coffee, follows him into the office.

"Have some juice. I thought you might need this too."

Tanner peeks in the bag, and Beanie pulls out a breakfast sandwich.

"It's a little something to tide you over. Erica is safely deposited at work. That poor kid needs the money. There's an officer pretending to be the janitor with her. Art had called me. He has a retired friend who said he'd help. He's the janitor. We can pay him as a contractor. I verified that we can. Okay?"

Leafing through the stack of messages on his desk, Tanner issues an exhausted, "Okay."

"What time did you finish at the hospital?"

"One a.m."

"The Mayor called, and he wanted to know how you were. He said he was checking up on your progress. Knows how hard you've been working." Beanie rolls her eyes. "He never calls unless he wants something. Now, what?"

Tanner fills Beanie in on the meeting with Garrett and the Mayor.

"Does he think all of this is made for TV like you can have all of that by tomorrow?"

"Yeah, I guess he does. Beanie, I forgot my briefcase. I'm going home to read the file." He grabs the bag and his coffee, smiles, and is gone.

Tanner calls Irene. "Perfect Woman. What do you have?"

"Well, a couple of things. Nothing too great. The sticky note was definitely from the same writer as the note on the fridge in the Summers case. The book was checked out by a girl named Alyssa Kirschenbaum, a student at another university campus, and again, three weeks ago by Anne Johnson."

Ding, ding, ding, ding, ding. Tanner's bell is going off.

"The book is in great shape. It couldn't have been in the flower bed for more than a week. You know, all this rain we've had, but the book is dry. I've contacted the University about mandatory readings for Anne's classes. I found out that not one class required this book, and she's a math major. I had a friend search the student files for more information on both girls. One small stain in the book is being tested. Oh, and another thing, did you notice the unusual smell? Faint but a little bit unusual. Well, we came up with roses and something we couldn't identify. Were there roses in that flower bed?"

"I can't remember, but I'll call Constance."

"I'm going to the library with a picture of Anne."

"Irene, be low-key. Call me if you get anything."

Tanner trudges up the steps. *Home!* He opens the briefcase and pulls the Kaplan file out. He's fighting sleep. *Mr. Kaplan, I've got to rest my eyes.* He finishes his sandwich and the last drop of coffee. As Tanner stretches out on the couch, he descends almost instantly into sleep. His mind paints a series of dark scenarios...

> Running, being chased by a mountain lion. Running through the rose bushes. Thorns poking and tearing. Yelling loudly, "Run, Libby!"

Tanner wakes up in a cold sweat, unaware that he is home. He jumps to the sound of his phone, his private cell.

"It's Beanie, Sir, the doctor called. Please call him." Beanie gives Tanner the number.

"Lieutenant Tanner, I have some news concerning Beth Adams." Tanner is instantly wide awake.

"Yes, I'm listening."

"The young lady has a hairline fracture in her finger. She, in fact, does not have a sprained ankle. It's broken. She has major injuries to her knee, and she has scratches all over her, like puncture wounds from thorns. We pulled some out. It looks like she's had contact with barbed wire and has scrapes on her legs like she's climbed a chain-link fence. She has no needle marks, but we believe that she ingested some kind of plant substance. We're running tests now.

"At some point, something was smeared all over her body— a kind of paint or clay in an oily base. The inside of her clothing was covered with the substance. Whatever the stuff is, it created paralysis of the muscles. Traces of PCP and Rohypnol, better known as the date rape drug, were found in her. There are also other substances we are trying to identify. No marks of her having been tied up, but there's tape residue across areas of her body. It appears she'd been taped down to something. One tooth is broken in the back, indicative of a seizure.

"This kid's a mess, but we can tell by her muscle structure that she's very healthy. Her mouth and her teeth indicate that she's not a drug user. It was hard to see last night, but she's actually very nice-looking. Someone whacked little pieces of her hair off. Looks like they did it with a knife, not scissors, and the color has been changed. Her fingernails have all been trimmed.

"We're flushing her system and keeping her hydrated. She's starting to have some loosening. There's more flexibility to her muscles, and her eyes look more coherent. Lieutenant Tanner, are you still there?"

"Yes, I'm taking notes. Continue."

"We are looking at some more exotic plant profiles than we have here in the states. My guess is that this was some kind of ritual. Looking at her, I can't imagine that she was a willing participant. I'm sending some of the samples to Irene's lab."

"Good, make sure she knows it's my case. She'll know what to do. Tell her we need a lid on it. Doc, thanks so much, and remember, *no one* sees 'Beth.'"

"Tanner, I suspect she's a good kid. Whoever did this is a psycho. I'll have a whole file typed for you. Do you want me to call with updates?"

"Yes, and thanks again. I'll stop by after I've had time to review the file and follow up with you myself."

"One more thing, Tanner, it's been a pleasure, and maybe we'll work together again. It seems as if we have a mutual friend in Irene. I'll call when we pin something down or if this kid comes out of it."

"Good, let me know."

Tanner, why did you become a police officer? Maybe you should've been a florist. Books and flowers and roses and thorns and plants and stuff, PCP, date rape. His mind is whirling. Libby, Emily, and Travis were told to call in and take the day off. *Thank goodness.* It gives Tanner pleasure to think of them all sleeping. Tucked safely away. *Erica's okay, Beth's okay.* Relief. *Now, Mr. Kaplan. Let's see what you have to say for yourself.* Tanner starts to open the folder. *Oh, my God, I promised Art I'd see him this morning.*

"Beanie, is Art in?"

"No, his wife is making him spend the morning with her. She's got a massive honey-do list. I suggested that he take the day off with pay."

"Beanie, you are a good woman. Wasn't last night crazy?... Are you worn out yet by yesterday and all the things I had you do?"

"Actually, Sir, as I said, I am honored that you trust me. I feel horrible for Erica and poor little Beth, but it was exhilarating. I had a fresh view when I woke up. I feel like my life is going somewhere, that I wasn't going to slowly fade away and be forgotten. An epitaph that reads: She was great at shorthand. Was that what I was looking at? Some future. I'm sorry that I've really stepped over the line."

"Beanie, I think your future is bright. *You* are bright, and Lord knows you've helped me. Thanks."

"You're welcome, Sir."

"Call me Tanner."

"No, I like Sir, if it's okay with you."

"It's okay."

"What are we going to do about Mr. Kaplan?"

"Get the locksmith and meet me at his store in an hour. You know the drill. Call Sheryl and make something up."

"Yes, I know. I'll be there. I've been thinking, and I have a couple of suggestions. I'll tell you then. I'll bring flashlights because I bet the power's off in Kaplan's store."

"Wow! I wished I'd have thought of that. Beanie, get Susan from forensics and come in her car. Tell her to bring a forensics kit. Tell her you want it to appear like you girls are going to lunch."

The Mayor's friend got his money's worth with this detective. What a complete file— dry cleaners, gas stations, names of friends, ex-relatives, business contacts, where he bought his underwear, and then nothing. A copy of the "going out of business" ad, but no sale. How does someone clean out his entire apartment, and no one notices? Why did he leave his whole inventory in the building? All his siblings are dead or live out of state. One half-sister, deceased. Nieces and nephews and spouses all checked out. Look for the holes, Tanner. Where are the holes?

Tanner re-tracks through the relatives. *Nothing about the other half-sister.* Tanner reads on, dates and notes. *Who's the other half-sister? Nothing interesting. Blah, blah, blah, blah, blah. On and On. No card. No money missing. Not one clue. Sounds familiar. I better head over there.*

As Tanner is getting out of his car, the police locksmith arrives. Tanner lies, "Someone reported sounds coming from the store last night. Thought they saw a light. Thought I'd come by and check myself. The Chief used to know Mr. Kaplan." *Yeah, that was easy.*

"Anything else, Lieutenant?"

"No thanks. I'm fine. I appreciate it."

As the locksmith is driving away, Beanie and Susan drive up. They both have very large bags with them. "Shopping, girls?" Tanner's amused.

"You said to make it look like lunch, not forensics." Beanie winks at Susan, and they laugh.

As they step into the dark shop, Tanner tries the lights. As the lights come on, all three raise their eyebrows in surprise. The threesome makes their way up and down the aisles. Nothing appears out of place. Mr. Kaplan's store is a reader's dream. Teabags in little baskets and coffee pots. Couches and chairs arranged in cozy sections.

Wow! No sign of anything wrong. Exactly as the private investigator had written into the file. "Take some shots, Sue, and I'll see if anyone has changed anything." Tanner sits on the stool behind the counter. "Sue, dust the register and this whole area."

He tells Beanie to sit on the couch and look around the room. "So, is there anything that strikes you as significant?" Tanner moves to a chair beside her. "Do you see anything?"

"I don't know what I'm looking for."

"Holes. Things that should be there but aren't. Things out of sync. Use those female instincts." Tanner waits...

"It's like he was coming back. The photos are still up— Mr. Kaplan smiling, the Mayor, the Chief, letters from authors, and writer's awards on the walls. Memories still here, and the lights are on."

"Sue, is the water still on?"

"It's on."

"Come on, Mr. Kaplan, tell us where you are."

"Sir, perhaps he's hiding. Maybe he wanted to disappear for a while. This would be almost impossible to take along, and because he planned to come back, why bother? I'm guessing that he's left the state. I think he traded his car in after leaving, and that's why we can't find it. Maybe he hid it, too, and got another one. You know, he sold his house about eight months before this. He moved into a very upscale apartment. I checked. I think we should see where Mr. Kaplan lived." Beanie informs Tanner that she had spoken with the manager and that they could see the unit if they were interested.

"Sue, I'm going to have someone come over and stay while you finish." Tanner calls for the closest patrol car but tells them to make it look casual and to stay until Sue is done. "Meet me later, Sue, after you've had lunch. It's on me. Don't tell anyone about this. It's very private."

"Thanks, Lieutenant, I won't." Beanie and Tanner wait until they see the patrol car coming.

At Mr. Kaplan's apartment, Tanner and Beanie pretend to be shopping for housing. "Can we look around for a bit?"

"Sure. Lock the door when you leave. You'll need to sign out at the door and give the doorman the key before you go." Beanie shows the manager her I.D. and takes an application from her. The manager hands her a card. Beanie says they will be in touch if they are interested.

Wow! Mr. Kaplan, you have some taste and money, too.

"Tanner, can you believe this place?" Beanie's mouth is hanging open.

The manager told them that the apartment had been paid for six months in advance. The tenant had broken the lease due to health reasons and that he was moving out of state. They released the contract because the apartment was perfect, like it had never been lived in. Mr. Kaplan told them to keep the down deposit as a courtesy for releasing the lease. The manager said that Mr. Kaplan came and went, but it appeared like there was never any furniture.

As they left the building, Beanie engages the security guard in conversation. She asks a myriad of questions. She asks him about furniture. He said Mr. Kaplan had furniture delivered in big boxes. "It must've been brand new."

"A moving company?"

"No, a U-Haul with two guys. The old guy had brought boxes in for the first few weeks, and then nothing. He always tipped and was a nice guy." The guard thought that he didn't cook because he always carried a bag with him when he came at night. Sometimes, he could smell Chinese or Italian.

Beanie was gleaning information by pretending to be terribly concerned about the moral standards of the previous tenant. She concluded the conversation with, "Leave this wonderful gentleman a nice tip, dear."

Once out of hearing distance, Tanner teases, "I didn't know you were such a snob, dear."

"We got the info now, didn't we? We need to talk to U-Haul and find those guys."

"Yep. Yes, ma'am, we do."

"Sir, I'm sorry, I—"

"It's okay, Beanie, you're on a roll, and I'm so glad you are." As they drive back to the station, Tanner tells Beanie he's turning the case over to her as long as— 1. she stays in town 2. doesn't quit her job until she finds Mr. Kaplan, and 3. makes him look good with the Mayor.

"Sir, I will try." Beanie is making a list.

Then, it hits him. Tanner flips a u-turn and drives back down the street.

"Where are we going?"

"We're going to need help. We've only got twenty-four hours. I'm taking you to see an old friend." Tanner explains about the Chief and the book and everything.

Partners

"Constance, thank goodness you are home. I've got someone I want you to meet. Constance Carter, meet Bernice Orr." Beanie shoots Tanner a look of disgust. She hates her real name.

"Call me Beanie. It's a pleasure to meet you."

Tanner fills Constance in and asks her to help Beanie. He hands Constance his file from the case. "Will you do it?"

"Oh, Tanner, I was so depressed when you didn't call yesterday. I felt old and forgotten. You really know how to show a girl a good time. Heavens, yes, I will help! Beanie, tell me what we need!"

"Do you have a car? Can we use it?"

"Of course, dear. We're partners. Anything I have is at your disposal. Mrs. Constance Carter at your service." Mrs. Carter looks like she's about to cry.

Tanner scoots before she can start. "Give Constance my private number, and you girls be careful. Call Sue and get her report from today." *Libby...*

"Call Libby, Sir."

"Lib, are you okay over there?... Keep a low profile, I'm working on something else right now. Play Monopoly or cards. Don't go out. Listen to Travis. Tell him what I said and Lib, I love you. Last night, you were amazing... I'll see you later. Call me if you need me. Be careful." *I know*

Beanie will check up on Erica. She's like a mother hen with that kid. Okay. Irene. Call Irene.

"Hey, Irene, did you get a package today?... Great. Seems like you know Dr. Lovett well... Oh, really? I didn't know. You're full of surprises. Surprise me again. Help me with the package and quickly... I knew you would, and seriously, did you get my message?... Great... Call me later. We need to catch up on a lot of things, it seems." *Irene dating the Doc. Could be good for business. Police business. He must be a good man. Irene, the perfect woman, has great instincts. The Doc. I better get to him before he goes off shift.*

Tanner catches Jamison right before he is leaving. "Hey, Tanner, I was just thinking about you... Yes, you told me to courier it over to your office. It has the security officer report in it."

"I forgot."

"Let me update you. The plant material is usually found in the Caribbean. Brings on hallucinations and seizures. The stuff on the body was clay and oil from a type of South American plant, like the stuff you see in the movies with the poison darts. Not frog poison, but plants. Irene has the entire package. Let's see what she comes up with before we draw conclusions... Beth is doing well, holding her own. Looks like she'll be okay. We guessed at the antitoxins and began to introduce them through an I.V. She's going to make it physically. I hope her mind comes through intact.

"Newsflash! About fifteen minutes ago, a delivery boy brought flowers. He didn't know the girl's last name but used the first name Anne. He was from House of Flowers. The receptionist told him that, unfortunately, the only person brought in last night had expired and did he want to leave them for the family? The kid made a phone call, paced back and forth, and appeared extremely nervous. He finally took the flowers and left, but it seemed that he didn't know what to do."

"I do."

"See ya later, Lieutenant."

Tanner tries to remain calm. A plan begins to form in his mind. He calls Jamison back and asks him if he can wait. He tells him that he's coming to get the reports himself.

"Travis, I want you and the girls to go to House of Flowers and pay cash for a delivery to Room 118 at Memorial Hospital. Make sure to use the name Anne. Then, bring the girls with you to the hospital. You won't have time to take them home... Yes, this is a fishing expedition."

Doc waits as Tanner pulls his car up. "Doc, I don't care who's in Room 118, move them. Create a fake situation, and let's see what we catch... Yep, let's see who shows up."

Tanner goes back into the hospital and heads to Room 118. *Travis, you and the girls better do a bang-up job of acting.*

Just like Doc promised, the patient is being moved. The room was being set up with respiratory machines and other necessary equipment.

Tanner places a call to Jack at the Narc Division and says he needs a blonde female officer in an ambulance and to make sure she ends up in Room 118, ASAP at Memorial Hospital. *Thank goodness for Jack. He doesn't ask a million questions. Should be a great evening. I love night fishing.*

Tanner can hear the sirens as he walks out. He gets in his car, drives around, and parks a couple of blocks away. He puts on a ball cap, takes off his jacket, pulls his shirt out, and heads back to the hospital.

As he nears the emergency entrance, Travis and the girls are pulling into the parking lot. Tanner waits beside the columns. "Hey, buddy, what are you doing here? Long time no see." Tanner whispers to Travis, "Find Jamison. He'll get you ready for your part. The girls need to stay out of sight."

"I'll find somewhere to tuck them away in case it gets bad."

"It's been great seeing you again." Tanner winks at Libby and smiles. "Have a good night, ladies."

❧

Constance is shocked. "Mr. Kaplan was an old friend of my husband! This is very odd, Beanie, and I agree. Mr. Kaplan was or is planning on coming back. Get the phone book." They divide up the U-Haul places and begin calling.

"Wait, I'm going to have Jim make these calls. It will be much more official and quicker with all the department's computers.

"Jim, this is Beanie. The Lieutenant wants you to take care of something... Yes, I know you have all those reports ready for him, including the others from before... I know you've been waiting to go over them with him. He said to tell you he appreciates it, and he will review them with you when things quiet down a little. He needed to take care of something for an old friend. Now, he has another assignment, all very hush-hush. You're in charge. We're looking for a rental from U-Haul, from about six to eight months ago, or maybe some other brand of rental."

Beanie gives him the timeline, Mr. Kaplan's name, the address and then fills him in to also find out who the two guys might be. "Like I said, all very private, for the Lieutenant's ears only." Beanie tells Jim to keep her updated.

Constance has her house phone in one hand and is leafing through an old address book. "Here she is! Bonnie!"

Beanie's got a questioning look.

"I still have some connections, you know." Constance is glowing.

"Hi, this is Mrs. Carpenter... Yes, Bonnie, it has been such a long time... Yes, you're still my girl. I need phone records for Mr. Albert Kaplan," and she motions to Beanie for the file. "Yes, find his record from within the last year or longer if you can. ASAP..." She gives Bonnie all the information on Mr. Kaplan. "Yes, dear, quickly! It's very urgent. Aaron would be so grateful. Mr. Kaplan and he went way back from years and years before... Oh, wait a moment. Beanie, where can she send the information to?"

Beanie looks panicked. "Give me a second." She pulls the card from Seaview Apartments out of her purse and calls Erica. "Can I have a fax sent there?... Thanks."

Beanie gives Constance the fax number and tells her to send it undercover, attention to Erica. "Okay, here's the fax number, Bonnie!... It's a lot of pages?... Okay, it will be there within the hour? Thank you, Bonnie... You are right. Fast technology is great. Remember the old days when it would have taken us forever to get all this done?... Yes, I know, I will come to see you. I'm feeling so much better. I'm going to be getting out more. I promise I'll call. Bonnie, thank you... You, too."

Beanie calls Erica. "Erica, slip it somewhere out of sight when it comes. Everything's okay?... Good. Does it make you feel safer with Art's guy there?... Good, keep your eyes peeled. We'll be there shortly to get it. Be careful."

Constance hears Beanie say *we*. She's up and headed to change her clothes. She reappears. No dress. Some slacks and a top with the cutest red loafers.

"Well, Constance, Mrs. Carter, you look—"

"What, dear? Younger? I feel younger. Let's get moving." With that, Constance gets a big shopping bag and puts all the files with the address book and her notes into it, slings it over her arm, and announces, "I'm ready. Oops, I almost forgot." She grabs a tiny picture of the Chief off the desk and sticks it in her purse. "For old time's sake. He'd love this. Beanie, thank you. You'll never know how much this means to be in the loop again. Thanks for taking me along."

"Well, Sir gave us this assignment together, and we're partners."

❋

The ladies arrive at Seaview.

The faxes come in, page after page. "Here, you take half, and I'll take the other half."

"Erica, is there somewhere we can go to read these?"

"Yes, my apartment. You know where it is. Here's my key."

❋

Once seated at the dining table, the two women realize they need markers and highlighters. One call to the office, and Erica appears with a handful. "I didn't have any, so I went to Anne's. I knew she had a bunch." Erica can see the look on Beanie's face. "It's okay, the forensic people have already been there, and they've got everything covered. They looked at everything. Art told me."

Beanie and Constance start marking off anything significant. Writing numbers that reappear, especially looking for the out-of-state numbers. An hour later, they lay their pens down. "Let's start calling." They say it simultaneously, so the "partners" giggle.

"Constance, I'm going to check in with Jim.

"Nothing yet?... Okay, call me when you get the information. And Jim, thanks for being discreet."

Immediately, Constance is dialing out from Beanie's phone.

"Wait, we need to use the office phone so we can both make calls. We also need to make up a story to use when we make the calls."

✱

The partners appear at the office. "Erica, we've got to make calls from here. Can we go in the back?"

Erica walks them into the owner's messy office. She shoves the papers around and sorts them into neat piles. "I constantly have to clean up, or it will always look messy like this."

"Erica, may we use the phone?"

"Of course, use line 2." She places it in front of Constance.

The partners come up with a spiel to use for a cover. They claim to have found a very expensive leather-bound edition book stamped with Mr. Kaplan's Bookstore. Their number was on a paper inside, and they are trying to return it to the owner. Quickly, the women decide which of the local numbers each one will call.

They work through the list of drug stores, shoe repairs, dry cleaners, restaurants, and miscellaneous personal numbers. Dead ends. All the local numbers with no bells going off and no leads. "Okay, let's go blue." Blue highlighted numbers were in the state but not frequently called. Customers, restaurants, some of those were take-out, some were friends and wonderful customers. Lots of them recognized Mr. Kaplan's name, and some were concerned because they hadn't seen him in a while. They didn't know how to get a hold of him.

They filter through the pinks and blues with no bells going off and no leads.

"Okay, let's do the yellow, the out-of-state." Same story. One guy, in particular, was extremely concerned and asking questions. "Sir, all we are trying to do is return a book to the owner."

"Stop!" Beanie says, "We need to look for the holes. Study your list." On each yellow highlighted list, one number appeared often and in spurts. "There's the hole. Less frequently called. A long period of nothing. Nothing, and then sometimes more than once in one week, then nothing, and then one last call before Mr. Kaplan disappeared."

Constance has the phone book open before Beanie can say it. "That's a Northern Arizona area code. Does that ring a bell?"

Constance is almost shaking. "I forgot! Aaron told me that Al had a sister there. You do the honors, Beanie."

Beanie takes a deep breath and whispers a prayer. Constance closes her eyes. A woman answers. Beanie starts her spiel, and the woman is quiet.

To Beanie's amazement, the woman says, "Just a moment." Beanie hears her speaking to someone. She hears a man in the background saying, "What is it? I don't remember a book like that."

"Ma'am, is that Mr. Kaplan? Is Mr. Kaplan there?"

Silence and a long pause. "Are you still there?"

"Yes, this is Beanie Orr. Is Mr. Kaplan there?"

The woman whispers, "Al, I'm sorry."

A gentle-sounding elderly voice answers and says, "This is Al Kaplan. Whom am I speaking to? How can I help you?"

"Mr. Kaplan, thank God." She begins to tell Mr. Kaplan who she is and how concerned his friends have all been. "Are you okay?"

"Yes, I'm fine."

"Mr. Kaplan, what are you doing in Arizona?... You what?"

Mr. Kaplan tells her he's writing a book about the disappearance of an old bookstore owner.

Beanie wants to laugh with relief but becomes very serious. "Mr. Kaplan, may I call you back?... No, you're not in any trouble. Everyone will be relieved... No, we don't have to tell anyone where you are... Of course not, I would never give away your storyline... Yes, sir, not a word to anyone about that. My boss won't tell. We'll call you back. It has been a pleasure speaking with you. I'm so relieved to hear your voice. Lieutenant Tanner will call you later... No, Mr. Kaplan, you will not be in trouble. Everyone will be relieved."

"Call Tanner, now. A case with a great ending." Constance takes the little picture of the Chief out of her bag and kisses it. "Aaron, don't we wish they could've all been good endings?"

15

TIME FOR TRUTH

Linda is busy preparing. Having put in the marinated roast, she's rolling potatoes in rosemary and other spices and oil. The fragrance is almost intoxicating. Individual salads properly arranged, with little mandarins and strawberries peeking out from under the leaves of spinach and radicchio, and other various kinds of greens. "Jan, I've planned for you to join us tonight. I forgot to ask."

"Linda, I would love to, but I need to be home this evening, unless Dee Dee or you need me. I want to reorganize my thoughts and take a hot bubble bath. I'll meet Chief Garcia tomorrow."

"Jan, it's okay. I feel better about Ben coming. If I need you, I'll call you." *God knows I've put her through enough today. I wish we could just hang out.*

"Linda, would it be okay if I lay down? It looks like you've got everything under control." Jan winks at Dee Dee and laughs.

"Well, why break the tradition?" Jan gives them both a hug. "See you tomorrow." Jan slips out the kitchen door, hops on her bike, and rides off.

"She's amazing."

"You are too, Linda. Wake me up so I have time to change. Here's my phone. If Ben calls, please pick it up."

It feels so good to lay down. Marty's words about the stone. Pastor Don's words, words, words, stones, and words.

❉

"Dee Dee, wake up. Ben Garcia called, and he'll be here in about an hour. He's getting a rental car and waiting for his baggage. He knows how to get here."

Dee Dee looks surprised. "He does?"

"Well, I did give him directions. Everything will be fine. I'm actually relieved. I guess everyone should have a Ben like you do, a boss that's so concerned. Get pretty." Linda closes the door.

Why is she so flustered? Get pretty? Something feels ugly now, ever since Marty's words. I need to ask Marty what she meant about the stone. I feel a tug from the pendant. *Stop it!* I press my fingers onto my heart. *Actually, I'm starting to feel relieved that Ben is coming.*

❉

"Look at you! Linda, you look beautiful."

"So do you, Dee Dee. Let's make a good impression. Don't worry, I'll follow your lead with Ben. You only have to deal with what you feel comfortable with." The doorbell rings. "Dee Dee, Chief Garcia is here.

"Please come in. Ben, what a pleasure to see you."

That handshake lasted a little longer than normal. "Hey, Ben."

"Dee Dee!"

Ben engulfs me in a big hug and kisses me on the top of my head. "Ben, you make me feel like a kid."

"Yeah, that's what you are, my kid."

Linda is fluttering. "Please sit down. You two visit and get caught up on things while I get dinner ready. I hope you like what we're having tonight."

Ben starts. "Dee Dee, I've been wanting to check up on you. I've come to walk you through much of what you've missed while you were at Fairstone. Look me in the eyes and tell me that you haven't been nosing around making contacts with the police."

"No, I have not." I'm relieved that Ben phrased it that way so I don't have to lie. Ben tells me that he's contacted the detective in charge of the case.

"Dee Dee, do you know anything about what happened?"

"Only what Linda has told me. That it was horrible."

"That's why I'm here. I know there are things that you need to know."

Dinner is ready. Ben grabs me and twirls me around. "Let's not let this go to waste. Your aunt has knocked herself out."

I notice a slight touch to Linda's shoulder as Ben holds her chair for her. "Linda, this looks superb." He's smiling at her.

"Ben, it's some of Dee Dee's favorites." Dinner is making a good impression. Ben talking about California and what's been happening over the last six months. He has a suitcase full of cards and gifts. He tells me that everyone at the department really misses me, and so does the gang.

"I'll bet."

"Dee Dee, you know you have people that love you."

"Aunt Linda, Ben was making a joke. He was being snide. It's a real gang."

Linda looks embarrassed and says, "Oh, I thought you were being negative."

Ben pats Linda and says, "It's okay, Lin."

Lin? Lin? Did he just call her Lin? Now, Ben looks embarrassed. "What's going on here? Aunt Linda, you've been running around like a schoolgirl. New hairdo, make-up perfect, the onslaught of cleaning. What's going on? Lin? Lin? I've only heard one other person call you that, and Gloria isn't here!"

"Tell her, Benjamin. I can't stand it anymore."

"Dee Dee, your aunt and I have known each other for years." Ben tells me how he met Linda when I was being checked out for undercover work. "I, well, Lin, I got a call from her... Linda introduced herself and told me who she was. She informed me she was coming out to meet me. She wanted to see the person her niece was going to work under. She was checking me out. Linda told me the whole thing about Allen, your uncle, your parents, Adlin, and you. I was shocked to see that such a tiny person, well... I guess she was kind of intimidating in a very sweet way. Let me know off the bat that she would hold me personally responsible for your well-being, me, and God, of course. Therefore, we've met many times, and well, this event with Adlin has brought us closer."

I am dumbfounded. *All these years? Some detective. Dee Dee, what a dupe!* "No wonder you had no trouble passing the time when you came to visit. While I was working, you two were dissecting my life." *Here comes the rage!*

"Deidre, it wasn't like that. Ben felt it was endangering you to know he was close to me. I agreed. Besides, what business is it of yours who I know? Why should you resent my feelings of concern for you? The need to know the person taking you into a very dangerous life was important to me. Good grief! All the prayers, all the love, do you think that I could casually let you be out there so far away without having anyone to talk to? The Lord knows how you cut us off. Pretty much cut us off from sharing your life. I am not going to see that ugly temper raise its head. I curse that in the name of Jesus."

Well, I guess she got that off her chest.

Ben is staring at Linda with his mouth open. After a moment, he begins to clap. "Well said, Lin, well said."

Linda is crying. "Dee Dee, I'm sorry. Something inside went off when I saw that dark look come over you. The Lord has something better for you."

Ben looks alarmed. "Dee Dee, are you okay? You're pure white."

I'm clutching my chest. That stone. That pendant, almost burning inside. "Yes, it's subsiding." I tell them about Marty, the prayer today, and the trip to the hospital.

"I don't know what it is, but the Lord does. We aren't going to put up with whatever it is." Linda begins praying, and Ben pulls me close to him. I can't hold back the tears.

"It's okay, kid, you've been through a lot. I know there is one who watches over us, who is going to take this all away. Look at me, right here in the eyes. This is exactly why I told you to stay away from this case. You weren't well enough yet."

"But, Ben, I'm better."

"Yes, you are, but you have really got to let this stuff go. It's the devil's territory when we have that kind of anger— unholy anger."

16

NIGHT FISHING

Erica and Constance lean forward as Beanie calls Tanner. "Sir, I have some very good news. Mr. Kaplan is okay. He's in Arizona writing a book. He doesn't want us to tell anyone. I hear noise in the background. Am I interrupting?... Going fishing?... Night fishing? Does this have something to do with last night?... I hope you catch a big one— a really big one. Erica, Constance, and I make quite a trio... We'll keep this end going... I will. I'll tell them both. Jim is ringing in. Be careful. Enjoy fishing... Yes, I'll call Sheryl.

"Jim, tell me what you've got... You found the U-Haul truck and the guys?... You already have checked them out?... Thanks, Jim, we needed your help... Yes, the situation with the old friend is working out. You really took a load off of us. Have a nice weekend, and keep this under wraps. See you Monday."

"Erica, have you ever thought of working in, you know, something a little more exciting than apartment management? Dear, you are just darling. You look so innocent. You're perfect for certain assignments."

"Oh, Mrs. Carter, you are so sweet, and I hope when I'm—"

"Eighty? You can say it. Old."

"Yes, I hope I can be as strong and smart as you."

Beanie is amused. "I love this kid."

Constance asks Erica if she would enjoy having dinner and spending the night at her house. Beanie had told Constance how afraid Erica is.

"Beanie, will you join us for dinner and drive us home? Remember, we came in my car. You'll have to join us. You're going to have mercy and humor an old lady."

Beanie calls Art's "janitor" friend and asks if he could be available for more "cleaning"... "That's great, I'll let Art know.

"Constance, I have got to use the lady's room. Would you talk to Art?"

"Arthur... Yes, it's me. How did you know?... Oh, I'm the only one besides your mother that calls you Arthur. Arthur, isn't that sweet? Miss Orr was assigned to run errands today, but she wants you to know that Tanner will see you on Monday. I know he appreciates you very much. Have a nice weekend, Arthur... Oh, you might be seeing more of me... I'm feeling so much better. Thank you for asking.

"Arthur was always so quiet, but Aaron liked that about him. He said he could keep a lid on things. His wife's a bit of a nag, though." They laugh as Erica turns the desk over to the night manager.

All About Anne

"Roscoe, drive to check on Anne. I haven't seen her since she came to work on the new project. She seemed so interested. I certainly hope she's okay. She hasn't called, has she?"

"No, Jacob, she hasn't."

"Do I offend some of the people from my lectures? I really need research assistants. I can't do everything I used to. The University will only fund for Stuart, so I need volunteers. I know you worked with all of them, but they always seem to disappear. Is it something I'm doing?"

"Maybe?... I guess I never really thought about it. You know, college kids come, are flakey, and sometimes just lazy. You never know; maybe Stuart has ruined it." Roscoe couldn't stand not getting a barb in at Stuart. "Jacob, I'm equally concerned with, I mean, about Anne."

Irene had worked all day. She tried to squeeze her own work into the mix. Tanner's needs far exceeded her own. She still had a deadline to meet, though, or her grant would be cut back. The package that Jamison had sent was being processed, but she needed some rare botanical books on ancient medicines to be sure of what she was looking at. She hadn't run onto Jacob all day long. He could've looked at the samples and known exactly what they were.

She had gone to the office to ask for the book. Rose kept some of the most valuable and interesting books. Some she had written after trips to meet with medicine men, those who use plant medicines in various parts of the world. The nature of some of the material involving occult practices led Rose to never publish them. She didn't want novices in aromatic medicine to confuse practice with the validity of the chemistry and effects of plants on human and animal systems and diseases.

Rose had kept a straight line of faith in the God of the Bible. Irene had always valued her knowledge but truly believed that it was her faith that kept her research pure and selfless. Rose could've made fortunes if she'd given in and sensationalized her materials through publication. She would always say that the road to truth and God is narrow.

After Rose's death, Jacob had been allowed, because of his medical credentials, to continue her research. Traditional allopathic Western medicine offered her no help or relief as cancer ravished the once vibrant life. Jacob and Rose worked continuously with alternatives, and though Jacob begged her, she would not try anything that would, as she put it, compromise her relationship with the Lord. Anything that hit her spiritually wrong, was immediately rejected.

In the end, she told Jacob she'd see him later. She was going to God's Garden, and if Jacob remained until the Lord came, she'd see him in the Resurrection. Everyone who knew her mourned her passing.

Jacob was a crushed man and refused to practice medicine. He was a brilliant surgeon, but he couldn't do it anymore. The University didn't want to lose Jacob. His name was too famous. He and Rose had brought millions in donations to the University; therefore, Jacob was allowed to switch his field, and continue Rose's research.

Where's Jacob? I need his help. Irene picks up the phone, but there's no answer or message machine. *Stuart's comment about Fort Knox was odd.*

Jacob always had a machine to pick up his phone calls. Everything is definitely odd.

Irene hangs up her lab coat, slips on her sweater, and picks up the keys to her car. *I'm going to see Jacob. I'll have time to get back and have dinner with Jamison.*

It had been almost five years since Irene had been to Rose and Jacob's. Shortly after Rose passed, the invitations were further and further apart. After Rose's grave had been desecrated and her body had been taken, the invitations stopped altogether. Jacob was a broken man.

The night air feels good. Irene is surprised to feel the faint ding of her bell. *No one's following. Come on, Irene.* Out of habit, she reaches into her glove compartment, takes the revolver out, and slips it into her purse. As she rounds the last curve to the house, a van sweeps to her side of the road. Irene swerves in the nick of time and stops, but the other driver never even slows down. *Was that van coming from Jacob's house? There are only four houses on this road.* She sees the entrance to Wilderness Walk on the right and knows that she's close. She had forgotten how beautiful and how far the drive was. *Maybe I won't be able to get back in time for dinner.*

She's almost to the house but turns around and heads back towards town, down the hill to meet Jamison. Their schedules are so full that a quiet dinner is a rarity, and she knows from past experience how quickly the flame of love is extinguished by the wind of neglect. Irene's work has blown out more than one flame. *Not this time! Jamison is special.*

As she's coming up to Wilderness Walk, she sees a car coming out, heading down the road in front of her. *Goodness, that looks like Stuart's car.* She speeds up to get a closer look, but the sun is going down, and it's impossible to go much faster. The curves are dangerous. For some crazy reason, she hears Tanner's voice speaking, *"Be Careful." Yes, Sir, Lieutenant Tanner. Tanner!* She hasn't heard from him.

Irene pulls the phone out and calls Tanner. It's ringing. "Tanner, were you going to call me, or was I supposed to? Supposed to—"

The next voice she hears is Jamison. "Irene, I'm working with Tanner here at the hospital. Umm, it has something to do with the package I sent you. We may not be able to have dinner."

Irene interrupts him, "I'm on my way. I'll be there in fifteen minutes. Put Tanner on.

"Tanner, I'm coming. You can brief me. You've ruined my dinner date, so the least you can do is tell me why."

Tanner gives her the shortened version and tells her to try not to be visible. "Did you bring make-up?"

"Yes, it's right here in my purse. She pats the gun."

"Good girl. Be careful."

"You take care of Jamison... And Tanner, you be careful too."

As Irene pulls up to the hospital, she sees the side entrance and decides to drive around and take a look. She pulls out of the lot and covers about a two-block radius, something she learned from an old friend. An old flame. As she's coming back towards the hospital, a chill, a tingle, a ding; there's a van parked on the side of the street about a block away from the hospital. On the back side, it looks like the same van that almost ran her off the road. In the front lot, she gets an additional shock. There's the car she was trying to follow down the mountain. She goes on past it, and it has a University parking sticker. *It has to be Stuart's.* She parks on the side of the building by the garbage dumpster. She hangs her purse over her shoulder and puts her hand in it, holding the gun. As she enters the door, security greets her.

"Good evening, ma'am. We've had a patient go loose from the psychiatric ward, and we're not permitting anyone in or out."

"I'm with Dr. Lovett. Call him."

The guard politely asks her to wait while he calls Dr. Lovett. The door opens, and the guard tells her he'll be right down. "Please have a seat."

Irene moves away from the door and sits in the far corner, with her back to the wall to have a full view of the entrance and lobby. A magazine covers her face. She is pretending to read. The lady janitor looks vaguely familiar. *Oh, my goodness, it's Jessy from the Narc Division.*

She sees Jamison coming towards her. He is in scrubs, and he's treating her like she is a family member of a patient. "The fish is in the building, but we don't know where."

"Oh, Doctor, that's such good news." She whispers to him about the van and Stuart's car. Jamison pretends that his pager is going off. He calls Tanner from the front desk phone.

"Tanner, Irene's here." He relays the story of Irene's drive back to the hospital.

"How did they get in?"

"One came through the Emergency Room in a wheelchair. They're busy tonight. Seems like the guy is healed up and moving. We don't know about the other one. He was delivering flowers."

Right then, Irene spots Stuart at the elevator in his lab coat with a clipboard in his hand. "Fish entering the elevator."

Jamison dials Tanner. "Fish entering the elevator."

Irene can't imagine what is going on. *How can this be? Stuart has always been such an open person. Rose loved him. What is going on?* Irene sees Travis is running to the elevators. *He looks great, like Dr. Kilgore!*

"Hold the elevator." Stuart holds the door for Travis. The "janitor" moves her cart to the middle of the hall and plunks the big mop bucket down beside it. Then, she lines the vacuum up beside it. *Nice. A nice barricade.* Jamison squeezes Irene's knee and pats her arm.

"I'll be back."

"You better be." Irene's skin is prickling, and then there's an insistent ding. *Where's the guard? It's like something really sinister has entered the hospital. Evil coming. Irene, you're losing it.* She sees the guard open the door, and a very large black man enters dressed in a very expensive suit. He glances in Irene's direction, stops, and turns towards her. *Oh, dear God, blood of Jesus.* The man turns and strides directly to the elevator. *Tanner, we're wrong. The fish wasn't in the building, but it is now. He isn't even trying to hide.* Irene calls Tanner and gives him the description. Irene begins to pray for protection, for angels to come. She sees the guard kind of shake his head. She gets up and stares at him. He looks blankly at her. "Who was that?"

"Who are you talking about?"

"That man you let in."

"No, ma'am. No one came in."

Irene's heart is pounding. *Pray, Irene, and stay put.* She sits back down and begins to beg God for help and for His protection over Jamison, Tanner, and everyone.

Jamison's back. *Oh, thank God.* "There is... I don't know how to describe it." Irene's babbling, telling him about the man, the one the guard let in.

"We got the guy, but not the one you're describing. We didn't see anyone like that."

"Hunt for him! He's dangerous!" She's trying to keep up the pretense of her being a family member and him being the doctor. She tells Jamison that they're all in danger. "Believe me. He's here. I saw him go up the elevator."

Jamison turns white and calls Tanner. "Check Beth Adams! Now!" Tanner takes the steps on a dead run, but at the top of the steps, "Doctor Tanner" begins whistling "Amazing Grace" as he opens the door.

He cheerily greets the black, well-dressed man at the counter. "Sir, visiting hours are over, and you're not allowed on this floor without an escort." The man apologizes. He says he's obviously on the wrong floor and returns to the elevator. Tanner rings the bell to be let in, and a sweet-faced nurse appears as the doors are closing to the elevator.

"It's okay, just make sure no one gets in tonight." The sweet-faced nurse is Melinda. Tanner always thought she was a great officer. Tanner calls the undercover officers parked in the front lot and tells them to follow the well-dressed, big man leaving the hospital. "Tell the others, I don't know which door he's going out of, or if he's going out at all." He hears an officer saying that he's going out the front door.

Walking south, the man is thinking, *I know I was told to go to the third floor.* He gets into the van, and the driver slowly pulls away from the curb. *Disturbing, very disturbing.*

Irene is still praying when Tanner and Jamison appear. Travis has Stuart handcuffed. Stuart looks like he's going to faint. "I was only following them."

"Who is them?"

"I don't know."

"Why were you following them?"

"I'm not sure... Irene, thank God! Irene, tell them who I am!"

"At this point, Stuart, I'm not sure. That was you at Wilderness Walk earlier, wasn't it?"

Tanner and Travis look at each other. "Were you there? Have you been there before? Often?"

"What is this all about? I don't know what I've done. Am I in trouble? Irene, help me!" Travis and Tanner look puzzled. The undercover janitor is bringing another young guy to the front, and the officers are coming from every direction.

Irene asks Jamison, "Who's that other young man?"

"He's a delivery guy."

He's saying, "Don't get me in trouble. I just deliver stuff and run errands. I'm a nobody."

"Who sent the flowers?"

"I don't know, and I couldn't even tell you what he looks like. I don't know what I've gotten myself into. I just get calls from him. I pick up cash and run errands."

"Where do you pick up cash from?"

"Different places. Like—"

"What kind of places?

"Like phone booths and under rocks. Crazy stuff."

Irene happens to notice his tattoos. She nudges Travis to look down at his wrist. It's a most unusual symbol on the inside of his left wrist.

"I think we should take him in."

"But all I do is make deliveries. Come on."

Stuart is staring intently at the kid's face. "I know him. I've seen him somewhere before, but I can't place him."

Travis turns pale and darts behind the front desk. "Oh, my gosh, Libby and Emily!" Libby and Emily appear from behind the closed door.

"Were you coming to get us? It looks like we missed out on everything." Libby is glaring at Tanner. "Out of sight, out of mind?"

"Libby, I'm so sorry, but I needed to be clear-headed. When I'm worried about you, I can't think clearly." He gives her a soft kiss on the lips. "If anything happened to you, I wouldn't be able to take it."

Travis apologizes to Emily for locking them in.

"Irene, do you mind coming to the station with us?" Tanner asks Jamison if he will walk Irene to her car.

"I'll do better than that, I'll drive."

Irene says, "It's two blocks to where your car is, Tanner. We'll drop everyone off."

Boy, she's good. She sees everything and remembers it, too.

Travis smiles at Emily and volunteers. "Tanner, I'll take Emily home."

More Than A Nap

Jacob was still sleeping and dreaming about Rose. *Rose.* Rose saying, *"Jacob, wake up! Jacob, wake up! Wake up, dear!"* Jacob tries to get up, but he can't. He's awake, but he can't move. *Roscoe, where's Roscoe? Voices, that voice. That accent. It's Desmond. Desmond can help.* Jacob can't move. *Why is Desmond here?*

Jacob hears Desmond saying, "Why did you send me there? Your directions were wrong. There was nothing on the third floor except a whistling doctor. He was whistling a most irritating tune. What a waste of my time! This was supposed to be a special visit!"

Desmond, help me. Jacob's mind is racing, but he can't speak or open his eyes. *He's coming.* Jacob hears the door open. He knows someone is staring at him. *Help me.* Jacob hears a chuckle, a familiar, raspy sound. *Roscoe, Roscoe!*

"No, he's still here sleeping like a baby."

Jacob hears Desmond's laugh. "That's good. I don't want this trip to be wasted. We only have a couple of days before everything's right. Roscoe, what about that stupid delivery kid?"

Roscoe chuckles, "Yes, helpful, but dumb."

If Jacob could see the two standing in the hallway, he would've been totally confused— the big black man and a strange-looking young woman about twenty.

"Roscoe, you're always so full of surprises." Desmond is chuckling, and Roscoe is laughing.

"Yeah, I had to get this one out of the garden. Do you like my flower?" Sinister laughter. The two begin to chortle. The "girl" has a small tattoo on the inside of her left wrist.

Jacob's mind is whirling. *Why is Desmond here, and what are they talking about?*

&

"Lieutenant Tanner, we lost the van in the hills going towards Wilderness Walk."

There is clanging in Tanner's gut. "Okay, call it off and be discreet." Tanner checks in with the third-floor staff. The flower kid, Bryan, and Stuart, are being transported by the Narc Squad. Some of the "janitors" and other officers are staying. "Travis and Emily will go together in Libby's car."

Room 118 is locked. Irene and Jamison are ready to drive Libby and Tanner to his car. The security guard at the front waves goodnight and apologizes, but he's still baffled as he locks the front doors. He sheepishly is being escorted downtown by an officer dressed in a surgical gown.

"This is like a circus. We are going to be up all night. Libby, let me take you home."

She replies, "It's in or out." She's still miffed at Tanner for being tricked and locked in the supply closet.

"I'm sorry, Libby. I didn't want you to get hurt."

"Tanner, I need to tell you something... what I was saying about that feeling, something evil. It sounds crazy, but Emily and I, at a certain point, quit being angry. We were glad we were in that closet. We prayed the entire time. We were terrified. I've never felt anything like that before. I felt like the air was being sucked out. Tanner, this isn't just a killer. It's like the devil showed up. It's out there, waiting."

17

TRAVEL PLANS

After dinner, as Ben presents Dee Dee the gifts from the California "gang," the phone rings. Linda cups her hand over the phone and whispers, "Madelyn's worried."

"Linda, I went to bed, and I dreamed about roses and a garden...

Rows of beautiful flowers. It was a huge garden, and I saw a girl. There was a horrendous, indescribable sound that started. The girl tried to run from it. The earth began to heave and quake, and the girl kept falling. The roses weren't beautiful anymore. They seemed to have taken on a life of their own and were trying to trap her with their thorns. They were scratching and clawing at the girl. It was horrific! She was bleeding all over. At first, I couldn't see her face, but she dropped something when she fell. After she got up, I could see something silver in her hand. Then, there was a beam of light and I saw her face. It was our Dee Dee.

"I'll be praying. Linda, this was a really scary dream, and I can still feel the evil. Dee Dee's in danger!"

"Are you okay, Madelyn? Do we need to come over?... Madelyn?... Really?... All right, but call us if you need us." At the sound of Madelyn's name, Dee Dee stops mid-sentence and listens intently.

Linda is white as a sheet. "Ben, we need to fill you in. Madelyn's had another dream." Ben looks blankly. "It's bad, Dee Dee. Get Ben one of the folders, will you?"

As Dee Dee leaves the room, Linda whispers, "The girl in the dream was Dee Dee." She puts her fingers to her lips and whispers, "Don't." Ben nods.

As Dee Dee returns, she hears Linda telling the stories of Madelyn's dreams. Dee Dee hands Ben a copy of the account that Jan had typed. He's reading as Linda speaks. After recounting the dreams, Linda says, "And now, oh dear Lord, she's had another dream." Ben tries to interrupt, but Linda won't have it. She shares the new dream but leaves the part out about the face.

Dee Dee asks, "Did Madelyn recognize the girl?"

Linda lies and says, "No."

Ben never flinches, but says, "You girls give great credence to the dreams. Well, don't you think it could just be the imagination of an old lady?"

Linda and Dee Dee laugh. "Obviously, you haven't met Madelyn."

"Good point. I haven't."

Ben, the only one out of the loop in this little love fest.

Linda lays out the timeline of Madelyn's dreams. She gives the final blow to Ben's mind. She tells him about Adlin's hair. "Ben, there's no way Madelyn could have known that! Absolutely no way!"

"Only, now, we're into a whole different realm. I've only dealt with a couple of cases like this. One was in L.A. a long time ago, and someone in Miami had some bizarre events in a case. Really weird. I wasn't directly involved in those events, other than a couple of meetings. They came to California, something involving the Cartel." Dee Dee can see Ben replaying those cases in his head. "Dee Dee, initially I came to share some things and perhaps escort you to Oak City, but I'm not sure now."

"Oh, I'm going! I've been tricked into staying here and having lunch after lunch. You were playing me."

"Dee Dee, stop it! I don't like it when you have that dark look. I've already addressed the issue with that anger. I take authority over it! This ends! I command this away from Dee Dee!"

Dee Dee feels like the chain on that pendant is swinging slightly. Linda notices Dee Dee's quick hand movement to her heart, but she doesn't say a word. Ben sits motionless with his eyes closed. Putting up his hand, signaling to be quiet, he opens his eyes and announces he's calling Lieutenant Tanner.

"Lieutenant Tanner, this is Ben Garcia. I'm still at my stopover." Ben gets very quiet. The conversation drags on.

Tanner, that's the guy working Adlin's case. Linda had mentioned his name earlier. I've seen that look on Ben's face many times. There's been a breakthrough or something. Dee Dee and Linda sit perfectly still, listening. They hear Ben telling Lieutenant Tanner that he's coming as soon as he can get a flight out.

"Linda, please get me a flight. The next flight to Oak City or any place close to there."

"Make that for two. Wait, let me call Jan. I promised.

"Jan, are you still up?... Want to go on a trip?... How soon can you be ready?... We'll be waiting for you."

Ben is protesting. "Dee Dee, you are not going!"

"As far as I know, I can make my own decisions. Jan and I can go on our own. Dot's taken care of that. Dot had the car dropped off earlier, and the money is in the bank." Ben surrenders, and Dee Dee tells him about Jan, not the secret of her health, but the rest. "I'll have someone who is street-smart with me."

Linda is on the phone making arrangements for Ben. He stands up and walks with his phone into the other room.

I wonder who he's calling?

"Okay, I'm set. Get movin', Dee Dee."

An hour later, Dee Dee sees a strange car pull into the driveway. *What now?* Much to her surprise, she sees Jan slide out of the driver's seat. Jan's coming up the walkway, wheeling a computer case behind her. Dee Dee opens the door before Jan has a chance to ring the bell.

Jan laughs and says, "Compliments of Dot," pointing at the car. "We also have a flight booked at 10 a.m."

Linda introduces Jan to Ben. "Ben's flying out at 9:00."

Jan smiles and rolls the computer case towards him. "Here's the whole thing; almost everything we've got is in the computer. The code is IMJR, and the file is under BMW45. Dee Dee is laughing as Jan winks at her.

"Jan, you look pale." Dee Dee is whispering out of the hearing of the other two. "Are you okay?"

"I'd love to say never better, but we need to get this show on the road. Don't ask, Dee Dee, don't ask." Dee Dee feels a lump forming in her throat. Jan hugs her and says, "Don't, Dee Dee. Dee Dee, pull yourself together."

They go back into the living room to join the strategic planning session. Ben tells Jan and Dee Dee that there will be someone to meet them at the airport when they land.

Oh, that's what his phone call was about, but who's picking us up?

Linda is calling the girls, the Big 10, about the change in plans. Dee Dee hears Linda say, "Yes, she knows."

Those sneaks, what a bunch of actresses. Dee Dee starts to feel that anger again. Linda's words pop into her head. She laughs and thinks, *clever girls.*

Ben and Jan have been huddled in the corner. Dee Dee sees the look on Jan's face as Ben hands her a folder. Jan is opening it, and whatever is in there, really affects her. "Jan, are you okay?"

"Yes. You know, I've been kind of dizzy all day. Too much going on." Jan closes the folder and hands it back to Ben. He puts it in his briefcase and clicks the latches.

What was in that folder?

Jan announces that she's got to lie down. She's sleeping in Allen's room. Dee Dee walks her to his room. They leave Ben and Linda sitting on the couch, quietly talking.

"Thanks, Dee Dee. I hope you know how much it means to be included on this trip."

"Gee, I wonder if I can sleep without that goodnight kiss to the forehead. I think we'll have a great time "shopping." I can't wait to see what sort of finds we'll make." They both laugh. "Night, Jan." *It's starting to feel like Christmas. Red October in a box with a big, red bow. Shopping for Red October.*

18

Q&A

S tuart is frantically trying to explain to Jim how and why he was at the hospital.

"Answer the question. Did you know Anne Johnson?"

"No, officer, I just followed the van."

"What van?"

"The one I saw at the Professor's house earlier."

"Why were you at the Professor's house?"

"He's my boss, and he's been acting strange lately."

"Strange how?"

"Well, not really anything I can put my finger on, but there's always this guy named Roscoe who answers his phone when I call him. Jacob is always sleeping or something. Out, you know, gone."

"Roscoe, who?"

"I don't know who, but—"

"Answer the question. Why were you at the hospital?"

"I already told you."

"Don't get smart."

"Did you see the van at the hospital?"

"I'm the one asking the questions!"

"Irene Carpenter can tell you what I know about Jacob."

"Who's Irene Carpenter?"

"For God sakes, she's right out there." Stuart is pointing towards Irene. Stuart defiantly slumps in his chair and crosses his arms against his chest. The questions keep coming. He says nothing. Jim tells Tanner that the Stuart guy is not talking.

Tanner enters the room. "Irene tells me she knows you." Stuart shoots Jim a glare.

"Jim, it's okay. I'll let you know if I need you.

"Now listen, Stuart, you are in a lot of trouble. It could be a case of being in the wrong place at the wrong time. Could I see the inside of your wrists?"

"Sure. Listen, Lieutenant Tanner, Sir, I'm telling you something weird has been going on with my boss. I can't explain it." Tanner was surprised at that and doesn't interrupt. "It's just something."

No tats on his wrists. "Give me an example."

"Well, after one of his lectures, I always used to take the list, type it, and put it in our database. For almost a year now, he types it, hands me a copy, and then I type it into the database."

"And this is significantly more than redundant?"

"Well, one day, I noticed a name missing. I knew because I really wanted to ask that girl out. Her name is Alyssa Kirschenbaum. I mentioned that to Jacob, and he said he'd ask Roscoe. That's when he started typing the list. He said he'd check it out. The next day, Professor Jacob said that apparently the girl had called and wanted to be removed from the list."

"And?" *Ding, ding, ding. How is this connected? That's the name Irene gave me when she researched the library book that Constance found.*

"Well, after that, because it bugged me, I put out a numbered sheet. The Professor had a fit because he said, 'People are more than a number.' As people would come and sign in, I would make a mark on my hand or something. We had over two hundred, so remembering each one was impossible, unless it was someone like Alyssa. I started to keep count at almost every lecture, and Roscoe's list was at least one short, sometimes two. We used to pass out cards to everyone, but not anymore. I think only certain people get cards with Jacob's personal information on it."

"What do you mean only certain people?"

"Well, like the lecture at the library. I saw Jacob give her a card outside. I was going to follow, but when I saw Professor Jacob following her, guess where we ended up?... At the girl's apartment. At Cynthia McGuinness's home. I saw Jacob just walking down the street, looking, and writing something."

"Why?"

"Wait, Lieutenant, it gets better. Sure enough, her name isn't on Roscoe's list."

"Then how did you know her name? Did you know her, talk to her, or what?"

"Nope, I took some shots of the Professor's table. I put the sign-in sheet there so I could catch it from the balcony. I pretended that I felt ill and used the bathroom on the second floor. So, when I enhanced the zoom, I had a copy of his precious list. There were thirty-nine on that list that came from Roscoe, but this time, there was a switch in the names. Cynthia wasn't on the list. Someone else was on it, though. This really freaked me out. I thought he was on to me. I went looking at his house. I'd been crossing the woods to the back side of his house, watching him."

"Why didn't you ever talk to anyone about your concerns?"

"I did, right after the trip that we went on to Haiti, but I was informed that the Professor was fine. Dollars, Lieutenant Tanner, dollars."

"What trip to Haiti?" Stuart relays the events of his trip. Corina's warning. All of it.

The ding is ringing. Tanner remembers the accent from the guy on the third floor last night. "Stuart, would you recognize the guy you know as Desmond?"

"I couldn't ever forget him." Stuart shivers.

"Stuart, I'm going to keep you in custody."

"Why? Don't you believe me?"

"Yes, unfortunately, I do, but I'm concerned that someone, as you say, is on to you. I am going to have you re-cuffed, and it will appear that you are being charged. Make a fuss. Pretend like you're actually being arrested. I'll find someplace to put you for a couple of days. For your safety, don't screw this up and start playing detective again. Do what you're told, or you *will* be charged."

"Yes, Sir."

"Stuart, were you at Wilderness Walk a couple of nights ago, sometime past 8:00?"

"No, are you kidding? That place is so creepy. So dark and secluded. I always get out of there before dark when I hike."

Smart boy, Tanner thinks.

Bryan sees the ruckus with Stuart as he's hauled off. Tanner appears, looking serious. "Well, Bryan, looks like we don't need much more from you. I think we've got the information we needed. Just one more question."

Bryan rolls his eyes and smarts off. "Like you haven't asked me enough questions. I've been here for hours. I tried to do a customer a favor, and look what it got me into."

"Enough, Bryan! What does that tattoo represent? Are you involved in a gang?"

Bryan grabs his wrist. "I can't really tell you how I got it. I had been somewhere partying and woke up with it."

"Woke up with it? What kind of party were you at?"

"You know, a mosh. I haven't gone to one since. It really bugs me. I can't remember a thing from that night. It took days to get right. I think someone slipped me something really bad."

Tanner is doodling. Actually, he's drawing the tattoo. "You're free to go, Bryan. Keep your nose clean. Do you want me to pull you in again?"

"Yeah, sure. Can I go now?"

"Yes, someone will take you back to get your car at the hospital."

As Bryan leaves with an officer, Tanner tells the night dispatcher to have some plainclothesman follow Bryan from the hospital and surveil him all night. Tanner motions his old friend into the office. "Irene, look at this. Do you know anyone who can tell me what this tattoo is?"

"I don't recognize it as any gang symbol I've ever seen. I think we can find someone, but not at this hour. What are you doing with Stuart? How is he involved? Goodness, who would have guessed? I've known him for years. I've never even—"

"Irene!" Tanner knows what she's thinking. "You didn't lose your touch. Stuart is benign but gave me some good info. I'm tucking him away for a while. Tell me what you know about Professor Jacob Warren."

Irene gives Tanner the whole story about Jacob and Rose, Rose's death, Jacob's breakdown, and his behavior lately. "Rose is the reason that I believe in anything good. Really good. In the cynical world of altruistic upper academia, Rose Warren walked like a light in the darkness. She was my inspiration. Her stand for Christ changed me and changed my thinking and my perspective. She made me a better person and a scientist. I wish you could have known her."

"I was out of state during that time testifying for a case. We never did a review together. Why do you think Rose's grave was robbed?"

"I don't know, but Jacob's never been the same since."

"How long after his trip to Haiti did that happen?"

"You know about that trip? Stuart told you? He never talked much about it. I've always wondered what they found. In answer to your question, I think about two months after they got back was when the grave was disturbed. There were never any leads, and Jacob didn't want to talk about it. The police couldn't get much out of him. I could understand. How horrible and sad for Jacob."

"Oh, one other thing. Do you know Roscoe?"

"No, he's the mystery man. I've never seen or spoken to him. I know Stuart can't stand him."

"Irene, do you know Stuart has never met him either?"

"Of course, he has! Jacob told me Roscoe had worked with Stuart on a couple of things at Rose's research garden at the house."

"No, Irene. Stuart says that he has never met him, and I believe him. He also said that he hadn't been at the research plots in months, maybe over a year."

Irene's eyes are as big as saucers. "Who's been helping Jacob? I've seen pictures of the plots, and they're planting and logging all the new botanicals, his plants from Haiti. Jacob couldn't possibly catalog all that and keep it weeded. Roscoe? We need to meet Roscoe."

"Yes, we do. Can you get us into Jacob's property tomorrow?"

"Sure, we'll drive over there. Jacob's a wonderful, sweet man. He loves to show people around, well, at least he used to. I'll set it up. Tanner, if I can't meet my deadlines for funding, I may need you to pull a few strings for me. Don't laugh. This has got me behind on putting the last of the data together."

"Perfect Woman, I'll get you what you need. I promise." *The Mayor is going to owe me a favor.* "Gotcha covered. Get us over there, but don't tell him why we're coming. I've got to clean up some papers in the morning, so I'll let you know when I can go."

"Tanner, remember, Ben Garcia is coming."

"Oh, my gosh, I forgot to call Beanie." Tanner makes a mental note to call Beanie by 7:00. "Sure, make it over lunch, around 2:00 if you can. I have to finish something, and I'm getting some fresh staff on the Adlin Summers case. I might bring a guest. Looks like the Doc and maybe one other person. Be careful."

Irene hugs Tanner. Jamison has his arm around her. As they exit the station, Jamison promises Tanner he won't leave Irene alone. Tanner hears Irene teasing Jamison, "You really know how to show a girl a good time. Some dinner date."

Jamison says, "Speaking of dinner, let's make it breakfast."

It's 3 a.m. Travis finishes interviewing the security guard from the hospital. "I'm letting him go. He has no connection to that guy. It's weird, though, he has no memory of letting anyone in. The only person he remembers, other than the call to stop letting people in, is Irene. We had him tested for drugs, and a background check was run while I questioned him. He comes up clean. I can't explain it, but I believe him. He's very worried that this will get him fired. I assured him that we'd take care of it. Will we?"

"Yes, if he's really not involved. The one tailing Bryan is calling in."

"Tanner, the kids at home. Drove straight over there. Lives in a dump, but it's his home... Yeah, I'll stay here and watch. Send someone to watch the back."

"Oh, didn't you know, you've got someone already there?"

"Give me a code or a number, and we'll communicate... Yeah, I know Ricky... Goodnight, Sir."

Tanner is running a checklist in his mind. *Erica, Beanie, Constance- check. Irene and Jamison- check. Bryan- check. Stuart- check. Now, my best girl- check. Emily and Travis- check.* "Travis, thanks."

"Tanner, this has been one of the craziest two days of my life. Sir? It's been great working with you. I want to tell you, I might be nosing in, but I would keep Libby if I were you. She's a fine woman. A real lady and, Sir, do you suppose it would be out of line... well, if Emily and I went out?" Tanner raises his eyebrows. "I'm sorry. Did I overstep my boundaries with the Libby thing? I mean, and, I, won't ask Emily out."

Tanner's thinking, *Aah, to be young.* "Travis, I appreciate that you see what a great person Libby is. Sweet, smart, and pretty. As for Emily, go for it. She is a good friend. One of the best people I know. By the way, where are the girls?"

"They're in your office. I'll take them home. I'm going to stay again."

Ooh, she's beautiful. Libby is at the end of the couch, curled up asleep. Emily's at the other end. Tanner can see by the look on Travis's face that he thinks the same thing about Emily. "Libby, Emily, girls, it's time to go home. Libby's going with me.

"Travis, take Emily in your car. Be careful."

Travis is all smiles. "Yes, Sir."

Tanner is driving and humming "Amazing Grace," as Libby sits snuggled up beside him in the car. Libby kisses his shoulder. The evil seems far away. He's with Libby, and everything is clean. She smells heavenly.

19

TEAMING UP

Tanner wakes up at 6:00 a.m. He was so tired that the usually irritating center lump of the couch didn't make him toss and turn. His mental day timer says, *call Beanie.*

"Beanie, I'm sorry I'm calling you so early. Once again, I need your help. Could you, would you?... I know it's Saturday, but here's the deal. I need someone discreet to pick Chief Ben Garcia up at the airport on time."

"What time?"

"He's flying in from Little Rock. He'll probably have a briefcase. Use your instincts and give him a big kiss. Boyfriend, brother, I don't know, it's your gig. Look for someone who looks like California... Stop it, Beanie. I don't think he'll have sandals on. You know what I mean. Like I said, use your instincts."

"Where am I taking him?"

It seemed like a logical question to Beanie. Tanner's at a loss. "I don't know, let me work on that, Beanie. Where are you?"

"Well, Erica and I stayed at Constance's last night, and I'm still here. Was your fishing successful? Did you catch anything?"

"Yes, but not the big one I wanted so badly. I'll fill you in when we brief Ben Garcia later."

"We?"

"Yes, we. That is if you're going to be available. You don't have to."

"Oh, I'm available. Figure out when and where we're meeting."

"I'll be back with you as to the time and a place to pick Ben up… Thanks, Beanie, and I'm glad you're okay too. I'll call the Mayor."

Libby floats into his thoughts. Tanner softly opens the door to his room. She's still sleeping safely. Tanner closes the door and makes coffee. *Ooh, wake-up juice; it's the best part of the day.* As he sips on his coffee, he chuckles. *Libby's the best part of the day.* He can't wait for her to wake up, but he decides to let her sleep. *The Mayor, he deserves to get up.* Tanner dials the Mayor. His wife sounds upset, grouchy, until he tells her that it's Lieutenant Tanner with police business.

"No, no, Tanner, it's okay. What did you find out? Let me get my robe, and I'll call you back on my cell." Tanner tells him the number. Ten minutes lapse. *Hmmm, the Mayor's a slow dresser.* The phone rings.

"Tanner, I'm sorry. Wow, I owe you an apology. I needed to get my cell so no one could listen. So, good or bad? Did you find him?"

"It's good. Kaplan is fine. He's visiting out of state for an indefinite period of time. I don't think he wants anyone to bother him. Might be something with a lady. She answered the phone… No, I haven't spoken to him. My colleague did, and he is fine… I will, Sir. I will most definitely encourage Mr. Kaplan to contact all his friends and assure them that he's okay… Yes, Sir, it's a good ending… Well, Sir, I'll get back to you on that offer… Anything I want? Sir, you might want to rethink that… Alright, I'll get back to you. I'm working on something else. Will you call Garrett and let him know the good news?… I knew you were stressed… No offense taken, it's my job… Well, thank you, Sir. I appreciate that. I hope this makes your friend feel better… You, too. I'll give you a run-down after I talk to Mr. Kaplan personally… You, too." *There's always a first. Two apologies in one day from him. He's sorry for being a pompous, overbearing jerk the other day and that his wife is nosey. Maybe he's not as big of a dimwit as I thought. He sounded genuinely relieved that Mr. Kaplan was okay.*

Next, the mental tick list. Where to put Ben Garcia. Tanner starts to feel like a cruise director: room assignments and schedules. *Let's see, you could… That's deceitful, well, not quite. It's perfect. Mr. Kaplan's apartment. It's perfect. It has four bedrooms, and I can have everyone in one place. It's large.*

He dials Beanie. "Beanie, here's the plan for Ben Garcia and whoever else is going to end up involved in this case. Call the nice lady at the apartment and tell her you are commandeering Mr. Kaplan's apartment. Explain that we were checking it out the other day. You still have her card, don't you?... I knew you would."

"Tanner, Sir, I'll explain to the manager how it will be like a giant slumber party. Command Central."

"Beanie, I need Mr. Kaplan's phone number. I told the Mayor I'd call him personally... Actually, Beanie, he was really decent, very grateful, and even apologized. Beanie, are you still there?... I know it's a shock. The guy might have a heart after all." Laughter. "You know, I couldn't have done this without you. Beanie, I really need the apartment. I'm worn out from trying to make sure everyone's okay. Can you make it happen, please?... Thanks, mom." Laughter.

"Libby, Libby, I need your help." Tanner's gently waking Libby. He's waving coffee near her. "Are you in?" At the sound of those words, Lib opens her eyes, stretches, and stands up.

She salutes, "I'm in, Sir."

Tanner kisses her. "Good morning, Miss Libby. Your assignment is to shop. Shop like the wind. Today, I need furniture." Libby is looking around the apartment. "Not for me, for Mr. Kaplan." Tanner fills Libby in on his plan. She loves it. Tanner hands her his credit card and says, "Go forth. I'm taking you home. Look pretty. Have some coffee. I'm going to shower. I'm sorry I had to wake you."

"Thanks, Tanner." Libby hugs him. "I love you, DJ Tanner. I'm getting Emily up because she is so slow and will need to start getting ready now. It's seven, and see, it needs to be done by four, at the very latest, five.

"Hi Travis, get Emily up. You two get ready. Tanner is sending us shopping. We have to hit the stores at 9:00. Travis, of course, you're going to take care of police business. Emily's slow about getting ready... You know?... I forgot. You've been with us for days. Sorry. Use my bathroom. Good thing you didn't have time to take your suitcase home. Do you have anything clean?... Wonderful, I hope Emily does." Laughter. "We'll be over shortly."

Tanner appears from the shower. Libby is dressed and looking like she's ready for business. "Tanner, you look like you haven't been up half the night. You are amazing."

Tanner's already on the phone. "Mr. Kaplan? I'm so sorry to disturb you, but this is Lieutenant Tanner, and I need your help. My assistant has told me... No, sir, you're not in trouble. Quite the contrary." Tanner explains that he needs to use the apartment, and if the lady there gives him any trouble, will Mr. Kaplan work it out?... "Yes, you could say that we're working together... Okay, I'll call you Al. Call me Tanner. Okay, if we're working together, can you do me another favor? Could you call your friend in Tennessee and let him know you're fine?... No, you don't have to tell him everything. I have told my source and inferred that it might be a woman thing. Mr. Kaplan, you dog... Thank you, sir. I really would like to meet you, and in the future, we'll do that... Mr. Kaplan, thanks. I'll call if I have problems with the apartment manager. I'll be back to you over the case I'm working on." Tanner was tickled that he had made Mr. Kaplan's day. *I have got to meet him. What a hoot.*

"Libby, would you drive? I've got another call to make."

"Yes, Tanner, but I hope we don't have to have that thing surgically removed. There is so much more to life. You need a partner. You need to get off that phone some of the time."

"Yes, I do, and I finally realized I have a partner. I love you."

"Yes, I've been waiting for years for an invitation. You know, I became quite good with phones and tasks. It happened shortly after I grew up."

Tanner realizes he thinks of Libby as the kid she was when they first met. "I can't help it; you'll always be twenty-two in my heart. You're my baby." Libby can't believe Tanner said that. He can't either, but his kiss confirms the truth of it. "Partners?"

"Partners forever."

Beanie laughs as she gets another call from Tanner. "Yes, Sir, it's done. I tracked the flight. I know the arrival time, and I'll be there... Yep, I have my plan. We're going to the apartment. The lady over there was almost euphoric at the mystery of it all, and helping the police was very important. She felt honored... Okay, it won't be ready until four? What do you want me to do with Chief Garcia? His plane will be here at 12:00 sharp... You'll meet us somewhere for lunch?... East Café?... See you then.

Don't call me again. Just kidding, but you *are* on the phone entirely too much. We have to quit talking like this."

Irene is calling. "Tanner, I can't get Jacob. He's always been an early riser. We'll keep trying, but Jamison and I thought—"

"Don't you dare go out there if you can't get him. Finish your paperwork, and I'll go with you at 2:00. So is Jamison there?

"Jamison, good morning to you too. Doc, don't let Irene talk you into going out there, or anywhere even near it. Are you going with her when she goes to the University?... Good. Don't let her out of your sight. We're all going at 2:00, and not a minute sooner. Doc, be careful."

"Are you done now?" Libby's waiting.

"Yes, Libby, I am. Well, almost," as he pokes her teasingly in the rib. "Now I'm done. I can't believe Chief Garcia is going to be here, and I haven't moved any further on the Summers case. He's going to be disgusted. Well, all I can do is all I can do." *Good grief.* Tanner's house phone is ringing. It's Travis.

"Tanner, what's wrong with your cell?"

"It's dead from never charging it. I've got it plugged in."

"The station called me because they couldn't get you at home or on your police cell."

"They were both dead. What's up?"

"Call the station. Stuart's got something. He won't talk to anyone but you. They wouldn't give me the number where they've stashed him."

"This is Lieutenant Tanner... You've been trying to reach me?... Give me a number. Thanks.

"This is Lieutenant Tanner. May I speak to Stuart?" Tanner hears Stuart in the background.

"Stuart, are you doing as I asked?"

"Yes, I woke up in the wee hours."

"Stuart, it was the wee hours when you left the station... Okay, I'm listening."

"Like I was saying. It may be nothing, but I did remember one thing. You know that girl that was in the papers last October? I know I've seen her before. I could see her face in my mind this morning, but they wouldn't call you until a few minutes ago. You told me to tell you if I thought of anything else. I feel like an idiot. Is all this connected?... But I am telling you everything. When am I going home?"

"Not yet, but Stuart, you keep trying to remember."

"I wasn't really trying, but that newspaper photo kept popping into my head. I can't quit thinking about Alyssa either."

"Stuart, thanks. I'll be back atchya today. Eat some breakfast and try to remember everything you can." *Ding, ding, ding, ding, ding, ding.* Tanner's bell is clanging. *Maybe we didn't catch the big one, but Stuart has been quite a catch after all. Adlin Summers, the girl from October. Lord, great timing with Ben coming. Maybe there's a connection, no matter how remote. Maybe something. I need something. Come on, Stuart, think, remember.*

"Lib, I'm finally ready. Will you drive? I hope Travis and Emily are ready, too. I've got to think."

"About what?"

"Libby, Ben Garcia is arriving today."

"Tanner, that's so exciting!"

"Well, he told me Adlin Summers's sister is coming on a later flight. There are two others from Meadow Brook coming as well. I'm nervous."

"Don't be. I know you need help. I think this is a God send."

"Really, Lib? You think so?"

"It's more than a thought. It's a deep awareness. This is a blessing."

"Okay, partner. I'm going to quit worrying. I love your optimism, Libby."

"I love you, too. Travis, Emily, and I will not let you down. See, there they are, peeking out the door. They are excited, too. I'll see you later."

"Thanks, Lib. Give me the keys. I'm going to the station. Call if you need me. Be careful."

"I will. It's going to be a great day!"

As Tanner scoots his chair forward, he's back in his element. The familiar feel of the desk is like a touchstone to reality. The events of last night were surreal.

Okay, I'm back. Libs right. It is a great day, and I do need help. I hope Ben Garcia doesn't think I'm crazy.

❧

Ben, on his flight, is studying the material on Jan's computer and thinking about his conversation with Tanner. *He's so busy with that case of the girl at the hospital, I hope he has time to think about Adlin's Project.* He smiles. Linda was adamant that he used the word project. He's sorry he didn't get to meet Madelyn. *This is far-out information. I wonder how this will be received by Tanner. He sounded paranoiac and overly cautious. He's created a cover for me. I wonder why? Who's meeting me at the airport?*

The plane is landing. Ben closes the computer and locks his briefcase. *Lord, please don't let Lieutenant Tanner think I'm crazy.*

As he exits the plane, he is greeted by a friendly person who promptly gives him a kiss. This is part of the cover and the code. He kisses her back. *Lin wouldn't like this.*

In the car, Beanie introduces herself and tells Ben that Tanner wants her to brief him on the events of last night. "For some reason, Tanner feels there may be a link to the Summers case. It's a feeling, but no evidence yet."

Ben unlocks the briefcase. He is taking a notebook out when Beanie tells him there's a complete file waiting for him, and he'll have a briefing from Lieutenant Tanner.

❧

Tanner sits gazing blankly out the window of East Café and is startled by the sound of Beanie's voice. "Well, it's been so long, DJ." She's smiling. "I couldn't resist coming over here. I'm sorry if we interrupted you. You looked like you were deep in thought. It's so wonderful to see you again."

Tanner stands and hugs Beanie and extends his hand to Ben. "And this is?"

"This is Ben, my fiancé. He flew in this morning. He's moving here. We're going to set up the apartment today. We're having a little get-together tonight. Maybe you could join us."

"Please join me for lunch. Let's catch up on old times." As the couple joins Tanner, he is thinking. *Beanie is more than your ordinary secretary.* To the average on-looker, it would appear like old acquaintances having lunch together.

"So tell me, Ben, how was your flight?"

"It was good, but I could hardly wait to get here." Beanie and Tanner quietly share events of the last days with Ben. He politely listens and asks no questions.

Finally, he says, "Is there anything on the October incident?"

Tanner is so relieved to be able to say, "It may be something, or not. I want you to go on a little ride with a couple of friends and myself. I'll show you around while Beanie gets the apartment set up. Let's see if my friends are available and ready to go. Beanie, call Travis."

"Thanks, Travis. I'll tell him it's a go.

"Forty-five minutes to design on a dime! Sir, they're right on time. Everything will be delivered by 4:00. I'm going to pick up the other guests at the airport.

"Ben, I think it's so nice DJ has invited you. You probably will enjoy the drive." Beanie kisses Ben, and away she goes.

"Shall we go?" Tanner insists that it's his tab, even though Ben tries to pay.

❊

Tanner is driving to pick up Irene and Jamison. He's briefing Ben as fast as he can. He asks Ben to take in everything and to keep his ears and eyes open as an objective bystander.

Irene and Jamison are ready. It's 1:45. "Nice to meet you, Ben. What brings you out to this part of the world? Are you here for a long time?"

"Well, I have an engagement, and I don't know when I'll be leaving." Ben glances at Tanner.

Oh, this guy is good.

"Tanner, I never could get Jacob on the phone. I'm worried." Tanner's mind is whirling as they make the drive. Irene and Jamison are pointing out the various sites as they drive along. Ben is very conversational, but Tanner can tell he's taking mental photographs, particularly of Wilderness Walk.

As they pull into the drive of the Professor's home, Irene seems very nervous. "What is it, Irene?" Jamison's voice sounds concerned when he sees Irene's hand slip into her purse. Ben notices it, too.

"I'm worried about Jacob. I'll go to the door first. You all stay here." Irene's effort to get someone to answer the door proves futile. She begins to go around the side of the house. The three men are out of the car, moving quickly toward her. Irene is startled by what she sees posted on the gate of the high stucco wall heading to the planting area. The yellow and black sign says, "KEEP OUT!" Property of the University. Stuart's words about Fort Knox are pounding in her head. She grabs Jamison's arm. "It was never like this. Jacob and Rose were always so inviting. Always welcoming to visitors."

Ben gives Tanner a slight nudge to back up. As Tanner pretends to clean his glasses, he notices the cameras.

"We've got to get in. Jacob, oh Jacob, what's wrong?" Irene is running back up the front steps to the house. She's pounding. The guys have their guns out but not in sight. They're ready.

Tanner is speaking a little louder than normal. "Irene, I guess there's no one here. I'll get to meet your old friend another time." The others expressed their disappointment. Jamison is squeezing her arm to let her know to back off.

"Okay, well, I do hope he's okay. We'll come another day. I'm so disappointed. I really wanted you to meet him and see his research. I think we should at least call the police to do a wellness check, shouldn't we?" She's speaking a little louder than usual. They all agree it's a good idea.

Once in the car, they wait until they are partway down the hill. Ben speaks first. "Irene, is there top security on Jacob's research?"

"I don't know what he was working on. Stuart would be your best bet for that." She tells him of Stuart's comment about Fort Knox. "Call a patrol car to check it out. Please, Tanner."

Tanner calls dispatch and asks for a patrol wellness check. As they reach the bottom of the hill, a marked car is entering the road upward. "We're all going to a place I have picked out. Ben and his fiancé's apartment. We have an announcement to make."

Ben's phone rings, and they hear him say, "Joe, you've arrived?... Good, you've already connected with Miss Orr. We'll see you later."

"Tanner, you're full of surprises. Now, I have one." As Tanner drops Irene and Jamison off, Ben invites them to his "engagement party."

Two policemen emerge at Professor Jacob's house. One goes to the front door and the other remains at the squad car. On the third ring, the door swings open, and the officer is greeted by a slender, slightly gray-haired man in glasses. "Professor Jacob? Jacob Warren?"

"Yes, is something wrong?"

"Sir, some friends had been here. They were worried. Is everything okay?"

"Visitors? Oh, I'm sorry. I must've been in the research plot working. I am perfectly fine. I truly apologize for your trouble. How nice to have someone worried about me." He tells them that his wife, Rose, had died about five years before.

"Professor Warren, I'm so sorry to learn that. Professor, do you have a cold, or are you ill?"

"I already told you that I'm fine."

"Glad to be able to report that you're okay. Have a nice evening, sir."

"You too, officers."

"Who was at the door, Roscoe?" The guest is asking from around the corner. "... The police? The police!"

"Somebody was here before, looking for Jacob. I guess we were busy outside. I really hated to get Jacob up, but when I saw it was the police, I knew they'd want to see him."

"Where is Jacob now?"

"I put him back upstairs. He's lying down again. He hasn't been able to shake this off. Poor Jacob."

The dispatcher tells Tanner that Professor Jacob answered the door and gives the description.

Irene is shaking her head. "It's Jacob."

The only thing the officer said was that his throat was so raspy. They asked if he was ill, and he said no and became slightly offended. The officers thought that he might have a mechanical voice box or something, so they dropped it. "He was very polite. He seemed fine."

"Jacob's voice is not raspy!" Irene is confused but adamant.

Tanner asks the officer to describe the voice. "He sounded, well, like I don't know how to explain it, but a throaty, raspy sound, really irritating." Now, Jamison, Ben, and Tanner are confused, too.

20

THANK YOU, MR. KAPLAN

At baggage claim, Jan and I are greeted by none other than Joe—Joe Landry with a sign that reads, Big 10. "Ladies, I'm your escort and your tour guide. Sorry your plane was delayed. Mine was on time, which worked out well so I could meet you. Our ride is outside!"

Did he mean to say, babysitter? Throw a dart through the universe, Joe Landry. I remember Joe saying, "If you need anything, let me know." Jan doesn't seem nearly as surprised as I am. I feel that tug. *There's no time for rage. Stop it, Dee Dee!*

"Ladies, this is Beanie."

§

Libby is supervising the finishing touches on the second floor. Two women from Sugar Plum Services are busying themselves, placing sheets and comforters and pillows in all the right places. Each room is perfect, with two twin beds and all the bathroom accents and towels. Travis is helping the moving guys arrange the last of the furniture in the great room, all under the guidance of Emily. He announces, "Okay, I've had all I can take of this, Emily."

Emily looks at her watch. "Not quite." She stacks the pens, pencils, papers, and notebooks in piles. Travis drags all the stacks towards the massive dining room table with twelve chairs and arranges them neatly. Emily checks the kitchen. Travis has put all the glasses, microwave plates, paper plates, and silverware away. The center of everything is the coffee pot. "Hey, Emily, when is that delivery guy coming with the groceries?"

"Wait a minute, I want you to see this. Come on, let's look upstairs."

"It's beautiful, Emily." Travis is impressed. "I just thought you were, well, a chick at the linen store."

Indignant, Emily informs him that, in fact, she has a degree in design.

"Well, I would've never known by the way your room looks."

"That's why I never tell anyone. I'm a slob at heart. Think of it like a hairdresser whose hair is always a mess."

Travis laughs. "Emily, the whole place is gorgeous. You and the other Sugar Plums have done a great job! Look at this! I would want to live here!"

Even the gals from the decorating service are impressed. "You put all this together in how many hours? People like you are in high demand. People need help with ideas." They want a card. Emily takes their numbers instead and promises to call.

Emily is thinking, *this could be a career door-opener.* Even Libby is ecstatic over Emily's ability.

Travis is slouched on the sofa. "Where is the grocery guy? I'm starving!"

Libby announces from the balcony, "He's here! He's downstairs! Well, actually, there's three of them." Travis puts on his jacket and puts his gun in his pocket. "The doorman wants to know if they can come up."

Travis says, "Yes. How much did Beanie order, Libby?"

"A lot, I guess." The guys appear to be legitimate; however, Travis stands in the doorway to the kitchen as they stock the fridge and pantry under Libby's direction. He can hear Tanner's, *"Be careful."* That's why Libby had to not let the gals from the decorating service out of her sight. Travis had been with the furniture guys every minute. Emily had directed the entire effort.

As one of the guys reaches up to stock the top shelf of the pantry, Travis sees a mark on the inside of his left wrist. "Hey, great job! You guys deserve a tip, but the girls have spent all my cash. Would you write your names down for me and a phone number? I'll get with you... No, I don't want to send it to the store. You know you'll never receive it." Gratefully, the guys comply, and Travis puts the paper in his wallet.

❈

Expecting to see Tanner and Beanie, Libby is shocked to see three people with Beanie, and no Tanner. "Where's Tanner?"

"Would you like to meet these people?"

"Oh, I'm sorry, Beanie. Yes, I'm Libby."

"Emily, Libby, Travis, please meet Joe Landry, Jan Raskin, and Dee Dee Summers." For a moment, it's silent. They're all thinking, *Adlin Summers's sister.*

Pulling herself together, Emily bows and says, "Welcome to our humble abode." As the guests look around, humble is not a term that comes close to describing the apartment. Almost simultaneously, they all ask if they may use the restroom.

Travis is sure that they're checking the place out. Beanie smiles and mouths, "It's okay."

When the group re-enters the room, Beanie encourages us to get acquainted and that Tanner and Ben will be here shortly. Beanie plays hostess, and soon, we begin to relax.

❈

I keep looking at my watch and Beanie assures me that they will be here. "Dee Dee, would you like to help me, dear? Since you know Chief Garcia, well, what should I order for the "engagement party?" Mexican or Italian?"

"Anything would be good." *If Aunt Linda could hear about Ben's engagement, hmm, bet she wouldn't be happy.* I chuckle.

"What, Dee Dee?"

"Oh, nothing."

The doorman rings. "Yes, send them up." Beanie announces, "They're here."

I head to the bathroom. My heart is pounding. I feel nauseated, not Christmas. *This is the guy who hasn't done anything to help Adlin.* Rage. A twinge. I hear Linda's voice in my head and I calm down. A weird, dark thought flits through my mind. *You can get even, later. Hunt for Red October.* I stare at myself in the mirror. *Deidre, be nice. Get everything you can.* I hear the Whisper, *"Help me, Dee Dee."*

As I walk into the room, Ben motions to me. "Hi, Ben. I thought you would never get here. Where were you?" *I feel like hitting him.*

"Dee Dee, this is Lieutenant Tanner."

"Lieutenant Tanner, finally, we get to meet." *I feel like hurting him. Here comes that rage. Blinding rage. Linda, Linda.*

Libby must have sensed something. She's running toward me.

Tanner's yelling, "Libby, don't—"

I fall backward as Libby softens my fall. "Libby, how did you know?"

"I heard a voice in my head saying, *'Help her!'*"

"Jan, Jan! It's happened again."

Jan stops Beanie before she dials 911. "Don't, she's okay! This has happened before. Dee Dee, are you all right? Come on, let's get you up."

"Jan, call Aunt Linda. It's something. I can't explain it."

"Linda, Dee Dee passed out again! Pray! Get the 10 and pray! Pray for all of us... No, we had a great trip. Lieutenant Tanner's right-hand girl took care of us... I'll have him call you again later... I'm not sure. Dee Dee can't speak right now but wanted me to call you."

Ben whispers, "Tell Peaches we're okay."

Why is Ben telling Jan that? "Ben, I can take it. Maybe this keeps happening because I'm out in the dark. I'm sick of being left out! Adlin was my sister! My only sister! I have to help her! I can take it! I can take it! Tell me the truth!" I grab my chest.

"No, everything's okay, Linda. Dee Dee's just upset. Pray, Linda. Pray."

Jan marches over to me. "Stop it! Stop this right now! Whatever keeps happening is not productive to you or us in finding the truth. You know how much this means. It's about everyone that loved Adlin and all the people who love you."

She's furious. She's so pale. Oh, this is not just about me. "Jan, I'm sorry. You're right. Lieutenant Tanner, everyone, I apologize. There are some things that I am still working through." Jan's crying, and all the other women are too.

"Ben, take me in there with Lieutenant Tanner and tell me the truth." *I feel like Marie Antoinette being led to the guillotine.* "You all decide what to do... No, Jan, I don't want you in this right now. Tell everyone everything. I mean everything! The dreams, the whole deal. Don't give me that look, Jan. You and Joe, fill them in. You all take notes. The village idiot is going to hear the truth. Yep! That's what I am. The town dummy." *I'll bet they all even know each other.*

❋

"Miss Summers—"

"Call me Dee Dee, Lieutenant Tanner." I'm practically snarling.

"Okay, Dee Dee, but call me Tanner."

How can anyone who looks like him be so stupid? I can feel that rage starting again.

"I can see and feel your intense anger. Based on what you said in there, I want to clarify. This is the first time I have met Ben, and I have only met your aunt when she came to make arrangements for your sister, and we had some phone calls. As for Jan, I only know that she is your friend. I didn't know until this afternoon that you were out of the mental facility or that you were coming. I was starting to think that you didn't exist. If you think that you have been in the dark, so have I. Initially, I thought Mr. Landry was simply an escort with you. Imagine my shock when Ben told me he brought him in to work on the case. I mentioned the creepy overtones in passing to Ben, which may or may not be linked to Adlin's murder. That's why Joe Landry is here."

I'm shooting darts at Ben.

"Dee Dee, I had a Chief like Ben once upon a time. You should be grateful that he cares enough to protect you. Your sister has consumed my thoughts for months, to the point that Libby thought that I was involved with another woman. I've crossed the threshold of paranoia. I'm constantly telling everyone to be so careful. I don't know who's who, and that evil I felt is still out there. A monster could be stalking someone else. Now, having said all that, if you want me off this case, I'm gone. Get someone else to help. I wouldn't blame you. All these months and nothing."

How could I have been so stupid? Tanner is a good guy. "Lieutenant Tanner, I think we can work together. Ben, show me the file. I have to be able to take it. Show me, Ben."

"Dee Dee."

"No, it's okay. Linda is praying. Praying with all of them." *I can't believe I said that.* "Oh, these can't be pictures of my baby sister, Adlin. These can't be you. Where were you, God? Where were you? Adlin screaming." I feel a scream coming to my throat. Rage. As it's building, a voice, a Whisper, *"Dee Dee, help him. Let them help us. Help me."*

Tanner is asking if I have questions. I can't even speak. Ben, sitting on the bed, putting his arm around me. "Linda told me it was horrible. She didn't tell me how horrible. How could she? There's really no way to describe it. It looks like she was smashed, not beaten."

"Almost every bone was broken in more than one place. Her skull was completely disintegrated. The only part that was not damaged was her feet. The creature that did this actually took his time to rebuild her body and wash her off. He put everything back inside. Remounted her jaws and eyes. It was unbelievable. It would've taken hours to do that so skillfully. Then, they meticulously cleaned up her apartment." Tanner relates the entire thing as Ben holds me close. "It was so hard for the coroner to tell, but he determined that past the first blow, Adlin didn't feel anything else. The forensics team confirmed that. They think she was hit from behind. She was so pulverized, it's hard to know, but the fracture in the back of the skull seemed to be different from the rest. Dee Dee, your sister was beautiful, and I..." Tanner is starting to tear up. "Well, somehow, she touches my heart. She was special. It's like I almost hear her voice."

"I, I know, I know what you mean. She had that effect on everyone. You would've liked her, Tanner." *He said she's special. He does think about her.* "Do you have anything yet?" Tanner relays the whole thing about the events at the hospital and Stuart's comments. "Would you call him and see if he can remember anything?"

"Stuart, did you get anything?... Okay, keep trying. Irene told me you made a comment about Fort Knox. What did you mean?... Thanks, buddy. Hang tight for one more night, and we'll get you moved, probably tomorrow."

Ben and I chime in together, "Nothing yet?"

Everyone is waiting. This certainly explains why no one ever told me. I kept pretending like I never went crazy over Adlin's death. What would I have done? Exactly what they did out of love. Dee Dee, stand up. "Let's find this one, Red October. Let's plan a hunting trip."

✽

The doorman is ringing. Beanie directs him to send them up. Jamison and Irene appear, dressed for the occasion with a bottle of champagne. Right behind them is a man practically falling down from carrying the huge order of Mexican food.

"Dee Dee, you sit at the end."

Good grief, it's like lunch at Dot's.

"No, Ben, you sit there." Beanie points to the chair.

Travis and Emily, Tanner and Libby, Irene and Jamison, Beanie and Ben, Jan, Joe, and me (Deidre). Ben is saying grace. *Thank goodness for love. I don't know these people, and yet it seems right that we're all here together.* Ben is also praying for all the others. "Amen."

With that, Tanner makes a toast. "Here's to you, Mr. Kaplan!"

Dinner is full of everything except light conversation. Irene is particularly interested in Madelyn's dreams. Ben seems to be interested in listening. So does Joe. *Why is Joe here?* "Joe, why are you here?"

"Well, to watch over you and Jan."

"No, why are you really here?"

Ben quietly says, "Because I asked him. Tanner asked me about a case, and Joe and I had worked on a case out of Miami a long time ago. It was of a spiritual nature. I needed someone who had encountered that stuff before. Dee Dee, stop it. I know what you're thinking, but I didn't know where Joe was. I contacted a couple of people, and Joe called me back." Joe is shaking his head in agreement.

"Does Peaches know about you, Joe?"

"She does now. Dee Dee, she wanted me to come and help you. It makes her feel better to know I'm with you and Jan. What Ben told you is true. Dee Dee, God has to be in this. What are the odds that Ben and I would know each other? Maybe the case we worked on together has nothing to do with Adlin, or maybe it does." Everyone's mind is whirling. "What if we lay down the normal view of this and move with the precept that God is orchestrating, moving us all together?"

"Joe, you may have really hit the crux of this. Let's clean the table off." Everyone begins to clean together.

Notebooks are passed out, and everyone is looking at Ben. "Tanner, tell them what you felt from the beginning."

"Yeah, but first, Ben, would you pray again?"

"Tanner, I believe Joe should."

"I would be honored. Dear Father, as we come humbled under the care of your unseen hand at work here, we ask for knowledge. We know little about things beyond our reason, but you know all things. Forgive us for our hardness of heart and all our foolish beliefs that we can do anything in and of ourselves. We surrender the concept of our routine ways and ask you to expand our vision. Establish a new way over our walk. May your hand lead us in the paths of righteousness and protect us from evil. We pray this over ourselves and those that we love."

As Joe closes, "In Jesus' name," the room is silent. Everyone committing themselves to the One that has come into the room. Everyone is aware of His presence.

Joe was asking for God's love and protection and surrender to His wisdom. I hear a small crashing sound inside. *It's my heart. Something is letting go.*

Crashing Down

"Roscoe, did you hear that?"

"Yes, it was really… I don't know how to describe it. Frightening. Where's it coming from?"

"I don't know, but there isn't much time to waste. It can be really bad for us if he shows up or sends someone. Remember?"

"Yes, it worries me for Jacob. What if someone, you know, finds out and gets to him before we can intervene? He's key to completing this project, and we can't afford not to finish. There are too many others depending on this."

"Who do you think is trying to interfere in the project? Check the cameras and see if there's anything odd. I'm going to check on Jacob. If you need to, get some security to make some calls. I don't like whatever is going on here."

21

CONNECTING THE DOTS

Jan is the last one to lift her head. Speaking softly, she says, "Joe, you have brought clarity to this whole series of events. I couldn't quite put my finger on it, but there was something so dark, so evil. I couldn't grasp how one could capture something like that with a set of handcuffs and a gun." Jan is tenderly touching the little gold symbols on her necklace.

"Dee Dee, I know I have stood at arm's length from embracing the truth, and so have you. All those ladies surrounding you and me, pouring out love. You and I have been semi-deceitful. We have simply wanted to catch a killer, but this is about much, much more, and we will catch the killer. I felt that originally, the frenzy of the last few days was simply marking time. Initially, I thought some of the things about the journals and luncheons were stall tactics— a bunch of bored women, needing to be needed and to keep Dee Dee busy.

"The way I feel right now, the shame is overwhelming. May the God you pray to forgive me. I have seen the light, as you all would say." They all laugh. "Now, in the light of my being humbled and my confession, I feel that what is in those journals and photos is very pertinent. May I share them with you? This is where the foundation is."

Jan unfolds the story of Dot and the plan of the Big 10. I feel the shame as Jan continues recounting how the women followed a plan step by step as God led them to help.

Jan shows the pictures and videos that have been loaded into the computer. I see the group entranced but notice that especially Tanner is engrossed. Jan stops at certain places and, from her copy of the journals, reads various women's comments and thoughts. Jan details all the events and occurrences through the eyes and ears, and hearts of the ladies, the Big 10.

Jan concludes her presentation with a question directed at Tanner. "What do you think?"

Irene interrupts, "I'm sure I know who the old guy is." Everyone is staring at her. "Jan, can you go back to the part where he's going into the church? Can we zoom in on that? See, there's those shoes. I know it's Stuart! When you talked about Gloria's comment about Obsession, I knew it was Stuart."

In unison, Jan and I ask, "Who's Stuart?"

Irene quickly explains about Stuart. "My question is, why was Stuart at the service?"

"Mine, too." Tanner is once again on the phone. "Hey, Stuart, good news. I'm moving you tonight. Let me speak to someone from the night watch." Tanner gives them the address and tells them to make it look like a visit. "No squad car.

"Looks like we'll be getting the answer to that question shortly. Hope Stuart enjoys the hot-seat."

Libby pops up and asks, "What about the lady and the other gentleman? How are they connected? The only feeling I got when I saw them was sadness, like a lost feeling. What do you think, Jan?"

"I don't have any idea, but it's odd that more than one of the ladies mentioned the pearl bracelet that the woman had on."

"It's doubly odd that in one of my gifts Peaches gave me, there was a silver bookmark, and at the end of it was a little pearl. She told me Adlin had made it and that she had found the pearl in her car." I reach into my bag to get it.

Ben says, "It's impossible for it to be merely a coincidence."

Joe adds, "And that Peaches gave it to Dee Dee."

"May I?" Tanner is reaching to touch the marker. "Dee Dee, can I keep this until we're finished?"

"Of course, but is there any link to these people?"

"Jan, can you send a photo to the station from the computer?"

"Sure, if there's a line to hook into."

Beanie is putting down her short-hand notes and leading Jan to the den. "I'll take care of it, Sir. You want the department to search where?"

"Start with missing persons and their families, too. Give them some of the verbal descriptions from the journals." Tanner does not discount the women's instincts. *Libby has great instincts.*

Joe is on the phone with Peaches. "Peachie, we're looking at the bookmark you gave Dee Dee. Try to remember when Adlin gave it to you. Do you know about what time of the year she found the pearl?... She gave it to you the night before your birthday?... Oh, so that was sometime before August 23... Of course, I remember. Did she say she found it? Did she say when she found it?... Right before she came?... Getting her car cleaned out right before her visit?... You're still my best girl, Peachie. If you remember anything else, call me immediately... Yes, I'll tell them. I love you...

"So, it looks like Adlin found it sometime before August 23."

"Libby, tell Beanie that it was sometime in June, July, or August. That's the time period they need to research for missing people and send pictures of Alicia Parsons and the man named James." Tanner is hoping it will at least be the beginning of a timeline.

"Peachie says she's praying. They all are. This could be something or nothing, but I agree that the lady in gray and the guy named James are together. Libby, tell Beanie to use their names, Alicia Parsons and James, as part or whole names in their search. Thanks."

"There's one more item concerning the pearl." Jan flips to her notebook about Madelyn's first dream, about the guy picking up something off the floor. I give Jan a nod. Ben is nodding, too. Jan, clearing her throat, says, "There's more in the dreams." All eyes are glued to Jan as she reads the copy of the first dream.

Emily is the first to ask, "Jan, what about the scent of cherries? There's a clue there, but what?"

"We draw a real blank about that one, but there is one about Adlin's hair."

Ben interjects, "This is the clincher that made me not discount this dream and the subsequent ones as the ramblings of an old lady."

Jan continues, "Well, in Madelyn's dream, Adlin's hair was red with highlights. The only people who could've known that were Linda, the Coroner, the Police, and the Funeral Director. The casket was closed. Remember that Madelyn had that dream before Adlin was murdered." Jan could hardly get those words out, hoping that Dee Dee's reaction was normal. She glances her way.

Ben adds, "Only those people, Red October, *and* the hairdresser—"

"The salon list!" Jan and I had forgotten the list.

Libby looks at Beanie. "Who's the hairdresser, the gal from the salon?"

"Jan, call Dot, Gloria, somebody. Get that list."

"Dee Dee, it's late, Dot will be in bed."

"I want to meet the hairdresser. He or she was maybe the last person to speak to Adlin. I also want to meet that girl that found Adlin, the one that saw her in the apartment."

"Dee Dee, we can't do that. She's had a complete breakdown."

Rage.

"Dee Dee!" Jan is grabbing me. "Dee Dee, stop it, before—"

Tanner quietly and gently tells me, "We'll set up a meeting tomorrow. You, me, and—"

Libby intervenes, "Tanner, I think it would be a good idea if I get my hair done."

She's winking at me, smiling. "Don't you, Dee Dee? Then, we'll visit, you know, salon talk." The rage subsides.

"Yes, that's a good idea." The relief is apparent in Joe's voice. "Thanks, Libby."

The doorman is ringing. Beanie says, "He'll be right down."

Tanner goes to meet the plainclothes escort and gets Stuart.

Stuart is oblivious that he's about to be stripped clean. "Wow! This is some place, Lieutenant!" As he walks into the room, he sees everyone sitting and staring at him. "What is this?"

"This is the place where you bare your soul. Have a seat, Stuart. Take mine."

"Yes, Sir."

"You are at the end of this. Stuart, tell us why you were at a certain funeral service."

"I wasn't! I—"

"Don't! Stop it, Stuart!

"Beanie, are you done with the computer?"

As the video begins to play, Stuart acts like he has no idea what is going on.

"Jan, pause it right there.

"Stuart, Irene believes this is you. Is it?" Irene is staring at Stuart. Sheepishly, Stuart nods his head yes. "Why did you lie— that stuff about trying to remember the girl from the October incident? How sick. Why didn't you tell me the truth?"

"Because of what you just said, how sick. I thought you'd think it was pretty twisted to go to that funeral. It would make me look like I was, you know, involved."

"You are involved!"

"Not in murder! All I've been—"

"Stop! Level with me." Irene's voice is terse. "What were you doing there?"

"I can't really explain it. I thought it was odd after seeing the newspaper clipping. Tanner, I was trying to tell you when I made that up— the part about the girl from the newspaper last October was popping into my mind."

"Stuart, did you kill Adlin Summers?"

"No! Honest, no! Like I was saying about the newspaper clipping—"

"What clipping?"

"The one in Professor Jacob's book."

"Okay, tell the story, and it better be the truth. Stuart, you are wearing me out."

"Well, you know about the lists, the sign-in sheets." All the others wonder, what lists? "One morning in October, I didn't even see the paper yet. Jacob came in but immediately decided to get coffee. He left a book on his desk. I noticed something folded, sticking out of it. Lieutenant Tanner, I told you I was snooping. Well, anyway, here's the whole story about that girl. It hit me. He had to have cut that out first thing when he got up. I have never known Jacob to be interested in newspapers." Irene is nodding in agreement. "After that, he came back, and I casually said I hadn't picked up the news that morning, and asked if there was anything interesting in it? Irene, you know I read the paper every morning." Irene is nodding, yes. "Well, Jacob tells me, no, and I about fell off my chair. Says he doesn't take the newspaper, but Roscoe does. That made me start looking through the lists, but that girl wasn't on any of them. I decided to go to the funeral, and if I showed up like myself, I would get sucked into some bad situation."

"Did you take a flower? Why did you spend so much time at the front by the casket?"

"My God! It's like you were there. Were you?"

"No, but you just mentioned his name. God was."

"Oh, this is spooky."

"Answer the questions. Why did you take a flower at the casket? Come on, Stuart."

"I don't know. I thought if, I, well, went up there, maybe I'd see something or sense something. I thought I should tell her I was sorry, so I did. When I smelled those roses, I took one to see if it was from Jacob. You know, one of those special hybrids. I'm sorry that I went there. I felt kind of sick, like a voyeur or something. So, I was really afraid to tell you about that."

"Was the rose one of Jacob's?"

"No, Lieutenant. I was so relieved it wasn't, but that's when I started sneaking the back way to Jacob's to watch through Wilderness Walk."

Libby, Emily, and Travis are wide-eyed. Tanner reassures them. "Relax, it wasn't him that night.

"Stuart, let's get back to the lists."

Stuart begins to tell them about the lists, and Tanner's phone rings. "We've got something. Beanie, Jan, somebody plug the computer in so they can send it to you... Yes, send an email. Here, tell them Beanie's putting the computer online, and Jan, give them the email address."

When the email arrives, it confirms the instincts of the Big 10. The lady in gray, Alicia Parsons, and the well-dressed man, James, are connected. They're the Kirschenbaums, the parents of a missing child.

Stuart is frantic. "That's Alyssa from the list. Cincinnati, Ohio? That's not where we were when I met her. We were at a conference in Florida. Yes, she was a student in Gainesville, Georgia. Tanner, it's like I suspected. The lists do tie to this."

"Beanie, get these people on the phone."

"Is this the Kirschenbaum residence? This is Bernice Orr. Lieutenant Tanner of the Oak City police department would like to speak with you... Please, calm down... We don't know. Please, wait... Don't." Beanie covers the phone. "Tanner, these people are really upset. All of you pray."

Quietly, Tanner speaks to the broken people, desperately clinging to the other end of the line. The room silently bows their heads and listens. Tanner asks the couple several questions. Libby is crying. Tanner needs to stay focused. He can't stand to see Libby cry. He motions to Ben and Joe. The three go into the den. The others are still seated in the great room and are reviewing the articles, pictures, and newspaper clippings.

Irene is looking quite puzzled. "Do you know that girl, Stuart?"

"Well, I didn't really know her. I met her at the conference in Florida. I was really impressed with her." Irene's eyebrow is arched above her right eye. "Okay, I was attracted to her. Tanner knows that story."

"I met that girl!" Everyone's focus is instantly on Irene. "I was leaving the lab, and she looked lost. She was looking for Jacob. Actually, she was looking for you, Stuart. I know it was on a Friday because you had left early, and you were spending the weekend with your friends who have a house on the lake. I walked her down to your part of the building. That's when Jacob told me where you were. Jacob greeted her, and I left. She was a very sweet person. The Kirschenbaum girl was here in Oak City!" Irene's words startle the three guys as they walk back into the room.

"What in the world is going on?" Tanner asks. "Everybody sit down and take notes." Irene relates the story of her meeting Alyssa Kirschenbaum in Oak City. Tanner replies, "Well, lots of things are coming to light." He announces, "I know what the scent of cherries is."

In unison, the others blurt out, "You do?"

"I do indeed. Alyssa Kirschenbaum is Cherry. Kirsch in German is cherry, and baum is tree. Cherry tree. Cherry was in the library. Libby, you were so right. The sadness, the sadness. The Kirschenbaums have felt like they have been completely alone in this. This is absolutely miraculous that this connection has been made. They have been praying. They said they needed to be here with others who care. They would've given up, but they got a word from the scriptures. 'They that wait upon the Lord, shall renew their strength and rise up as on wings of eagles.' They have been in prayer for days. Mrs. Kirschenbaum said she knows Alyssa's alive. She had a dream— Alyssa saying, 'Don't give up! You're eagles! Fly, and you'll find me! Hurry!' She had that dream before they got the scriptures. They believe they're supposed to fly here and find her."

Libby says, "I hope her mom is right."

"Libby..." Tanner is so tender. "You know, Lib—"

"I know, Tanner. I know." So does everyone in the room. The chance that Alyssa is alive is slim, extremely slim, after all these months.

Stuart is having a complete crushing meltdown. "Why wasn't I there? I must have missed her by minutes. Now, she's—"

"Stop it, Stuart! You didn't know."

"I did know! I knew something. I should've confronted Jacob and Roscoe. I knew something was wrong."

"There's something else, the pearl." Once again, all eyes are on Tanner. "Mrs. Kirschenbaum said that the bracelet was slightly scratched and two of the pearls were missing. They found the bracelet in her dorm room after she disappeared. It belonged to Alyssa's grandmother. It was a very expensive heirloom. That means, if this pearl is one of the missing ones from the bracelet, Alyssa was alive when she left here. She disappeared after she went back to school. We're still left with a problem. How did the pearl show up in Adlin's car?" Tanner addresses his thoughts out loud. "What was it that Madelyn said about the pearl? The Pearl of Great Price. It's in scripture. Why two pearls? One at the library and the other one, where? How did the pearl get into Adlin's car?... Whew!" Tanner looks at his watch, "It's really late. We all better get some sleep." Irene and Jamison are getting ready to go.

"Where are you guys going?"

"We are going home, and for the first time in a while, we've decided we are going to church tomorrow. Ben and Beanie, congratulations! This has been quite an engagement!" Irene kisses Tanner on the cheek. "As always, Tanner, it hasn't been necessarily fun, but it has been real. This has been an indescribable evening. A real blessing in many ways."

"She's the perfect woman."

Jamison is laughing. "Yep, the perfect one for me. Does anyone need a ride?"

Beanie replies, "I do. I'm going to leave my car in case someone needs it. I need to check up on Erica and Constance."

Jamison speaks to Tanner privately. "Tanner, the hospital just buzzed me. I need to check on Beth Adams. Irene will be with me. I won't let her out of my sight."

"Call me with an update."

"Of course, and Tanner? I really do hope we can find the Kirschenbaum girl. I think her mom's right. I think she's alive, but I know we've got to hurry. Irene and I can pick up the Kirschenbaums when they fly in. Let me know when they're arriving. Does that help you out?"

"If you weren't a guy, I'd kiss you. Yes. That would take a big load off me." *Irene, the perfect woman, may have found the perfect man. I really trust this guy.*

Emily, Travis, and Libby have joined forces. They want to go back to the apartment tonight. Libby gives Tanner "the look."

"Joe, something seems very familiar about all of this."

"Ben, that's what I kept thinking all evening. I know, I was blown away by some of the elements of that case you and I worked for the feds. At that time, I had no idea of the difference between bad guys doing evil things and blatant manifest evil. I had a hard time after that— thinking about things that go bump in the night."

22

CAMEO FROM THE PAST

The happy group seems oblivious to the unusual stillness. The increasing motions of the little patterns of the waves lapping on the dock go unnoticed. The effect of the moving wavelets and the wafts of gentle air flowing across her body have a narcotic effect. She is being lulled into a deep sleep. Fifteen minutes… twenty minutes…

Wakened by a sharp, shrill whistle, she sits up, straining to focus and to move her muscles. She sees the cause of the shrill warning. The men in the boat are signaling to the woman. The little corks are bobbing far out into the waters. A strange drift, like an invisible hand, is pushing the inner tube out into the middle of the lake.

Droplets of rain begin to fall as Julia plunges into the cold water, swimming frantically towards the tube. The men are rowing against the drift, and their efforts are weakened by the wind, revealing its strength, blowing them back, away from the little corks. It's moving them farther into the middle of the lake. The puffy clouds are wearing angry, dark expressions.

The pastoral scene has changed. The powerful waves slap over the woman, desperately trying to grasp the inner tube.

The little bobbing corks begin to scream, "Mommy! Mommy!" Rain is pounding, coming so fast that the catch between the churning spillway and the girls collapses. They're going to get sucked into the violently moving channel. The woman sees one last glimpse of the men in the boat. Dark pounding rain is split by lightning. A crack in the universe and the boat is gone.

The woman grasps the inner tube with almost supernatural strength. "Oh, Father, help me!" The waves are pouring over her as she gets below the water, holding her breath and pushing the tube with all her might. The little girls grab onto the place where her hands are above the water, and miraculously, the tube is caught by a current.

The woman coming up for breath sees she is about fifty yards from the far shore of the lake. Using the last of her strength, Julia shoves the inner tube. It squeaks into a crevice between two of the massive rocks, like giant hands cupping around the rubber nest. The girls are safe. The little colored corks search for her hands, their mother's hands, but the lovely slender fingers are limp, and Julia disappears. The little girls are alone, screaming and crying for help.

The storm rages. Liquid forces keep tugging on the inner tube, trying to loosen it from the safety of the rocks. The screaming and desperate crying of the girls are drowned out by the voices of the thunder and the sizzling snaps of lightning strikes. The older girl is aware they are trapped. There is no way she can lift her sister up the face of the towering rocks. She keeps screaming for help. Darkness has enveloped them, and no one can possibly see them where they are lodged.

Into the night they scream until their small voices can barely whisper. The older girl holds the little one close to her as she hangs on. Their small bodies drape over the tube like rag dolls.

A voice. "Dee Dee! Adlin!"

"Daddy! Daddy?"

"Everything is going to be okay." A strong man in a slicker is reaching for Adlin and standing on something. Dee Dee can't see what he's perched on. He lifts Adlin up and disappears around the side of the rocks. Dee Dee is almost unconscious as she feels herself being lifted by two strong arms and carried to safety.

"Daddy?"

"No, but he sent me to get you." A glimpse of the face with the beautiful eyes, smiling, a policeman, an angel man. He kisses Dee Dee gently on the forehead, and exhaustion overcomes her. She's asleep.

ভ

The rescuers found the girls sleeping in a small clearing in the woods right above the rocks. Their inner tube was shredded at the bottom of the spillway. Their bodies were toasty warm, like a giant blanket had been placed around them. It was miraculous.

The tragedy of the loss of their mother and father, uncle, and cousin was in all the newspapers, along with the miracle of the girls. People still talk about that unbelievable storm. It's still referred to as a demon of a storm, coming literally out of nowhere on a beautiful day, like something unleashed from the pit. The media all requested that the officer who saved the girls come forward. No one ever came. Dee Dee's angel man, the policeman, was never found. The reward offered by the Aunt was never claimed.

23

CLAIMING BRYAN

Party Planners

"How are we going to finish all of this in time? I don't know how the Boss expects us to get all this in place by Friday." He shudders. "Tomorrow is Sunday."

"You always make too much of that. We just have to find more recruits and decorate for the Boss's arrival."

"I know I can be up for a great evening of celebration. It's a real honor that he's actually coming to this."

"What about that kid?"

"Bryan?"

"Yeah, I've heard you speak about him. Do you think he could rise to the occasion?"

"Maybe he could." Laughter

"See, that cheered you up, now, didn't it? Maybe he's even got a couple of friends that could come, too. It never hurts to have a couple of extra bodies around to help." Sinister laughter.

"You think you're so funny. I'm gonna give Bryan a little jingle."

&

"Lieutenant Tanner, it's Bryan, you know, from the other night. Can you meet me? I need to talk to you. I don't want anyone to know."

"Yes, where?"

"Could you pretend that I've been arrested?"

"Yep, get in your car in about ten minutes. Speed and I'll have you pulled over. They'll take you in if you smart off to them. I know you're good at that, so it will look natural.

"Travis, before you go, call the stakeout guys and have them stop Bryan and arrest him. Tell them to let him speed a little while. I'll go to the station."

"Not without me, you won't."

"Travis, stay put. Jamison is ringing in."

"Beth Adams is coming out of it. Some of the things she's rambling about are questionable. If I hadn't been with the group listening to dreams and so on, I would take her straight to the full psyche lockdown. It's out of my league. Trained people need to hear this. Ben and Joe should come."

"They're on their way. Sorry, girls. Libby, you and Emily are not coming with me."

"Tanner, I told you, in or out."

"I need you to go with Ben and Joe to the hospital. You were so good with Anne the other night. I think you could help get some answers.

"Travis, I know you want to go, but I need you to stay with Jan and Dee Dee. Most of all, to keep an eye on Stuart."

"But Tanner, I really want to be part of this."

"Buddy." Tanner puts his arm around Travis and walks out of the living room, away from hearing range. "You are. It makes me nervous to leave Jan and Dee Dee alone with Stuart. Jan looks so pale, and she seems sick, so please keep everyone together here. Think of this as Command Central. I don't want Dee Dee going out and getting mixed up in all of this. You keep everything locked up, and don't let them out of here tonight, please. Okay?"

"Okay.

"Hey, Stuart, let's get some leftovers. Jan and Dee Dee, it looks like I'm the house mom for tonight."

"Jan, you okay?" Dee Dee is whispering.

"Dee Dee, I think I'm losing fast. The pain is pretty bad again. Wait until Tanner is gone, but if you need to go with him, throw a fit. He'll know to let you go."

"No, I promised Ben. I need to stay put. I'm exhausted anyway."

Please, God, don't let anything happen to Jan. She needs to finish this, and then you can heal her or the other way around. "Hey, guys, we're headed to bed. Thanks, Travis. And Stuart? You be good tonight. No snooping."

Travis starts to ask if Jan's okay. Dee Dee gives him the high-sign to not ask. "Jan, you get some rest. The stuff you put together was amazing. You don't know how much that meant to Tanner. I could see how impressed he was." Travis hugs her. "You are a great lady and a great cop."

Jan is surprised at his last words.

"I know, it shows all over you. How many people have little gold handcuffs on their necklace?"

Jan hugs Travis. *Wow, this kid will be great at doing police work. Who knew? He's so quiet and sweet. I'd never have guessed that he's that sharp.*

Tanner gets the call about the speeding, smart-mouthed kid. Seems he's gotten quite pushy, and they're bringing him in. Looks like he's been drinking. "Oh, great, a drunk." *That call from Bryan was probably a drunken needy thing. No, he sounded perfectly normal before. What's up?*

As Tanner drives in the dark, he finds himself praying and humming "Amazing Grace." *That's a twist for me, Lord. It's been a long time since you and I have had a heart-to-heart. When I was a kid, everything was so clean and clear. I guess the years and all the bad stuff has made me numb. I'm so sorry. Please help us find Alyssa Kirschenbaum, and may she be alive. Give Ben and Joe wisdom at the hospital.* He goes on and on as he pours it all out at the foot of the Cross.

✤

He waits for the elevator. Tanner almost turns around as he's aware of someone right behind him, but he only sees his reflection in the metal doors. There's no one there. It's not a good feeling, prying eyes and ears. Tanner prays in his mind for Bryan and their conversation to be covered by the Lord. Tanner is singing "Oh, the Blood of Jesus," as he travels along to his office. He feels like he's in a capsule, a bubble of safety.

As Bryan enters the office, Tanner can see the fear in his eyes. He touches Bryan's arm. *Oh, my gosh, this kid is shaking all over.* "It's okay, you don't need to be afraid. Someone's got you covered. Don't say a word."

As Tanner shuts the door to his office, he starts. "What's up? You reek of booze."

"I thought it would help when I got pulled over. I pretended to be drunk. Lieutenant Tanner, what's the deal? I was so freaked out. How did your guys know where to find me? You never asked me where I was."

"Bryan, I guess you could say I had my guys watching over you."

"You mean watching me? I'm a nobody!"

"No, Bryan, you're somebody! You're my only link I have to a murder case."

"Oh, my God! I didn't kill anyone!"

"I know, I believe you didn't. Tell me what's going on."

"Well, it's really strange. Remember when you asked about the tattoo? Well, I started putting some pieces together. Right after the tattoo showed up, I started getting calls, but something was weird with that. My phone rings and then I really don't remember talking over it. I started thinking if it's like a signal. Do you think it could be some kind of hypnosis or some creep that has taken over my mind, like the mind snatchers? I've met a couple of other people in the clubs with the same tattoo. They have the same story. They can't remember how they got it, either. Hanging out with gothic types, and you know, some of the stuff from the dark side of the force. People in that world, well, it's kind of spooky and fascinatingly interesting. We don't think much about God. I'm terrified. I've been trying to find God. I even bought a used Bible."

"Bryan, do you believe in God?"

"Well, I don't know. I've been thinking about this girl I met. She was having some flashes. Crazy stuff like being buried alive and hearing chanting. She had the same tattoo. Ever since she told me that stuff, I haven't seen her. No one has. She said she needed to get help. She said she had a friend who was a Christian, and she was going to try and find her. All last night, I kept thinking about finding her and wondering if she found her friend. I don't know any Christians like she was talking about. She told me all kinds of things about God. I don't know why, but I let her pray over me once. She said her friend had taught her to pray a long time ago. I guess I always had an issue with God, but when she prayed, something happened to me."

"Do you believe in God?"

Bryan doesn't answer but says, "I kept hearing a voice in my head all night last night. It kept saying, 'Lieutenant Tanner will watch over you. Tell him.'"

Tanner is stunned and ashamed. *This kid thinks I'm something, Lord. You know how I've been. He's seeking your help. He's like a pitiful stray cat.* A voice speaks to Tanner's heart, *"And you are going to give him my help."*

"It sounds like God has been working on you for a while, Bryan. It's like this. You commit your life to Jesus and surrender. Ask Him into your life and to forgive you of sin, the stuff we all involve ourselves in. He will save you."

"Can I do that right now? I can feel that awful thing coming."

"Let's pray." Heads bowed, Tanner takes Bryan through by what the church calls the sinner's prayer, but for Bryan, it's the embrace of God. Tanner and Bryan are both touched by the unseen hand of His love. Clinging together, they are crying. Both men have been changed instantaneously forever. Bryan stepped from being a rebellious punk to a young man of God. Tanner is restored and released to be the man he was always meant to be.

"Bryan, is your phone vibrating?"

"Yes, I have to answer it. Pray, Lieutenant." Bryan deliberately slurs his words as he responds to the call.

"Yeah, I've got to get out of here first. I got hauled in. This Lieutenant is a real nutcase... Sure, I think I could work on that... It pays how much?... Okay. I'm all over that... Friday night?... Okay. Let me know where and what time... No, I can't meet tomorrow, my grandma is coming to town... Well, she goes to church, and I have to give her something. She always throws some money my way... Yeah, you know, huh... Thanks for getting me this gig... Oh, you want me to bring other people?... They get the same deal?... I've never met you... Yeah, I'm sure it will be a surprise... Your boss is going to be there?... Why would he be interested in me?... You think it could be a permanent position?... Okay, let me know when... Thanks again." Bryan is shaking.

"Bryan, you were fantastic. You might consider an acting career. Do you think he knew?"

"Not if God doesn't tell him, Lieutenant."

"Call me Tanner."

"I think I'll call you, Sir. That will be a first for me— respect! Sir, this is really dangerous stuff. I can't even express how sick it made me. That conversation, that sound of his voice, so raspy, mechanical, and creepy. Do you know what, though? I don't feel that fear anymore. Wow! I remember everything he said and what I said."

Ding! Tanner's wondering if it's the same voice that the patrol heard when they checked on Professor Jacob. "Bryan, would you recognize that voice if you heard it again in another setting?"

"Yes! If you heard it, Sir, you'd never forget it."

"Bryan, I'm going to charge you and keep you here tonight. But you told him something, so we need a grandma to show up. Tomorrow's Sunday, and you're going to church. I'll work everything out." Tanner writes down Constance's phone number. "Call this number, and your "grandma" will be down to bail you out. Go with her to your apartment. I won't see you until tomorrow, Bryan." Tanner is hugging him. "Meeting you has changed my life. God bless you."

"You too, Sir. God bless you. I've met "churchy" people, but no one like that girl told me about, that is, until right now. When you prayed, and what you prayed, I knew you must be a lot like her friend."

"Well, Bryan, act like a jerk one more time when I tell you to get out of here."

"I will, Sir."

"Get this little piece of work out of here and book him!" Tanner doesn't even look at him as the officer hauls Bryan off.

"Constance, I know it's late, but I've got a cat I need to be rescued. It needs a grandmotherly type— bossy and rich, who loves her kitten. I know you've been wanting a cat, so here's what you have to do… Oh, yeah. I forgot you have house guests. I'll call you about 7:00… When does church start?… I don't know if I'll be able to make it at 10:30, but we'll see. Thanks for the invitation. Constance, I'm so glad you called about cats so many times. Goodnight, and God bless." *Lord, bless Constance Carter and let the Chief know that she is still carrying on the good work. I'm going home to sleep in my own bed. Lord, I entrust all these people and myself into your hands. Help Ben, Joe, Libby, and Emily. Bless Beth Adams. What a relief, knowing you can do a much better job than I can of protecting everyone. Thank you for Bryan, and watch over him. He's your boy now.*

Party Planners Continue

"How did it go with that kid? Is he coming?"

"Yes, and he's bringing friends. I thought he blew it when he got arrested. He was driving drunk."

"Doesn't he know how dangerous that is?"

"He's been driving drunk, careening around curves, going places he shouldn't. Rebellious, stubborn drunk. Well, he's due for a change. I heard you say that he might get a permanent position."

"I think the Boss would enjoy meeting Bryan. Underneath all that, he's probably got some good potential."

"I think so, but he's got to go to church with his grandma. I'll wait until Monday. I hate Sunday. It always seems to make a break in the flow of the week."

"How is the family?"

"Good, they are really getting big, growing like weeds. Well, they're more like flowers and are starting to bloom. They should be up before you know it. It's been a long day, and I just want to enjoy what's left of the quiet evening. So, you're going to have to scoot." *I thought he would never leave. Well, Bryan, this is going to be a busy week for you, too.*

Libby and Emily are startled by the transformation of Beth Adams. "Emily, it's astounding, isn't it? I wish that Tanner was here to see Anne." *She's beautiful.* Emily sits on the chair next to her bed and starts singing "Amazing Grace."

"I know you, don't I? I've met you before. Where did we meet?" Anne's scooting away, curling up towards the head of the bed. "It wasn't at the bed in the garden, was it?" She appears to be really afraid.

"No, we met at Wilderness Walk. You rode here with us. Remember, we were singing together." Emily starts singing again.

Anne starts singing, "Flowers everywhere. Flowers in her hair... Where's the girl that pushed me through the glass? She was nice. I think you are too, not like those things in the garden, plant people." Ben and Joe are intently listening.

Emily asks, "What plant people?"

Anne seems agitated, "You know, the ones that claw at you. Oh, you're the girl that pushed me through the glass. I'm sorry I couldn't take you with me. I lost the book. I dropped all the flowers." Anne is crying.

Emily says, "It's okay. It's okay. How did you get out of the garden?"

"I ran, just like you told me. Remember, you told me, no matter how much it hurts, to keep running. I did it!" Anne looks like she's waiting for Emily's approval.

"You did it! I'm so proud of you!"

"They almost got me at the wall when that guy pulled me up."

"What guy?"

Anne doesn't reply and keeps on talking about the barbed wire and the chains at the wall. "The black cloud, thundering, was trying to fly over and find me. That guy gently pushed me down and laid on top of me. He told me to be quiet. He smelled like fresh rain. Everything was shaking, all shaking. That other guy stomped around and around. The cloud kept trying to find me. Suddenly, the guy gets up and tells me to run. I ran until I got so hot I had to take my jacket off. That's when her notebook fell. I couldn't find it. It was too dark. Are you mad at me? I really tried to keep the flowers safe." Anne is rocking and mumbling again.

Emily quietly whispers to Anne, softly stroking her head. "It's okay. Do you know my name?"

"It's on your notebook."

The astonished group is startled by Jamison's phone ringing. "I'll be right there.

"Pray. Jan's been brought in by ambulance. Stay with Beth as long as you'd like. I've got to get to the Emergency Room."

❋

"Jamison, thank goodness you're here. I can't express how much Jan means to me. Help her. It's cancer."

"Dee Dee, I'll do my very best."

"Jan, can you hear me?" A weak nod and a slight movement of her hand signals that she is hanging on. "What's your blood type?" The pale lips form an O. "Positive?" A tiny nod and Jamison orders a transfusion. "Stat!" Jamison closes his eyes and clasps Jan's hand.

"Dee Dee, I think Jan is going to be back with us shortly. How long have you known?"

"Actually, Jan told me the first day I met her. We had one of those instantaneous bonds. No one else knows. That's the way she wants it."

"From what I've learned about all her friends, I imagine the women already know, at least, they know something."

A nurse hands a note to Jamison.

"Madelyn must have had a dream. A lady named Marty has called about you and Jan. Isn't she one of the 10?"

"What? How strange. Marty couldn't have known where we are. She wouldn't have known who to call. No one even knows we're here or that Jan's in trouble." Dee Dee's reaction is somewhere between relief and fear. She feels that pull on the pendant. Jamison moves quickly toward Dee Dee as she touches her heart.

The beauty of life fading from Jan's face and the limpness of her fingers remind Dee Dee of her mother, Julia. Dee Dee shakes the memory away. *All right, Jan, please don't die. Run the race. Finish it. You need to finish this.*

"Jamison, I'm fine. I'll ask Jan if I can tell the other women."

24

EVERYTHING'S FINE?

Sunday's here. Tanner awakes refreshed. He hasn't slept like that in years. *Thanks, Lord, I really needed to let it go. How long have I been asleep?* He breathes a sigh of relief that the clock says 5:45. *Lord, thanks for last night, for Bryan's life. Forgive me for, I guess, judging a book by its gothic cover. Your love brings light into the darkness. Bring your light into this whole situation and cover us with your power. The Kirschenbaums, where are they?*

He gets a call from Ben Garcia. "Hi Ben, you're up early... What?... All right. I can't finish making calls until 7:00. As soon as I'm done setting up some things, I'll get back over there. Where's Libby and Emily?... I appreciate you taking care of them... Yes, I have a lot to tell you, too. Is Stuart still with us?... Good."

Tanner's making another list, always a people list: Constance, the Kirschenbaums, Libby.

"Libby, what are you doing? You're up?"

"Tanner, we've got to get back to Wilderness Walk in the daylight. We've got to find that notebook that Anne had."

"Lib, I'm coming over as soon as I get some details worked out." Tanner quickly explains about Bryan and what he needs to do.

"Hurry! Tanner, some girl needs our help."

"I know, Lib, and so does God. I love you, Libby. Are Jan and Dee Dee—"

"They're fine, Tanner. Everything's fine. Do what you need to, but hurry."

Hmmm. Are we sure everything's fine? What's going on? 6:45. "Constance, you must have thought I was a nutcase calling about cats... Oh, you want that kitten?... Great! Could you be ready in about an hour for him?... Yes, it's a male. He's very special... Is Beanie there?

"Hey, Beanie, it's me again." Tanner explains what he needs. As always, Beanie comes through. She'll take Constance to pick Bryan up. "Beanie!"

"Sir?"

"The kid's okay. Whatever is after him is really evil. I don't know many details yet, but pray! I don't know if it's incarnate or something else, but it's dangerous. You know what you need to do, Beanie."

"Yes, Sir, I'll be careful. We are going to church, so it will be a restful Sunday. You take it easy today, too. When Erica wakes up, tell her Beth is better. She still can't see her, but she's better. Tell Erica she can go to work with the "janitor" tomorrow... What do you mean she's quitting?... Constance is hiring her, and so are you!"

"I've got to hear this one, but it'll have to wait."

Tanner is running through his usual list in his head. *What a wonderful Sunday!* As he finishes his list, he mentally folds it and tucks it into the back of his mind.

Tanner drives to the apartment, Mr. Kaplan's apartment. *Thanks, Mr. Kaplan. It's so nice to have your hospitality for all the guests. It's so much easier for me. Maybe Libby and I can even lease your place.* As Tanner arrives, he sits quietly, looking at the building. *I really like this place.*

As he greets Sam, the doorman, he feels like he's greeting an old friend. The key in the door feels right. There isn't that hesitation as he steps into the room, the one that the Adlin Summers murder created. *It's like we're all family.* He's glad to be home. He sees Libby in the kitchen. *She's beautiful.* "Libby."

"Hi Tanner, I missed you."

"I missed you too. I'm going to talk to Ben and Joe for a minute, Libby. Where's Jan and Dee Dee?"

"Tanner, Dee Dee, and Jan went by ambulance to Memorial last night. Dee Dee said Jan's been losing blood. We didn't know what happened until Jamison got a call when we were with Beth. He was with Jan and Dee Dee all night."

"Why didn't you call me?"

"Jan didn't want us to, and neither did Dee Dee. They both know how stressed you are. Jamison said she'll be okay. She needed a transfusion. It's cancer, and it's very aggressive. Dee Dee said for you to take care of business. It's only a matter of time, but Jan will be out of the hospital in a couple of days."

"Libby, baby, don't cry. We'll pray. That little gal has already wriggled her way into our hearts. You know that God's heart is towards her."

"But, Tanner, she doesn't believe completely."

"I know, but he's still the maker of miracles and the lover of souls." *Bryan is an example of God's power.* "Lib, let me tell you about last night, but first, I have to ask, where's Stuart?"

"That's why Jan went by ambulance. Travis wouldn't leave Stuart and didn't want him at the hospital again."

"Smart boy. Wait until you hear the story of Bryan." Tanner makes a quick call to Jamison.

"She's pinking up. Her color's back, and it's like she's being transformed back into Jan. That white alabaster person who was transported here last night looked nothing like Jan. Tanner, I'll take good care of her."

Ben and Joe are sitting at the table. "Tanner, Joe has something he wants to go over with you. There were several things that Beth said last night. We both have some thoughts." Ben is speaking very softly to not be heard by the others.

Joe is flipping through a little notebook. "Where do I start?" Joe closes his eyes for a quick, silent prayer. "In 2000, I contacted Ben over a case involving the disappearance of a couple who had been on a vacation. They had gone missing from a cruise to the islands. It was one of those Millennium Cruises."

"I remember something about that, but it seems like it got reported and then nothing was put out about it."

"There's a reason for that, but I'll back up to that in a moment. The couple was not actually a couple. I mean, they weren't married. They were undercover tracking jewel thieves targeting older women on cruises. I was sent to investigate at the federal level because it was linked to the Cartels. The ship was docked at Port Au Prince when the agents disappeared. They didn't return to the ship. They had vanished. The agents had been brought to Miami from California, and that's how Ben and I got acquainted."

Ben leans forward and softly says, "Tanner, if this is what we think it is, everyone is in real trouble. None of this is of this world."

Tanner feels like he's back at Adlin's apartment, looking at the bizarre scene.

"During the investigation, I uncovered a situation that was impossible to grasp. Initially, we thought that the jewel ring had uncovered our agents and simply had taken them out. The ring only had an indirect connection to the disappearance. What I encountered was, I don't know quite how to say this, but it was black magic, Voodoo. Well, Ben asked me to help profile the killer in the Summers case. He told me about you and your feelings about this case, Adlin's murder. I couldn't shake that old feeling. I thought I was completely off-track until I got here. Last night at the hospital was the clincher. Tanner, you have somebody involved in Voodoo, or several somebodies."

Ben's adamant. "Tanner, we have to go back to that place where you found Beth Adams. We both understood her last night. We've got to go find that notebook. We need to get to that hairdresser as well. I know there's something there. The gals, Linda, and the others have spoken to the salons. They found the right one. Jamison gave us a complete rundown on the condition of Beth when he examined her. Tanner, it's the same stuff Joe found in Haiti. It's here. Your instincts of evil are right on. This is not police business as usual."

Joe is measuring his words. "Tanner, we only have a few days. It's going to be a full moon on Friday."

"Libby, get a hold of that salon tomorrow. You get an appointment and take Dee Dee with you."

"I thought we were going to look for the notebook."

"We are, but first we're going to church. Libby, I need you to get to that hairdresser and take Dee Dee along with you. Make an appointment for two. We need two sets of eyes and ears."

"Tanner, I'm picking up Dee Dee at the hospital. Jamison and Irene are going to Jacob's house to visit today."

"No one can be out there alone!"

"Tanner, it's okay. Beanie lined up some backup, unseen backup. They'll be discreet. If someone else is at the Professor's, they will distract them so Irene can get to Jacob. The plan is to take Professor Jacob to lunch at noon. Emily and Travis are keeping Stuart busy today. They're going to church and the library."

"Well, it looks like we're all going to church. We're going to set the precedent of putting the Lord first and then, we're going to hunt."

Memories

"Roscoe, I've been so ill I can't tell reality from dreams. Am I speaking to you? Am I awake?"

"No, Jacob, it's a dream. You're dreaming. Sleep. It's only a dream."

"Okay, then I'll dream about Rose instead of you." Jacob's gone out of Roscoe's spell.

"Jacob, don't start that again. You'll lose your focus. Rose... how can someone dead have so much control? It's not good control. It's always bad, leads Jacob down the most unproductive path."

Jacob is smiling and talking to Rose in his sleep.

"I don't know why I have to put up with something like this. Crazy fool. It's infuriating. All the meddling from twits like Stuart and those police at the door. I'm about ready to—"

"Get a hold of yourself." Desmond's voice is deep and firm. "We have much to do, and you better not lose your temper. I was told about your temper tantrum."

"Who told you? Come on. You're not all-knowing."

"Others have certain powers, intellect, and hearing. I've been listening."

"Not surprising with all these birds that information is getting spread. Damn crows! Bunches have been clustered on the walls for days. They better not try to get the plants. Desmond, did I ever tell you about when I worked with the Queen of England?... No, not Elizabeth. Mary, a long time ago. She was quite the woman. She and I worked very closely together. This project so reminds me of her. It was so exhilarating to walk out onto her balcony. Her little mini-garden. You know, they even made up nursery rhymes about it. Bluebells, cockle shells, and pretty maids all in a row. All those years of being locked away really made her receptive to things and innovative ideas. A religious fanatic is one of the best partners to have because they have vision."

"This is quite an interesting and touching insight. Bloody Mary. Who would've thought? Roscoe, you are something else. I'm not sure what, but something else." The two are laughing hysterically, but Roscoe isn't laughing inside.

You, Desmond, making fun of me? I know how Mary would have handled you, and your head would have been in her garden. Black magic. Voodoo. Does he really think he has any power? What a dupe. Now, Roscoe is laughing grotesquely. He is swirling and laughing as they enter the research plot.

Jacob is pulled from his dreams by an insistent pounding sound. The chime of the doorbell is ringing over and over.

As he opens the front door, he's surprised and delighted to see Irene and a friend. "Irene!"

"Jacob, this is Jamison. We're here to take you to lunch! We'll wait for you to get ready, and we're not taking no for an answer."

"How thoughtful! I'll leave Roscoe a note."

"It's a gorgeous day for hiking. The last time I was here, it was pitch black so let's travel up the path. I think I can find it." As the three hikers travel upwards, Tanner relates the evening they found Anne, "Beth Adams." "Here, this is about where I went into the brush." Tanner is pushing back the undergrowth. "There, up ahead, at the edge. That's where Travis pulled her back, but it's all caved away." The three men are standing about five feet from where Anne was rescued. The whole section, several feet, has crumbled down into the ravine.

"Tanner, if you hadn't gotten her, she may not have been found for weeks." Ben is peering over the sharp incline at the pile of dirt and rocks almost 150 feet down the wall of the ravine below. "How do we get down there?"

"I think we'll have to travel up further and loop back down."

A fifteen-minute climb up the path brings them to a point where they can go back down. There's a small path to the left that leads upward. They can tell it's been some time since it was a route used by hikers. It's overgrown. At the top of the incline, they are surprised to find themselves with a perfect view of what appears to be Professor Jacob's house across the ravine. "Is this what I think we're looking at?" From where the men are, they can see over the wall into the growing plots and the front drive. The whole property is in full view. "This is where Stuart has been watching the house from. Why didn't we bring him along?" Tanner thinks he sees Irene's car in the front of the house.

Joe's nudging Tanner. "Yeah, I think Jamison and Irene are making their house call. It looks like Irene's car is in the front."

Ben thinks he spots a possible route to the bottom. The men begin to descend without a path, moving from tree to tree along the steep incline downwards. It takes them almost an hour to reach the floor of the ravine. Looking upwards, they locate the missing area where Anne was.

"Was there a wind that night? If there was, it could be anywhere. On the other hand, if there wasn't a wind, we may wish there had been one to carry it out away from all this." Joe is facing a massive pile of dirt and rock. "This would be quite a load to move."

Ben walks to the other side of the pile. He's praying. "Guys, come help me! I can see it!" Ben is lying flat on his belly, pointing into a pile of rocks and dirt. "There's a tiny little bit of pink sticking up in a crevice. He begins to lift the rocks, tossing them away and scooping at the dirt.

"Hold it!" Tanner's aware that their effort to excavate is causing the pile to shift. "Get something to brace this up." Slowly and carefully, the two position the broken tree limbs to hold it back. Pushing with all their might, Ben gently works his arms amongst the small rocks and dirt under the pile towards the pink notebook. "Ben, I'm about to give out! Hurry! The weight is shifting!"

"I've got it!" With a swift motion, Ben runs his hand into the crack that he's created and jerks the notebook out. He yells, "Run!" Tanner and Joe let go of their timbers, and the entire pile begins to collapse. Not looking back, they hear the rumble of the dirt and rocks. A huge cloud of dust covers all three of the men.

As the quiet in the ravine is restored, Ben wipes the cover of his treasure with his sleeve. It reads, "Property of Cherry K." The men stand silent, astonished. This is Alyssa Kirschenbaum's notebook. An observer would have thought that they had uncovered King Tut's Tomb. They are so excited.

Joe is mystified. "How did you ever manage to see that notebook?"

"Well, I tripped on my shoelace and landed flat, and there it was. I guess you could call it divine providence. Wasn't that the sermon in church today? 'That which is hidden shall be brought to light.'" Ben tucks the book carefully into his jacket and zips it up. "Maybe there's fingerprints or other evidence of some sort."

The upward climb takes a team effort. At the top, before heading down the path, the team pauses to view the house. The car is still there.

Tanner calls Jamison. "Hey, Doc, we had a successful surgery. What's on your agenda today? Wanted you to examine what we've extracted... Oh, you're visiting an old friend with Irene?... You're all going to lunch?... Okay, we'll give you a call so I know when you're free. Call me when you leave... Oh, you're leaving now?..."

Tanner is directing Ben and Joe to look towards the front of the house. They could barely make them out, three figures moving to the car. They're dumbfounded, blank.

Joe grabs Tanner's arm. "Tanner, don't even think of it. We are not going to that house. I'm telling you, we are not prepared if it is what I think it is. Have you two noticed anything unusual about all of this?"

Nodding, Ben says, "You mean like no sound? Like complete silence? Off. Everything seems very off."

"Yeah, I've been thinking that it's strange too. No birds, no animals, only trees and rocks. Do you think someone's watching?"

"No, I don't have that feeling. It's eerie." Ben's looking around. "Let's go, there's nothing here. Maybe it's all the noise we made. We haven't exactly been quiet hikers." Laughing, they head down to the parked car.

As they turn to leave the area, Tanner thinks he sees someone standing in the trees again. He stops the car and stares, but there's nothing there. "I think my imagination is getting out of hand."

"Gee, we could only wonder why." Joe is laughing as he pats Tanner.

Ben is patting the bulge in his jacket. "Thank the Lord for letting us get what we came for." All the guys say, "Amen."

Voices in the Woods

Not visible through the trees of the park, two are meeting. "I like this place. It's so far from the noise, and it's rather picturesque."

"Don't go flying off the handle again. You, my friend, have got to get a hold of that temper. Learn to savor the moment. You know, let things evolve. You always create a real mess. I can't believe you let that little snip actually outsmart you. You need to be more diligent in business. The Boss really wanted that girl included in the team. Have you located her yet?"

Roscoe is sulking, almost pouting. "You know this assignment has been frustrating. The United States is quite a bit different from other parts of the world. It's been a real strain to figure out the system here. I don't know, people always surprise you and disappear on you. The Bible Belt Region has a language all of its own. I know human nature is the same all over, but this is some kind of place."

"Yeah, that "good ole boy's system" hasn't always worked out for you. So many young recruits have dropped out. They get to a certain level of expertise and all fun and games, but when it gets down to the hard work, only a couple have continued on."

"I'm frustrated! Like that kid, Bryan, he's really got potential, but he's so, well, slow. That girl, Missy, I had to, oh, let's say, plant her in another part of the project. She was very smart but couldn't work well under orders. Kind of always trying to figure everything out. She just needed to learn to follow the plan. Back to the original subject you brought up. I think I did a fairly adequate job in cleaning up my mistakes, and the end effect was a nice outcome. Don't you think?"

"Well, I guess it was. In defense of you and your efforts, it was a beautiful ending. Good save, Roscoe. Maybe that word save is a little off. Let's call it a clever retrieve. I know, it was not easy to find a place to live. You had to really hustle to find adequate housing. How's that working out?"

"Quite well... to think that I was simply invited in."

"It has such wonderful access to much that would give you a home and a place to work from. Actually, I've been quite impressed with your progress."

Roscoe is beaming. "Yes, I'm not treated like a tenant. I'm, in every sense of the word, a true house guest."

"Well, I've got a couple of people calls to make. We'll get together soon. Keep me updated."

"Wow! What is this national park visitor day? That was unexpected, and now for my scheduled meeting."

"This is a great place to meet— private, quiet, pristine. I enjoy this time of day in the cool of the evening, so to speak. It's almost exhilarating, refreshing, energizing as the business of the day ends."

"I know the way you feel. Enough chatting. Why did you want to meet? You know I hate being checked up on. The home office should know by now that I'm a conscientious worker."

"Your work is not in question. Here's the message. Don't go flying off the handle like that again! Get back on the page! You really made a mess. Your actions could have ruined the entire effort." The voice is almost a snarl.

"You can't imagine how bad it is. Well, when you spend so much time and effort, and then you find out again that you've been tricked. I hate to have been outsmarted." His voice is seething. "I better not find out that I was laughed at, or there will be hell to pay. I thought I did an excellent job of cleaning up. The end effect, well, I don't mind saying it, added something of interest to the project."

The other voice is laughing, dark laughter. "Yes, you're right, it was a great, defiantly clever moment. I heard the Boss got a chuckle out of it. You do give an eye to detail."

"Good, I bet it hacked those jerks at headquarters off. They're so jealous. I hope the Boss really gave them a tongue-lashing. It's hard enough to do fieldwork without interference. Some are always wanting to be the top dog."

"You know, personally, I thought it was brilliant."

I hate suck-ups. Don't try to worm your way into my project. "This is my project. I have my orders from the Boss. Sent me to the wrong place. If I find out who did that, heads are going to roll." His voice is almost shaking with anger. "I will find out."

"Let me assure you, it wasn't me. I only check the field reps. Well, it's like the Boss always says, 'You can't trust anyone.'"

"Do you know who it was?"

"No! Absolutely not! Well, I've got to get going. It's almost dark. The night gives me a chance to catch up on loose ends... No, I told you, I've got a couple of calls to make. Anything else?... No, I'll give this information to the Boss. He can't be everywhere at once, but really likes to keep up on the field projects. It's been interesting as always."

Hmmm. I bet it has. I didn't even tell him everything. He doesn't deserve to share in the new developments. "Tell the Boss I've managed to get at least two potential leads." *Back to business.*

Jacob is safely deposited in the front seat. Jamison is driving. Irene starts. "Jacob, I'm so glad you came today. I had come to visit the other day. When you didn't answer, we were concerned. We sent a patrol, the police, to do a wellness check."

"You did? I'm sorry, I must have been gone. What day was that?"

"Thursday."

"No, Irene, I was home all day. You know, I don't feel well sometimes. I may have been sleeping, or maybe I was out in the back. I probably didn't hear the police, either. Thanks for checking on me, though." Jamison is looking in the rear-view mirror right into Irene's eyes.

"Jacob, the police said they spoke to you. You answered the door."

"Irene, I don't remember them being there. I'm really having trouble remembering. I feel like I'm walking around in a dream most of the time. I went to the doctor. He took all kinds of tests on my heart, and everything seemed fine. Maybe I'm going crazy again. You know, that stuff with Rose and her grave. I had a breakdown—"

Irene interrupts, "I know Jacob." *Oh, Jacob, he seems like my old friend again.* "Jacob, I have heard so much about your house guest, Roscoe. We could have taken him with us, you know. I've never met him."

"You haven't? I could have sworn he told me he had met you. To tell you the truth, when you asked me to invite him, I didn't. He's been a great help, but every time I bring up Rose, he gets snotty. Irene, you know how much I miss her. Do you think that makes me unfocused to think about her?"

"No, Jacob, it seems natural after forty years of marriage, that you would want to think of her. I would want someone to remember me like that." Jamison is looking at Irene in the rear-view mirror again, smiling. "Jacob, did you know Stuart says he's never met Roscoe, either?"

"What? Why would Stuart lie like that? I know for a fact that Roscoe and Stuart have worked on the project together when I wasn't feeling well. What in the world has gone wrong with Stuart? He's been so strange ever since we came back from Haiti. I would've dismissed him, but Rose liked him so much, and he's so knowledgeable about her research. Roscoe says, 'Stuart is trouble,' and that he doesn't like him. How could Roscoe know that, if he's never been with Stuart? How can you dislike someone you've never even met?"

Irene's thinking, *I dislike Roscoe, and I've never met him.*

Jamison diverts the conversation, "Speaking of research, how is it coming?"

Jacob is off talking to Irene about finding plant substances that rejuvenate tissue. He's doing research on plants with lab animals which have reduced tumors. Jamison is intently listening. "Do you think I could come over next week and see some of your data? I believe that there are some solutions that Western Allopathic Medicine has ignored for years."

"You know, Jamison, I was a surgeon."

"Yes, I know, and that's why I wanted to come today. I wanted to meet you. When Irene told me she was an old friend of yours, I was so excited."

Irene listens quietly as Jamison and Jacob exchange medical experience. *This is the first time I've seen Jacob like himself since Rose passed away. Thank you, Lord. He sounds like Jacob.* It's almost like Jamison has read her mind. Irene hears Jamison.

"Jacob, have you had any difficulties with your throat lately?"

"Why? Do I sound funny?"

"No, but when the officers came to your house, they thought whoever answered the door had trouble with their throat. They thought the person had a trach, kind of like a dull, mechanical voice."

"It must've been Roscoe then. He has a very unusual voice. He said it was from an old injury."

Jamison is giving Irene a sign with his eyes in the rear-view. Irene knows not to comment. "Jacob, how would you feel about me checking you out? I could run some tests to get to the bottom of your tiredness. If you're open to it, I'd like to put you in for a couple of days. Have you out by, hmm, Tuesday or Wednesday. Then, we'll take a look at your data."

"Jacob, I think you should let Jamison run some tests. I've been worried about you for a long time. You know that. I know Rose would want you to be well."

"Irene, I know I've got to feel better. I'm at some kind of turning point in the research. Jamison, I'm going to take you up on your offer. This week is crucial, and I've got to get things back on track. I still want to have brunch, and I need to get some clothes at the house."

"Jacob, I'll call Roscoe. I'll get you whatever you need."

"Jamison, do you know where Mama's Restaurant is? I feel like having Italian. Ooh, that's such a great restaurant. Okay with you, Irene?"

"I love that place, Jacob. We had such great times there."

✳

As they eat, Jacob is excitedly sharing with Irene. He keeps repeating how wonderful it is to be with people. He's chatting on about the project he's working on and how difficult it has been to get any part-time help. "I had hoped to use my lectures to get my solid part-time staff. Every time I've got someone, they come a few times, and then I never see them again. I can't get in touch with them. I've given up. Roscoe told me not to give up, but it's all so disappointing."

Jamison and Irene are looking right into each other's eyes. "Well, Jacob, you know kids today are not quite as dedicated."

"I know Jamison, but Irene, you know when you feel that connection. When you see that spark in the eyes of a student. I know they were interested. That spark was there, so I would give them my personal card. They would come, and within a few days or weeks, nothing. Rose and Stuart never had that problem. They had whole groups of workers with them."

"What does Stuart say about this?"

"I don't know. He was so rude and snapped at Roscoe one day. Said he was tired of being treated like a field hand. When Roscoe told me, I felt I had probably burnt Stuart out. So, I pretty much kept him at the office or in the lab at the University. He hasn't done physical work on the project in months."

"Did you tell Stuart what Roscoe told you?"

"No, Roscoe didn't want to cause a further breach of their relationship. He wants us to all get along. That's why Roscoe has worked so much in the greenhouse and on the new plantings. He's really helped me. If he didn't have this issue about Rose, I would have given him a lot more reign. See, that's what is hard about asking him to leave. I need help."

"Yes, you do. If you had told me, I could've doubled efforts with you and shared some staff. We'll get you help. How about next week? When Jamison comes, I'll come too with some others. We'll put a team together."

Jamison winks at Jacob. "We'll take care of a few things for you."

"I'm so excited! You don't know how much better I feel already! Wait until Roscoe hears! I better call him. He can start getting things in order."

Irene is speaking very softly. "Jacob, why don't we let Jamison get you checked out? I'll fill Roscoe in for you. You need to rest. We'll let him know you're okay. Let's not get the cart before the horse. First steps first."

"I think Irene's right, plus she'll need to get some of her work finished, and then you two can put a plan together."

"Perfect! You have really given me hope. Irene, Rose would love this."

"I know, Jacob, she would be so pleased."

"You know how long it's been since I felt encouraged? Roscoe's helpful, but sometimes he makes me discouraged. He's always pushing. You'd think he has some kind of deadline. Well, here's to everything in its season." They lift their water glasses, laughing and toasting their new venture.

House Guests

"Jacob did what? You let him go? I thought you were concerned about saving his strength?"

"Listen, I know it would have been trouble. That woman was the one that sent the cops the other day. She could have brought too many nosey people here. Besides, it's only lunch. Jacob didn't invite me. I only heard the conversation as they were leaving." *It was bizarre. Usually, I can tell when someone's arrived. I must have been too engrossed out in the garden. Normally, I can read Jacob like a book, but not today. He must be feeling stronger.* "He'll be back. He's too dependent on everything I do for him."

"Yes, you better hope he stays well. You'd be in real trouble if he's gone. Your project would be ruined. It will be a shame after all your hard work."

Roscoe is trying to stay calm. *Oh, it would tear you up to see me fail. I'm sure.* "Thanks for the concern."

"I hope you're not wearing out your welcome."

"Never. Jacob is very appreciative of my companionship."

"Looks like you have nothing to worry about then. I'll be back later."

The phone rings. Roscoe lets it go to the answering machine. "Roscoe, this is Irene Carpenter. I'm sorry I didn't get to meet you today. Jacob wanted me to call and let you know he's having some tests run. He'll be back on Tuesday or Wednesday at the latest. He's working on data with another doctor. He wants you to keep the project moving forward. He has shared how much you have done for him. I'll be excited to meet you. If you need anything call this number. Jacob said he has caller ID."

"Sure. I told you he's fine. Letting him get out for a change was a good decision." *This could work out well. I won't have to constantly think about Jacob. Taking care of him has been like dragging around a ball and chain. His state of mind has been a continuous problem.*

"Would you write that number down in case I need information?" At that exact moment, there's a power surge. The surge is only a blink of an eye, but enough to delete the number.

"Check the generators in the greenhouse. The temperature has to stay perfect. Check the thermostats. Never mind, I'll go, too."

Roscoe's thinking, *stupid power company.*

25

GETTING WHAT YOU WANT

Tanner takes the notebook to the forensic lab at the hospital. "Let's unveil the thing."

It's evident that it's a botany field notebook. The fine dust that poofed all over Ben and the notebook reveals human fingerprints. Some appear to be more like the paws of an animal with claws, rats perhaps. Lots of dried plant material and sketches of plants. Where the flowers should be, many are dislocated or missing. Tanner recounts Erica's dream about Anne to them— her picking something up, putting it in a notebook, and pressing it. The lab people are shooting pictures of each page and documenting where the plant material or flowers were found in the book.

At the back of the book, wide smeared lines form the word, "HELP," in a brownish material. The tech swabs it, and it's positive for human blood. It's been written by a blood-soaked finger. The swab is tucked into a vile for future testing. The musty, dank odor of the book is noticeable. Ben can smell the same scent on his jacket. It's the smell of dirt or a basement, a dead smell.

Ben and Joe are shaking their heads as Tanner says, "That's it! It was all over Beth Adams when we found her." Tanner makes it clear that no one other than Ben, Joe, Dr. Lovett, and himself can have access to this information.

"Lieutenant, we won't be able to process all the rest of this until tomorrow."

"Guys, I'll bet this stuff is a perfect match to everything in Irene's lab."

Ben's phone is ringing. "Ben, can you come over to the hospital? It's Jan. She wants to talk to you."

"Yes, Dee Dee, we'll be right there. We're headed that way anyway. We are here in the lab. Tanner wants to know if Libby's there... Tell her to meet Tanner in the main lobby in about fifteen minutes."

❉

"Hey Libby, I'd hug you, but I'm still covered with dust. Did you get any more information from Beth?"

"Let's go see Jan first. Ben and Joe are up there."

As they ride the elevator up, Libby explains what Jamison said about Jan's condition.

"Hey Jan, you look better than you did." Ben hugs her. "You gave everyone a scare."

"Everything's been scary, why shouldn't I follow suit?" Jan's little raspy laughter catches Ben off guard, and he's laughing. Jan's poking fun at Ben. "I'm glad you haven't lost your sense of humor. Actually, I wasn't sure you had one."

Ben is smiling. "Seems we're both full of surprises."

"Ben, I need you to talk Tanner into letting me get on the third floor with Beth Adams. I know that kid needs me. Has Tanner had any luck finding her family?" Jan's almost begging.

"No. Nothing."

"See, she needs me. Please, Ben, I know it's important. I want to help in some way."

"I'll talk to Jamison. You need to rest, but first, Jan, may I have the honor of praying for you?"

"Yes, if it makes you feel better."

Ben prays and lays his hands on Jan. "Dearest Lord, I bring Jan before you.

Fill her with understanding and wisdom. Surround her with your angels. Lord, we ask that she be healed in Jesus' name."

Jan takes Ben's hands and holds them to her face for a moment. "Thanks, Ben. Promise you'll ask Jamison and Tanner? If I have to stay, I might as well be useful to someone."

"Jan, maybe you can be helpful to a couple of people. Jamison called. Tanner is here, and the Professor is coming in for tests. Lunch went well for Irene and Jamison, I guess. Wait until Dee Dee fills you in. Jan, rest up. There are more visitors here.

"Dee Dee, let's move to the sunroom."

"I have probably developed more lifetime relationships in this short amount of time than I have ever allowed myself to have. Jan has helped me realize that I have a fear of getting too close. You've been like a dad to me, so you and Adlin were closest to my heart. It feels good to begin to live. I wish that Adlin could know."

"She does, Dee Dee. She does."

"Ben, I trust Jan. Help her. She needs to be involved, and she's so worried she will be left out. Let her give what she can." Tears are beginning to form in Dee Dee's eyes. I promised Jan I wouldn't tell. I don't want this to be the last thing she does."

"Dee Dee, I'll make sure she's involved. Actually, we are going to need her to keep it together here so it will be real. I trust her, too."

"Ben, there's one more thing. I'm sorry I was so mad at you and Linda. I think it's wonderful that you are close. It's actually comforting. If things don't go well—"

"Dee Dee, you're going to be fine. I'm glad you have given me permission to court your aunt. I probably would have pursued her even if you didn't approve, but this is great. By the way, I've told her you're fine. I didn't say anything about this crisis with Jan; I'll leave that to you. I have something to tell you. We found the notebook."

"Ben, is it Anne's, I mean Beth's?"

"The front reads, 'Property of Cherry K.'"

"Oh, thank you, Lord. Libby had filled me in today about Beth and the ramblings. It's true. She was with Alyssa! She might still be alive!"

"Yes, and they were together somewhere. We are getting closer to finding out where. You probably heard that Professor Jacob is coming. I don't know all the details, but Tanner and Joe are meeting with them right now. Dee Dee, I can see that look. I promise you'll be informed. But promise you won't go off again and get in trouble. Remember? Jan needs you. We all do."

"I know. I promise." *For once, Dee Dee, you are going to think of someone else first. Ben's right; Jan needs me.*

"Jan, you don't even look sick." Tanner is so surprised to see her and how well she looks.

"Amazing what a couple of pints will do." Jan's laughing and chatting with the nurse.

"Jan, don't kid around."

"I'm not. I'm seriously okay. Did you hear? I'm being moved to the third floor. I'm going to have a new roommate. I think her name is Beth."

"Yes, I heard. Frankly, I'm concerned. I have reservations about that. We don't know much about her other than Erica's account. She hasn't known her long either."

"Don't even start this Tanner. I appreciate the concern, but I'm going to help that kid. I know she needs me. Tanner, you don't know this, but I have an extensive background in mental health. I'm totally comfortable with being Beth's roommate."

"See, that's what I was telling you." Libby is shaking her head. "See, she won't take no for an answer. Ben thinks we can try it out for at least one day and then see what Jamison thinks. Remember, you have extra staff there in case."

Yeah, Melinda, there and two others. "Okay, but this is my case, and I feel responsible for you."

"Maybe God's responsible for me. What I'm dealing with is pretty much in His hands, according to all of you. Before you say it, I'll be careful. Yes, Libby's informed me of how you are. Tanner, you have one terrific woman. Libby is special."

I guess Jan caught me there on the issue of turning things over to God.

Libby is blushing as Tanner says, "And beautiful."

"Girls, has anyone seen or heard from the three amigos?"

"Yes, they have left the library and are going to grab a bite.

"Tanner, Beanie called. The Kirschenbaums arrive tomorrow at 8:00. The original flight was canceled. They left a message with Sheryl in Traffic. Your phone must need charging."

"Traffic? Oh, Lord, I've had it on silent all this time. Yep, there's their call. I feel terrible that I forgot those poor people."

Jan pipes up. "See, I'm not the only one that isn't perfect." Laughter.

"Who's picking them up? Jamison looks like he's tied-up with Professor Jacob. At some point, Doc will have to go home and sleep."

"Ten guesses as to who's going to the airport." Libby's smiling as Tanner guesses.

"Beanie?"

"You got it! Tanner, that woman deserves a raise."

"I know, Libby, she's amazing. When this is all over, I will let you plan something special with me for Constance and Beanie."

"What? I don't get anything?" Jan's teasing.

Tanner teases back. "Well, you'll have to get something going on the third floor. Then, if you're very, very good, we'll see." Laughter. *I hope you get healing Jan. I hope that's what you get.*

Libby reads his thoughts and squeezes his hand. "We love you, Jan." She's starting to show the effects of the medication. "You rest, we'll see you later." Jan doesn't answer. She's drifted off. "Sweet dreams, Jan."

Tanner clicks his ringer back on. "Beanie, how's the cat?... Thank you so much for connecting him with Constance. I hear you're picking up the parents too... Great. Thanks for covering for me with them... You are one terrific lady. Please take them to Kaplan's... Are you at the house with Erica and Constance?... Oh, you're all on your way back from church and lunch?... How nice. Did you take the cat?... Could I say hi to the little guy?...

"I've been thinking about you, Bryan. I'll be over later. You've been nice to them, right?... Keep your eyes and ears open. Take care. Be a good watch cat. Love ya, buddy." Libby is looking at Tanner like he's lost his mind. "I told you about Bryan. He's the cat. It's a private joke between Constance and myself."

"Tanner, I didn't know you loved cats so much."

"Now, you do." *I really do love Bryan. Amazing.*

As the "three amigos" are having brunch after their visit to the library, the conversation is fascinating to Stuart.

"Emily, explain again how you knew where to go in the library."

"Well, I guess you could have called it women's intuition. That, or plus reading the account of Madelyn's dreams— the history aisle and the wrong turn. I think that we mustn't make a wrong turn. But was it really a wrong turn? If Madelyn had stayed on track with history, she wouldn't have seen Adlin at the table. My question was, what did Adlin take out of the book? So, I thought we needed to find the book. Step one, was Adlin there for a reason? What's the reason? Seems funny that she got her hair done and then went to the library. It's logical to me that she was used to going there, so she probably had a card."

"Travis, it was so cool when you flashed your badge."

"Did you like the part where I let her know that it was a very top-secret investigation? Made her feel part of it. Tanner taught me that people love to be in on things, like on the inside, and helpful. So, we don't boss them around. We subtly invite them into the "club." Frankly, we did need her help. The rest of the conversation was like a trip into Adlin's world. She was reading some pretty hairy stuff during those last few weeks. Nothing like that before then."

"You don't think she was getting involved in something, do you?"

"I don't think so. I don't know why she was reading that stuff, creepy stuff. Stuart, how did you know what she was reading that night?"

"While you guys were opening every book on the occult, I simply asked the lovely librarian a question. Who was stocking books on October 21? Did she have a payroll or a volunteer sheet for that day? She said they only have three regulars at night to restock books. One of them happened to be working today, Terra Smith, and boy, was she helpful. She knew Adlin from her frequent visits in the evening. Terra said that Adlin was such a nice person. She remembers the evening very clearly because Adlin had changed her hair. She initially thought that Adlin was another person who frequently came to the library.

"When she saw Adlin reading books on Voodoo, out of curiosity, she asked Adlin why she was reading about it. She said she was doing research for an old friend, someone she knew a long time ago. Miss Smith told me she was relieved because she said Adlin was too sweet to be involved with that sort of material, as she called it, from the dark side. She remembered the book. When it came out in the papers that Adlin had been murdered, she immediately pulled the book and called the police. The officer blew her off and didn't think it was connected to the case. She never got a return call."

"Tanner is going to be furious!" Travis is thankful it wasn't him.

"If we go back to the dream, what did Adlin take out of the book?" Emily and Travis are staring at Stuart. "Okay, I was snooping again. While you all went to bed, I was reading Jan's folder. I was curious, and I am a researcher, you know."

"You sneak!" Emily is punching him. "For a minute, we thought maybe you had some of God's insight."

"I actually have another question, though. What about the woman who looked like Adlin? Who was she? Another big question is, what about the guy who picked up the pearl?"

"Stuart, there *is* a connection to the guy. I kept thinking about the pearl in Adlin's car, but there are two pearls. The guy *is* a clue, but what was he checking out? He definitely checked something out. Maybe Terra Smith knows who the woman is." Emily grabs Stuart's face and kisses him right on the mouth. "You're brilliant! Maybe we can figure out who the guy is, too. We've got to go back to the library!" Travis looks as shocked as Stuart.

"Hey, Emily, I don't like—"

"Jealous, are we, Travis?"

"Okay." Emily kisses Travis, deliberately as the one she gave Stuart, but it has a whole different meaning.

"Emily? Travis? Let's get outta here before it gets too thick. Looks like I've got a date with Miss Smith."

&

The library closes at 2:00 on Sundays. They are getting ready to shut the doors as Travis flashes his badge again. "We need some more information, Miss Smith. We'll help you stock books while you and Emily visit.

"Come on, Stuart, let's get busy."

"Miss Smith?"

"Call me Terra."

"Okay, Terra. Do you know who the woman was that looked like Adlin?"

"Sure, it's Leslie Cartwright. She's been coming here regularly in the evenings, but I haven't seen her in months."

"Really? Can you pull up her card and see what she was reading?"

"Diane, will you help us?"

"Officer, does this still pertain to your investigation?"

"Absolutely! We need your assistance to retrieve the information."

Diane, the librarian, searches. "It looks like books about plants and flowers, botany material. Let's see... she checked a book out on September 19. I remember now. In the last entry, she returned that book on October 20. She paid a fairly large fine. It was a special edition which you can only check out for a week. It was a research book on exotic plants. She said she was moving and turned in her library card. I asked her where, and she was reluctant to answer. When she didn't tell me, I didn't press the issue. She kept glancing nervously around the library, and then she got a book from the section you were looking in. I saw her writing on something, and she stuck it in the book."

Trying not to hyperventilate, Emily asks, "How did you notice all this?"

"I know everyone thinks librarians are boring, but we kind of see everything. We are astute studiers of people and things."

"Thank goodness. On October 21, right before closing, a man checked out. Can you—"

Diane works her magic on the computer.

"Diane, you are a genius! Can you print that list?"

"Yes, but I'm sorry, I wasn't working that evening so I can't help you as to anything about them. Five men checked out from 8:00 to 9:00."

"Do you have their addresses?"

"Are you going to tell them where you got this information?"

"Absolutely not. Like the officer told you, it's all very secret."

"Before I give you this…" Diane is holding the printout away from Emily. "The point is, I don't want to get in trouble. Do you promise?... Okay, if this helps in the case, let me know."

"Oh, Diane. You'll be one of the first to know, and we'll be back. You and Terra deserve lunch on the department."

"Well, that would be lovely. Will those two cute officers be joining us?" Diane is nodding in the direction of the guys.

"One of them is taken."

"Which one?"

"That's for me to know and you to find out." Laughter.

"It's a date. Don't forget, I want to help."

"I won't, believe me, I won't. Tell Terra she's invited, too. Thanks so much. *I will never think of librarians as boring again.*

26

PUZZLE PIECES

L ibby touches my hand as we reach for the door, "Dee Dee, you can do this."

Adlin would've liked Libby. Somehow, that gives me comfort as we enter the lair, the salon, the kind of place I would've avoided. The salon seems like a trip into a secret kingdom. I hadn't been around so many females in one place. Strangely, it doesn't fill me with the usual disgust. *One last touchstone with Adlin. The last afternoon of Adlin's life was spent in this place.*

As we delve further into the salon, I hear the hum of the gossip line; women chatting and sharing secrets. Giggles and laughs. The cute little hairdresser with spiky hair is coming straight at me.

"Are you Miss Summers?"

"Yes, and you are?"

"I'm Deidre. You sort of look familiar, have we met?"

See, she's my girl, she knew Adlin. I tell her no, and that it's a pleasure to meet someone with the same name but that I go by Dee Dee. She immediately has an expression on her face, an inquisitive expression. "Call me Dee Dee."

I see a lightbulb go on. "You're Adlin Summers's sister. That's why you looked familiar. Miss Summers, I want to tell you how sorry I am. I called the police immediately when I read the newspapers. I can't believe you're here. It's so special that you ended up here. Thank God! It's been hard for me after I realized I was probably one of the last people to be with Adlin. She looked so beautiful. Adlin had been my client for quite a while and my friend."

I am filled with the oddest sensation. One of the last places and people Adlin was with before she became a memory.

Deidre is speaking very softly. She gives a quick, slight motion with her head. I know she doesn't want anyone else to hear. She points to a chair in the far corner. She tells the clerk that she's moving to Marie's chair today. "My client has a horrible headache, and it will put us away from so much of the noise."

Libby never moves from reading her magazine and waits for her appointment. She gestures with her hand, and I stand to follow Deidre across the room. As I cross the salon, I feel like I'm retracing Adlin's steps. Deidre lightly chatting, asking questions about hairstyles.

When the cape is in place, and she starts washing my hair, I hear her say, "There are things I know, but they wouldn't listen. Adlin was researching something for an old acquaintance, some really creepy stuff. I was concerned. She had asked me a lot of questions. What are you looking for, I mean, what kind of look do you want? Do you have something in mind?"

She wouldn't want to know what I really have in mind.

"You have such thick hair we could probably do anything. Nice layers?"

"I'll leave that up to you, just something easy to maintain." *Last thing on my mind.* "Did you know my sister well?"

"Well, Adlin and I both were new to the area, so we would usually have lunch together when I was done with her hair. That day was different. Because it was a highlighting job, we scheduled it towards the end of the day. We had planned to have dinner, but she told me she was helping someone research some things at the library. It sounded pretty creepy. I kept wondering if we had gone to dinner or maybe a movie or something if Adlin might still be alive. I feel guilty."

I wonder, too. "Do you know who she was helping?"

"No, but I know she was surprised. She ran onto them one day shopping."

"Do you know how they knew each other?"

"No, but it sounded like that person was really in mental trouble."

"A guy?" *Red October?*

"No, Adlin always said she. Listen, whatever was happening was bad. Adlin asked me if I knew anything about the resurrection of the dead."

"You mean, like in the Bible?"

"No, I mean like in a horror movie. You know, zombies."

"Do you?"

"No, but I guess she asked me because I watched horror movies. Well, I don't anymore. I keep feeling like something hunted her down. I never thought things like that really existed. Now, I'm not so sure. I don't want to see it or read about anything even remotely connected to monsters and all that night stuff." Deidre is white as a sheet.

"Deidre, did you notice anyone with or someone watching Adlin that day? Anything unusual?"

"No, not at all. Nothing bad. Only one thing stands out about that day. One of the other gals thought Adlin was her client when she left. She jumped me about doing her client's hair. Stealing clients is a big no-no here. It turned out that after Adlin's hair was done, she looked a great deal like Rita's client."

"Really? Who was her client?"

"I don't know. I don't remember, and Rita's not here. Just a second, I'll check with the receptionist."

Deidre walks to the front and returns with a name and a phone number. "Leslie Cartwright, but she hasn't been seen in months."

No coincidence. Months. Adlin's look-alike, where are you?

"I tried to call the police because I knew she was going to the library. I guess they thought I was a stupid, ditzy hairdresser. I never got a call back."

"Well, the police were here and spoke to you, right?"

"No, they did not." She's adamant. "They never came here, not to my knowledge."

"Deidre, Lieutenant Tanner would've interviewed you."

"The first I've heard was when some lady called a few days ago." Deidre finished my hair. "Look, do you like it?"

"Wow! I can see why Adlin liked you. I barely recognize myself. It's great. I look like a real girl."

"You look like Adlin, other than the color."

"Deidre, how can I thank you? You've been a real help. If you have any more information or need help in any way, call me or Lieutenant Tanner." I give her a card of Tanner's with my cellphone on it. As I pay her, she's reluctant.

"This is way too much. I can't take this."

"Yes, you can and have that dinner that you and Adlin were supposed to have. She would want you to have this." As I hug her, she begins to cry.

"Catch that evil thing," she whispers. "Adlin told me it was a secret, but I know you're a police officer of some kind, aren't you? Adlin always thought it was so funny that you and I had the same first name. Maybe that's why we became such good friends right off the bat."

"Deidre, find out if, in fact, the police were here, and I'll tell the Lieutenant what you told me. Thanks for being Adlin's friend. We will deal with this evil thing."

"I want to help. I'm not going to tell anyone who you are. It's our secret."

Libby was waiting for me. Her hairdresser didn't have to do so much damage control.

As we leave, I see a man walk into the salon next door.

"Beanie, I never thought a mundane Monday could be so enjoyable. Nice to be at my desk in my office, looking out and seeing you at your desk. Could you get a hold of Jim?... He's walking your way?... Send him in.

"Jim, thanks for being so patient. Let's see what you've got." Jim hands Tanner all the reports and starts explaining each one. "Looks like you've almost memorized these. Why?"

"Well, I think a couple of the reports are off. They don't make sense. They don't feel right. I knew you were working a case, so I didn't bug you."

"Thanks! Give me your opinion."

As Jim lays out his thoughts, Tanner hears that familiar ding. *He's right. Something is wrong.* "I'll check on these two. Jim, not a word to anyone. Thanks for your insight and diligence. I knew I could count on you."

"Sir, it's my job!"

"Well, Jim, it looks like we'll be working closely in the future." *Wonders never cease. I never knew he had it in him.*

As Jim walks out, he looks taller, like he just got a medal.

Tanner catches up on all the stacks on his desk and makes numerous calls. He's recompiling the Kaplan file and sees the sticky note about Susan. "Beanie, call Susan. Let's go to lunch. I owe her for the favor at Kaplan's Bookstore."

As the three are having a casual and leisurely lunch, Libby calls Tanner.

"Hey, Tanner, can you pick me up at my apartment? I dropped Dee Dee off at the hospital, and I'm headed home. No rush, but the salon was most interesting."

"Okay, Libby, that was clever. You knew I'd speed my day up to hear the news. I'll be there at four."

Beanie and Susan are still laughing at Tanner as they leave for the station.

"Tanner, Dee Dee and I had a great day at the hair salon."

"Yes, you did. You look, well, scrumptious. Besides coming out looking ravishing, did you get in on any gossip?

As Tanner walks into the apartment, refreshed by making the drive with Libby, he's surprised to see the gathering. At the large table, he sees the three amigos that he now formally refers to as Emily, Travis, and Stuart. They are so concentrated on each other with a cellphone and a notepad. Travis is the first to acknowledge Libby and Tanner.

"Hi, guys! I hope you had a good morning."

"We had a very successful day at the library yesterday. Where's Ben, Dee Dee, and Joe? How's Jan? Is she okay?"

"Stop with the questions, Travis, what's up?" Tanner knows Travis well enough that something besides the library is going on."

Travis looks sheepish. "Tanner, I, well, I may have overstepped my boundaries."

"Okay, that's good for a start. Please explain."

"Libby, your hair looks great." Emily and Stuart are admiring the new style. "Do you like her hair, Tanner?" Tanner ignores the question.

"Travis, what and how did you overstep your boundaries?"

"Well, we needed to find a person, Leslie Cartwright. I called the station, and I told them to find her. I said you wanted the information."

"And why did I want to find her?"

Stuart pipes up in a blast of words and explains the events of the morning and the library yesterday. Cheerily, at the end of the flood of reporting, comes, "See, that's why you want to find her."

Travis sighs, "Thanks, Stuart." Emily is waiting expectantly for Tanner's reply.

"Really good job. Excellent initiative, Travis." You could hear the sigh of relief from the three. "Have we found Leslie Cartwright?"

"Not yet, Sir. We're waiting for a file on her."

Libby's in the den and sees the email coming through. Looking at the file, Libby screeches, "Tanner!" On the computer screen is someone who appears to be Adlin Summers or almost her twin. "Tanner, I didn't tell you because Dee Dee wanted to, but she's the one the salon told her about!" Libby's screech not only attracts Tanner but the whole group who are clustered in the den.

Emily is pointing excitedly. "There's the one Terra and Diane told me about!"

Libby and Tanner respond with, "Who's Terra? Who's Diane?"

"The re-stocker at the library and the librarian. The one Stuart was telling you about. The woman that left the note in the book is *that* woman." Libby and Tanner look blank. Emily continues, "Remember the dream?

The part when Adlin took something out of the book? Adlin was reading that book! We found the book. The note was from Leslie Cartwright."

"We need a printer, Libby. I forgot. Will you get one? Call Beanie. Yes, tell her we're all having dinner tonight. I want everyone to meet Erica, Constance, and Bryan. Some kind of synergy is going on, and we need to meet before the Kirschenbaums arrive."

❦

"Hi, Jan."

"Wow, Ben, I feel privileged. You came to see me again. Missed me, didn't you, or did you miss Dee Dee?"

"Where is she?"

"Some sleuth you are. She's right behind you."

Dee Dee steps out from behind the door.

"Aren't you going to compliment her? I thought she was getting ready for my funeral, but I decided to fool her and live."

Ben is so concentrated on Jan that he is oblivious to Dee Dee. "Wow, there's my girl, Dee Dee. You look fabulous, daahling." The wispy layers frame Dee Dee's face and soften her whole appearance. She looks twenty. Ben kisses her right on the forehead. "You are transformed. I'm taking you out tonight. Dee Dee, you look so much more rested."

"I have been concentrating on others since the other night instead of myself, and it's like something is letting go."

❦

As Dee Dee and Ben walk into the apartment, they're shocked to see everyone sitting around the table. Everyone's clamoring to get their chance to tell their story. Joe quickly bows his head, and they all pray. Joe says, "Everyone gets a chance to tell their story. Everyone's name goes in the pot."

Joe conducts the meeting. "Let's go back to the dreams, the last day of Adlin's life. Dee Dee, you're on."

"I went to the shop where Adlin had her hair done. Libby and I met the beautician, the hairdresser. She thought I looked familiar, and she put the pieces together. I have the name of a look-alike and a phone number for one, Leslie Cartwright. When I asked Deidre if anything unusual had happened, she told me about an incident with another hairdresser, thinking that she had stolen her client. She also told me Adlin was talking about an old friend whom she was researching occult materials for. All Deidre knew was that it was a friend, but no name. Because Adlin knew Deidre was a dark movie buff, she asked her some strange questions about resurrections of the dead… No, not from God's standpoint, definitely the dark side. There's no bad link with Deidre. I believe she truly was Adlin's friend. Oh, I almost forgot. They were supposed to have dinner that evening, but Adlin told her about the research and that she needed to go to the library. Deidre was upset because the police blew her off when she called the station. No one ever came and interviewed her. Tanner, did you hear that? No one ever came and interviewed her."

"Did everyone get that? Travis, what's your story?"

"Well, Stuart, Emily, and I went to the library. Emily was brilliant. With the help of my badge, we found out that Adlin had a look-alike. We also found the book that Adlin was reading in the dream. That look-alike wrote something and stuck it in the book. The importance of the lady was brought up by Stuart. That's why we went back to the library, to find out who the woman was."

Emily pipes in, "Since we're all moving in a different realm than traditional science, I felt that there were two elements of the dreams left out. The note and the pearl. I thought if we could find the note and the guy linked to the pearl, we might be somewhere in the case." Emily tells them, "The woman is Leslie Cartwright. She's the one who wrote the note or whatever was in the book Adlin was reading." She relates the account as told to her by Diane, the librarian. "Terra, the re-stocker, confirmed that Adlin was reading the same book. We have the names of five men who were at the library in the checkout line or at least the ones who checked out books. Maybe we can locate the connection to the pearl.

"Tanner, Terra also called the police because she pulled the book. No one ever called her back, so eventually, she had to put the book back on the shelf. It's a hairy one, dark stuff with rituals, sketches, and symbols—those sorts of things. You can't check it out because it's very valuable. One more thing. Leslie Cartwright had been checking books out on Botany, plants, and natural medicines."

Everyone's frantically taking notes, and the conversation continues. Tanner introduces Erica and tells her to calmly tell her story. Beanie had prepared her for the huge group.

Tanner didn't tell me about Erica. That's strange. That twinge. Stop it! There's nothing deceitful about Tanner. Dee Dee, stop. Do not ask. Let the kid talk.

Erica is going on about her missing friend, Anne, and her car in the parking lot in the back by itself.

Oh, Lord, this is the green car under the light. How does this tie to Adlin? It's part of Madelyn's dreams. One more round of applause from Adlin. All right. What was the significance of the car at the church? Good grief, if this kid hadn't been invited... Miraculous that she ended up on Tanner's list of phone calls. I write, "Is someone at the police station involved?"

Tanner is introducing a lady named Constance. She tells us about a book in her flower bed, the book checked out by Anne. She's so excited, as she puts it, back in the loop.

I can relate to being in the loop.

She describes how she and Beanie found Mr. Kaplan and acquired this apartment.

So that's how we all got to this classy place. I didn't ever think to ask. I must be losing my touch. I guess I thought maybe Dot had sprung for it. The girls, Linda, and all of them flood my thoughts.

Constance's words bring me back from my thoughts. "Dee Dee, it is such a privilege to meet you, and I'm so sorry for your loss. If you need anything, let me know."

I smile and tell her, "Thanks for helping, and I appreciate your offer." *The one I really want to thank is Beanie.* She's whizzing away, taking shorthand, writing it all down so the gals at home have a record. *Home? Yes, home.*

I hear Tanner asking Beanie if she wants to share anything. She shakes her head no and waits for someone else to speak. Bryan's name is pulled out from the pot.

As Bryan starts to relate his recent change of heart, his salvation experience, I feel that tug. That thought slips in. *Sure, he says that now...*

Stop it, Dee Dee. Look at him. You can see that clear look in his eyes. He's holding up his left arm, exposing a very unusual tattoo inside his left wrist. Bryan is relating the strangest story about phone calls. He's talking about having no memory of how he got that tattoo. He pauses and says he needs to back up.

I hear him as he says, "The reason I started thinking about how weird everything was getting was when I met this girl in a club. She was talking about the weird stuff she had experienced. She had the same tattoo and no memory of how she got it. She was going to contact a Christian friend she used to know. When I met Tanner, I knew I needed his help. Constance and Beanie have helped me a lot, too. For the first time, life is beginning to make sense. I hope I can help. I want to find this girl from the club just like Erica's friend was found. I owe that girl a big favor."

I write, 'Who's the girl?'

Tanner says, "Let's give Beanie a break, but the rules still apply. No questions about this case. Just chit-chat to get acquainted."

Constance is whispering, "Dee Dee darling? You're in law enforcement, aren't you?"

I'm speechless.

"I have very good instincts." With that, she winks and moves over to Stuart chatting away."

I need to tell Beanie how much it means to me and the others back in Meadow Brook that someone is writing it all down. "Beanie, I am so glad you're here, and I know how much this will mean to all the ladies Jan was telling you about."

"No thanks necessary, Dee Dee. I'm sure you were feeling pretty disgusted with all of us out here. Tanner almost went crazy over all of this. I praise God that some pieces are coming together. We all want to help. Interesting how God has brought us all together. I'm deeply sorry for the tragedy to you and your Aunt. Have you called her?"

"Oh, I was so concerned with Jan, I left that all to Ben.

"Ben, did you call Linda?"

"Dee Dee, you were supposed to call her."

"Linda... Yes, it's Dee Dee... Linda, there's some good news... No, we haven't caught Red October, but we're getting the pieces put together. There are many people working on this. That's the ones you hear in the background... I do like Lieutenant Tanner. He's actually nothing like I expected. I've got to get back to the meeting, but you girls will be getting a prayer update." *I can't believe that came out of me. Seemed natural. Hmm.* "Good for Joe, at least someone has been staying in touch... Thanks. Tell Peaches and everyone hi and Linda, thanks... I love you, too. Ben will call after we are done here... We'll be seeing Jan later."

Tanner is standing at the head of the table. "I wanted to get this all down without opinion. There are some details that are pertinent, but Irene and Jamison are picking up the Kirschenbaums, so they aren't participating in our group puzzle. I don't know if all this information is good for Alyssa's parents to hear. I decided we should get it all on the table before they arrive." All heads are nodding in agreement. "Dee Dee, in your gut, do you believe Alyssa K. is still alive?"

I'm caught off guard. I guess I hadn't given her much thought other than sympathy for her family. *Why should she be alive when Adlin isn't?* The whole group is looking at me. I feel that tug. That pendant tugging is tightening. I hear myself saying, "Yes. Actually, I do. Why would Madelyn have those other pieces in her dreams? Adlin would want Alyssa to be alive, and so do I." I hear a small snap, like a tiny cracking noise inside. Everyone is applauding. Ben's hugging me.

"See, Dee Dee, not only do we want to get this animal, but we want to help prevent another atrocity. Your focus is getting on center." He kisses me right on the forehead.

"We've got to find Alyssa." Stuart is almost in tears. "I feel so guilty for not being there that day."

"Dee Dee..." Tanner's voice seems far away. "Dee Dee, will you give me your list of observations?"

"Sure, almost everything is based on dreams, but new revelations are confirmed in the natural, other than the pearl." *Why is Ben looking so deep in thought?* "Leslie Cartwright is important. Where is she? Who's Bryan's friend? Is she the same person Adlin was doing research for? Who is she? What was the significance of the green car at the church? The guy with the pearl. Who and why? Who in the police department would blow off information in a case like this? What is the significance of the tattoo?

Who's on the other end of the line when Bryan gets calls? Why haven't you gotten any more calls, Bryan? Why do you have that look on your face, Ben? Is there something you're not telling me? What was written by Leslie Cartwright?" Everyone is silently nodding. "I'll ask you again, Ben. Why do you have that look on your face? Do not sluff me off. Something's going on."

"Dee Dee, I'm just trying to listen. I don't want to convolute everything with my thoughts. I agree with your list completely, except for one missing item, which came up before, but indirectly. Who's Roscoe?"

Candidates

"Those kids were a snap. Offer them a few hundred dollars, and they'd fly right off a cliff."

"So, your advertising campaign worked. You've got new recruits. Do you think any would be willing to pour themselves into the project?"

"Too early to tell, but they are a pretty loose bunch. It might be fun working with them. People always surprise you, especially those of the individual, self-purporting types."

"Remember, pride goes before a fall."

"Yeah, I've heard that forever. Been there, done that."

"Don't do anything that is below the Boss's standards. We want prime candidates."

"Oh, you wait. I have one that I've been keeping under lock and key, so to speak. Someone very special. They will add so much meaning to our efforts. I was very fortunate to meet them. Kind of a stroke of luck that we ever came in contact."

"Did you ever locate the lead person you had picked out?"

"No, not yet. I'm hoping they show up again soon. I can't wait."

27

MAKING FRIENDS

Jamison's infinite wisdom has put Jacob on the third floor to keep an extra special eye on him. Jan has been quietly asked by Jamison to do some visiting.

"Hi, my name's Jan."

"Mine's Jacob, Jacob Warren, Professor Jacob Warren."

"It's so nice to meet you, Professor."

"It's a pleasure to meet you. Are you doing well?"

"Better. What are you being held captive for?" Laughter.

"I'm having some tests run. Dr. Jamison thinks I need to get some rest and find out why I've been so tired."

"Dr. Jamison is my doctor, too. Isn't he a great guy? How did you end up with him as a doc?"

Jacob gives Jan the whole rundown on Irene and Jamison. Rose is in the conversation also. All the history, the incidents, and Roscoe.

Jan's unable to stand the suspense anymore. "Tell me more about Roscoe. Does he work for you?"

"Well, not really. He likes to think of it like working *with* me. Since Stuart quit coming to the research beds, I've had to depend a lot on Roscoe."

"Well, Jacob, I'll let you get some rest. It's been such a pleasure to meet you. Can we visit tomorrow?"

"Oh, that would be wonderful. I need friends. This is kind of an unusual place to be—"

"I know, but Dr. Jamison knows we both need some major rest, and this is one of the quietest floors in the hospital."

"Oh, okay, that's great, but you're able to come and visit?"

"Yes. They have a sunroom also."

"All right, we'll do something tomorrow."

Jamison is checking with Melinda to make sure Beth is okay and that the room is ready for Jan. "How are you, Anne?"

She doesn't answer. "Doc, Beth has been in art therapy. She keeps sketching the same person over and over. The crazy thing is that she's not an artist, but she's drawn him with her eyes closed, and sometimes she said she's painting with her soul. Take a look at these; they're quite good." Melinda slides the portfolio towards Jamison.

"Is she agitated? Do you think this someone is responsible for causing her condition? Involved in some way of kidnapping her?"

"No, she said he gives her peace. That he always saves her in the dreams."

"So, he was in a dream?"

"Maybe, but I don't think so. I can't explain it, but I felt peace when I began to look at the drawings. I think he's a good guy from her past."

Jamison opens the portfolio. Staring full-faced at him is a man, picture after picture of the same man.

"Exactly the same man. Some drawings were made with Beth's eyes closed, and some with her eyes opened."

"Wow, this girl is something. These are terrific sketches. Next time, ask her where she met him."

"I did. She said at the wall."

"Melinda, I have to take these along to have them reviewed. Don't let down your guard here. Tanner is working on stuff and it's all linked to something more. Irene and I have to get to the airport, so take good care of Beth, and you know she has a new roommate?"

"Yes, I've already met Jan. I kept her in the sunroom until we had a chance to talk about Beth."

"Okay, good. Jan will be allowed to come and go. Oh, and the same rules of protection apply to Professor Jacob Warren. No one gets in or out. Understand?"

"Perfectly."

As Jamison leaves the hospital, he calls Tanner.

"Tanner, good news. I'm picking Irene up from her friend's house and getting the new arrivals. Tell Beanie we've got it covered... By the way, I want you to see these drawings Beth Adams has created. They'll blow you away... Thanks, Tanner. God bless... Yes, Tanner, I will. I'll bring them right to the apartment. Thank you."

At the airport, Jamison and Irene are waiting at the end of the concourse as the Kirschenbaums arrive. They recognize them immediately from the funeral service pictures and news articles.

"I'm Jamison, and this is Irene. We were sent to meet you. Are you interested in 'cherries?'"

"Yes, indeed we are. Thank you for coming. No baggage. We only brought carry-ons. We'll pick up whatever we need. We brought pictures, though."

Irene is pretending to be sisters, hugging Mrs. K.'s arm and chatting away. It appears as one happy family reunion.

Once in the car, Mrs. K. begins to cry and clutches Irene's hands.

Jamison calls Tanner. "Lieutenant, we have our guests with us. Are you ready for dinner?... Okay, we're on."

Irene prepares the Kirschenbaums to meet the team. James begins to share about the things leading up to Alyssa's disappearance.

"We got a call from Alyssa that she was driving with friends to a university. She said she had been at a seminar and was interested in pursuing botanical research. She went on and on about how excited she was. We didn't think much about it, considering she's a grad student, and we knew her friends. It seemed like she was fine even when she got back to school. Later, we got the call that she had disappeared."

"Why did you go to that funeral?"

"We had been searching and praying for God to show us something. The police had no leads. I guess we were looking for cases. We saw the headlines about the Summers case, and because we knew Alyssa had been in that town, we thought maybe there was a link. Maybe it was a basic need to reach out in some way. Basically, we felt compelled to go to the service. We felt like the odd couple showing up together, so we acted like we came alone. That also gave us a chance to view things from different perspectives. It might sound sick, but we had heard that sometimes killers actually go to the services, so we were trying to be observant. We both felt like we were being watched. It looks like we weren't wrong."

"Tell us about the bracelet. Why did you wear it?"

"Well, Alyssa was wearing it on that trip."

"Really, how do you know?"

"Well, she felt so bad because she lost two of the pearls during the trip. It was her grandmother's. I told Lieutenant Tanner that on the phone. She was concerned we would be angry if we came to visit and saw it was damaged. She's always been so truthful." Tears.

"She told us that she was coming out of one of the shops with her friends, and a young guy grabbed her wrist. She thought he was trying to get the bracelet, so she jerked away, and apparently, she lost the pearls or loosened the mountings. He apologized and said he was mistaken. He said he thought she was an old friend. She said the whole day was horrible, like she had been touched by something.

"Later on, she accidentally got in the wrong car when they came out of another shop. She said all her friends were laughing when she hopped into the back seat of someone else's car. She wasn't really sure where she lost the pearls but realized they were gone that evening on the trip.

"I guess I wore the bracelet because it was like contact with her. You know, not one thing was missing from her room, and her car was still parked in her regular place. She vanished. We don't understand why the bracelet is so important to Lieutenant Tanner."

Jamison is looking at Irene in the rear-view mirror. "Irene, would you share a little bit about the relevance of the pearl?"

"Well, I don't know how to explain it, so let me ask these questions. From what we understand, you believe in dreams? Is that accurate? I mean, dreams from God?"

By the time the four arrive at Mr. Kaplan's apartment, the Kirschenbaums are prepared to meet the team.

❁

"Grace and James Kirschenbaum, this is Lieutenant Tanner." Grace begins to cry and lays her head on James's shoulder.

"Baby, we'll find her. Don't cry."

"I know. I'm sorry, Lieutenant. It's such a relief to know that someone cares."

"Actually, Mrs. K., several someone's care. Everyone, meet Grace and James, Alyssa's parents."

Each person, one by one, introduces themselves to the Kirschenbaums. Joe begins to pray. The couple is stunned, shocked by the presence of God in these people.

"This is not what we expected. What a surprise! I guess we thought it would be one more sterile police station. I so wish we could've spoken with you when we called the station." Everyone's bells are dinging.

"James, you called the station?" Tanner is white.

"Yes, several times."

"Who did you speak with?"

"Well, I don't remember, but we always got transferred to Traffic. That lady was nice and would transfer us back, and then we'd get cut off."

"Dee Dee, put that on your list, please."

"I will. I want to speak to Grace and James alone.

"You don't know this, but I'm Adlin Summers's sister. Could we go in the den?"

"Absolutely. We are so sorry for your loss and have prayed and prayed and prayed for her family."

As the three leave, Jamison shows Tanner Beth's drawings. Ben and Joe join them at the table. "Heavenly Father, what is this?" Ben, Jamison, and Tanner are staring at Joe. He is visibly shaken. "It's Oliver!"

"You know him?" comes out in unison.

"He goes to our church."

"What? He goes to your church?"

"Yes, he and Marty are Russian. They volunteer and clean our church. I thought he was an okay guy. I must've lost my instincts. How is he involved in this? How international is this?"

Jamison quickly relates the story of the pictures and the fact that Beth said he always saves her in her dreams. "When Melinda asked her where she met him, Beth said, 'At the wall.'"

Ben is rapidly whirling through the encounter with Libby and Beth. "You've got to be kidding. That kid was not just rambling when she talked about the man pulling her up the wall. If that part is true, what about the cloud and the rest? What are we dealing with here?"

Tanner quietly speaks, "The devil. Ben, I haven't been able to share with you a couple of things about another dream of Madelyn's. It involves Dee Dee, so let's sit on this a little and find a time to quietly talk."

"I agree with Ben." Joe's voice is lower than usual. "This needs to be handled very carefully and we'll need some backup on this one. Also, remember that your instincts are right, Tanner. Something weird is going on with someone at the station."

"Hey, what are you guys all huddled about over here?" Stuart is curious again.

"Medical stuff about Anne, I mean Beth. I'll have you look at the lab results later, okay?" Jamison is handing the folder to Tanner. "You can go over it later with Irene."

Stuart's excited to think he's been included in the medical end. "Sure, I would be happy to do that."

Ben gives him the high sign.

"We want to accommodate the Kirschenbaums and Dee Dee right now, so let's get some dinner." Tanner's uncomfortable with interrupting the three in the den.

"Libby, would you and the other ladies figure out what to order? Here's my card. Get something really special for everyone."

"Tanner, Beanie and Constance are already on it. We have a smorgasbord coming: Chinese, Mexican, German, something for everyone. Constance has great connections, and she paid for it."

"Travis, I know you need to go home and get some clothes."

"Nope, Tanner, we did that before we went to the library."

"Okay, then Stuart and I will go to my apartment. You, Libby, and Emily go to the girls' apartment. I want Ben, Joe, Dee Dee, and the Kirschenbaums to stay here."

"I changed the linens for them, and you're right, I do need to go home."

"Libby, you are my girl." *Ooh, she is really going to be my girl.* He pecks Libby on the cheek.

Dee Dee and the Kirschenbaums emerge from the den.

Dinner with Grace and James is a most unexpected treat. They are intelligent and gracious people with a deep foundation in God. Tanner realizes that they don't need to filter information from them. They are rock-solid emotionally and spiritually, assets to the group and the investigation.

He informs the group that they should share the entirety of what they have accumulated from the people. "Joe, Ben, would you give them a full rundown other than the "medical stuff" we discussed earlier?"

Travis pops up, "Sir, do not say it! I'll be careful and will take care of the girls."

Tanner informs Stuart he is spending the night at Tanner's apartment. Stuart, in relief, asks if he can go to his own place and get some clothes.

Tanner takes Beanie, Constance, Bryan, and Erica aside. "Here's the new assignment for the partners and your new guests. Find Leslie Cartwright. Beanie, keep a lid on this.

"Dee Dee, are you going to be okay here tonight, or do you need to see Jan? I'll take you over if you need to see her."

"Tanner, Jan is doing her job. I had a call from her, and she sounded great. She told me to get some rest. She's met Jacob and is with Beth. She's doing what she wants to. She's working the case." Laughter. Dee Dee hugs Tanner and whispers, "Thanks." Tanner hugs back and kisses Dee Dee on the forehead.

"Lib, when this is over, we can make some plans. I've come to realize some things, but this one I've known for a long time. You are the love of my life. You are *my girl* forever." Tanner shocks himself as he kisses Libby with a long, passionate kiss in front of everyone. The room bursts into applause. Tanner blushes as he says, "Okay, I'll be leaving now. Come on, Stuart."

❧

"Hi, Anne. I'm Jan. I'm going to stay with you. We will be roommates for a while. What do you think?" There's no response, so Jan gets in the other bed and curls up with her notebook.

"I had a notebook."

Jan is shocked that Anne is talking to her. "You did?"

"Yeah, the nice girl gave it to me, but I lost it." Anne starts to cry. "She needs me to get it to someone. She needs help."

"Anne, it's okay. They found the notebook, and they're going to find her." Silence. Crying. Jan gets up and sits on Anne's bed, gently touching her leg. "It will all be okay. Everything will be fine."

"He's going to help her. He told me he would."

"He, who, Anne? Who's going to help her?"

Anne points to her new drawing. "Him, the man I see in my dreams."

Oh, boy, more dreams. "Are you an artist?"

"No, my hands are drawing. It's my soul."

Whoa, this is wild. "Anne, tell me about your dreams."

Anne is shaking her head. "No, the plants might know and come here."

"What plants?" Jan hasn't heard this before.

"You know the plant people, they have thorns. They grab and scratch you." Anne is speaking very low, looking around, fearfully shaking.

"Where do they come from? Where did you see them?"

"In the garden, when I was running." Anne is starting to curl up and rock.

"Hey, Anne, I'm going to read for a while. Why don't you sleep for a little bit."

"See, look." Anne is holding out her arms. Deep scratches are all over. A mass of angry welts covers her legs.

"They really did hurt you. I'm so sorry."

"At least the dirt wasn't over me anymore." She's starting to hyperventilate.

"Anne, let's not think about that right now. You need to rest." Jan isn't sure that either she or Anne are ready for whatever Anne is going to tell. "I'll peek outside and see if anything is out there." Jan uses her pass key and opens the door. "Nope, nothing in the hall. Nobody's going to get in here. I've got the key."

Anne seems to calm down.

"Let's go to sleep. We're safe." *Yeah, I've got the key, and I've also got a gun. Anne, you're safe. This poor baby, what has she been through?* Jan shivers and tucks Anne in, and for some reason, kisses her on the forehead. Feeling completely drained, Jan lays down and closes her eyes. *If it's the last thing I do—*

The thought is interrupted by, "Thanks. You're nice. He told me."

"So are you, Anne. So are you." *I wonder who she's talking about. Poor baby.*

❧

"Anne, are you awake?"

She's singing "Amazing Grace."

"Anne, are you awake?" It sounds like more than one person singing. *What's going on?*

The door opens, and Melinda peeks in. "Jan, are you okay?"

"Yes, are you hearing this?"

"I thought you had a radio on, but there's no radio in the rooms. What is this?"

"I don't know." Jan and Melinda are staring at each other in disbelief.

Anne keeps singing, stops suddenly, sits up, and says, "Where am I?"

"You're in Memorial Hospital."

"How did I get here? Oh, I know, he brought me here."

"He, who?"

No response. Anne has laid back down and is sleeping again.

"Jan, are you all right? You are pale. I can get you a real nurse."

"I'm fine. I have a strong impression that I need to see Professor Jacob. Can I get out and go see him?"

"Yes, but sit tight. There's a bell at the front."

Losing Hope

"I don't know how much longer I can keep myself in hope." She repeats the scriptures, "Yea, though, I walk through the valley of the shadow of death…" The young woman shivers in the dark. One small blanket is wadded up under her head. Soon, it will be used to cover various parts of her chilled body. Her fingers are sore from using the shard of glass, making a small incision to write her message. The moon overhead looks like it always does, but there's something that makes it seem ominous. It's almost full. "How many full moons does that make?" After the weeks of being confined in the semi-dark realm of the underground prison, time is a blur. She misses her notebook; at least it was something to look at. "Where are you, mom and dad?" Thinking of them makes her smile. She lays down to dream of home and of the girl she sent out as the messenger for help.

Grace is ringing Tanner's phone. Tanner's already awake and dressed.

"Lieutenant Tanner, I dreamed about Alyssa. She's somewhere underground. The musty smell of dirt, death, and flowers was real. I could smell it even when I woke up. She's barefoot, and she can barely stand. It's really bad. We have to find her quickly. She's losing hope. You need to tell us the truth. The dream is very spiritually dark. Alyssa is surrounded by evil and death. What is really going on?"

How can I tell someone, let alone a mother, that some monster from the pit has her child? Not over the phone. "Grace, I'll be there. I'll be right over. Get James up and meet me downstairs in thirty minutes. Bring Joe with you. Tell Ben to keep an eye on Dee Dee."

"I'm going with you." The phone has awakened Stuart. He's already pulling his pants on.

"Stuart!"

"Listen, Tanner. I'm not staying here alone. I've been in and out all night. I feel sick. Something is wrong."

"Hold on, Stuart. My phone is vibrating.

"Hello, Melinda, what's up?... What do you mean some officer you didn't recognize came to the third floor?... No, he was not sent by me... Good girl... Thank you for playing dumb... I'm coming over as soon as I can, but I have to meet with some other people. Get to Jan and tell her. Give her a heads-up... You did the perfect thing. Send Jan to Professor Jacob's room... Yep. His personal early morning nurse. Change shifts. Melinda, I owe you big time... Thanks. Call me back if anything is wrong. Don't take any chances. Not cleaning people, no one gets to Jan, Beth, or Jacob... Thanks, and be careful.

"Stuart, you were sure right. Something is wrong. Let's get moving." *Lord, why didn't you tell me? Please protect everyone. What's going on?*

Tanner calls Travis. "Travis, I'm sorry to get you up. There's a new development. Looks like the mystery of the officer is about to be solved. Take care of the girls, and I'll be back to you. I'll fill you in as soon as I can."

He calls Joe. "Joe, did Grace fill you in?... Call a taxi and meet me at the All-Night Diner on 22nd and Lexington. I'm not coming to the apartment. Something's up... Thanks, Joe, and please pray."

"Why aren't we going to the apartment?" Stuart's voice is shaky.

"I don't want to be followed there. A police officer showed up on the third floor of the hospital. He said I had sent him."

"Oh, dear God! Jan and that girl and the Professor are there at Memorial. How could he have known? Tanner, this is creepy."

"I know, Stuart. Maybe I should drop you off at Libby's to be with Travis and the girls."

"Tanner." Stuart's researcher mind is voicing, "You don't think one of those cops you sent me with is him, do you?"

"Why? Do you? Let's talk in the car."

They take the stairs and go out the back of Tanner's apartment building. There doesn't seem to be anyone around. Tanner slides into the driver's seat, and the strangest feeling comes over him. "Stuart, we can't go yet. I forgot to turn off the air-conditioner and the coffee pot. Your "aunt" is going to have to wait to see you. I can't believe she came in on such an early flight."

"Tanner, I forgot the flight info." Stuart is smart enough to play along. "I'll go up with you. I was half asleep when she called. I don't know where I wrote it."

Calmly, they exit the car and go back up to the apartment. When the door shuts, Stuart whispers, "What was that? I had chills all over my body."

"Me too, Stuart. I don't know. I'm not taking that car, and I can't really tell you why." Tanner is whispering, too. "Yep, I left the pot on." Tanner's voice is normal. "Find those flight numbers and times."

Stuart pretends to be rummaging around, looking for the flight information. "I found it!"

As they step into the hall and head toward the elevator, Tanner texts Joe and tells him to go to the airport, to United Airlines. When they approach the car, Tanner pretends he can't find his keys. "Well, it's good your aunt's flight isn't coming in as early as you thought. Stuart, now I can't find my keys."

"Sorry, Tanner. I guess I was really out of it. I'll call a taxi."

"Jacob, hi. Remember me? How are you? I thought I would come and sit for a while. Is it too early? I can't sleep."

"No, I was already awake. Jan, I'm sorry I haven't checked on you. I can't seem to shake off this lethargy. This will sound strange, but I keep having these dreams. You probably don't believe in that sort of thing, do you?"

"How very interesting you would ask that. Actually, as of recently, I've come to realize the importance of things we can't explain. Speak on, Professor. What have you been dreaming?"

> "Well, I keep hearing my wife saying things to me. For instance, I'm in the research garden, and she's saying things like, 'Wake up, Jacob. Wake up. Why can't you see what is here? It's unholy. You've been blinded.' I start to run, and everything is shaking, and there is this sound, like wind. Rose is saying, 'Jacob, plead the blood! Jacob, plead the blood of Jesus! Hurry! Speak!' but I can't talk. I try to wake up, but I can't. Finally, I feel like someone shakes me, and I wake up."

"Jacob, you need to tell Jamison about these dreams. What does he say is wrong? Have you gotten back any tests?"

"Well, it seems that I have something in my bloodstream. You know, I was in Haiti, and I may have picked something up there."

"Really? Something exotic? Something strange? When did you begin to develop symptoms?"

"You know, I'm not sure. But I told you about my wife, Rose, didn't I?"

"Yes. She must have been a wonderful person."

"Yes, she was. I don't think, though, that I told you her grave was robbed, did I? I don't remember."

"No, Jacob, you didn't. How horrible! Is that when you started having symptoms?"

"I had a major breakdown. That was the final straw, I guess. After Rose's illness, I felt so hopeless. I lost it for a while. I quit the surgical field, and like I told you, I continued Rose's research. I had been reading some of her data and became interested in plants in Haiti. I applied for a research grant through the University. Stuart, Rose's associate, and I went there for a month to study plants and native medicine. It was very confusing. The people we were supposed to work with had some kind of miscommunication and were actually out of the country.

"Fortunately, we were invited to an estate and ended up not staying in the city as planned. I contacted the University and discovered that we didn't have any guide for our arrangements. I didn't want Stuart to get upset, so I acted like that was the plan. I was concerned that he would think I was crazy again. To tell you the truth, I'm starting to wonder exactly what did happen. I barely remember anything after I arrived at the estate.

"Jan, I guess it was after we got back that I felt so detached. Then, the tiredness started. Memory loss, too. I haven't ever bounced back. Then, Roscoe showed up. No, wait, Roscoe came about two weeks after I got back. Desmond called, and I told him how poorly I was feeling. He said that he had a friend who needed a place to stay. Would I like some help? Stuart was acting really strange, so I told him yes.

"The next day, Roscoe came. He has been a great help. I've been very dependent on him. Lately, though, he started to irritate me. You know what?"

"What?"

"Maybe that's why Rose keeps coming in my dreams because Roscoe always cuts me off when I talk about her."

"Why wouldn't he want you to talk about Rose? It seems normal to me to talk about someone you love. I wonder why he doesn't like that?"

"I don't know, but he always says, 'That is in the past...' and that it makes me unfocused."

"Unfocused on what?" *The ten-million-dollar question is, who is Roscoe?* "What does Roscoe do?"

"I'm not sure. He is a recruiter for some company. He's always talking about his boss. He said he's coming this week, and I will get to meet him. His company is having some big celebration on Friday night, but Roscoe wants to have it at my house so we can show off the research garden and the project."

"Really? That sounds like quite a big event. Are you up for that?"

"Roscoe is taking care of all the arrangements, so I won't have to do much, just host."

"Are you inviting any of your friends? You don't know any of those people. I, myself, would want to have a few friends of my own there."

"Jan, since Rose passed, I pretty much have cut myself off from everyone."

"Jacob, I know you have wonderful friends, and they would be honored to come." *Boy, I could introduce you to people who would love to meet Roscoe and see your home.*

"Would you like to come?"

"Yes, most definitely. I would be honored. That is if they let me out of here in time. Maybe you could show me some of Rose's data. I am so in need of help. Maybe she ran onto something that would work for me."

"You know, I should invite Irene and Jamison. They could invite some of their colleagues, their friends. Irene has been a wonderful friend. She and Rose were very close. She would enjoy being back at the house. She used to call our house her home away from home."

"Jacob, I got so engrossed in our conversation that I forgot to ask you if you've had any other visitors."

"No, I haven't seen anyone except one new nurse. She checked in on me. Funny, she asked me the same question. If I had any visitors, I'm glad they didn't let me see them. I might've missed out on our conversation. I've got to call Roscoe and tell him about the extra guests."

"I wouldn't worry about that. You need to find out what is going on with you. Roscoe will have all week to get ready."

"Yes, he's very efficient. Jan, I haven't even asked about you. What is it that you do? You must have worked with people a lot. I feel better already just talking to you."

"Jacob there are people who would tell you that they did not feel better when they were around me, but lately, I've been developing the gentler side of me. I guess when faced with one's mortality, one begins to re-evaluate our stand on many issues."

"Isn't that the truth."

"Yes, Jacob, it is."

28

JOINING FORCES

Lord, It's almost 5 a.m... "Airport, please." Tanner and Stuart ride in complete silence. He texts instructions to Joe where to meet "Stuart's relatives."

Arriving at the airport, they hurry in. Joe, Grace, and James are all sitting in the arriving passenger area. Stuart plays the part well with hugs and kisses. "Let's get some breakfast while we wait for your luggage." The small group seats themselves in a secluded area of the food court.

"Joe, would you tell Grace and James what else we know?"

Joe begins to cover some of the unexplainable occurrences, and that some elements seem very similar to his past experiences in Miami, California, and Haiti. Grace and James are visibly shaken but simply nod their heads in agreement.

&

"Dee Dee, I've got some news. We're going to Jacob's for a big evening event."

"What are you talking about?"

"I've been visiting with Jacob."

"Jan, it's only 7 a.m... No, it's okay. I was awake. Are you all right?... Really?..."

"Well, I think I know part of what's been happening. I want to tell you in person, not over the phone."

"Jan, I'll be there as soon as I can... Thanks. I'll call Tanner.

"Tanner, this is Dee Dee. Where are you?... The airport?... I just got a call from Jan. Something is going on. She wants to tell me in person. It's information she got from Jacob about a big event."

Tanner's ears are about to break from the clanging, more than a ding.

"You've got to go to the office?... Okay, Ben and I will go and see Jan. I'll call you later. Tanner, be careful."

Tanner's thinking, *that's a switch. Someone's telling me to be careful?* "You too, Dee Dee, and thanks."

"Joe, would you take James and Grace to Memorial to meet Jan? There's a new development."

Grace pleasantly replies, "Oh, Dee Dee told us she was so close to her. You do consider us as part of the team."

"James, we're part of this.

"Thanks, Lieutenant."

"Grace, call me Tanner.

"You too, James."

"Tanner, what about Beth and the Professor?"

"Joe, you have some great instincts. You'll know if that introduction is timely or not. Keep everyone in-tact."

"You know I will. How about if Stuart goes with us so you can take care of the business at the station?"

"Stuart, are you good with that?"

"Are you kidding? I won't be glued to your side. Sounds great to me."

"Stuart, no snooping."

"Yes, Sir."

"Joe, pull your group together for a meeting tonight around 8:00 after everyone's had a chance to rest and eat."

"Sure thing, Tanner. See you tonight."

Tanner has the taxi drop him off a couple of blocks from the station. Whistling as he enters the front door, one of the officers Jim had mentioned is going up the stairs. *That's fortuitous, Lord.* Tanner takes the elevator. As he starts to turn the corner to his office, he sees the officer standing up against the wall next to Beanie's office out of Beanie's line of vision.

"What's up? Did you need to see me?"

The officer practically jumps out of his shoes. "Sir, you scared me!"

"Really? I'm sorry. What brings you up here? Come on in."

"No thanks. That's okay. I was going to ask Beanie about my time from a week ago, but I'll do it later. I need to make a correction on a report."

"Sure, okay, I'll mention it to her. Thanks." *I'll bet he needed to make a correction.*

"Hey, Beanie. How's the World's Greatest Secretary?"

"Sir, I'm fine. Last night, I could hardly sleep from thinking about the events of the last few days. When I finally did, it was heavenly. I feel like I've been rejuvenated."

"Beanie, I know I've overloaded you, but thanks for helping me so much. Let's hurry and take care of business. I have some new developments."

"Okay, so do I."

Finally, the day-to-day work is finished, and the phones are transferred to Sheryl in Traffic. Beanie puts a sign on her door, locks it, and walks into the next room with Tanner.

"Who goes first?"

"Well, Sir, I got a call from Constance. She and the rest of the team have managed to find Leslie Cartwright's mother. I'm telling you, those two, Erica and Bryan, are great. I think they both would be great undercovers. Erica is so intelligent and bubbly, and Bryan is so street-smart. Who would ever suspect them? Both are very instinctive."

"You think so?"

"I know so, Sir."

"I'll take that as an endorsement. There's some new information from Jan. She's been visiting with Beth and Professor Jacob. It seems as though we'll be going to a big event at Jacob's on Friday night."

"What? The sound of that gives me chills."

"I'll know more tonight when you all come for a meeting. Joe and Ben will have all the details by then. The Kirschenbaums are meeting Jan today and perhaps Beth and Jacob. Maybe we'll have more information on Leslie Cartwright then."

"Sir? After all the frustration, look at all these pieces that are coming together. I'm concerned that we need to find Alyssa. I know she's still alive."

"Me too, Beanie. There's another issue. Jim ran onto something in those reports he's been collecting."

"Jim?"

"Well, I believe I had one confirmed this morning. I want you to have cameras installed outside your door and inside your office so we can record who's coming and going."

"I'll get Art and his "janitor friend." He has installed surveillance equipment since he retired. They would be able to equip the building. How soon do you want it done?"

"Tonight."

"I'm on it, Sir. I'll see you tonight."

"Is everyone coming?"

"Yes, Sir. When this is all over, we need to have a wonderful gathering of celebration for the Lord."

"Amen, Beanie. I agree. I'll stay until Art comes, and then I'll walk you out."

It's almost 6:00 by the time Art and his friend arrive. Tanner pulls the two reports in question, puts them in his briefcase, and greets Art. "Hey, Art, I really can't thank you enough."

"Sir, it's my job."

"So, you are Lieutenant Tanner? Art's told me much about you. He said it's like having Chief Carter back, only more high-tech. It's a pleasure to meet you."

"Murphy, I hear you were an asset to the department. We really need your expertise. Can you have it done tonight? Leave a bill, and we'll take care of it. Be generous with yourself. Beanie will make sure Art gets overtime—"

Beanie interjects, "You know I will. Art's been here for me every time. He and Murphy visited Erica and are even considering learning to like Bryan."

"Goodnight, guys. Thanks. I'm going to walk Beanie to the car. Art, keep the office key, and I'll see you tomorrow. We'll be in a little later in the morning, so I'll call when I get here."

Art's grinning as he says, "Aren't you going to ask if my wife will get upset?"

"Will she?"

"No, she's out of town." The four all burst out laughing.

"Beanie, I forgot to ask you. Did you send all the folks in Meadow Brook the notes you took?"

"Typed and sent. Did you really need to ask?"

"No, I didn't. You're amazing. See you and your bunch tonight at Kaplan's."

❧

Beanie opens the door at Constance's house (her home away from home) to a barrage of chatter. "What is going on?"

Erica is excitedly jumping up and down. "Sit down, Beanie, we've got news!"

Constance pulls a chair up to the table. "We found her."

"Her?"

"Leslie Cartwright. Yes, the one and only. You're on, Erica, tell Beanie."

"She'll be here in three hours. We are picking her up. We had Bryan use his sweet voice and trick her mom into getting her on the phone." Erica is glowing as she tells Beanie about all of it. "Bryan, because of his tech skills, found her sending out resumes. He pretended to be from one of the companies. Once he had her on the phone, he explained about Lieutenant Tanner. We told her to call the Oak City Traffic Department to verify the information about Lieutenant Tanner. She was very afraid, but she looked up the number and called Oak City Traffic. Constance had already prepared Sheryl. We knew you'd be here soon. We know that Grace and James said that Sheryl was safe territory. Constance told Sheryl they'd explain later but needed her help. We were on needles and pins, afraid she'd run, but Leslie called us back. Wait until you hear what she said about being afraid of the police. She only wants to speak to Tanner in person. We assured her there would be protection and a safe place to stay."

"I'm calling Tanner."

"Can I let the cat out of the bag?" Bryan uses that sweet smile, asking Beanie if he can call Tanner as he grabs Erica's hand. Constance and Beanie laugh as Beanie hands Bryan her phone.

"Beanie?"

"No, Sir, it's your favorite stray cat."

"Bryan!"

"Yes, Sir, I've got some excellent news. We have found the item you were looking for. The package will be here in three hours. Thanks for retrieving this cat for Constance. I've learned so much from her and Beanie. I received another call last night. I've got a time pinned down... Yes, I'm okay... Oh, there's a meeting tonight?... Well, we will hand deliver the package then... Yes, we'll be careful... See ya later."

Lord, how amazing are your ways. A stray cat turns into a prince. Wait until Libby hears this one. "Lib, what are you doing?... You got the part?... I didn't know you were doing casting calls anymore... That's awesome. You didn't go alone, did you?... Emily got a part, too? Wow!... My news is almost as good. Are you guys at Kaplan's now?... Great, because I'm going to change and head that way. We're having a meeting tonight. Libby, thanks for everything... Thanks. Everything is coming together. I know we'll find Alyssa... See ya later."

Stuart is on cloud nine. "Jacob was like the old friend I used to know. I had such a good time reminiscing about Rose. I told him many things about the projects that he didn't know. Life is great. Thanks, Joe, for letting me see him. I think it meant a lot to him. That little peek that Jan let me have confirmed that Anne was one of the lecture attendees. She was sleeping, but I distinctly remember her face. That poor girl. We've got to find Alyssa too. What about the girl Jacob was following that night?"

James is startled. "You mean there might be more?"

"Tanner's been concerned for a while about that but had to stay on track with the Summers case and finding Alyssa. I think your daughter is one of the most beautiful girls I've ever seen."

"Thanks, Stuart. Her mom and I think she's beautiful too. Apparently, she noticed you, too. After all, she made a special trip to see you at the University."

"Don't make me feel bad again. I feel so guilty." Stuart starts to choke up as Grace gently lays her hand on his head. She prays for God to comfort Alyssa and to intervene and reveal where she is.

Ben and Dee Dee join the group.

"Well, we're all here again, one big happy family." The announcement from Stuart makes them all laugh.

"Joe, how did it go today?"

"Tanner, it was revelatory. That's the only word to describe the visit at Memorial. I talked to Jan. She said Dot wants the Big 10 to gather and the call to be on speaker phone with all of us. They have something to share with us. Something about cars and license plates. I guess Jan had tried to research traffic tickets. I didn't totally understand it, but Dee Dee seems to."

"You've got to be kidding. How does that play into all this?" Tanner is boggled.

"Jan wouldn't tell us but said it's a doozy. She didn't want to steal the other gals's thunder."

"Well, Beanie, Constance and the kids are bringing a doozy of a guest. I guess this is going to be an evening to remember. Since there's a time difference, they weren't able to call until about 10:00 our time. Think everyone can stay until they call?"

It's a chorus of, "Yes!"

Moments after Beanie and Constance, and Erica and Bryan arrive with the guest, Dee Dee answers the call and puts it on speaker. "They're all here."

Dot's lovely voice greets everyone. "Yes, we're all here. Let me have them introduce themselves." One by one, all the Big 10 introduce themselves to the team. "Where's Beanie?" Dot says they all want to thank her for sending the transcripts of the meetings.

"I'm here!"

"Beanie, we were all so blessed by you. Reading all that you typed truly made us feel like we were part of all this. Ben and Joe gave us updates, but those transcripts were superb. They filled in all the blanks for us."

"Well, you ladies were so special. Like Jan said, you are the foundation. The ones that got this whole thing moving. Thank you."

"Lieutenant Tanner, you better take very good care of Beanie. Give her a raise and a vacation to come here. We all want her to come to Meadow Brook so we can meet her."

"Ladies, you can be sure I will. You're right; she is amazing and brave."

"Where's Stuart? We have got to hear his voice. We all know something was unusual about Leon at the funeral."

Stuart is as red as a beet. "Ladies, I'm sorry."

"Stuart, we love you. You were a living break in the case. We look forward to meeting you once again. This time, as yourself."

Dee Dee interrupts the sweet ladies and says, "Turn it up. We have a special guest to add to your prayer list."

Constance gives an introduction. "We have found her, and now here she is, Miss Leslie Cartwright."

As Dee Dee turns around, she bursts into tears. She's almost identical to Adlin. She feels a tiny pull of that pendant. *Not this time.* She heads straight toward her and says, "You could pass for my sister. It's a pleasure to meet you."

Leslie reaches out and asks Dee Dee if she could hug her. Everyone is shocked as Dee Dee hugs and gently pats the crying guest. "I'm sorry for you, Miss Summers. I didn't know your sister, but by the looks of this crowd, she was really special.

"She was, Leslie. She was, especially to me, and she had that same effect of the ladies on the phone."

Tanner suggests that it's time for Leslie to tell her story.

"The guy I had been dating is a police officer. I kind of liked the mystique of all that cop and robber sort of thing. As the months progressed, though, there were funny little things beginning to happen.

"He always told me how special I was. I had met him at the library. I was looking for plants and herbs to grow in my apartment on the balcony. He was very involved in medicinal herbs and plant medicines. He said the old ways were much more effective. We had a lot in common.

"Sometimes, I felt like I was being watched, even when I was at home. He was always talking about all these street kids and stuff. At first, we had a lot of fun. We went out on botanical searches in different areas.

"One time, we were at Wilderness Walk, and I suppose that's when things began to change. He told me to go ahead to the car. He was going up further, said he was supposed to meet someone undercover, a connection. I went back down to the car or pretended to, but I guess curiosity got the best of me. That's when I decided to sneak back up there. What I saw was beyond comprehension, not of this realm. Carlton was speaking to a man, or so I thought, and all of a sudden, it was like the man started to transform. I don't think there were words to describe what he became. I couldn't get close enough to hear what they were saying, thank God. The guy was a monster, and this wind came up out of nowhere. It was like a black cloud swirling. Carlton didn't seem affected or shocked by it.

"I started to move back down the hill as quickly as I could. It was getting late, but I didn't want him to know I had seen anything or heard a sound. I guess being practically paralyzed with fear helped. When I got near the bottom, I twisted my ankle and scraped one leg badly, so I sat down on the path and began to cry. When Carlton got there, he thought I had fallen and was very sympathetic. I managed to get out that I had stupidly tried to cut through the woods instead of winding down the path and had fallen. I had to play the part of my life. I asked him to take me to the hospital. I pretended that I was worried and that it was fractured.

"When I got to the hospital, I also pretended that I was sick. Actually, I was, from what I had seen. The doctor said maybe he should keep me overnight. I was so scared to tell the doctor what had happened because of the police connection with Carlton. I was afraid to tell also because they would've put me in the psych ward. I called one of my co-workers and set it up for her to pick me up when they released me. I didn't know what to do, but I knew I had to leave. It turned out I had a really bad sprain. I told Carlton and my work that I had a fracture and wouldn't be in for a couple of days.

"I spent the next few days looking for what I saw. I found it in one of the books at the library. I went to the bank, cleaned out my accounts, paid my rent up and my bills, and canceled my cards. I sold my car, took only my valuables, and stuck them in a deposit box at a mailing place. Then, I went to the library. That scared me because I was worried Carlton would show up. For some reason, I felt like I needed to give someone a warning, so I went back to the book and left a note about what I had seen in this section where I found the picture of that "thing." I had a taxi waiting, and he took me across town to the bus station, and I left. That's how I ended up visiting the Benedictine Monastery. I needed to get somewhere safe.

"How did you find me? I even wore a wig on the bus and changed my clothes."

Tanner explains tracking the phone call to her mother.

"Yes, I told her I found religion and needed some time re-evaluating my life. She was shocked because I've always been at least agnostic, if not an atheist. You tracked my cellphone, as you must have really wanted to find me... Oh, dear God, it's involved with the murder of that Summers girl! It's my fault, isn't it? I should've told someone. I wasn't sure who was who at that point. If I had known the things about God back then, she might be alive."

Tanner replies, "I don't think so. How would you prove something like that? They probably would've blown you off, and Carlton would have known. I think you did the right thing even under the circumstances."

"Tanner, you were right!" Travis is unglued, furious. "Carlton Prince! What in the world? How could he?"

"Travis, stop! We'll get him.

"What are you ladies screaming about?"

"The person driving the green car was a police officer, too! That's what we had told Jan today. We finally found the rental. It was delivered to the airport and returned there. We used the date of the funeral as a center point and finally found it. His name is Hammond, Bretton Hammond. Dot had to use some real connections to get us that information. Is he a real officer?"

"Yes, unfortunately, he is. He's a rooky in the department." *Jim was right. He's the other one.* "Thanks, ladies. You are all great!"

Travis looks devastated. "Bretton was becoming a friend. Tanner, I have a hard time believing Brett would be involved with something so sick."

"Me too, Travis. He had real potential. We'll get to the bottom of this tomorrow.

"Leslie, we are so grateful you are here. It's very brave of you to come back. We'll take care of you. Don't worry."

"I won't worry. I know God is with this group. Bryan deserves some credit. There was something about his voice that gave me peace. Maybe I can get this out of my dreams now."

Bryan, my stray cat. Maybe Beanie's right. "Thanks, Bryan."

Both groups are clapping. Bryan grabs Erica's hand and hugs her. "Erica was with me through the whole thing."

Beanie winks at Tanner and mouths, "See."

Constance is chuckling and patting Erica and Bryan on the back.

Tanner is about to move on as he realizes they haven't introduced James and Grace.

"Hello, ladies. We have heard much about you. We know you have been praying for Alyssa and for us. Pray we find her."

Tanner relates the creepy events of the last night. "Uncle James and Aunt Grace and Joe were meeting us at the airport. Stuart played the part perfectly. Initially, we were picking them up in my car. We knew there was something significant about an officer saying that I had sent him to the third floor of the hospital. Melinda didn't recognize him. We knew something was up. Stuart and I had the most unusual feeling when we got into my car and so we took a taxi to the airport." Stuart shivers at the memory. "I also had an encounter early this morning with, guess who?"

The whole room asks, "Carlton Prince?"

"Yep, so we are having cameras installed in the office. We'll see what we catch, if anything." Leslie looks frightened but Bryan and Emily go over and quietly reassure her. "Leslie, you will not be near the station or Carlton, and there will always be someone capable of protecting you."

Bryan gets a phone call. Dead silence from both groups. "Seven o'clock on Friday night at 322 Wilderness Walk Road. I'm supposed to bring friends."

Irene and Jamison come into the room at exactly the time Bryan is giving the address out. "That's Jacob's house! Oh, dear Lord! Tanner, everybody, that's Jacob's house!" Irene is shaking.

Stuart blurts out, "Irene, we are all invited by Jacob; at least Jan and I, you and Jamison, are."

"What?"

"That's what Jacob told me. I saw him at the hospital today. He was himself. He explained what happened in Haiti. We are good. Lieutenant Tanner, we have got to make a plan."

"Yes, Stuart, we do." Tanner walks closer to the phone. "Ladies, I can never thank you enough. Without you, we may never have figured this out. Is Madelyn there?... I didn't think so. Would someone please make contact with her and tell her that we are so thankful that she's a dreamer."

Everyone can hear a chuckle from the Big 10 group. "We will, Lieutenant Tanner, and may the Lord bless and protect you as you find Alyssa. Thank you for making us a part of this."

Dee Dee clicks off the speakerphone. "Dot, thank you for listening to the Lord and starting the investigation. I love you. Once an investigative journalist, always one. Matthew would be so proud of you. Love you all."

Grace and James suggest that because it is so late, everyone should go home and pray and seek the Lord about a plan and about finding Alyssa. "We know this is all tied together. We also know that Alyssa is still alive, but we think there are others. The Lord had impressed us about that." With that, they excuse themselves and go to their room.

I know I heard Adlin's Whisper. There's more, much more. Jan knows that, too. "Leslie, you can stay in my room with me if that makes you feel better. You don't know this, but I'm a police officer. You'll be safe."

The whole group sees the relief on Leslie's face as she nods her head and accepts Dee Dee's offer.

Ben and Joe quietly speak with Tanner. "Don't forget, we need to speak tomorrow about the thing concerning Dee Dee."

"What thing?" Stuart has popped in again.

He has a nose for news. "Come on, Stuart, I'll brief you later." *Much later.*

"Tanner, Art called. He and Murphy are done. I'll see you in the morning. Maybe our remote fishing has caught something. I know you love night fishing. Maybe you'd like morning fishing, too."

Tanner laughs as he hugs Beanie. "See you tomorrow, World's Best Secretary."

29

EYE SPY

"Art, thanks. I owe you."

"It's my job, Sir."

"Thanks anyway. How come Murphy didn't leave an invoice on Beanie's desk?"

"I'll talk to him about it."

Tanner and Beanie start to review the security tapes.

Joe rings in. "Tanner, something unbelievable has happened. I didn't want Dee Dee to know, but this morning she told me she had dreamed about her mom and showed me pictures of her parents. They were the agents that were in Haiti. After we rescued them, we removed them off the radar, and I never saw them again. The jewel thieves were all gruesomely murdered, but we found the jewels, other than one pendant. You and I need to meet with Ben before everyone else, and develop a plan."

"Wow! Joe, what a way to start the day. Are you okay?... I'll call you back. You and Ben stick close to everyone at the apartment. I'll make sure Travis comes over. Libby and Emily can come to be with Dee Dee and Leslie.

"Beanie, don't ask. I'll tell you when I get my head wrapped around it."

"Yes, Sir. Let's look at those tapes... Well, look at that. Might be evil, but he's not smart. The crack of dawn, picking our lock. Must've freaked him out to find out the reports weren't here. Look how frantic he is. Run, Carlton, run. I'm sorry you can't tell Jim right now. He'd be so proud. He probably saved you from exposing Grace and James. If he's involved, he may know where Alyssa is. Who knows what might have happened to her?"

"I know, Beanie, I know. What should we do about Carlton? What about Brett?"

"Sir, I prayed last night, and every time I thought about Brett, I would see those pictures of Stuart dressed like an old guy. I don't know what it means."

"Beanie, I think I'll visit with Brett and feel out the territory. I think I'll take him to lunch. Would you like to go?"

"Yes, it's a date."

"Get it set up. We're going day fishing."

"Brett, I'm so glad you could join us for lunch, especially since it's your day off."

"Sir, I feel honored that you invited me. I don't have many friends here."

"Travis speaks highly of you."

"He does?"

"Yes, he likes you."

"Well, he hasn't been around lately, so I didn't call and wasn't sure."

"No one else has befriended you?"

"Lieutenant, everyone's nice, but you know the rookie always gets the brunt of jokes and pranks."

Tanner replies with a laugh. "Yeah, I had forgotten." *This kid can't possibly be involved in evil.*

"You mean none of the other guys, not Jim, Art, Carlton, or the others?"

"Miss Beanie, it's okay. Carlton wanted me to go to some kind of herbal plant thing, but I'm not interested in all that. He's always around some pretty strange kids. I think they're in some kind of club."

"Really? Why would he be with a bunch of kids?"

"Don't get me wrong. Maybe he uses them as informants or is trying to make a positive influence on them. I'm too new to know who's okay and who's not, so I didn't get involved. I wanted to ask you a couple of questions about Carlton, but you've been pretty busy. Is anything happening with the Summers case?"

"Why, have you heard anything?"

"No, Sir, I'm sorry. I'm overstepping my boundaries. I heard how awful it was and feel sorry for her family and you. My sister was killed by a hit-and-run driver. We never found the person who did it. I know how awful it is to never see justice served. That's why I went to the Academy, to help others."

"Brett, why did you go to Adlin Summers's funeral?"

"Miss Beanie, I've been—"

"Stop, Brett. Lieutenant Tanner and I know you were there."

"Sir, am I fired?"

"That is not what this is about. Tell us the truth."

"Well, I saw the notice about her funeral, and I don't really know why I went there. Initially, I was going to the service to find out anything that would help you. When I got there, I realized how stupid I was. I parked by the church and prayed. Miss Summers was a student here, and I realized that some of her friends might recognize me. It was your case, and I knew I'd be in trouble because it wouldn't look good."

"Tanner, it's like when I was praying. Now, I understand why I kept seeing Stuart. He is like Stuart. They were both there trying to find the truth at the funeral."

"Miss Beanie, who's Stuart?"

"Oh, you'll get to meet him, Brett."

"Would you come to my office and go over a couple of reports?"

"Yes, Sir, but I don't understand. Did I fill out something wrong?"

"Depending on what we discover, I may need you to go undercover for an event."

"Sir, I'd be honored. Are you kidding?"

"No, but don't tell anyone. Act like you're in the doghouse when you get back. Come and see me. I'll explain later. Just do it."

Beanie pats Brett's hand. "Trust us. I'll call you to come up."

"I'll be there, Sir.

"Miss Beanie, thanks."

"Beanie, I think Bryan got another friend to show up. Who else can we recruit?"

"Sir, Erica wants to go."

"Absolutely not!"

"I think you should speak with her. Without her, you might not have found out about Anne. She's not fearful anymore, but she's really upset about Anne. She saw her today. Please, Sir, at least listen to her."

"Okay, Beanie, but only because you want me to."

"Thanks, Sir. Constance has a lot to tell you, too."

"Emily, did we ever make any progress on the guys from the library?"

"Gosh, Travis! I guess in the middle of all this, we dropped the ball. Stuart started traveling with Tanner. We were so excited about unraveling other mysteries from the library it got left out once we found the Kirschenbaums."

"I woke up this morning thinking about the guy at the library and the pearl. Help me find the guy. Do you think Tanner would let Stuart work with me on it? I have Beanie's list. I have the dream list in my folder at Kaplan's. Is Libby up?"

"Did someone say my name?"

"Good morning, Lib. I want to take you and Emily over to Kaplan's. We need to find the link to the guy and the pearl at the library. Tanner is tracking down the police connections. He won't want you guys to be here without me. We've got to find Alyssa. There may be others. We have got to find them.

The library is the strongest link. Remember, Leslie said she had met Carlton at the library. Maybe the guy in Madelyn's dream is connected to Carlton and all of this. Let's get to Kaplan's. Tanner wants me to come to the station. Something's up. He wants me there for something with Ben and Joe."

"Ben, can we see the folder? Grace kept dreaming about the folders."

"Sure, James. I'll need you to keep an eye on everyone for a while. Travis has to go to a meeting with myself and Joe. Tanner's working on the police connection." *I'm not telling you why we are really meeting— all about Dee Dee.*

"Stuart, you're already up?"

"Ben, I could feel the vibes. What are you two up to? Don't get that look on your face. I can't help it. I can feel things."

James is smiling at Ben and Stuart. "When you get it, you just have it. We need to redirect some of that, Stuart. God's got a plan for you. He told me you will find Alyssa." Dead silence.

Stuart and Ben are staring at each other. "Wow! That was kind of a boom to my brain. Are you serious?"

"Yes, Stuart, I am. Whatever comes your way today, pay attention. You'll find something big. Stay on track."

Travis arrives with Libby and Emily. Emily runs to Stuart. "Thank goodness you're here. I need your help today."

"I'm all yours."

James adds, "We all are."

"Ben, get that folder for James and Grace."

The second that Travis sees the folder, he remembers the piece of paper in his wallet. "Here, Emily, you might want to check on these guys. They were the ones that delivered all the food. Might be nothing, but maybe there's something there."

"I've got my file and I'll put it in there.

"Stuart, we've got some mysteries to solve. Coffee is already made, and I set out rolls and cereal." The whole group had slept late. It's been an emotionally crazy time for everyone.

"Thanks, Ben, you always take care of me."

"That's sweet, Dee Dee.

"How are you, Leslie?"

"I haven't slept like that in a long time. No bad dreams. No being startled awake. What do you need me to do?"

"Stay in. No one goes out. Travis and Joe and I have a meeting with Tanner. No one goes out while we are gone.

"Dee Dee, James and you are in charge.

"Joe, pray and let's get going."

"Lord, give us all your wisdom and protection over each life. Help us find Alyssa."

❧

"Beanie, page Brett on the intercom..."

"Did everyone think you were in trouble?"

"Yes, Ma'am. Beanie, that sound in your voice was so stern."

"Some others will be joining us shortly. Look at your report and Carlton's. Tell me what's wrong and why."

"Sir, I guess I was trying to account for my time, and I goofed up. I was on duty, but the location was wrong. I was tailing Carlton." Tanner and Beanie are dinging. "Carlton's whole report is a lie. He was with those strange kids, but when he got in the van—"

"A van?"

"Yeah, a white van. I followed him until they turned towards Wilderness Walk. I turned around. I thought it was one of Carlton's plant excursions. It probably was. There's one thing that's accurate. He did go to that upscale tattoo parlor, the one that looks like a salon. That's where the white van was, behind the building. Carlton parked back there and left his unmarked unit. Those kids appeared to be waiting for him."

"Boy, Brett, you have done some good detective work, very helpful. Brett, are you a believer?"

"Yes, Sir, ever since I was a little kid."

"You're going to need Him to grasp all of this.

"Beanie, do you have your folder? While I'm with the guys, will you walk Brett through all the events?"

"You mean about the Summers case? You're reading me into it?"

"Yes, but I guess you brought yourself in." *Thanks, Lord, for bringing him in. What a decent kid. He'll be a great detective.* "The guys have arrived."

❈

"I saw Brett. Is he okay? I saw him in an interrogation room with Beanie."

"Travis, you have no idea how okay he is.

"Ben, Joe, lay it on me. What about Dee Dee?"

Ben lays out Madelyn's dream about Dee Dee: the roses, the sound, something silver in the moonlight.

"I hope Linda didn't tell the gals yet. Peaches will be freaked out."

"No, Joe, I'm the only one that knows. Linda told Madelyn not to share that with anyone else. Madelyn promised, and Linda told me that Madelyn never violates a promise."

Tanner is in agreement. "Thank God! We can't share this with anyone. Those rows of roses were the ones we saw when we were behind Jacob's. I'm guessing at least two acres. That expanse was massive."

"I haven't seen it. Do you think we could do a flyover? Aerial surveillance while it's light?"

"Travis, that's a great idea. We'll take Brett when Beanie's done. I'll call Sheryl and get one of those traffic helicopters, a big one."

Once at the helipad, Tanner gets another Beanie surprise. A cameraman is seated next to the pilot. "Hey, guys, I got a call that you wanted some really good footage of our trip today. This baby will do it." He pats the camera strapped to his shoulder. "I was told you didn't want to fly too low."

"As always, she's on it." The others nod in silence.

The pilot asks where they're going and seems pleased that it's a trip over scenery instead of traffic. Wilderness Walk looked totally different from the air. The vast, raw beauty erases the ominous and dangerous memories.

"There, take it down a bit, but not too low." Jacob's house is coming into view. "Take some phenomenal shots of this whole area. The University has a research area here. They may want some of the footage."

The five guys sit silent as the pilot follows directions from the cameraman. Round and round, back and forth from every angle. The guys feel like they're on a roller coaster. "Wow! I had no idea the University had this beautiful area under its control. I'll get some great shots."

Well, they used to, and they will be getting it back. Tanner replies, "Isn't it interesting."

"Well, I think I've gotten every square inch of this place. Enough, Lieutenant?"

"Yep, that should do it."

As the helicopter starts to go, he spots a very large guy walking through the potting shed area.

"Film that."

A swirling cloud of dust appears to be moving along as the guy is walking. The pilot hovers the helicopter for a moment until the cameraman announces that he zoomed in and got it. The man seems to be oblivious to the guys hovering to the south of the property.

The pilot looks at the cameraman. "What was that, kid? Some kind of dust devil? That guy didn't even notice it. Did you guys see that?"

"Yes, I think it was one of those devils." After Tanner's reply, no one speaks, not a word.

Back at the helipad, Tanner tells the cameraman to send him an invoice.

"How about you don't pay me, and if the University wants to use it, I'll get credit."

"You've got a deal. Give me a card. Jake, give me a call sometime, and I'll share with you the results. You'll get credit."

"Do you need me to edit the footage?"

"Maybe later. Can you load it on something we can view on a computer for now?"

"Yep, here's the stick. I'll store the original for the University."

"Lieutenant, do you need to go anywhere else?"

"No, that was it. That was a great ride."

"It's my job. I couldn't believe it when Sheryl called, and I thought it was going to be for Traffic. This was wonderful, peaceful, no crime scenes, no accidents."

No crime? If you only knew.

❦

The guys can hardly wait to get it to the big screen in the briefing room. There's a sign on the door that the unit is out of service and a little card in the corner signed, "Beanie." Laughter.

"No one else will bother us. She thinks of everything, doesn't she, Tanner?"

"Yes, she does. You guys have no idea."

"Brett, if you don't want to be in this, it's okay. If you're in, one word leaked, and I will fire you."

"Yes, Lieutenant, Sir. I'm in.

"That was some kind of camera, like Disneyland. Look at the detail he captured. You can almost see the petals on the roses. What are those bizarre areas that look freshly dug? What are those pipes sticking up? Looks like vent pipes. Those signs on each one... do you think those are plant descriptions? I can't see because of those thorny vines."

"Well, Brett, are you done?"

Brett sheepishly replies, "Thanks, Travis. I guess I got carried away."

Ben and Joe are clapping. Ben laughs as he says, "That was quite a review. Too bad we couldn't see the guy's face, but he's big. What kind of clothes was he wearing? He didn't even notice that something was swirling, that dark thing right behind him. He had to feel that momentum."

"I'm going to close out the day with Beanie.

"Okay, Ben and Joe, you're on. Fill the young guys in."

❋

"Beanie, what's been happening? Thanks for holding down the fort."

"Sir, I've cleared out all your calls."

"I forgot."

"I know. I kept a tick list on the calendars. The lady who keeps calling is fine, just needed some reassurance that we are here for the citizens. She was a nervous wreck, so I prayed for her. She was shocked but loved it. I applied the Bryan technique. I'm sorry I didn't go in to see the footage, but I've been catching up on some loose ends. What are you going to do about Carlton? Friday's coming. Emily and Stuart have made a connection with the list from the library, but they need Travis. Irene called. She has some information on the tattoos. Memorial called, and they finally have the book completely analyzed."

I'll call Irene first. "Hey, Perfect Woman."

"Tanner, I showed that tattoo drawing to one of my colleagues. He said it's a very ancient symbol most commonly related to Voodoo. He wanted to know why I was asking about it, but I was uncomfortable giving him details."

"You are a brain. Thanks, Irene. I had the notebook tested in forensics at the hospital. Don't get mad... Don't get mad. I wanted to get it away from Jacob's vicinity and the station. Since he's temporarily out of the picture, I want to send it over to you... Wait, I'll bring it to you... Okay, you're headed to pick Jamison up?... Perfect, I'll meet you there. I'll give you the clearance to take the materials.

"This is Lieutenant Tanner. I'll be over to get the samples and blood collections: all of it and the notebook. I really appreciate it. You have been great. Irene Carpenter will be there. Since you're an extension of the University, she'll sign too. Thanks. Have the paperwork ready."

Tanner peeks into the briefing room. "Hey, guys. Are we all on the same page?... Good, let's get these guys and find Alyssa."

30

A TELLING "TAIL"

"Tanner, we've got to find Alyssa. We think, based on the notebook, she's on that property. Remember, Beth kept talking about the wall and chains? Thank goodness we crisscrossed back and forth over the property, and the cameraman shot from every angle. The potting shed has two levels. From one side it looks like one level, but it has a basement or something like that on the other side. It has ground-level windows covered with thorny vines. One of them was broken. Beth must have gone out that window. Remember, she talked about the girl who shoved her through the glass?"

"Travis, why didn't Stuart tell us about the shed having two levels?"

"Well, he never heard what Beth said. He was hauled off that night. There's a good possibility Alyssa is in the shed."

"Wow, Travis! How are we going to get on that property? A judge would think we were crazy. Jacob is too respectable."

Ben pops up with, "Stuart! He had a good visit with Jacob at the hospital. We need written permission from Jacob."

"I've got to go to Memorial and meet Irene. The "Three Amigos" have made a connection to the guy at the library based on Madelyn's dream. Ben, Joe, you go with Brett and see if you can tail Carlton. Apparently, he's always cruising at night. I'll bet business is good at that tattoo salon after dark. Ben and Joe, do you need something to carry?"

"Nope, we're good to go. You should know by now that Ben and I are good Boy Scouts, always prepared."

"Brett, be a good tour guide and be careful."

"Ben, I've arranged a different car for you from the rental on Sixth. They're waiting for you. It has tinted windows and all the necessities, but not too obvious. I couldn't help but hear you guys. The door was open a crack."

Ben hugs Beanie. "Tanner, pay this woman more."

Tanner's phone is ringing. "Libby, what's wrong?... Travis will be there shortly. He's already on his way. I'm headed to Memorial to meet Irene. Then, I'm coming to Kaplan's... I know Lib. I'll be there as soon as I can. Tell Stuart to calm down."

"Beanie, go and have dinner with your bunch. I'll keep you updated."

"Stuart, you can't leave. I'll have to knock you on your can."

"But I know who the guy is. He owns that fancy tattoo parlor that he calls a salon. He knows where Alyssa is."

"Stuart, I'm Alyssa's father, and I'm telling you to stop."

"But you said I'd find Alyssa."

"Yes, but not by running out. It's almost dark. What do you think you can accomplish all by yourself with no plan?"

Grace hugs Stuart. "I know how you feel, but remember, Stuart, we want her to live, and then there may be others."

"Stuart, I called Travis. He's almost here. He said he needs your help."

"He did?"

"Yes, he did, so calm down and wait for him."

"Okay, Libby."

Travis swings the door to the apartment open, "What's going on?"

"Travis, no one would let me go. We've got to go to that tattoo salon, that hell pit, and arrest that Phillips guy, the owner."

"Well, Stuart, on what charges? For being in a library? For being in an older woman's dream? For picking up a pearl? Give me a break! Let's all sit down. You've made everyone upset."

"Dee Dee, I don't like your color. What's wrong?"

"I can't explain it." *Rage. The pendant.*

"Sit down, Dee Dee." Emily sits next to her.

"Grace, pray for her, please."

"Emily, was he like this all day?"

"No, we were so excited that we made the connection. We think one of the guys on your delivery list is also a creep. Stuart went nuts. Travis, Beanie tried to tell him you were tied up and that you had your phone off."

"Stuart, you are not the center of the universe."

"No, but the guilt I feel over Alyssa overwhelms me. Yes, that sense of helplessness."

"Stuart, I've got a real job for you. A really big deal. We need you to get Jacob to give you written permission to be on his property."

"Did he hurt Alyssa?"

"No, but we're really on to something. Help us, Stuart. Help Alyssa."

"Okay, Travis, I can do that."

"All right, let's get a plan. Use your brilliant mind."

"Well, Jacob told me about his new friend Jan. Maybe Jan could be helpful with Jacob. Let me think. Tomorrow would be better. Jacob would think it was odd if I came tonight. Can we get something to eat? I'm starving."

"Stuart, you're back." Emily is relieved.

The entire room breathes a sigh of relief. Stuart is back. Libby and Grace have already prepared dinner for us.

Travis blocks Emily from kissing him. "Before you say it, I admit I'm jealous. Emily's my girl."

"Dee Dee, are you okay?"

"Yes, Travis. It's just old emotions." Adlin's Whisper, *"Help me. Help us, Dee*

Dee." "I think Grace's comment earlier was right, and there are others that need rescuing. Leslie is hiding in the room. Stuart freaked her out."

"Tanner, sorry to bug you. Emily and Stuart figured out the connection to the library. The guy that owns that upscale tattoo parlor, excuse me, salon, is the guy from the library."

Ding, ding. "Travis, I'll touch base with the guys. They're with Brett, heading toward the tattoo place doing a little surveillance. Carlton might show up... No, they're hoping to find him and tail him. Is Stuart back on track?... Good, get that permission from Jacob. Tell him I said so. Thanks, Travis. As always, be careful."

"Looky, looky, who's coming down the street? Our buddy, Carlton. He's a busy man. Is our luck on, or what? He's driving straight to the club where a bunch of those goths hang out."

Ben gently touches Brett's arm. "Sometimes, they change. You haven't met Bryan yet."

"Not with someone like Carlton. He'd take them under in a minute. Okay, he's moving again. Hey, look back at that cluster coming out of the club. Wonder where they're going? I'm going to pull over, and I want to see where they're walking to... They're headed towards the park."

"Brett, let's drive to the other side and watch. We'll be closer to the tattoo place." Everyone sits in silence.

"There!" Joe spots a white van pulling around the corner. They all duck down into the seats as the van drives past. It slowly drives around the park two times. Joe peeks up and sees the whole group loading into the van. "Okay, Brett, make sure he doesn't know he's being tailed."

Ben calls Tanner. "In case this van turns up Wilderness Road, we will need some kind of distraction so we can tail them."

"I'll send an ambulance to get to the intersection before they turn. Get in and ride all the way.

"Jamison, I need an ambulance. Now!

"Irene, sign for the stuff and get me out of here."

Jamison calls the ER, and Tanner gets into the ambulance. He flashes his badge and tells them where to go. "Put the pedal to the metal.

"Ben, are you still on them?"

"Traffic's heavy; there's been an accident."

"Ben, we'll be there in about eight minutes."

"Guys, we're gonna have to run the rest of the way. Tanner's coming from the other direction, so he won't be in this mess."

Brett pulls the car right up on the sidewalk, flashes his badge, and they start running.

"Three blocks, guys, we can do this. Here they come."

As the van starts to move, another ambulance comes around the corner, and the guys slip in. "Sure as shootin', they're taking Wilderness Walk Road. Keep the light on and run that van off the road if you have to. Go to the end of the road and then turn around. We'll pretend you couldn't find the right house." *This has to be the van Irene saw.* The ambulance passes the van and turns around.

"Now what, Lieutenant?"

"Let me think a minute... Ben, you're the victim of a fall at Wilderness Walk."

They unload the stretcher and go into the woods, returning with Ben covered. The sirens are back on.

Tanner commands, "Drive slower. We have an injured person here." The whole group is laughing. As they pass Jacob's, they see Carlton directing the goths into the back, inside of the walls.

"Ooh, I'd like to jump him right now."

Joe softly speaks, "Not yet, Brett. We don't know what we're dealing with."

At the picnic area, Tanner tells the driver to drop them off. "Bill the department for this ride, but not a word, or I'll get you fired. Thanks for the ride, and keep the sirens on."

"I won't tell a soul, Sir."

As the three sit in the dark, the sound carries their way: drums and faint chanting.

Joe says, "Maybe they're practicing for Friday."

Two hours slowly drag by. Tanner calls Jamison.

"Tanner, you weren't in the ambulance when it got back. Bruce wouldn't tell me anything except that you might need a ride. Where are you?... Why are you there?... Lord, protect you... Okay, I'll call Libby and tell her you got called out. I won't tell Irene... You're turning your phones off?... Call me when you need a ride.

"Let's get closer to see when they come out."

"Tanner, it's far up there. We want to get those kids when they unload. I see lights coming." The van is starting back down the hill. "Joe, call Beanie. She'll get someone on that tail. We want the kids, not Carlton right now."

"Beanie, call me when you have it set up. They should be at the intersection in about 15–20 minutes. We need undercover at the corner of Wilderness Walk Road and that intersection. Call Jack immediately. Tell him what to do. He never asks questions. Tell him we want the passengers, not the driver, so don't pull him over. Wait until he unloads and leaves. Tell him to make something up as far as a cause. We'll be there as soon as we can.

"Jamison, can you come and get us?... Leave in about twenty minutes. Head close to the picnic area. We'll see you. We're out of sight. Park."

Take A Night Off

"Good little workers, Roscoe. I think they're ready for Friday, so nothing tomorrow. Don't want to wear them out."

"I'll tell Officer Prince to let them have the night off to get ready for Friday. Desmond, what do you think about that ambulance?"

"Probably some stupid hiker got lost in the dark. Too bad he didn't come this way. We could've taken care of him."

"Oh, wouldn't that have been fun?"

"Beanie, did you get Jack on it?... Really?... He's on them and knows what to do? He laughed, huh?... What? Another, Tanner? He's a real jokester. Give me a jingle when he rounds those kids up. Thanks, Beanie.

"Let's go home, guys. You don't have to go to lockup with me. I'm going to pick up the rental car we left on the sidewalk unless they towed it to the pound. I'll call Traffic...

"Aah, Brett, they towed it. Jamison's here, though." They emerge from the trees.

"Tanner, what in the world is going on?"

"I'll tell you some on the way to lockup. I'm pretty worn out, so I'll explain everything tomorrow.

"It's Beanie.

"Jack got them?... We're headed there right now.

"Guys, they got em.

"Libby, I'm okay, but I'm headed to interrogate some folks. You and Emily are staying there? ... Oh, yeah, I forgot Stuart. I don't want you and Emily driving home alone... Good. You got clothes there?... I'll see you in the morning. Ben and Joe are with me."

"Tanner, it's good to see you. Hope we picked up the right visitors for you. We still haven't figured out what you're up to."

"Jack, I owe you a couple favors now. You have many great qualities, but the best is that you never ask questions. I promise I'll fill you in later. Jack, meet Ben, Joe, and Brett."

"Hey, guys. You look familiar to me, Brett. I've seen you making rounds."

"Ben and Joe are from out of town."

"Whoa, this is a big deal, isn't it?"

"Jack, that was a question."

"Okay, Tanner, I'll lay off. One more. Are these the right guys that we picked up?"

"Yep, they are. Joe, you know the most about what we need to question them about. You pick one out and go for it."

"Tanner, I think Bryan might be helpful. Can you get him down here?"

"I'll call Constance.

"Constance, this is Tanner. Yes, I'm sure you recognize my voice. Is the cat handy? Thanks."

"Hey, Sir, what's up?... You're kidding, you need my help?... Old-style Bryan?... I'll be there shortly. Can Erica come?... Constance said we could take the car. Where do you want us? We'll be there in about thirty minutes. We'll have to dress for the part, like stray cats... Thanks, Sir."

"Joe, Erica and Bryan will be here in about thirty minutes. Do you want to pick one out and start?"

"Yep, give me that nervous one in the corner. Make sure you guys can hear the conversation and see what's going on."

❁

"Have a seat. You look really rattled. Heard you had a club meeting tonight... Look, Andrew. Isn't that your name?... Your license says it's Andrew... Okay, Andy, spill it. What were you doing at Wilderness Walk?"

"I don't know. I got a phone call, but I don't remember. We got in a van, and then we got dropped off."

"Have you been drinking?"

"Yeah, we all drink in the van. That's all I remember. Ugh, I feel sick."

"Oh, too bad. You're shaking all over. Let me see your arms. Pull those sleeves up. Were you shooting up?"

"No, Sir, I don't use that stuff." On his left wrist is the same tattoo that Bryan has.

"Where'd you get that tat?"

"I don't remember."

"Are you playing a memory loss game?"

"No, I really don't remember. I was at a party, and I woke up with it. It was weird, and I had lost a whole day. Then, I started meeting other guys and chicks with the same tats. It's the same story. They don't remember how they got them. I guess we've all hung together trying to figure it out. Chip said he'd help us."

"Who's Chip?"

"You should know him. He said he's a detective, and he's been undercover working on a case. Said we could all help each other."

"Really? How's that working out?"

"Not good. Some of the group disappeared. Chip said he had reassigned them, but no one has seen them. We're starting to get freaked out. He keeps saying they're fine but never tells us anything. King showed up to find his sister, but she had disappeared. Before she vanished, she kept talking about an old friend helping her, and poof, she was gone."

"Did she say anything about the friend?"

"Yeah, crazy stuff, all about the Bible and God. She was really off the deep end."

"Andy, this has been very enlightening. If I were you, I wouldn't tell the others what you just told me. Keep your mouth shut, and I'll see what we can do. By the way, I don't think talking about the Bible and God is a crazy idea. You need all the help you can get. Think about that. You're on a seventy-two-hour hold, so keep quiet. I'll see what we can do."

❉

"Wow, Joe, that kid was a powerhouse of information."

"Yeah, Brett, I was blown away by how easy that was. If the rest of them are as freaked out as this kid, this could turn out to be a very successful night."

"Lieutenant, Sir, what do you think?"

"I love night fishing, and this is quite the catch. Which one is King?"

"Tanner, let's wait for Bryan and Erica." Ben's in agreement with Joe.

❉

"Whoa, Bryan, you look like you're one of the bunch.

"Erica, what happened to Miss Bubbly and fresh? You look like a stray cat dragged you down here."

"Stop, guys, it's not funny. We're here to help."

"Okay, Bryan and Erica, this is Brett."

"We're here undercover."

"You're the Bryan they told me about that I hadn't met yet. Ben must really like you. He said it would change my point of view."

"Thanks, Ben. Oh, I know these guys, but why are there no girls? That's odd." Joe gives Bryan all his interrogation information he got from Andy and his comments about King.

"I don't know him, but I recognize some of the others. Throw Erica and me in there and we'll get something going. Sir, do you remember the girl I told you about?"

"Yes, but I'm leery about Erica being in there."

"Sir, I'll be all right. There are two of us, and it may soften them up without long interrogations. Lieutenant, I helped break some of this case, and you're going to command me to stay out? Let me go in there with Bryan."

"Erica, it's really unusual. We put women in separate holding tanks."

"I'll make up some reason. Please let me do my part."

"Okay. Make it look official.

"Lock them up.

"Erica, come up with something good." Tanner hugs them both. *Lord, we need your help.* "Let's get some coffee and pray that these kids get a breakthrough."

✳

The clock shows two hours have lapsed. Tanner is jolted by the buzzer.

"The girl in the holding tank needs to use the restroom."

"Yeah, and bring her to the office when she's done."

"Sir, it's a miracle. These guys are scared to death. It's like Bryan's story all over. The phones, the memory loss, the whole thing. That guy King started crying when he saw us. He is really concerned about his sister. It turns out that Bryan knew her. He has offered to help find King's sister and the rest of their other friends. Can you get someone down here to take blood samples and see what's in their systems? They all have agreed."

Tanner's calling the lab. "Put a rush on it."

"Bryan was amazing. He shared his testimony and told them how dangerous this is. They even let us pray for them. They all want to find King's sister and their other friends. There are more people missing. What about the Carlton guy?"

"Oh, we'll have a visit with him later. Get Bryan, and I'll take everyone home... What do you mean he's staying? Send him in here.

"Bryan, you can't stay here tonight."

"Why not? I used to be one, and I know God wants me to stay with them. I'll be fine."

"Well, since you put it that way, I guess it's all right, but keep that phone on you."

"Brett, will you handle getting Bryan out when he's done? Call Jack and set it up. Keep an eye on Carlton, too."

"You know I will, Sir. It's been great seeing all of you in action. Thanks, Lieutenant. Don't worry, I'll take care of everything here."

"Erica, I'm impressed. You must've done something really special in that cell."

"Lieutenant, I loved playing the part. Ever since I was little, I wanted to do something exciting but was always so afraid. That fear is gone. I'm still cautious, but that's common sense. That innate fear is really gone, and I'm free. Bryan has been so good for me. He's intelligent and street-smart. We both want to do police work."

"Erica stop, I know. Beanie and Constance are already on me about you and Bryan."

"It's okay, Lieutenant, we'll talk later. Thanks for letting me experience tonight."

&

"Miss Erica, you were really something. A great little actress and a very fine person."

"Thanks, Joe, that means a lot."

"Look how beautiful it is right before daylight, pink and glowing."

"Erica, it's your morning."

"Oh, Ben, that's so sweet. Look, Constance has the light on for me. I'll bet she's going to ask a million questions."

"Does Bryan have her keys?"

"Yes, he does."

"Well, I'm sure she'll be excited to hear the news. You were a genuine investigator."

"Ben, thanks for the comment about the morning, and thanks for all the rest of your support. I respect all of you so much. I can't explain how much you have changed my life. Isn't it something how a bad thing happens, and God turns it into good for so many?"

"Erica, that's one of the greatest mysteries of the Lord. Goodnight, Sweet Pea, or should I say morning?"

"Thanks, Ben. You guys keep praying for Anne. She's better but still doesn't recognize me. Thanks for the ride."

As Erica reaches the porch, the door swings open into the arms of Constance, wrapping around her. Tanner gives Constance a thumbs-up and pulls out of the drive.

31

SLUMBER PARTY

"Guys, let's go home. What a night! What a morning! This is beautiful.

"Libby, you slept out here all night?... You and Dee Dee talked all night?... Is she okay? She's been low-key for days."

"She says there's something, but she can't quite put her finger on it. She's been spending a lot of time on the phone with her aunt. She says they've been reminiscing about the past. I don't ask a lot of questions."

"I'll talk to Ben tomorrow and see what he knows. He's very close to Dee Dee's aunt."

"I know they are, Tanner. I think they're making plans for the future."

"Really? He told you that?"

"Come on, Tanner. You're not the only person with good instincts and intuition."

"Are we making plans?"

"Yes, Tanner, we are. Every precious minute. You can share the room with Stuart, and I'll finish sleeping on the couch."

"Libby, Stuart is—"

"Get up there, and I'll be fine right here."

Tanner gives Libby a sweet kiss on the forehead. He can't shake that uneasy feeling about Dee Dee. *I wonder what she's dealing with. Does this have something to do with Madelyn's dream?* "Night, Lib. I put the deadbolt on."

℀

What is that? Fortunately, I left the light on. As Libby sits up, she has a clear view of the room. "Dee Dee, what are you doing?"

"Libby, I've got to get out of here. I'm going stir-crazy. I keep feeling like I'm supposed to be somewhere, but I don't know where. I thought if I went for a walk, it might let up."

"I don't think you're going anywhere. We'll do something later today. I'm sure Leslie and Grace would love to get out, too. Please, Dee Dee, don't make me wake the guys up. They're exhausted. Please."

"Okay, Libby. I feel bad that I woke you up. I'll go back to sleep."

"Dee Dee, come on. You can lie down here at the other end of the couch. Lock the door, and let's finish our slumber party."

"I'm going to go to the bedroom. Leslie's still asleep."

The figure standing in the hallway outside turns and walks away as the deadbolt clicks back into place.

℀

Static

"Did you put out that call?"

"Yeah, I put out the message several times. I even sent a courier to pick it up. It seems like there's always some sort of static interference. The package can't be delivered to us right now."

"Keep working on it. The Boss won't be satisfied until we get the package. Friday's coming."

"Desmond, get off my back! I'm working on it!" *We have this great project, so why must I fool around with a special delivery? Well, with everything I've done, now this again. Static. Static, static.*

Libby awakes to a quiet sound in the den. "What are you guys up to?"

Tanner is the first to speak. "Lib, did you sleep well?"

"Lightly. I need to talk to you about Dee Dee. Something happened after you went to bed. She was undoing the deadbolt, and she was getting ready to leave. I talked her out of it, but I'm worried."

Ding, ding, ding. Ben, Joe, and Tanner immediately know it has something to do with Madelyn's dream. "Is Dee Dee still asleep? Libby, come in and shut the door."

Ben gently pats Libby's hand. "Tanner, we need to tell Libby."

"Tell me what?"

"Joe, why don't you fill Lib in."

"Miss Libby, I am so blessed that you and Dee Dee are becoming friends. Peaches loves that girl, and so do I. We need your help to keep Dee Dee safe."

◦

Thank goodness I spent that time with Libby tonight. She's the childhood friend I never had. Strange that I'd have to get this old before I let another person, especially a female, get that close to me. I guess the memories that Linda and I have been sharing softened me up to have this evening with Libby. Why did I never see the beauty of another person's life? I believe Jan was the door-opener and paved the way for me to listen to someone's voice besides the one living in my head. What a skewed view of life, making my own emotional rules and building barriers. I built a fortress around me— trapped by my self-designed values. Hiding from the truth. Hiding from God. What a gift I've been given, starting with the Big 10 and one little old lady, Madelyn, loving me just because, with no selfish motive. Lord, forgive me. I promise I will change. I need you to help me find the truth. Why can't I remember certain things? Help me to surrender and receive that help. Help us find Alyssa. Grace and James believe you are watching over her. I promise when I wake up, I'm going to change. Goodnight, Linda. Goodnight, Adlin. Ah, look at Leslie. It's like watching Adlin sleep. It's amazing and comforting. They're almost twins. What kind of plan do you have for all of us? Everyone from Meadow Brook and Oak City all bound by a cord of life. The cord of life. Oh, that's beautiful, Lord. Finally, sleep...

"Dee Dee, wake up!" A frightened and pale Leslie is shaking her awake. "Dee Dee, thank goodness. Are you okay?"

"Leslie, what are you doing?"

"I woke up to the room filled with you talking to someone, and it felt like everything was shaking. Were you dreaming?"

"Yeah, it was a nightmare."

"No, nightmares don't affect other people. I'm telling you, everything was shaking. We have to tell the guys."

"No, I was only dreaming. Don't tell them."

"Well, I'm going to because I'm frightened. I've never been caught in someone else's dreams before, and I'm telling you everything was shaking! I immediately thought about my experience with Carlton. I'm going to tell them right now!" With that, Leslie runs out of the room.

A tap at the door of the den startled the quiet group going over the details of Madelyn's most recent dream. "Leslie, why are you up so early? You look like you've seen a ghost."

"I'm so glad you're all up. I was getting freaked when you weren't in your rooms. Libby, you're up too? What's going on? This is bad, isn't it?"

"Leslie, keep it down. All we need is for Stuart, Grace, or James to hear. Are you okay?"

"No, Tanner, I'm not! Dee Dee didn't want me to tell you, but I'm going to!"

"Tell us what? You better come in and sit down."

As Leslie enters the room, Dee Dee appears right behind her.

"Leslie, let me tell my own story. I'm always suspicious that someone knows something I don't, but maybe that's my fault. Libby, our slumber party last night made me realize that I keep myself distanced from the very people I need the most. Leslie, thanks for not letting this one be another secret. I keep hearing a Whisper. Adlin is saying, 'Help me,' and now, 'Help us.' I realize it's not Adlin, but the Lord using the one person who can touch my heart, my baby sister's voice. I went to sleep, and I dreamed about Madelyn again."

"Praise the Lord!" Joe's outburst breaks the silence of the group. "Tell us about the dream because we have a lot to tell you, too. Looks like this is a truth session. We're running out of time, so we better put it all out on the table. Let's pray first. Go for it, Ben."

"Dear Lord, hear our plea for truth. You are the way, the truth, and the life. You alone know how to direct our steps to lead us into the truth and perhaps save lives. May we all be truthful and bound with love for one another. I thank you for bringing us all together and for the precious name above all names, Jesus."

Dee Dee stands in the middle of the room with her eyes closed and shares the dream...

"I'm in some kind of garden. Initially, I have my eyes closed. I'm standing barefoot in soft soil. The scent of roses is intoxicating, filling the air all around me. All of a sudden, I hear Madelyn's voice saying, 'Dee Dee, open your eyes.' As I open my eyes, I can see in the moonlight, and rows upon rows of beautiful roses, all sorts of unusual colors. I'm aware that Madelyn is standing to my left and slightly behind me. I hear her saying, 'Dee Dee, turn around. Do you smell the other scent?' I smell cherries, but I don't know where the scent is coming from. There are no cherry trees. Madelyn is pointing at some kind of shed or some sort of building. As I begin to walk towards the building, I pick up another fragrance. The scent of cherries is becoming stronger, but the new smell is of something rotting. I try to pull open the door. I'm pulling and tugging, and at that exact moment, I hear Madelyn yell, 'Dee Dee, run!' I hear this horrible pounding sound, almost deafening, like gigantic stomping. It's like an earthquake. Suddenly, I see this black mist snaking towards my feet. I shout, 'Where do I run?' 'Run to him!' I see Madelyn pointing to the other end of the garden or whatever I'm in. I see a man in the moonlight standing against the far wall. 'Run to him!' I begin to run. I'm falling and running, and the roses seem to be clawing at me, trying to stop me. I'm almost at the wall, and I see the man again. He's smiling at me, and then I fall on my face and extend my hand upwards toward him. I hear Madelyn repeating, 'Receive the gift! Receive the gift!' The man bends down and drops something silver in my hand. The black fog has almost overtaken me. The man covers me with his body, and I could feel the earth shaking and the black mist swirling around us. It's almost like it's sucking the air out. It's stomping, and it's hunting and hunting. I guess it can't see me because the man is shielding me. I don't know what he handed me, but I have a flash of Madelyn saying, 'You did it, Dee Dee!' as she's smiling at me. I wake up to the smell of those cherries and the roses and that stench of death or something rotten. It was a nightmare. The man seemed familiar, but I couldn't place him, and his skin smelled like rain. I'd know him if I saw him again."

"I know what you mean about a nightmare. The case I worked on out of Haiti stayed in my dreams for years. All this is connected. Dee Dee needs to know the whole story."

"Joe, I'm not sure I want to know. I feel such—"

"Dee Dee!" Ben catches her as she clutches her chest.

How could I explain the rage? "I feel like my heart is being tugged on by something like a pendant or a stone hanging from a chain. When Adlin died, that rage from when my parents passed, began to grow. It's gotten heavier with time. I've learned to control it, but something triggers it, and then it's back."

"Leslie, calm down. It's okay. We're all here."

"Well, I think all of you would be upset if you had gotten caught in somebody's nightmare. Dee Dee was asleep, and I woke up to the room shaking! Ben, that shaking was exactly like the time I followed Carlton at Wilderness Walk. It all felt the same. Something followed me here."

Dee speaks softly. "No, Leslie, it didn't. It's looking for me."

"Dee Dee, don't say that."

"Libby, it's true. I know it is. I can feel it. I don't know why, but as I told you, there's something that keeps pulling on me. Otherwise, how did I end up here? You always tell us there's a plan. Suppose there's God's plan and a dark one, too."

"We all need to sit down and lay out the truth. Are you ready?"

I told God I would change. "Yes, I am. Tell me everything, Joe.

"Ben, I see that look. I'm okay now."

"Dee Dee, I knew your parents."

"Oh, my gosh! Joe, you knew my mom and dad?"

"Yes, Dee Dee. When I saw your old family photos, I immediately recognized them. They were working a case in Haiti. That's how Ben and I came to know each other. Somehow, this all ties together and what you said about the pendant and the stone. I know it's all connected. I believe you're right. It does have something to do with you."

"Linda's been lying to me all these years! Hasn't she, Ben?"

"Absolutely not! She never knew your parents were undercover, not ever. I never knew that those agents were your parents, either. This is all going to bring out the truth concerning Adlin's death; I can feel it. Something is happening Friday night and I believe we'll get to the bottom of this.

"Dee Dee, I was sent to Haiti to find the agents. They had disappeared. No one could make contact with them. They had used a cover traveling on cruise ships to catch jewel thieves and acted like they were married. After all that happened, they did marry, and those were your parents. Miraculously, I did find them. They had survived the experience in Haiti. Voodoo was involved, and the jewel thieves weren't so lucky. Their demise was beyond description. I had nightmares for years.

"The jewels were all recovered except for one very large stone pendant on a chain. I think that someone is looking for the stone. Is it possible that it's connected to what you keep experiencing? These were unexplainable things that went on in Haiti. A strong spiritual overtone. Your parents were amazing people, and I believe their faith spared them from a horrible fate."

Everyone's looking at me. Dee Dee, you promised to change. Stay calm. I can feel tears stinging in my eyes. *Mommy, Daddy. Libby is crying. Be brave. You asked for the truth.* "Go on, Joe. I'm ready."

"In reference to your comment about Linda, your aunt, knowing anything... Your parents didn't actually go into witness protection. We scrubbed all their files and said that they had died in Haiti. So, your Aunt Linda never knew. Somehow, all this comes together with what you've told us about the stone. It's all connected. I believe you're right. It does have something to do with you."

"Tanner, why are you leaving?"

"Dee Dee, Irene is calling me. I've got to take it."

"Hey, Perfect Woman, you're up early... What? Jacob's insistent on going home?... Get Jan involved. She's good with him. She's really good with him. We've had a big breakthrough, Irene. I'll go into it later... Yes, I'll fill you in... Guaranteed, you'll be a vital part...

"Okay, I'm back. We have to get moving. Jacob is completely agitated and wants to get out of the hospital. Irene is getting Jan involved. He seems to accept Jan as a confidant and a friend. Did you guys share about Madelyn's dream?"

"Madelyn's dream? I was sharing my dream about Madelyn. I'm confused. What's going on?"

"Dee Dee, your dream is parallel to Madelyn's dream. It was about you. We've known there is a place with roses and a shed. Somehow, Jacob's research plot behind his house is in Madelyn's dream and your dream."

"I'm supposed to be there, aren't I, Ben?"

"Yes, baby, you are, but it's really dangerous because we still don't know what the celebration is for that Jacob talks about. He said some big-shot is supposed to come. Maybe you're also a featured guest."

"Oh, my gosh, Ben! It just hit me!" Joe pauses for a moment. "I know what it's about!...

"Dee Dee, you look almost identical to your mother. Whoever is behind this thinks that you're her or that you have that pendant."

"Joe, that's why sometimes I'd see you looking at me with the strangest look."

"Yep. At first, I thought it was a coincidence, but you're almost a carbon copy of your mom."

"That's what Aunt Linda would always say.

"Ben, do you think we can solve Adlin's murder and find Alyssa?"

"Yes, Dee Dee, I do. This is like one big, divine plan. I also believe that we may save many lives."

Wow. Everyone agrees. "I'm in. Get a plan, and whatever I need to do, I'll do it."

"All we know is that this has to do with a bunch of street kids. Leslie, the stuff you shared with us has been of great value. It's like each of us is a piece in the puzzle. What seemed like random events are, in fact, fitted together perfectly. We can't move forward until we get feedback from

Constance, Bryan, and Erica. Those kids hold a key. Anne is also a key to much information. Hopefully, she comes out of the trauma she has experienced. I know everything's coming together."

"Are we filling in Grace and James and Stuart?"

"Yep, Libby. No more secrets. We're all together in this and need each other."

"Tanner, thank goodness. I'm tired of being nervous about giving information to the wrong person."

32

TIME CLOCK

Tanner's phone is ringing. "Bryan, you're up early. What did you find out? Did you find out when that lab work would be done?... Okay, you're gonna head to Constance's?... Call me when you get there. There have been some real developments on our end. Tell Jack thanks if he's still there, and tell Brett to stand by. Big stuff is coming... Tell all your cellmates thanks and that they have to remain incarcerated a little longer. I think we'll have a special deal for them... You what?... Yeah, Bryan, I agree. It's like being in the Twilight Zone, dark stuff... Okay, be careful. Call me when you get to Constance's."

Tanner calls Beanie. "Beanie, I need your help. You're always a voice of sanity. I want you to clear out my calls and have a sudden attack of something where you feel so ill you have to go home. I need you to go to Constance's and be there on standby all day. Put Art and Jim in charge of any calls that come in... Oh, my gosh! Mr. Kaplan called? Oh, boy, have I dropped the ball with him. Beanie, come up with something, you're a clever girl... Yes, Beanie, we are getting to the place where we might be able to solve everything... I'm deeply concerned, too. Thanks for praying like crazy... Beanie, you know I would never leave you out. That's why I want you to have the day off. As always, I need your help. You can wait at Constance's and get all the mundane stuff outsourced. Art's always helpful... No, I will not forget to honor him someday, and Jim's been a great asset, too. Thanks for the endorsement of Art; very glowing... Okay,

I'll take your advice. See you later and thanks." *I wonder what is happening between Art and Beanie.*

"Libby, what's going on?"

"Jan called, and Jacob is adamant he's going home today."

"He can't. It's too dangerous." *Think Tanner.* "We have to come up with something big. We need help. I know, I'll get Travis on it."

"Hey buddy, I need you to create an event. Didn't you work for the utility company or something?... Oh, you have an old friend there. Jacob wants to go home today, and we need to make it impossible for that to happen. Get the road blocked somehow. Water, gas, whatever... Thanks, Travis, I know you'll handle it. I know I won't worry while you're on it. Would you call me when you have it set up?... Thanks, I need to fill you in on a bunch of stuff... Oh, my goodness. Okay, thanks, Travis."

"Tanner, you didn't even let me finish. Anne's coherent. She's asking questions. Jan is with her now."

"Libby, get Emily and Erica and head over there. See what you can find out. She'll probably recognize you and hopefully remember you and Emily. Erica's been her friend for a long time. It's really important."

"Okay, give me a minute, and I'll get dressed.

"Joe, will you drive me?"

"You bet, Miss Libby."

"Tanner, could Beanie pick up Erica to save time? I overheard you tell her to meet you at Constance's."

"I'm on it.

"Beanie, could you get sick soon? Have that spell. I need you to pick up Erica from Constance's and take her to Memorial Hospital. It appears that Anne's up... Yes, that is exciting. Hopefully, she'll be completely coherent. I know she's got a lot to tell us and is a big key to this whole story... Thanks, Beanie. As always, I'll talk to you later... And once again, no, Beanie, you will not be left out."

"Irene, help is on the way. I'm sending Libby, Erica, and Emily to the hospital to talk to Anne. You don't have to worry about any of that. Travis is handling the situation with Jacob. He won't be able to go home today. Don't know what Travis will work out, but it'll be good. Irene, this whole thing is coming together. I want you to know how much I appreciate you and Jamison and all your help... Yes, I'll give the undercover gals the information... Really? You'll have to fill me in on what you found out. Thanks, Irene... I'll be back to you when I get some of this set in motion. We're all going to Jacob's tomorrow night for some kind of big celebration... Yes, you'll get to be there. That is, if you want to be there... Yeah, I knew you would. It could be very dangerous, though... I know, Irene. It won't be the first time, but thanks... Okay, I'll talk to you later."

Tanner calls Melinda in the psyche ward. "Melinda, it's okay. I'm sending some people to you... Okay, I'll give them the code... Ask them individually to recite it. They're coming to see Jan. Thanks.

"Okay, the code word is moonlight. Each of you needs to know it. Say it individually to Melinda, and she'll let you in. She knows you're coming to see Jan. I'm going to head over to Constance's and talk to Bryan and find out what's going on with our friends at the jail.

"Constance, tell Bryan I'm coming over... Oh, Libby has already called about Erica?... Good. Constance, there are some things I need to share, so have your notebook out and be ready when I get there. I need your help... I'm sorry I sound so bossy. Let me back up. Would it be okay if I come over?... Thanks, you're such a sweetie. I'm going to have Travis come over, too, if I can. I have him already working on a project... Yes, it's a busy day already, and you are going to be a big part of it... See you soon." *What a gift Constance is. Chief, you were right.*

On the way to Constance's house, Tanner realizes he's left Beanie off Melinda's list. "Hey, Melinda, there'll be a fourth person. You know her, Beanie... Let her in, too... Thanks always... What do you mean Carlton came up there? You didn't let him know anything, did you?... Good, don't. I'll explain later. Thanks."

Oh, good, Bryan's already here. Tanner's thoughts start to run to the Chief. *Chief, I'm struggling here. I feel almost panicked. There's a time clock ticking. What would you tell me to do? Lord, give me some wisdom. All this seems so crazy.*

Tanner is snapped out of his thoughts by Constance tapping on the hood of the car. "Gosh Constance, you startled me."

"You were somewhere else. Breakfast and coffee are hot now! Come in, let's eat. I bet you haven't had anything this morning, and it might be doubtful if you had anything last night. Bryan's already showered and ready to eat. Erica's gone to the hospital with Beanie. We have work to do now, don't we?"

"Constance, you're momming me, aren't you?"

"Sure am. Aaron always told me to keep you in my prayers. I'm attached to the heart with you. So glad you're back in my life. It's wondrous to feel needed again."

"Hey, Sir, you look horrible and worried."

"Thanks, Bryan."

"Maybe I can put a smile on your face. Can I say grace? I'm starving."

What a change listening to Bryan pray. What a change time can make. Coffee, aah, sweet coffee. "I might perk up, Bryan.

"Constance, you're every young man's dream."

As the food has been downed and the coffee has been swallowed, Bryan gets into what he learned from the lockup friends.

"Please take notes, Constance."

"Tanner, Sir, I can't put everything together, so I'll just tell you that all roads lead to Carlton."

"Why or how did Carlton get involved in this, Bryan?"

"Well, Sir, I found out that Carlton got involved with some group in Louisiana. He thinks he has a calling of some kind, that he has some sort of elevated status in spreading this weird gospel. King heard him talking to some big, black guy about it. The big guy had an accent and seemed to know all about Carlton. King had never seen that man before. King had started paying attention because he had come to find his little sister. He's not under the control of Carlton and doesn't have a tattoo. He also doesn't have a phone from Carlton. He blended into the group and whatever they were doing. I think he's our best source because he's been playing a part to get in on the inside. When they are all drinking or doing dope, he pretends. He's pretty freaked out.

"The house that belongs to some professor is the place that's the center of all this activity. It's some kind of research project. There's a huge rose garden and rows and mounds with pipes sticking out of the ground. He thinks the pipes are connected to a ventilation system. He overheard the big man telling one of them, what he calls diggers, that part of the project had failed, so they needed to eliminate that air pipe. King couldn't see who he was talking to. No one was there, so he assumed he was using a bluetooth. He heard the name Roscoe. None of the others had ever seen Roscoe, but apparently, he takes care of the research project for the Professor. King has never seen the Professor. The other guys said he moves around like a zombie and has a weird, raspy voice. He gives them all the creeps. Coming from them, that's bizarre. Pretty creepy bunch themselves. They are always given shovels and are digging up stuff. They never remember what, though. They're always covered with dirt when they wake up the next day. The Professor talks about new recruits.

"Something is going to happen tomorrow night. It starts at 9:00. The Professor hasn't been around for a few days. The big man has been running the project. King says there's a large shed, but no one is ever allowed in it. The others said they were told that the contents were very valuable and anyone was caught near it would be punished severely. In fact, they said the research plot could end up being their permanent residence. King thinks his sister is on that property somewhere.

"One of the guys gave me this. He said it was blown off one of the plant stakes. He picked it up and stuck it in his pocket. There had been a big wind, and it blew it away from the mounds."

"Bryan, this has a girl's name on it and the same mark as your tattoo. Who is this?" *Ding, ding, ding.* "What if the girl is on one of Stuart's lists as an attendee at the seminars?"

"Sir, that's exactly what I thought. What if King is right? What if the pipes are part of a ventilation system? What if there are people down there? I didn't tell King or the others what I was thinking. There's one more thing I learned. All the guys in lockup are freaked out. They're all in for finding out what's been happening to them. Carlton will need to look over his shoulder for the rest of his life, and I mean every minute. Sir, it was something special to find myself praying with all of them. They were like sponges, and I told them all about saving grace and protection from evil."

"Bryan, you and Erica were like vacuum cleaners sucking up all this knowledge from them. As I'm listening to you, it looks like you'll get some new recruits for yourself, only recruits for good. These guys are going to be valuable.

"Constance, what do you think? Did you get the high points of what went down?"

"I think you need to get the truth from that treacherous coward, Carlton. What a disgrace to the force and human decency. Tanner, you need to not get in a frenzy. I know there's a time clock ticking, but God knows that too. So, calm down. I know Aaron would tell you that."

"Constance, you and the Chief were really like one person. You're right. That's what he would've said." *Well, Lord, once again, you answered my prayer.* "Constance, thanks for being like my mom.

"Bryan, well done. I'm going to call Travis. We need to visit with Carlton."

Tanner rings Travis. "Hey, did you figure out how to block Jacob from going home today?... Oh, you got it set up. Thank goodness... Oh, a big water break, and the water's shut off. Good job, buddy! ... I've got another task. Would you round up Carlton and tell him we need him to I.D. someone from down in lockup? Have him ride with you. I'll meet you there.

"See, Constance, I'm a good listener. You're a wise woman."

"I want to go down there with you. I promise I won't get in your way, please."

"Okay, but you have to stay in the office in the back."

"I'll be ready in ten minutes."

"Sir, we can't take her. It's dangerous."

"Bryan, I know, but I can't leave her home alone. She'd be too depressed and worried. There's something about Constance you don't know. She used to do undercover and acted as an informant."

"Are you kidding? She seems like such a sweet and loving old lady."

"Bryan, she is, but she's a lot more."

"Here, I'm ready." With that statement, Constance picks up Aaron's picture, kisses it, and puts it in her bag. She looks at Tanner, "Oh, the Chief is going too."

"Bryan, you and Constance can drive her car."

"It will be a privilege. Miss Constance, your favorite cat will drive you there."

33

IT'S A GREAT DAY

"Beth, you have some friends here that you haven't seen in a while. They are so glad you're up and around and that you're recovering."

"How did I end up here? Where am I? Why does everyone call me Beth? My name is Anne. You seem so familiar, but I don't remember your name."

"I'm Jan, and your friend Erica will explain everything."

"Erica's here? Oh, my gosh, Erica!"

"You have others here, too. Can they all come in?"

"Yes, absolutely! Erica!"

"Let me call the nurse to let them in." Jan presses the call button. "Okay, Melinda, everybody can come in."

"Erica, help me. I don't know where I am. Everyone keeps calling me Beth."

"I missed you, you're back."

"Back from where? Why is everyone crying?"

"It's joy, we were all so worried. You were very ill. Let me introduce you to Libby, Emily, and Beanie. They're all true friends."

"It's so nice to meet you. You all look familiar, but I can't think where I would've seen you."

"Boy, do I have a lot to tell you."

"Erica, I'm really confused."

"You are at Memorial Hospital in a special ward. Some very bad people had drugged you." As Erica sits on the bed and hugs Anne, she explains that for her protection, they gave her the name Beth Adams.

"Oh, it's like we're undercover, and I'm going by the name Beth."

Beanie begins to take notes.

Libby steps into the hallway, and talks to Jan. "Jan, Travis is making it impossible for Jacob to go home today. Why is Jacob so insistent?"

"He says he keeps hearing a voice in his head talking to him and telling him he needs to get home. He said it sounded like Roscoe. He's almost frantic. He says it has something to do with the big event at his house tomorrow."

"Oh, I'm sure that evil is hammering Jacob. Tanner is working on some of the details, and we'll know by tonight. Dee Dee and Madelyn have had dreams that parallel each other. We believe that all this has a direct link to Dee Dee. When Joe saw the pictures of Dee Dee's parents, he knew them."

"What? Okay, back up and fill me in. Is Dee Dee in danger?"

"Jan, calm down. Let's go to the solarium because this will take a while. Would it be okay if we get Irene and Jamison to meet us? Let's call them. They also need to know this...

"Irene, this is Libby. Are you at the hospital?... Well, can you and Jamison be here and meet us in the solarium? Jan and I are here... Yes, on the special level. Erica, Emily, and Beanie are with Anne. She recognized Erica right off the bat... Yes, it's a miracle... Okay, come as soon as you can... Thanks.

"Jan, they'll be here in about thirty minutes. I wonder if Melinda could get us all something to eat. Let's mosey to the nurse's station and find out."

"Melinda? Could you get us some food from the cafeteria ASAP? Breakfast for seven, coffee, juice, and the whole works. It's a celebration. I'll pay for it."

"Jan, you don't have to pay for it. Tanner already put a card on file with me if the team needed anything."

"It will be up in about twenty minutes. Does that sound okay? I'll get some omelets, all the good stuff, and yes, lots of coffee."

"Great! I'll tell the others."

Peeking into the room, Jan informs the team that food is on the way. "Looks like it's all going good in there. Melinda had a nurse give Jacob a sedative, so he's sleeping. Libby, it's so good to see you. I feel like I've been left out, caged up, but Tanner needed me to stay here and keep a lid on Jacob and Anne. I've learned a few things too."

"Really, Jan? Jacob told you something?"

"Yes, and Anne did, too."

"Jan, you still look pale."

"It's okay. No energy, though, and I'm anxious to get out of here, but I'm okay. I spend a lot of time in the solarium because you can actually see outside. It keeps me from going crazy. You were talking to me about dreams. I had a dream about Marty. At the end of it, she tells me, 'We're coming, Jan. Don't worry about Dee Dee.'"

"Really? Isn't she one of the women down in Meadow Brook? I wonder what that dream means."

"Travis, did you find Carlton?... We're already here... Okay, go to his apartment and take Brett with you. Brett knows where Carlton hangs out... We'll wait for you... Find him. Travis, be careful... Oh, and Emily?... Okay, so she's at the hospital with Libby and Beanie and Jan. It seems like there's been a breakthrough with Beth." *Where is that slimeball Carlton? Lord, help me. Help us.*

"Constance, here's my phone. If anyone calls, answer and write the information down. Bryan and I are going to have a chat with the lockup friends. Promise you won't leave this office. The Chief would want me to take good care of his girl."

"Yes, Tanner, I will not leave. I promise."

"Andrew, how are you?"

"Good, Sir. I admit I'm better than the last time I saw you. I've had a change of heart and mind, and I'm getting my thinking back."

King pipes up and says, "We're all in but scared to death. It's like everyone is waking up after a long sleep."

"Sir, what has Carlton done to them?"

"I don't know Bryan, but we're about to find out, and if he doesn't spill it, I'm going to let him visit with all of you guys. So, do you like that idea?" Cheers and clapping. "Now, tell me one by one what you know about all this stuff."

"Beanie, this is Constance... Yes, I'm in charge of Tanner's phone. He's with Bryan and those street kids in lockup... Really? She knew Erica?... That makes me want to cry. Erica has been so frantically worried. Tanner told us about the big breakthrough revelations in the case... I know, me too. Is Miss Summers okay? This has been such a horrible time for her."

"Mr. Kaplan keeps calling."

"Are you talking about Al, the bookstore owner that we hunted down?"

"Yes, I know him. He was very good friends with Aaron. Give me his number. I'll find out what he wants. Al always called me his best reader. I loved his store. He's a brilliant and kind person and very funny too. Great sense of humor... I didn't tell you all this before because it seemed irrelevant. It will be pleasant to speak with him. He has a nose for news, though, so I'll have to keep it casual. Anything else I can do?... Wait, I can't follow all of this. Tunnels and whatever else you're talking about. You'll have to explain later... I'll have Tanner call you."

What's Next?

"Desmond, who was that?... What do you mean we have to fill containers with water?... They have to shut the water down today?... First, stupid power company, now stupid water company. Stupid, stupid people."

"Roscoe, don't start throwing a fit. That always makes a mess. The last time you caused such a stir, you blew the plant stakes down."

Oh, so I'm sensitive and upset, perfect Desmond. "Well, when will they have it fixed?"

"Tomorrow, at least by 5:00."

"By five? That means Jacob won't be here today. I had big plans for him. I've been calling him, and no one answers. He must be sleeping. Desmond, you know I'm ready, but Jacob is handling what he thinks is the catering. I can't wait until he sees the decorations. It will be something like he's never seen before. Is the Boss bringing some of my old acquaintances?"

"Yes, his private entourage is coming."

"Boy, will my street recruits be surprised! You know, I firmly believe in cleaning up the streets. I call it doing my civic duty."

"Good to see you can still tell a joke. We're going to have a bloody good time, as the English say."

"Desmond, that's hilarious. A bloody good time indeed."

"Oh, I almost forgot. Are you working on that special delivery package? That is the crown jewel of the celebration. It's been a long time coming."

"Yep, I think I'm going to get that punk Bryan to pick it up. I'll call him tomorrow."

"Don't disappoint the Boss, Roscoe. You know what that could mean for both of us."

"I know, don't even mention it. The very thought of it makes me quiver. Someone's calling. It's that broad, Irene. She's such a piece of work."

"Roscoe, answer the phone and see what she wants."

"No, she can leave a message."

"Hey, Roscoe, it's Irene. Jacob wanted me to call. He's been having additional tests run, and it required sedation. He'll be home tomorrow. He wanted me to tell you what time the caterers will be there. He has them coming about 6:00. I wanted you to know so you don't worry. I heard on the radio there's a big shut-down on the water, so I guess the cleaners can't come until it's back on. Did the county inform you? Great timing. It never fails, especially when someone has a big event happening. Call me if you need anything. Here's my number."

"Yeah, I need something. I need you to shut up permanently!" Roscoe smiles at the thought. *Catering will be the last of your worries.*

As Desmond walks away, Roscoe does one little stomp and a twirl in defiance. *Wonder what could be next.*

❧

"Jan, what are we going to do? We can't get a caterer on such short notice."

"Irene, Emily had a lady give her a card the other day. Some lady with a Russian accent. Emily liked the woman. She seemed so nice. I think she has her card. Let me get it..."

"Emily, do you have the card the woman gave you about catering? Thanks, don't ask any questions."

"Yeah, here it is. Fill me in later."

"Wow, look girls, Heavenly Planners and Caterers, even short notice. I'm calling her.

"Hello, this is Irene Carpenter. I need your help. We have a celebration tomorrow evening... I'm not sure about the time, but we are desperate... Yes, it's an evening event and a big deal for at least fifty people. We need everything— tables, set-ups, drinks, and food... Thank goodness you're free. I'll be at the University lab. Could you come meet me around noon?... Great! I'll take care of the deposits or whatever we need to do... See you then.

"Girls, she has nothing booked. She has a full staff available. She said it will be heavenly, and for some crazy reason, I think it will be. I really liked her voice. We don't have much choice anyway, considering it's such short notice.

"Thanks, Jan, for taking care of Jacob. I wish you could have known Rose. You would've been good friends. Let me give you a big hug. Sorry, Jamison got called away, but I'll give him all the details."

"Libby, you take care of Tanner. He's special, too. I'm so glad he has you. I'll let you know about my meeting with our Heavenly Caterer. Got to scoot. If you need me, call. I'll be at the lab."

"Wow, Jan. Irene is really something. No wonder Tanner calls her Perfect Woman. She is, inside and out."

"I can't tell you, Libby, how much she and Jamison mean to me. I wish I had known them a long time ago. Jamison is a great doctor. I have total confidence in him. I know you've got a lot to do, so let's see what's happening with Anne."

❋

"Jan? I remember you. You stayed with me when I first came here. I remember feeling so much less afraid. Some things are still cloudy, but some memories have started to come back. I'm really worried about Alyssa. It was awful. You aren't going to leave me, are you?"

"Nope, you're stuck with me. Anne, there's also another patient who is my assignment.

"Have you girls filled her in on everything?"

"Yes, no more secrets, but only the parts that are pertinent to her. We're trying to let Anne get her full memory back."

"Erica, you look like a new person."

"Yes, and I know you had a lot to do with that. You've been a comfort and a protector to Anne. Oops, we're still calling her Beth per Tanner's orders."

"Well, I suppose we could call her Beth Anne."

"Jan, you are too funny." Even Anne laughs.

"Erica, I've got to go. Do you want to stay or go? I talked to Constance, and she's with Tanner and Bryan. I'm going down to the lockup."

"Beanie, I'm going with you.

"Anne, God bless you. He is watching over all of us today. Like always, it will be a great day."

"Where's Joe?"

"Lib, Melinda found him an open bed. He was exhausted. He's got to take us home. Will you get him up?"

"Emily, maybe we should let him sleep and get an Uber."

"Libby, Tanner would be furious, and so would Joe. I don't want a lecture from Travis, either. I've got a design meeting at 2:00. Will you go with me? It's a big deal. Pretty lucrative."

"If there's a financial blessing, I'm all in. Speaking of Tanner, he's calling me.

"Hi Tanner... Yes, everything is good here. Emily has a design meeting. Joe will take us... Okay, I'll tell Emily... Don't worry about Dee Dee. Ben is with her."

"Tell me what, Libby?"

"Emily, Travis, and Brett are going to meet Tanner at lockup. He's finally found Carlton. Maybe that creep is getting what he deserves. Let's wake up Joe and get ready for your big deal."

"Hi, ladies. Erica, how did everything go at the hospital?"

"Lieutenant, it was wonderful. I've got my old friend Anne back. She's really herself again."

"That's great. Constance and Erica, you girls will stay here in the office out of sight. Fill each other in and write down any insights you get. You have my phone, so use it if you need it."

"Tanner, we will be very discreet. You get to the truth."

Erica is clinging to Bryan's arm. "Is he going to stay with us?"

"Sir, I should be mixed in with the guys. It's got to appear that I'm in trouble too. No red flags for Carlton."

"Oh, my favorite stray cat, you're right. I don't know how this is going to play out. Any other brilliant insights?"

"Well, Sir, actually, I agree with Constance. I keep getting the word, truth."

"That would be refreshing. Do you think Carlton is capable of telling the truth?"

"Yeah, I think so if you rattle his cage. I know he wouldn't want to be in lockup with all of us."

"Good point, Bryan.

"Beanie, I need your help. Are you game?"

"Sir, you know I'm always in. I'm always up for a good time. I love fishing. Remember, I'm your best secretary and fishing partner."

"Beanie, you're my only secretary, irreplaceable. You helped me catch all kinds of things. Let's set the stage. When Travis and Brett arrive with Carlton, I want you to bring them to the viewing room. That will throw Carlton off and make him nervous. He'll wonder why you're here. Beanie, I'll start and then turn it over to you. Follow my lead."

"You bet, Sir. I want you to know that Constance and I have a little surprise for you. Two bodies and one brain. Let's reel that creepy, little, prideful fish in."

"Oh, yeah, that's my girl. The stage is all set." *It might turn out that I like day fishing as much as I like night fishing.*

As Travis and Brett escort Carlton around the corner, Beanie steps out of the office. Carlton is thrown off by her sudden appearance.

"Hi guys, we'll be using the viewing room today. Lieutenant Tanner is waiting for us."

"I thought I was here to I.D. someone."

"Well, you are. That's why we're heading to the viewing room." Beanie cheerfully smiles. "Well, the Lieutenant needs to go over some important information. Call it a briefing so we're all on the same page."

❧

"Carlton, how nice you could join us. Apparently, the guys had quite a time locating you. Have a seat."

"Lieutenant Tanner, I—"

"Stop, Carlton. I'm glad you're here now.

"Travis and Brett, would you get the line-up ready?"

"Sure thing, Lieutenant."

"Thanks, guys.

"Beanie, would you get your notebook?

"Okay, Carlton, I sent the guys out to keep this private."

"I'm working on this case, so I couldn't come to the office today."

"The bean counters have found several discrepancies in your timesheets and call logs. We want to keep this under wraps. It doesn't look good if one of my officers is not on the up and up."

"Lieutenant Tanner, I apologize. Sometimes I get lazy, don't fill in my schedule, and then I get confused and forget and mix up days."

"Well, being slack and confused is one thing. Altering for some other reason might have some consequences.

"Beanie, you have a list. Why don't you ask Carlton to clarify?"

"Yes, Sir.

"Carlton, let's start from the most recent. Did you turn in the logs for last night? I couldn't find them, and I checked. You were working last night. I know you're off today, but those should've been turned in before you left."

"Well, I was cruising, shaking doors, checking on things, nothing happened. No big deal. Everything was quiet. I'll fill them in as soon as I get out of here."

"So, you didn't go anywhere outside your normal route?"

"No, why?"

"Well, you were seen by some officers driving a white van into the Wilderness Walk area. In fact, you were at a residence there. Weren't you? You had other passengers, too."

"That's a lie! Who said that?"

Tanner's thinking, *you're looking at one of them. Ugh, I can't believe this liar is in the department. No ethics and no morals.*

"Carlton, I have the records."

Carlton starts to argue with Beanie. He's getting abrasive and defiant.

"Hey Carlton, we're all having a great day, so don't ruin it. You'll be given an opportunity to clarify all this, but unfortunately, your records have been under scrutiny for some time. The errors have become glaring. What are you up to? I'm trying to keep this quiet and private, but that depends on you. Hopefully, you don't display that temper anymore. It could change the whole tenor of our visit here. Let's put that aside. I need you to I.D. some folks."

34

RISKY BUSINESS

Tanner uses the intercom to the line-up room. "Brett and Travis, are you ready?"

As the light goes on, they have five of the guys from lockup. In the middle is Bryan. "Okay, do you recognize anyone?"

"No, Sir. Pretty much all those street kids look the same."

"Next group, guys.

"Anybody here?"

"Same thing. They all look the same."

Travis and Brett go through the entire group. Carlton plays dumb.

"Sir, there's one more." With that, Beanie presses the intercom and says, "Travis, would you bring the last one in?" Beanie smiles.

There on the other side of the glass is Leslie Cartwright. "Do you recognize this one?... Carlton, do you recognize this one?"

Carlton's mumbling. "Where in the world..." Tanner can tell by Carlton's reddening face that he's off guard.

That's interesting. "Carlton, are you okay? Sit back down. I'm guessing by your reaction that you did recognize her." *Look, he's sucking air, starting to turn completely white. His little knuckles are white. Temper, temper. Oh, poor little Carlton. Beanie, your eyes are sparkling. Oh, Beanie, what a surprise this was.*

"I, I, I, hey, it's impossible."

"Yes, do you know her?"

"It's the girl that was murdered. What's going on?"

"Nice cover, Carlton, but you know who she is. Don't you? Looks like you might need a nurse. Do I need to get one?"

"No, Sir."

"It's truth time, Carlton. Who is she?"

"I want an attorney."

"Carlton, that's no problem, but you better rethink everything because you're not under arrest. That's why I wanted to keep this private, so the powers that be, specifically the ones you're involved with, don't find out what a loser you are. By the way, you're free to go as soon as Travis has all the guys released. We'll make sure and put the word out so it looks like you snitched them out. Oh, and Brett will be making some inquiries at that house you were at last night. Carlton, we'll get back to you over the log sheets and time.

"Beanie, would you meet with the internal people today?

"Carlton, you'll have to wait until we get the group released. By the way, you'll be working overtime at the station. Art called, and we're short-handed. You won't be off duty until about 10:00 tomorrow night. I decided to give you a chance to clean up your time and log sheets. I would hate to lose an officer." *Gag, gag. Please, Lord, make him bite on it. I hope he fears whatever's out there more than he does us.*

"Lieutenant, I'm off today and tomorrow. I have a previous commitment."

"Well, so you're telling me that you refuse to sacrifice a little time to save your badge?"

"You don't understand. I can't blow that off. That commitment is something big. I've been working undercover on it for a long time."

What a dope. So prideful. He must think I'm dumber than a post. "Well, I'm you're superior, so you're free to tell me what's going on.

"Beanie, get all this down for the internal review. Beanie, will you call Garrett, the D.A., and ask his advice here? What should we do with our uncompliant friend?"

"Sure thing, Sir." Beanie winks at Tanner as she leaves the room.

"Carlton, now that the lady's gone, I'm going to share a big secret with you. We know a lot about the special little project of yours. Therefore, we're going to let you go down in flames if you don't cooperate. Don't even think about calling an attorney because we're not pressing charges. We're going to let this play out however you want. You have options, but they don't look good. Kind of spooky, isn't it? Somebody you thought was dead standing on the other side of the glass. All eyes will be on you. We're going to make sure you're released, as all those other guys are coming out of the building. Remember, some people don't play by the rules. I want you to sit there for a few minutes and consider your options. Give me your phone because it belongs to the department, and we don't want anything to interrupt your thoughts. We'll let you know what the D.A. says."

Tanner exits and locks the door from the outside. He leaves the cameras on so he can enjoy watching Carlton panic.

"Leslie, what a surprise! I didn't know you were making your debut." Tanner hugs her.

"Tanner, I would've loved to have seen Carlton's face when he saw me.

"Thanks, Beanie, for asking me to join the lockup group and participate. I've been praying for an opportunity to really help Dee Dee. I still feel horrible about how Adlin died. She died because she looked like me. Maybe helping will relieve some of the guilt. Art made me feel so safe and told me he wouldn't leave me."

Constance and Beanie are brilliant. They are quite the team. "Art, I'm so glad to have you on the force. The Chief always said you could keep the lid on, and he was right."

"Listen, there isn't anything I wouldn't do for these two ladies and, of course, for you, Lieutenant."

"It's okay, Art. They are special, and we both know it. Do you want to stay?"

"Well, Lieutenant, I need to hold the station down, but I think Leslie wants to stay with the girls. Is that okay with you?"

"Sure thing.

"Leslie, you're officially one of the bunch now. They're in the office. Erica can fill you in about Anne."

"Thanks, Tanner. If Libby didn't love you so much, I'd kiss you."

Look at Art. He's so tickled. He's such a good man. Beanie's right. I need to do some kind of acknowledgment for him. Tick, tick, tick.

Everyone's gathered in the office watching Carlton. "I'll give Carlton about another hour. Travis, you and Brett tell the guys that lunch is coming. Stay calm. Somebody order food for that bunch. It's on me. Here's my card."

"Sir, I did that when I went out to call Garrett. We have food coming. It could be a long day, and everybody's in for the haul. You may need to call Ben. He's still at the apartment. I think you need to check on them; just a suggestion."

"Ben, are Dee Dee and the rest okay? I knew you could keep Stuart in line... Tell them we're working on Carlton and to pray for truth... Thanks, Ben... Yep, we'll have new insights and a video for everyone's enjoyment. Tell them we're getting very close to Alyssa.

"Beanie, it looks like our day fishing expedition is going to be good. Maybe better than night fishing."

"Sir, look at him pacing around talking to himself. He doesn't look well."

"What did Garrett say?"

"He said we have enough to hold Carlton and charge him. When I told him about missing people, he said Carlton could be labeled a suspect, and you could charge him for that, too."

"Wonderful, let's see if we can finish reeling him in, but let's eat first." *Too bad we don't have any popcorn for the show.*

❋

"Guys, don't get too restless... Oh, here it comes. I told you the Lieutenant would take care of us. He had some details he was working out.

"Brett, tell the Lieutenant that everything is good here. We're all on the same side."

"Bryan, you sure you want to stay in here?"

"Yep, this is my village, and we've got lots of bonding to do. Tell Erica I'll talk to her later."

"Lieutenant, Bryan is staying with the guys.

"Erica, he said to tell you he'll see you later.

"Sir, can I do anything else?"

"Yes, come in, Brett, and meet the group while we eat. You're part of the family now. No escape. It's a trap, but a good one.

"Everyone, this is Brett. He's officially one of us now, and I'm proud of him. He was the one in the green car behind the bushes at Adlin's funeral." The whole group gasps and then claps.

Carlton knows the consequences on both sides, but one side doesn't play fair. Considering how discipline is administered by his keepers, he's leaning towards cooperating with Tanner. It's risky business either way.

Tanner's decency won't let him do certain things. Maybe I can fool him into thinking I'm cooperating and still implement the plan. I've got to be at Wilderness tomorrow night. There's no running from this. There's no boundary. A tiny thought pops into his brain. Maybe it's truth seeping in. *What if I'm not in such high status as I think, and Desmond has plans for me, too? What if?* Shaking off the thoughts, Carlton begins to pace again.

The whole group is watching Carlton unravel.

"Do you think he's stewed enough yet?"

"Sir, I think when he sits down and puts his head in his hands, he'll be ready to surrender."

"Sir, I agree with Brett." All the other heads are nodding in agreement with Travis.

"Look, Tanner, he's sitting at the table. Oops, there goes the head in the hands. He looks physically ill."

"Boy, he does, Travis. Looks like your sidekick is right.

"Brett, any other suggestions? This is risky. I'll probably only get one chance of getting cooperation from Carlton, so pray.

"Well, have you made a decision? I guess we're playing truth or consequences. I hope you choose truth. I'm turning on the recorder."

"Lieutenant, wait! Can we make a deal first?"

"No, but if you choose to help, I'll do my best to protect you and your life. You'll be in big trouble, but it won't be from the department."

"God, they'll kill me."

Tanner clicks on the recorder.

"Who will kill you?"

"Well, there are humans, and there are others that are not in bodies."

"Are you talking about spirits, demons? Things from the darkness?"

Carlton's expression morphed into shock.

"Don't look surprised. Christians aren't simpletons. I know there are entities that exist. Carlton, why don't you tell me how you got involved in this? Go back to the beginning."

As Carlton begins to relate the events of his childhood and the fear that drove him to dedicate himself to evil, Tanner is blown away to think what seems like a horror story is real. *I didn't think it was possible for me to have compassion for him, but I do. He's pathetic, like a scared little kid. Brought into Voodoo.*

"So, you see, Lieutenant, I was commanded to work on this project with the Professor and Desmond."

"Who commanded you?"

"Sir, I'm not going to tell you the real name, but he goes by Roscoe here."

Ding, ding, ding.

"He was assigned to me and put in charge of me many years ago. He'll kill me if I don't obey."

"Carlton, what have they done to you? Can you stand up to it?"

"Well, he can't be everywhere at all times. So, I've been kind of free because he's usually at the plant plot. Desmond's been called here to be able to travel around. He has many powers and I'm terrified of him. His rank is higher than mine. I hate him."

"Carlton, if these entities are so powerful, how come they use humans?"

"Because they don't have authority in the earth. They have to link to a person. I guess man was given dominion. You always freaked me out, Lieutenant, because of the great spirit you have. I don't know how I ended up in this place where so many people move on the other side of the spiritual."

"Why are you here?"

"To spread and teach the gospel and ancient techniques. To introduce people to power."

"Carlton, you know Jesus is the greatest... Why did you cringe when I said His name?"

"Because He'll punish me."

"Carlton, that's not true. Maybe He sent you here to be released from bondage. He came to set the captives free, to save us from evil and ourselves and the crazy things we do."

"But Lieutenant, this is treason for me to even listen to this."

"Tell you what, I'm going to let you visit with someone. Listen, you said someone who I love freaked you out. Think about this. He must be greater than what you're serving. He can save you from this. He knows everything. So, in case you try to pretend or trick me, many people are praying. Can the entities read your mind?"

"No, but they can sense things and spot believers. Oh, my gosh, I realize I don't feel like there's any link or connection here. I'm always aware that something is watching. I don't feel that presence here. What's going on?"

"Prayer, Carlton, prayer. There's a whole group of people praying. They've covered this whole building and everyone in it. That includes you. If you want true power and freedom so you can have a life, you'll have to surrender. As soon as you're outside, you'll be subject to all that again. Why don't you tell me what the plan is and what you're involved in?"

Carlton begins to lay out the orders he's been given, the timeline, and what's supposed to happen on Friday. "I don't know everything that will go on, but it will be a full moon ritual, and there will be gruesome atonements. Sacrifices. We call them offerings."

"Maybe you want to rephrase that into "they," not we. Decide what you're going to do."

"I surrender. Tell me what I need to do."

"I'm going to send someone to help you with that."

Tanner presses the intercom. "Brett, bring Bryan to the viewing room, please."

"Carlton, you know Bryan. He'll be helping you do the right thing. Be wise and listen up.

"Bryan, you're on."

"Sir, do you think I'm qualified to do this?"

"Yep, I think you're called to share the truth with Carlton. He's never heard it before.

"Oh, and Carlton, I'll stand by Bryan's recommendation as to whether we help you or not. Life is full of decisions, and some of them are risky business."

35
REALITY CHECK

"Tanner, that was unbelievable! It was like listening to the script of a horror movie. Unreal. What are we going to do?"

"Keep praying. Constance, I need my phone. I want to check on Libby.

"Travis, you need to call Emily. I can see the worry on your face. We're going for a little drive. Would everyone else stay here and keep covering us all and the office and the building with prayer?

"Brett, you're in charge of the building.

"Travis, why did the entire staff leave?"

"I forgot to tell you. Jack sent everyone home. He's a pretty instinctive guy. He said you'd need privacy. He has his people on standby. They'll come back in when we call."

"Call Jack and tell him I'm almost done."

"Lieutenant, stop by the lab and see if they have any results."

Libby doesn't answer. Neither does Emily.

"Joe, the girls aren't answering. Are you with them?"

"Yes, they're getting ready to do Emily's presentation. They're fine. Don't worry, I won't leave them for a minute. I've got "the good book" with me.

Emily had one in her bag, so I'm reading. Travis should be honored to have her on his arm. She's a complete pure heart. It makes me miss Peachie. Tanner, I told them what we're doing. The group in Meadow Brook are all praying. After you brief us, they also want to hear the whole thing."

"Joe, call Peaches and tell her it went really well. We got a lot of information. There's been an unexpected turn of events with Carlton. Tell them to pray for him... Joe, I'm not kidding. I'll fill you in, but boy, the truth showed up today on our behalf. He showed up big-time. Joe, Bryan is talking with Carlton right now. You pray too... Call me when you're headed back to Kaplan's... All I can say is I'm always blown away when He shows up. He's always faithful... Can't wait to fill you in. Hopefully, we'll have good news about Carlton. He's got some decisions to make."

Tanner starts working through his mental list and makes calls. "Art, how's it going?... You told him Carlton was on a call right now?... Boy, you have good instincts... Yeah, I know who he is. His name is Desmond... You told him you'd have Carlton call him later when he comes in?... Yeah, he is creepy and imposing, but he's met his match in you. You can be very imposing on the good side and not creepy. Art, I can't tell you everything, but it went well at lockup. Thanks for keeping the lid on and taking care of Leslie..."

Next. "Jan, Erica told me what a great job you did with Beth... Yes, it went well with Carlton. We'll be making a plan... Of course, you'll be involved. We'll need you to be with all of us. Don't cry, Jan, are you okay?... What did Jamison say?... Of course, you'll be with Dee Dee shortly. Tell you what. I'll pick you up for dinner this evening if Jamison gives you his permission. I owe you. You're still a great officer and a trustworthy friend... I'll get it cleared with Jamison... What about Irene? She's doing what?... Well, I'll stop by and see her. I'm headed to the police lab. Thanks for telling me." *Oh, my gosh. Are we planning to place others in danger?* Tanner takes a deep breath.

"Travis, drop me off at Irene's office. I need to be in a meeting with her."

"Yes, Sir. So, I'll head to the lab and see if those tests are back. I'll call you. Would it be okay if I head over to be with Joe and the girls?"

"Actually, I think that's a good idea, buddy.

Next. "Ben, tell your group we're almost ready to make a plan for tomorrow. It went well at lockup. Tell everyone there to pray... We're almost done, but we can't take any chances. Everybody needs to be covered. Would you put Stuart on?...

"Stuart, would you get your list of the seminars together?... Look, if you need anything from your place, we'll go and get it... Calm down, you're not on trial, but we'll need to see those lists, and by the way, it's been a great day... Don't go nutty on me. Let's keep it as a great day. I need you to tell Dee Dee and Grace and James we're getting close... Stuart spend some time praying instead of worrying. That's an order. Get those lists together. I need your help. Review them with Dee Dee. Tell her I might be bringing a special guest tonight... None of your business. It's a surprise. Got to scoot. I've got to be in a meeting. Tell Ben I'll call him later."

"Tanner, before you get out. Can I ask you what kind of a meeting you and Irene are having?"

"Well, buddy, it will sound bizarre, but she's meeting with the caterers for tomorrow night."

"Sir, those people could be in danger. We can't take that responsibility."

"I know, Travis. That's why I'm here. Jacob told Roscoe he was handling the catering, so we're in a pickle. Thank goodness Jan gave me a heads-up."

"Yeah, no kidding. I'll pray you have wisdom. This is not a good development. Maybe we could substitute the staff with our officers."

"Maybe I need you to check on those lab tests and see Emily. Irene and I will figure it out."

ૐ

"Hey, Perfect Woman."

"Tanner, I thought you were working. What are you doing here?... Oh, Jan told you? I didn't think you needed this on your plate, too."

"Irene, we probably could get some food from the store, and Travis suggested our officers as staff. Irene, I don't think this is a good idea."

"Well, when I saw her card, I thought maybe it was a sign. She'll be here in about thirty minutes. Fill me in between with what went on. Did you get anything from Carlton?"

Tanner begins to tell Irene about the interaction.

"You told him the truth? Why in the world would you do that? Can you trust him?"

"Listen! I'll give you all the highlights. You'll get to see the video tonight. We need to set up a meeting at Kaplan's."

Tanner's only about halfway through relating the events of the day when the receptionist rings Irene.

"Yes, send her up.

"Well, here we go, Tanner. Read the vibes. Lord, help us."

There's a tap on the door, and Irene opens it.

I wonder if Irene feels that slight soft rush of air and that fragrance. Whoo, that fragrance. Irene seems pleasantly surprised. Does she feel it, too? Who is this woman? What a feeling of peace.

"Let's sit down."

Irene is motioning us towards the table. Everything is in slow motion. She's introducing herself. *Snap out of it, Tanner.*

"Hi, I'm Irene. Thank you for coming on such short notice. This is Lieutenant Tanner from the Oak City Police."

"What an honor to meet you, Lieutenant Tanner. I'm Martina. Here are some of my cards, and here are some for you, Miss Irene. Let me get my notebook out."

Heavenly Planning and Catering? What a name for a business. Is this you, Lord? Good grief, Tanner, don't read too much into it. You know there are no coincidences. I definitely need a plan, though.

"You know, there are no coincidences. I believe that each person that needs our service is special. There's always a reason that we meet them."

Is she a mind reader? Oh, look at that sweater. The buttons on her sleeves are crosses. Well, Irene told me to read the vibes. "I'll just sit and listen, Irene. You make all the decisions." *Oh, my gosh, the caterer just winked at me and threw me a little smile. Did she know what I was going to say?*

"Miss Irene, I worked up a tentative menu. Would you like to look at it? We'll make any changes per your request."

"Martina, all these entrees are my favorites. It's perfect. A nice variety, and the drink offerings you presented are spectacular."

"I didn't put wine on the list, other than champagne, because you said it was a celebration."

"Martina, you also provide staff?" *This is where I come in.*

"I always insist that my staff be present. I don't just drop off the food and set it up. They're all fully trained. I have an army of helpers. They're quite capable of handling, let's say, situations. I can guarantee that everyone there will be safe."

For some reason, I believe her.

"I sense that you have concerns about that, Lieutenant, so I want to say again that everyone will be safe.

"Oh, by the way, we use real crystal and silver. Miss Irene, I can tell you have impeccable taste. It will be extremely classy. What do you have in mind for linens? I brought several samples and a unique rainbow sample."

"Martina, these do look like rainbows. What kind of material is this?"

"Oh, something I ran onto years ago. Specially made, hand-crafted, and designed. I'm so glad you like it."

"I think the rainbow will be perfect."

"I have others to choose from, though. I do love His promise of the rainbow. He always keeps His promises, and so do I. This is your event, so we'll go the way you want it to."

"Tanner, what do you think? Look, I love it all."

"Lieutenant Tanner, I want to assure you that it will be a heavenly experience. What time does the event begin?"

"Nine o'clock."

"Marvelous, so we'll bring some beautiful lighting. It's always a joy to shine light on things."

"Well, Tanner, what do you think?"

"I'm almost dazed. I think it's up to you, Irene."

"Martina, you have a deal. What kind of deposit do you require?"

"Write, I promise, by the end of the receipt and sign your name by the amount. You must also sign, Lieutenant Tanner. No deposit is necessary. I know where to find you. This will be staged perfectly, and we will have a part for all of us to play. Thank you for letting me be part of your team. I'll contact my staff. What time do you want us there? We'll need at least two hours to set up. Since this is a residence, we'll need the address and someone to let us in. So, 6:30, 7:00, or earlier? Whatever you decide. Once we set up, my staff does not leave. What address is it? I'd like to have a look at the property to see where to park our vans. I'll google it. Well, I so appreciate this opportunity. May I give you both a hug? I feel like I know you both, like old friends. My kind of people."

As Martina hugs Tanner, she whispers something to him.

✤

"Tanner, what did she whisper to you?"

"You saw that?"

"Of course I did. What did she say?

"She told me everything would be okay and that my plan would be approved. That I would know exactly what to do and that it would be more than I expect."

"Tanner, I think we've been sent help."

"So do I." *Heavenly Planning and Catering, indeed.* "Maybe you're right, Irene. Maybe this is a sign. The Lord has a sense of humor, doesn't he?"

"Hug me, DJ Tanner. I've been worried. I can't wait to tell Jamison."

"Irene, speaking of Jamison, I've got to see if he thinks it would be okay for Jan to come to dinner and see Dee Dee. I told Jan I would talk to him."

"Tanner, he's in surgery today, so I'll talk him into it. Plan on getting Jan out of there. She's about to go stir crazy."

"Okay, you handle Jamison, and I'll call Jan. I guess I should have asked our caterer to fix dinner for all of us tonight."

"We can all feed ourselves. Take care of Jan, and I'll take care of the rest of us. Hang on. Let me answer this.

"You forgot to ask us?... You have all this food?... Enough for twenty?... Oh, that's why you were free tomorrow night? They canceled... Of course, you can finish cooking... About 7:00 would be great... No, I'm not offended that you asked... We really do need food for tonight... We'll pick it up... Okay, if you want to deliver, I'll have to call you with the address... Thanks so much, Martina... No, that's not pushy. Why should that all go to waste? Thank you so much.

"Well, Tanner, did that take some things off your plate? Write down the address, and I'll call her later."

"Irene, we might consider using caterers in all of our cases. Wow!"

Travis is ringing in. "Yes, I'm ready to go... Sure, stay there until Emily's ready to leave. Well, why don't you ask Joe to pick me up? I've got a lot to tell him. I'll sit in the park at our favorite picnic table. He'll need good directions. What about the labs?... Great! I'll see them tonight.

"Irene, I'll see you tonight. Remember to call Jamison." *That was some kind of meeting. Martina. I need to get fresh air and my feet on the ground. I hope she's right that a plan will work out.*

"Love you, Tanner. See you later."

"Hey, Tanner, I didn't want to honk and draw attention. You were deep in thought."

"Joe, I was caught up in memories. Memories of the Chief, you know, my old boss, Constance's husband. Traveling back in time."

"I'll bet he was a wonderful mentor."

"He was a great man, too. I learned so much from him. The Chief taught me to always look for holes in evidence and interrogations. I think that's why I was so open with Ben. Right out of the shoot, he talked about holes."

"Tanner, this case was definitely full of holes. Sometimes, I felt like the Haiti case was one big hole. Don't you think it's strange that after all these years, the door on that big black hole might finally shut? I'm hoping all my mental loose ends get tied up."

"Joe, I never dealt with something from this dimension before. That thought never crossed my mind. I'll bet this case has been like a double whammy for you."

"Yeah, and the memory of those scenes in Haiti constantly replaying in the night. Those dreams and thoughts were gone for so long, but they're back. Tanner, we can't make any mistakes. Nothing even close to the Haiti experience can be allowed to happen here. There are parts that I will never tell anyone about."

"Joe, you know—"

"No, Tanner, not even you. It's too unholy to even speak about. Well, I'm the driver of the day. Where are we headed?"

"To lockup. I want to evaluate the situation with Carlton. Let's see how our infamous Mr. Prince is doing. Bryan's been working on him."

"You've got to lay out all the details to me on the way. Carlton has got to tell us what is going on. I'm adamant. We must have every detail worked out. We can't let anything slip out of place. By the way, Tanner, did you notice all the crows at the park? They were landing in the trees near you. I had a flash of the day we went to the Professor's house."

"No, I didn't notice them. I don't remember ever seeing crows at the park." *Wonder what that means.*

❧

"Hey, Jack. Do you remember Joe?"

"Sure do. Good to see you again."

"Tanner, Travis called and said you were almost done. I felt like I needed to show up before you left. I haven't called my people yet so you can take your time. I see my office is full. I recognize some old friends. Constance is a hoot. They were all being very tight-lipped, clammed up when I came in." Laughter. "Whenever you're done with whatever this is, I can't wait to hear the story."

"Jack, let's all go to your office. This is about the Summers case." *I don't ever remember seeing Jack startled.*

"That's one creepy case, Tanner. There's something really off about it. I know you were stymied."

"Good instincts, Jack. I think we've made progress. You and your people have been a big help.

"Joe, I'll have Constance and Beanie fill Jack in. We're going to need him. I just know it."

Jack assures Tanner, "Read me in. You know I always have your back.

"And Joe, Tanner's right. I do have fairly decent instincts, and I also have your back. I trusted you from the first time I met you."

Tanner knocks on the door to Jack's office. The group is startled and clicks the monitor and the audio off to the viewing room. "Turn it back on. Beanie and Constance, would you give Jack a synopsis of this? Explain to him about everyone that's involved. No secrets. Joe and I are going to visit with our street friends. How's Bryan doing?" Thumbs in the room go up.

"Well, young lady, you look a little different than you did last night."

"Jack, this is Erica and... Jack? Are you okay?"

"Yeah, but this one looks like—"

"I know. Leslie is almost a carbon copy of Adlin Summers."

Jack's mind is whirling.

"Anyway, I guess you've been assimilated into the family."

"Beanie, what a sweet thing to say. Do I get some kind of a certificate or something for that?" Everybody laughs. "Ladies, I'm all ears."

❧

"Gentlemen, I want to apologize for the delay. You have helped us so much, and I want to assure you that you'll be released soon."

Andrew is adamant. "Sir, we want answers. Are we going to be charged?"

"We may have a deal for all of you. It depends on what we find out from Carlton. Hey, guys, no more of that language. No one is going to kill him, at least not yet. Just kidding. He'll be in shortly. You can visit with him then."

"Joe, would you mind sitting in with Bryan and Carlton?... Good. I hereby deputize you, Joseph Landry.

"Guys, you're all witnesses that Joe is officially an officer now. You're the witnesses... Yeah, I know. That's a first for some of you, but I expect you to back me up."

Tanner returns to the office to watch and listen.

❧

"Lieutenant Tanner wants me to be an objective listener. Officer Prince,

I'm Joe. Brand new on the force. I have some experiences with your spiritual beliefs. Tanner filled me in."

"Joe, Carlton is going to help us. What we can't figure out is how he can get saved without the other side knowing. Carlton tells me they can spot believers."

Carlton is trembling. "Sir, I'm terrified. If you've had experiences, then you know what I'm facing if they find out."

Joe closes his eyes and nods in agreement. "I also know the Word says it's better to fall into the hands of the Lord than into the hands of men. He has authority even over the dark side. He can hide you from them knowing."

"He's right, Carlton! Roscoe didn't know about me when I talked to him on the phone, and I remembered every word he said. I know he didn't know I had changed. He has no power over me anymore."

"Let's do it! I have to ask, what is the Word you are talking about, Joe? I mean, Sir."

"Call me Joe, and He's the Word, but I was talking about His Word, the Bible. Promises."

"Help me, guys, I don't know what to say. I don't even know the ritual words."

"Carlton, it's not a ritual. It's a conversation with God. I'll help you. Repeat after me. Heavenly Father..."

Carlton begins to sob and pour out his heart with confession and repentance. All the heads in the office are bowed.

After several minutes, Carlton gets totally quiet and still.

Joe adds, "Amen... Carlton, are you still with us?"

"This voice spoke to me. He said to not be afraid. That he would cover me over and protect me. It's like those words are inside of me."

"Carlton, welcome to the family of God."

It's a big celebration in Jack's office. Tanner walks into the viewing room.

"Congratulations, Carlton! You made the best decision you've ever made. If I ask you to go with Bryan to the lockup, will you go? I'm going to stick you in there with those guys. You need to explain to them what's been going on. In fact, you have a lot of explaining to do."

"Sir, I'm going with him."

"Thanks, Bryan. I knew you would."

"Time is running out, Carlton. You need to ask for their forgiveness. Well, before you go, let me give you a hug and a handshake. It's the first day of your new life. He is faithful. It will be okay in there with the guys. Bryan's already worked on them."

"Lieutenant, I probably will screw it up."

Wow, no narcissistic pride. "What you just said tells me you won't. I'll get the key, and you guys can let yourselves in.

"Leslie, you know Carlton better than any of us. What do you think?"

"Tanner, it's unbelievable. I watched him change. I could feel the same feeling as when I got saved. Boy, he was so humble. I didn't sense anymore of that arrogance and pride."

"I'm trusting you, Leslie. Do you think we can trust him?"

"I do. Actually, I can't wait to talk to the new improved Carlton. He's a new creation."

"How about you, Brett? Jack?"

"Tanner, it's unanimous. I thought you said the perfect thing. He has hidden my life for years while I worked undercover."

"Jack, I never knew you were into God."

"See, how undercover I was? I guess I never knew you were undercover, either. I didn't know you were a believer." Laughter.

"Touché, Jack.

"Brett, how about you?"

"I now understand what Ben said about changed lives. You know, I could hardly stand being around Carlton. I'll know if he's changed when I'm near him."

❧

Bryan unlocks the cell and goes in first. "Here's the deal... This will be your first opportunity to try out your new strength. We are having practice in forgiveness and acceptance. Our guest is Carlton Prince, otherwise known to you as Chip... Hold on. Lieutenant Tanner can change his mind about all of you, and so could I, so calm down and let the man speak. Then, we'll have a civilized discussion.

"Carlton, you're on, but first, we're all going to pray.

"King, would you do the honors?"

"What? Me?"

"Yes, you."

"Hey God, you're the best, and we all want to thank you for tripping us out with all the things we never knew or felt before. Thanks for caring when we were so bad and were filled with tough-guy stuff and evil. Thanks for forgiving us. Help us to be like you. Because of you, we are going to listen to Chip or whatever his name is. In Jesus, amen. Oh, and I want to thank you for Bryan, too. He's a stand-up guy. Take care of him, please."

The scowls on the faces of the guys soften slightly when Carlton begins with, "Thanks, King." They're also tenderized by the fact that Carlton's eyes are moist with tears, and his voice sounds choked up. "I want you to know that I would deserve whatever you could dish out to me. If you should do that, I am not afraid anymore. I surrendered today to the same Lord you guys did, but my trust must be proven. Hopefully, you will give me a chance to show you that he has changed me. After I'm done apologizing and asking for your forgiveness, I will explain as much as I can. You deserve to know what's been going on. Call it truth or consequences. I owe this opportunity to finally come clean to Lieutenant Tanner, Bryan, and of course, all of you." Carlton continues on as the lockup friends sit quietly listening.

❋

"Tanner, maybe we'll have to relabel lockup as Transformation Chapel. I have never seen anything like this before. How evil is whatever we're dealing with? It must be bad since God is invading the territory by transforming our street friends. This must be war!"

"Jack, you put lip to it. This isn't one case or a plan. It's war. Thanks, Jack. I knew we needed you in the family. Did you hear all that? Doesn't it explain everything?"

"Joe, what you said today about no errors. Now, we're on the offense and not defense anymore."

Everyone is praising? We're taking this to the next level. "Everyone be at Kaplan's at 7:00 for dinner. If this is the chapel, Kaplan's is Command Central. Use the rest of the day and write down anything the Lord gives you.

"Beanie, can you drive Erica and Constance home since Bryan is still with the guys? Stay there. Don't be out by yourself." *The crows are out.* "I've got to get a strategy going with Bryan, Carlton, and the guys at lockup. Brett and Joe are going with me."

Carlton and Bryan finish answering the guys' questions as Tanner enters the cell. "Well, gentlemen, what's the verdict? Does he live? Thumbs-up or thumbs-down?" All the thumbs go up. "Gentlemen, it has come to our attention that we need to design a war map. I need all of you to coordinate what you can remember about the Professor's property. Try to remember what you did there. You should all stay together tonight. Do not get off by yourself. Carlton, any suggestions?"

"Yes, Sir. They can all come to my place. I have a big apartment. We're all in this together. I have the van, remember?"

"Sounds good. Are you guys down with that?" It was met with a unanimous response.

"Lieutenant, we're going to need clean clothes and stuff."

"Carlton, you stop at their places and get what they need."

"You bet, and I'll feed them too!"

"I'll send someone with you!"

"Tanner, I'm going with them."

"Bryan, you can't—"

"I'm going with them. We're all in this together, or we're not going."

"Wow, Bryan, I guess I've been corrected. I've got to talk to Carlton for a minute."

Tanner and Carlton walk into the back hallway, out of hearing range. "Carlton, Desmond was at the station today looking for you... Wait, Art's got you covered. He told him you were out on a call and you'd call him when you came back in."

"Sir, what should I say?"

"Why don't you tell him you've been trying to bail the guys out of lockup all day and that they're not getting out of your sight from now on."

"Oh, that would make sense. He knows how unruly they are. How did you come up with that?"

Tanner points upwards. Laughter. "Let's pray for wisdom that Desmond doesn't have a clue."

"Desmond, well... Well, you know I can't be everywhere at once. I have to keep up appearances. I can't believe you came to the station... Yeah, Art told me, but I couldn't call you until now. I'm still at lovely lockup. Seems the recruits all got picked up last night... I've been here all day... Wait a second! I can't help how they are. I thought that's the qualities you wanted— dumb and involved on our side, so lay off. I'm doing my best. In fact, I'm taking them home with me. They're not getting out of my sight... Why do I deserve that on my day off? I think you could've been a little grateful. Roscoe's depending on me to deliver?... Okay, I know you don't want him to lose his temper. I don't either, so get off my back. I've got us all covered. I'll see you tomorrow night, and I'll call you for more instructions before we come. I've got to go. This was a bad time to talk. My boss is here waiting to discharge these guys. I'll call you tomorrow. I hope you guys hold up your end of the deal... Yeah, lockup took all their phones away. Tell Roscoe he'll have to wait until morning to make any calls... Yeah, I know that kid, Bryan. He showed back up, and he got thrown in too... No, it had nothing to do with us. I told you, I'm on it. Here comes the head of the lockup. Later."

"Carlton, you sounded like your old self."

"It made me sick, but I don't think he suspected anything. Do you, Sir?"

"No, I don't."

"I feel bad. I lied about the head of lockup coming."

"Carlton, the Lord knows you're undercover. Remember? But it's good you think like that. Let's get moving. You and the guys have drawings to make."

"Thanks so much, Sir, for a second chance."

Jack walks out with Tanner and the guys as they are leaving. "Tanner, I'll take care of our little friend at the tattoo parlor. Oh, excuse me, the tattoo salon. Well, when I'm done, I'll hang near Carlton's place. It's a little feeling I have. I'll keep those guys covered."

"Thanks, Jack. Make it look good when you release Carlton and the guys. You never know what's watching."

As Tanner and Joe reach the car, Joe motions with his eyes and a nod of his head. Tanner spots crows sitting on the building across the street.

"Did you see them this time? Are they following you or us?"

"Joe, I don't know, but I'm going to tell Carlton. Drive to the front, and I'll tell Jack. "Hey, Jack, give Carlton this." Written on the folded paper are the words, "THE CROWS ARE OUT."

"Tanner, do you think he'll know what that means?"

"Yep, I do, but we'll find out later. Head to Kaplan's. I've got to catch a little nap. My brain is fried. I feel like this day has been three days long. Joe, I need to call Jan and pick her up. She's going to be with us tonight. Could you and or Ben pick her up?"

"Tanner, I'll talk to everyone. I got some shut-eye time at the hospital this morning. You need a good little snooze."

"Call Irene first." Tanner falls asleep in the car.

"Dee Dee, where's Tanner?"

"Libby, he came in, handed Stuart a piece of paper, spoke to him, and went upstairs. Joe said he needed to sleep."

36

ON THE SAME PAGE

Dot has called a meeting of the Meadow Brook women, The Big 10. "Ladies, what a joy to see all of you. We're together, where our journey began. As you know, Jan was wise in her suggestion to divide into groups of two or three. Less travel and more coordination gave us more time to pray, to be faithful in support of Dee Dee and all those in Oak City.

"Remember that the Lord told each group separately that the recovery of the girl, Anne, would be the signal of change. As you know, Anne has her faculties back and appears to be perfectly healthy. The next stage is beginning. Dinah called me. She had an experience, and I felt it was pertinent to that next step."

Dot continues with prayer, "Dear Father, we come and humble ourselves in your presence. Give us insight and wisdom. We ask you to protect and direct the efforts of all those in Oak City, especially Dee Dee. She has been through such a battle and so much hurt. We ask you to reveal your plan. We commit to do your will. In your precious name, Jesus."

As Dinah stands, she bows her head and begins to sing in worship. Her sparkling voice moves through the air of the room. All the ladies have goosebumps. It's that same reverent presence from the day they started. "I felt like I had to let that out. There truly is something about that name, His name. Thanks for coming. I called Dot because I had a vision last night…

"We were all together with the group in Oak City. A dark mist formed and began swirling like a dust devil. The sound was deafening. Fear was thick in the air. The fear wasn't in us but all around us. The ground was shaking. I heard the Lord say, 'Don't receive the fear. I have not given you a spirit of fear, but of love, of power, and a sound mind.' He said fasting and prayer breaks the hold of this. Then, as crazy as this sounds, we were all in a large house. It seemed like a celebration with food and beautiful linens and lights. One of the waiters whispered to me, 'Now it begins.' These large doors opened, and I could see a huge garden in the darkness. I heard, 'Prepare for battle,' and we all began to sing and praise him. As we did that, we were all given silver shovels. A command was given to dig up the seed."

Dot is shaking. She's lifting her hands in the air. "Dinah, yesterday I had a flash of a dark-clawed hand planting seeds. It was a flash, but it came two times.

Carolyn's hand is raised. "What, Carolyn?"

"Well, I know if we fast, we do it very privately. He spoke to me days ago to fast. In light of Dinah's vision, is anyone else fasting?" Hands go up.

Dot asks, "Gloria, what is it?"

"One phrase keeps running through my head when I am quiet in prayer. 'War has come. Prepare for battle.' He said he has sent an emissary of His kingdom to go before us."

"Goodness! I haven't had any dynamic spiritual revelations, but there is news from Oak City. Joe told me there's a major turn. He told me it was war. They're meeting at 7:00 tonight. I spoke for all of us. I told him we wanted to be on with them.

"Dot, could we all come out here tonight?"

"Of course, Peaches. You know, anything I have is for the Lord. Can you all come?"

"I need to bring a guest. Clay also got a call from Joe. He said I'm not going unless he does."

"Pam, you're blowing me away. Timothy is flying in. He also had gotten a call from Joe. I need to bring him. I didn't even know he and Joe were close friends."

"Gloria, Clay said he knew another guy was coming. Did they talk, too? What is going on?"

"Pam, I don't know, but you can bet we'll find out. Ladies, can the guys come?"

"I vote yes. The Lord told me some were going, and some were coming. I didn't know what it meant until now."

"What do you mean, Claire?"

"Dot, you know that Oliver and Marty are out of town, and now Clay and Timothy are coming. This is what he was telling me. One more thing: Grace and James are going to set many free. He told me they are mighty warriors. See, there's the battle and the war theme again. Dee Dee is also going to be completely set free. I was with her at the church when she collapsed. It was very, ugh, I don't know, weird. The Lord told me yesterday to pray that the chain would be loosed and the stone removed. I have no idea what that means. I know Dee Dee will be freed if we pray."

"Oh, I didn't mean to upset you, Linda."

"These are good tears of relief. Dee Dee and I have been talking for days. She made me promise not to tell. All I will say is you are right on. You are precious, Claire. Ladies, I know we all have to get moving, so we need to close. Lareece, would you close in prayer?"

"Lord, I know you are bringing Dee Dee's journey to a close. Thank you for Adlin's life, and may her death not be in vain. Though we don't understand the whys, we know that she loved you, and you never forsake us. It has been a privilege to seek truth. You know, Lord, how much I have been changed. You have drawn us all closer to you. Help those in Oak City, especially Lieutenant Tanner. The burden of responsibility has been on him. Give him wisdom, give him rest, and renew his strength. We plead your precious blood over everyone involved and especially our Dee Dee. There is something about that name, and in your name, we close, Jesus. Amen."

"See you tonight, ladies. I took notes and will type everything and send it to Beanie. Claire already typed up the vision He gave her. I'll add the other comments, make copies at the house, and have them here tonight."

"Oh, Linda, that would be great. I know Ben would want to see what insight we have received."

"I'll send it to Beanie too. From the bottom of my heart, I will never be able to repay all of you for helping Dee Dee and me. See you tonight. I'll also tell Madelyn to pray and fill her in. She has been a big help. I almost forgot that Jan will be there tonight... I know. Isn't that wonderful?"

❧

"Dee Dee, thanks for organizing the lists. Would you mind helping me again?" Stuart and I had arranged the lists of seminar sessions by dates and places. Sticky notes began to look like feathers covering every paper.

"You're welcome, Stuart. You really kept yourself reined in. I know it was driving you crazy as to why Tanner asked you to do that."

"Yep, I kept control, though, and didn't run wild with imagination. Now, it's "wild time." When Tanner came in, he told me to let my mind go free and to think outside the box. He handed me this piece of paper."

"What in the world is it? Must have been a doozy if Tanner told you to unleash that brain of yours."

"It's an identifier for plants. You know, to tell you what you're buying. See, it says Fey Lougawou. It's one of the plants Jacob brought back from Haiti."

"That gives me the creeps, but how does that link to the list? Tanner must think there's a connection here. Stuart, what's that look? Don't go nuts on me."

"When I learned that Alyssa was missing, it kept dinging in my mind. Streptocarpus. I always felt that was odd. I tried to figure out the ratio of names against the possibilities of—"

"Stop, Stuart! My brain does not move at the speed yours does. Tell me what I'm looking for."

"Dee Dee, find any name that faintly reminds you of this card. You take this list, and I'll look at this one. Write down any possibility."

Maybe there are others. Adlin's Whisper. Jan and I knew there was much more.

"Let me show you Kalanchoe Pinnata, Fey Lougawou, the Wonder of the World. It's a healing plant." Stuart opens his computer and pulls up images of the plant. "What I'm wondering is why they used the Haitian name instead of the true botanical name. Oh! I've seen this plant before."

Why wouldn't they have used the true botanical name? One more piece to the puzzle.

James and Grace are still having a long conversation with Ben and Joe in the den. Libby had left Stuart and I alone at the dining table. She said that she was drained from the excitement of Erica's presentation. *I guess Emily got what she went after. I hope I get what I'm going after.* Travis and Emily went to celebrate. *I hope we all get to celebrate at the end of this.* The apartment is so still as Stuart and I pore over our hundreds of names.

"Dee Dee, use your detective skills. Let's pretend this is the game, Mad Gab. Maybe if we say the names quickly and quietly out loud, something will stand out." We quietly begin to whisper the names on the lists in a rapid rhythm.

"Stuart, here's one." Just as I say that, James and Grace appear.

"Dee Dee, could we interrupt for a few minutes? We need to speak with you." I hand Stuart my list with the names I found.

"What, James?"

"Joe and Ben have filled us in on the events of today. Are you aware of the things that have occurred?"

"No, Stuart and I are looking for a link to the Professor's seminars. What's happened?" *The serious looks on their faces are causing my heart to start pounding.*

As Grace and James and I go into the den, they begin to relate what Ben and Joe have told them. I find myself saying, "Stuart, you need to be in on this." *I can't believe I said that. Hope he doesn't get off the rail.*

Suddenly, Libby comes in, too. "What's going on?"

"Oh, Grace and James are filling us in so Tanner doesn't have to belabor the points tonight." Stuart, Libby, and I are like kids sitting on the edge of our seats. The whole story that James recounts seems like a dark fairy tale. Good versus evil.

"All this is coming to a close. Tonight, we're finishing our plan. Tomorrow night is going to be the finale.

"For us, the recovery of Anne has been so encouraging. It signals that there can be restoration for Alyssa, no matter what she's been through. We are strongly impressed that there are others. God gave Grace and me the scripture, 'Beloved thou doest faithfully whatsoever thou doest to the brethren and to strangers.' He told us the others are strangers. We will be caring for them. Dee Dee, there are others. You kept hearing Adlin's Whisper. Adlin's voice was the only one you initially would listen to. So, when He spoke to you, you heard it as Adlin's voice. See, you're not crazy.

"I don't want to offend you, but we have begun to feel like you are a beloved daughter. We will protect you, and you will be free. God also told us that He has sent someone to go before all of us tomorrow night. Evil thinks that it has control, but the Lord is greater. He's invading their plan. Adlin's murder was unintentional. Leslie was the target. There is a mystery about you, though. Tanner thinks that because you look so much like your mother, you have become a target.

"Grace believes that some of these people are actually entities and think you possess something they want. I do, too. When Joe mentioned the missing piece of the unrecovered jewelry in Haiti, Grace immediately knew that the description matched what you had been sharing with her about the pendant and the stone."

"Grace, I don't have any jewelry like that."

"Dee Dee, that's irrelevant. This spiritual group thinks you do. We think they caused the death of your parents. Don't ask us to explain that. We have a feeling many events are linked. We, as Christians, try to negate the dark powers, but they do exist. You're connected to that piece of jewelry. It's like Adlin's death reactivated something in the spiritual realm. Isn't that when you started feeling that tug on your heart?"

As I sit here speechless, my mind is whirling through my conversations with Aunt Linda, James, and Grace. I shove that faint tugging sensation aside and remain focused on what they're saying.

"Grace has researched those jewels based on Joe's description. She believes the stone belonged to a very famous woman. Her name was Sanite DeDe. She was brought to America as a slave who then bought her freedom. In the early 1800's, she was known as the first queen of Voodoo in New Orleans. It was her most powerful lodestone. Another lady had it mounted on a silver chain because silver represents salvation, and she believed it would protect her from evil spells. It was stolen from a collection several years ago. Because it was owned by Sanite DeDe, it was very valuable, especially in certain circles. It's supposed to be very powerful and in the wrong hands, to be feared."

"Okay, that's enough. I'm starting to feel sick. The fact that her name was DeDe really bothers me. I pray that's not significant."

"So do we, Dee Dee. This is all very dangerous. Apparently, you told the guys this morning to count you in for tomorrow. Are you sure?"

"I need to be alone for a few minutes." *Leslie isn't back yet.* I hurry up the stairs and quietly shut the door. *Amazingly, there's no tug inside and no fear. At least James and Grace had the decency to tell me the truth.*

When I initially determined to find Red October, my thoughts were consumed with Adlin and revenge. The isolationist attitude that I had, led me down the road of a prideful overdose of independence. It was a lesson in foolishness to think that I could make it all on my own. I didn't realize how emotionally crippled I was. I'm a better person for having received the help of this tiny army of people around me. The strength of Grace and James has been a true comfort to me. Talk about demonstrations of faith and courage. They are living examples. Our conversation earlier touched me deeply. Truly concerned for my being and all the others, all while their daughter is missing. I think they are true examples of trust in God. Mighty, selfless strength exudes from them. I feel terrible, like a traitor to my parents, but I'm beginning to think of them as substitute provisions. I so miss my mom and dad. I guess I'm called to finish what they started in Haiti.

I've got to get back to Stuart. I wash my face, put a smile on, and go downstairs. The look of surprise on their faces makes me laugh. "I know, you all thought that after that Voodoo stuff you spoke about, I would have another attack. It didn't happen this time. Actually, the truth has set me free. Libby, thanks for being such a great friend. James and Grace, thanks for thinking of me as a daughter. Stuart, you are amazing. Let's get busy and do what Tanner asked you to do. Thanks for letting me help."

"Boy, that was a bombshell, Dee Dee. My brain was exploding. I'm sorry, I didn't realize you were a target."

"Stuart, that's sweet, but let's find those names. Here's the one I found." I show Stuart the name Fayette Lugano. "Say it fast, Stuart. And, it sounds like—"

"Oh, my gosh, Dee Dee! I think this one is something. Let's keep going."

The next one Stuart found was Gemmissa Wede. "Look, Dee Dee, Jimson Weed. Also known as Datura Stramonium, devil's snare. In Haiti, they call it Concombre Zombi. The Zombie Cucumber."

"Stuart, why does this stand out to me? Gwen Madison."

After repeating it quickly several times, Stuart pulls up Jatropha Curcus. "Dee Dee, it's Haitian. It's Gwo Medisyen. It means good medicine. It's Voodoo. It purges evil spirits and releases the trapped souls of the dead. I think I've seen enough. This is really getting to me. I believe we've proved Tanner's theory. Only Jacob would be able to make these links. He picked Alyssa and Anne Johnson. He picked those other girls because of plant connections. How many more are there? How truly sick is he? To think he would defile Rose's legacy like this. He's a monster. I feel dirty for even knowing him."

"Stuart, stay calm. Jacob wasn't like this until his encounters in Haiti, was he? Perhaps, he's a victim, too."

"Do you think so?"

"Yes, I do. Let's print this information out for Tanner. The only question I have is how does Anne Johnson fit in? She's not on the list. How did she get into this mess? The only Anne I found was Anne Lacey King. Is she Anne Johnson?"

"Queen Anne's Lace!"

"What?"

"Well, Dee Dee, Queen Anne's Lace... Queen Anne was married to King James the 1st, and there's a whole legend about it, but it's a flowering plant. It's hard to tell the difference between it and poisonous hemlock."

"Stuart, this is getting way beyond my scope. I think we've got enough for Tanner."

"Dee Dee, would you present this to him? My mind is, you know, how I start babbling."

"No, we're going to put it together. You'll be great. This wouldn't be possible without you and your magnificent brain. You care, unlike other intellectuals who look down on people. What a great friend you are to everyone, a true tender heart."

"Dee Dee—"

"Not a word, Stuart. Be exactly who you are. Alyssa is blessed to have someone like you care about her."

I never thought I would be attached to so many people. As Stuart tucks the feathered lists into his briefcase, I'm touched by his purity of soul. *God has made a unique and intensely caring person. I'm learning to see others through His eyes. Wow, Dee Dee Summers, look how your point of view has changed.*

I'm snapped out of my thoughts by Emily and Travis arriving. Their joy and sparkle fill the entire room. "Emily, I heard everything went well today."

"Everything flowed."

"Emily was magnificent. Those strait-laced corporate guys were cracked out of their shells. When they walked out, they were all smiles and laughter. They loved Emily, but they better not love her too much." With that, Travis pulls Emily close to him and kisses the back of her neck.

"Emily, it looks like a couple of deals were cut today.

"Travis, those corporate guys weren't the only ones cracked out of their shells.

"Emily, it looks like you made two home runs."

"Dee Dee, this was a great day. I was so thrilled. I did a little dance at the end. I couldn't help it. They all stood up, laughing and clapping. They said I was refreshing and intensely creative. Can you imagine? I was so humbled. They practically offered me the world, and then, Travis...Well, that's for later. It's been a great day! Where's Libby? Where's Tanner?"

"In answer to both questions, they're upstairs. Travis, Tanner was exhausted when he came in. He'll need to fill you in on everything that's happened. Stuart and I just finished a project for him. Stuart's in the den, creating a folder for Tanner to review. Joe and Ben have gone to pick up Jan from the hospital. I didn't think Emily's sparkle could've gotten any brighter, but at the mention of Jan coming, she lit up."

"I love Jan. She has helped Professor Jacob and Anne so much. I've never seen Tanner have such an immediate closeness to anyone. He loves Jan. He trusts her."

"I love her too, Emily. She helped me from the moment I met her." *Oh, Jan, only we know how precious time is to us. I hope it's not the last thing you do, my beloved friend.* As the cloak of sadness tries to drape itself over me, I shake it off and quietly hang it up for another time. *Today is a great day.* I wipe away the welling tears and swallow deeply.

"Dee Dee, are you okay?"

"Stuart, I'm fine. I've had a good day. Maybe it will end up being a great day." *Tender Stuart.*

"Look, Travis. Libby's like a little girl on the floor snuggled up with a pillow and a blanket. Tanner looks so peaceful sleeping. He still has his shoes on."

"Emily, shh. Don't make me laugh."

Tanner opens one eye. "What are you guys doing staring at me? Where's Libby?" The two visitors point to the floor. Tanner turns on his side and peers over the edge of the bed. "She's beautiful, even when she's sleeping. Don't you agree?"

"Yes, Tanner, we do. Sir, you probably should get up. Ben and Joe have gone to get Jan. Everyone will be here in about an hour. Remember, you called a meeting?"

"Travis, yes, I did, and I feel locked and loaded. Shh, let her sleep." As the three exit the room, Tanner gives Emily a big hug.

"Kiddo, I'm so proud of you. Did it go the way you wanted? Were you a sugar plum?"

"Oh, stop, Tanner! It was more than I could have expected. I did a little dance at the end. It's been a great day!"

"Was it the "Dance of the Sugar Plum Fairies?" Let's have a great evening, too. I'll see you downstairs. I've got to wash up." *Lord, you know how I feel about Libby. We've had to put our lives on hold. Don't let all this ruin us. Give me strength, please. I feel so responsible for so many people. Adlin Summers looms in my thoughts all the time.*

❧

"Tanner, Dee Dee got a call from Jan. Jamison is with Jacob now. Irene is on her way."

"Stuart, I'll call Jamison right now.

"Hey Doc, what's going on?"

"Jacob is insistent that he has responsibilities for tomorrow. Tanner, we need to take him out of here. He won't do well without Jan. Irene just came. I'll call you back."

“Jacob, what are you so upset about?”

“Jan, you know I have to get everything ready. Rose’s project could lose a big sponsor. He’s supposed to come tomorrow night to see her plots. It’s a huge deal. I can’t let Rose down. I’ve got to go home.”

“Irene, you’re here. Jacob is frantic about going home.”

“Well, Jacob, about going home... The county has had a big water break, so there’s no reason to go there. The road is blocked.”

“Irene, the cleaning, the catering, everything ruined. I don’t even have anything to wear.”

“Good news, Jacob. I ran into the most wonderful caterer and party planner. See, here’s the menu. I also spoke to your tailor, and he will have a nice tux for you. We’ll pick it up tomorrow. You’ll have to come to my house tonight. Jamison will come, too, so you won’t have to worry about any medical needs. I called Roscoe and told him you had everything taken care of. You can call him tomorrow.”

“What about tables and servers?”

“The planner has all that covered, so all you need to do is rest and be the grand host at the party. Jacob, you should’ve known I wouldn’t let you or Rose down.”

“Oh, Irene, I’m so sorry. I cut you out of my life, and here you are, like always. Is Stuart going to be there? I know Rose would be disappointed if he weren’t there.”

“Of course, he’s coming with us. Maybe we could all go together like the old days, plus Jamison, of course.”

“Irene, you shouldn’t let this one slip away. Rose would’ve liked him. I like him. He’s right for you.”

“So, you’ll come to my house tonight? Promise me you’ll quit worrying.”

“Yes, I appreciate the offer, the shelter in the storm. I promise to quit worrying.

“Jamison, does this work for you?”

"Absolutely, my patients always come first— especially the ones Irene loves. Excuse me, I've got to make a call.

"Tanner, Jacob is coming with Irene and me...Yes, Irene's house... Can you send someone from the force to be with us?... Tanner, don't laugh. You know what I meant. We'll treat them like a house guest. I don't want anyone to sit outside in the car all night... Thanks. Give him Irene's address and tell him we'll be there in an hour. We'll take good care of him. Take care of Jan. I see Joe and Ben are coming in. Will you clear all this with Melinda so she keeps a special eye on Anne? She will be here, minus all of us... Tanner, I'm sorry we will miss the meeting tonight. You can fill us in later.

Jamison turns to Jan, "You have my number. Call me if you have any problems. It will do you good to get out of here. Tanner will take good care of you, and we will take good care of Jacob."

"Jamison, pray we finish this soon. What about Anne? I told her I had to leave to have some tests run."

"Tanner is giving Melinda special orders about Anne. Jan, I guess this is kind of a test for all of us. So, in case you feel like you lied to Anne, it's not a lie."

"Jamison, how did you know I hate lying?"

"The Lord does talk to me once in a while. I do pray for my patients. Hurry! Go! Have a great evening and dinner with friends."

"I love my doctor. Goodnight, Doctor Lovett."

"Tanner, is something wrong?"

"Libby, I didn't know you were up. I had to give special instructions to Melinda. Jacob is going home with Irene and Doc. I talked to Art, and he's going over there for the night."

"I'm sorry you have so much responsibility. I'm in this with you. We have a deal, remember?"

"Aah, Lib. I remember. I always remember us. I will never break our deal."

As Tanner leans down to kiss Libby, the buzzer rings. "Grace, would you see who that is? I'm wrapped up." Grace is still smiling as she answers the buzzer.

"Tanner, it's the caterers. He is with Heavenly Catering. Said they are early, but they need to set up."

"Thanks, Grace. Buzz him up."

"It's a fiesta! Look at all this food and the splendiferous presentation. Thanks, Grace, for taking care of this. I needed to spend some time with Libby."

"My pleasure, Tanner. Oh, there's a card for you."

Tanner opens the card. It reads,

> "Lieutenant, enjoy the time and the food. We've got you covered. Tomorrow night will be perfect. Martina."

Tanner's phone rings. "Irene, what's wrong?... You what? Sent her Jacob's address, but forgot to give Martina the address here?... She doesn't answer?... Well, somehow, the food all got here. What a caterer we all have stumbled across. She's got us covered. Take care of Jacob and Jamison. Did Art get there?... Good. I won't have to worry then." *Heavenly Planners and Caterers. Who is this woman?*

37

TOGETHER AGAIN

"Well, here we go once again. Strung together by a cord, which all started with a terrible tragedy. It seems clear to me that we were all connected over the years by some divine providence beyond explanation, just like this free and most wonderful dinner by Heavenly Planners and Caterers. I was so defeated and disturbed by Adlin's death, alone in it with no way to go. We are about to bring our quest for truth and resolution to an end. God always sends the very best. He sent all of you, as Dee Dee says, 'To help Adlin.'"

One look at Jan, and I have to excuse myself. *I'm back in the BMW on the first day I met her.* As I hide in the bathroom, a little note slips under the door. It's a poorly drawn tennis shoe with a broken and frayed lace, and signed with a smiley face.

I hear her raspy voice say, "I need to enjoy tonight. It's important. Please, Dee Dee. Come out. It's safe. I'm not cooking tonight."

Laughing at Jan, I open the door. "Jan, I—"

"I know, you forgot how short I am."

"Jan, you are always much taller than you appear to be."

There they are, my tiny army.

As I look around the room, it's like Jan reads my mind. "What a gift they all are. A tiny but mighty army of faithful friends. Let's enjoy them.

"Wow, this is some spread, Tanner! Did you cook all day?"

"Jan, from one police officer to another, you know I didn't." Laughter. "Ben, do the honors, please."

After a sweet but powerful message, Ben closes with, "The Master says come and dine." The amens are mere whispers. Jan is cracking everyone up. She's so witty. The sound of laughter spreads like a spring breeze banishing the serious gloom that was waiting— lifting it away. Even Tanner is laughing.

"Oh, Jan, what a great work you are doing, lifting us away from the stress." *A merry heart doeth good like a medicine.*

Before Tanner calls the Meadow Brook group, he walks over and gives Jan a big hug. "I needed that, Jan. I don't remember the last time I've laughed like that." Even Grace and James stand and clap.

"Wow, a standing ovation! I guess you could've called it laughing in the face of danger." Jan bows to her adoring fans.

Beanie passes us copies from the insights of the Meadow Brook Investigation Foundation. That's what Tanner calls them, The Meadow Brook Investigation Foundation. "Without all of them, we wouldn't have been able to go as far as we have. They are the foundation."

"Dot, is everyone there?"

"Yes, Jan, we're all here. Oliver and Martina are away, so Timothy and Clay came instead."

I notice Joe seems pleased that they are with the ladies. Tanner quickly lays out the day's events and asks Stuart to share what we found on the lists.

Tanner pats Stuart on the back and gives him a quick hug. The look on Stuart's face is priceless. Approval means so much to Stuart.

I hear Aunt Linda say my name. "Tanner, is Dee Dee going to be safe?"

"Aunt Linda, I'm surrounded by this army of people, as well as all of you. This is war, but there will be a resolution and justice for Adlin and Mom and Dad. We will find Alyssa. I can feel the prayers of all of you surrounding us here. Don't cry. I'm in good hands with Ben, Joe, Tanner, Jan, and all the rest. There are others I haven't even met.

"You have been given many insights about seeds of evil. This will probably shock all of you, but I believe what I'm about to say with my whole being.

"Adlin's death is like a seed planted which has burst forth and flourished into the lives of all of us. So many lives have changed, especially mine. Adlin's testimony of faith is now alive in us. God has used this heartbreak to bring forth something good. The enemy has planted seeds, but God has too. What the enemy means for evil, the Lord turns for good to those who love Him. All I can say is it was a big mistake for the enemy when Adlin was murdered."

Everyone is incredulous as Stuart begins his presentation. He recounts his trip to Haiti and the history of his research with Rose and Jacob. As he progresses into the current file about the lists, I can hear prayers going up. It feels like a giant shudder issued from both groups. I guess the mention of Voodoo and black magic created that shudder and the dead stillness following. *That's probably what had triggered Aunt Linda's question and concern for me. Not the most common thought for today. It's that place where spiritual and natural thinking collide.*

I immediately ask Tanner to explain to Aunt Linda how many people are involved in this. He starts by asking the group to pray for our missing members, the guys from the lockup and Carlton.

I hear Tanner explaining, "Carlton's group, led by Bryan, will be crucial. We'll have to wait until tomorrow to know how everything will come together. We'll see the plot plans and any additional information that flows out of their memories. There are missing components. Our plan will have to be finalized tomorrow. We're all like actors on a stage but not in a play. This is life and death."

It kind of reminds me of, '[Let's] Eat, drink, and be merry, for tomorrow we…' I'm not going to say that last word.

Dot pops back to the information that Stuart had laid out about the lists. "So, there *are* others besides Anne and Alyssa."

"Yes, Dot, we believe so."

Tanner had done such a clear and precise recounting of all the events from the beginning of my hunt for Red October. He tied so many loose ends together. I was so impressed by his deep gratitude for everyone and their contribution. He's a true leader and a gentleman.

As we begin to brainstorm through suggestions about tomorrow and attempt to develop a war plan, he even shares about the caterers. I don't think I have ever seen Tanner so in command. We feel the assurance and the comfort of his wisdom.

At the end of the meeting, everyone feels much better as to what part they are to play. The group Tanner refers to as the Meadow Brook Investigation Foundation will keep praying and fasting for us. We, in Oak City, will depend upon getting together with the group from Carlton's place. We need to develop a plan of exactly where everyone will be staged tomorrow night. I hear Tanner asking, "Ben, would you close in prayer?"

"Oh, dear Lord, thank you for bringing us all together. Lord, I feel especially pressed to plead for your protection and covering over Bryan, Carlton, and all the other guys. Watch over them and watch over Jack all through the night, Lord, and may you give divine revelation to them. Bring back their memories and let them see clearly what it is they're supposed to do. Father, we rest in the security and the knowledge that you know everything and see everything. You've known from the beginning what we we're supposed to do. May we be faithful and listen to do exactly what you tell us.

"Lord, I believe what Dee Dee said about Adlin. Out of this tragedy, you have brought forth something of greatness to help so many people. We pray for the others whom we do not know. We thank you for Stuart, and his amazing worth, and his intense knowledge. Lord, we ask you to protect over all of us and honor Linda's prayers for Dee Dee. Father, I thank you for the things that you've done in our lives and the revelations Linda has brought to us. I ask you to give us all insight and wisdom and speak to every person so we know what to do. We believe there are others. Deliver them out of bondage.

"Father, we ask for your protection over Alyssa. We thank you that Anne has come out of this. It's so much encouragement to know that others can be restored. We ask you to protect over Irene, Jamison, and Professor Jacob all through the night. Watch over Art as he takes care of them. In your mighty name, the name of Jesus, amen."

As soon as Ben prayed and the phone call ended, Tanner was back to his usual vigilance. "Beanie, are you staying with Constance and Erica?... I'm concerned because Erica told me earlier that she is nervous."

"Tanner, you know that I wouldn't leave them alone, but I have to go into the station tomorrow morning."

"Constance, do you have room for a couple more people?"

"Yes, Tanner, who have you got in mind?"

"Brett, would you go with the ladies home and stay tonight?"

"Sir, you know you can count on me.

"Mrs. Carter, I promise I'll be a good house guest.

"Beanie, I'll follow you girls home. I have to bring a friend with me, though," as he pats his pistol.

"Well, Brett, Constance, and I already have a couple of your friends' "cousins," so we are comfortable with that." Laughter.

"Constance, what is it?"

"Tanner, I need to speak with you privately for a minute. I got a call today. You had asked me to communicate with Al Kaplan. Well, he's coming home... No, he's not coming here. He has a small area in his bookstore. He'll be in tomorrow at about noon. I told him I'd pick him up. I couldn't put him off. He said he has something to tell you personally and won't take no for an answer. What are we going to do?"

"Constance, before you get to the bookstore, take him to lunch. It's on me."

"Tanner, who pays for the lunches, is the last of my worries. The timing is terrible, but I will be glad to see him. I know Aaron would tell us to carry on."

"Constance, you're so right. The Chief would tell us that. I'll meet you at the bookstore. Let's talk in the morning. Get some rest. Al Kaplan is not a threat, is he?"

"Absolutely not! He's a wonderful person!"

Boy, Constance is defensive. "I didn't mean it that way. I trust your opinion, and I'm glad you're excited to see him."

"Give me a hug, Tanner. I'm so sorry I flared up like that. Don't know why."

"Constance, no apology is necessary. I accept your endorsement of Mr. Kaplan and your stamp of approval from a truly great lady and a dear friend. You're in charge. Mr. Kaplan is a new caseload for you." Laughter.

As I'm listening to Tanner and Constance, I'm distracted by Leslie, "Dee Dee, Jan can have my bed. You can share our room with her."

Jan interrupts, "Thanks, Leslie, but I'll be fine on the loveseat in the den. Remember, I'm not too long. I get up and down, so I prefer being in there. I think Libby already has it made up for me. She's sleeping on the other couch out here. One of these days, everyone will be able to go home. Leslie, thank you so much. I appreciate it. This is like the world's longest slumber party."

"Libby, thank you for helping Jan with the bed. You're a constant. Always stay close to Tanner. Lib, regardless of how tomorrow goes, I want you to know that you have been a wonderful friend to me. Through our little slumber party the other night, I have realized so much about friendship. I didn't really confide with other people before. So, you and Jan are my first real female friends. Thanks, Libby. I hope you have a good night. Sorry you're sleeping on the couch. You could have my bed."

"No, Dee Dee, this will be great. I'll be out here on the couch, and Jan will be on the loveseat in the den, and it will be a great evening. We will all sleep well. Sleep well, everyone." With that, Libby kisses Tanner on the cheek.

"Tanner, you get some rest because we all need you to stay together, and remember, we are in this together."

"Oh, Lib, I always remember us."

As I head into the bedroom, I see Tanner, James, and Travis walk into Ben and Joe's room. *I wonder where Emily is.*

"Guys, Jack's on the phone. I want you to hear this straight from him."

"Hey guys, it's been an interesting evening. I started to get edgy as I was driving to Carlton's. You know, that uneasy feeling. I parked about a block away to have a broader view. Some big guy came down the street and went to Carlton's apartment building. He was dressed nicely. I could see him in the streetlight."

"Jack, was that guy Desmond?"

"Oh, yeah, Tanner, you mentioned him to me. Well, it gets strange. All of a sudden, crows were flying off the buildings and out of the trees, bunches of them. That was freaky. As he walked away from the building, they flew off in the same direction."

"Did you give that note to Carlton?"

"Sure did."

"Did you read it?"

"Tanner, you know I wouldn't read a note for someone else."

"Well, we gave him a heads-up about the crows."

"Wish you would've given me one. That really rattled me. It was like that old Hitchcock movie." Laughter.

"Sorry, Jack, but it gives you a sample of how bizarre this whole thing has been."

"I got the picture." Laughter.

"It's probably okay for you to go home now."

"Nope, I'm going to stay here. I'll use it as quiet time. I'll be here if Carlton and the guys need any help. I know your kid, Bryan, is in there too."

"Thanks, Jack, I appreciate that. Would you go check on them in the morning? Give me a call after that."

"Sure will, Tanner."

"Joe, you were right about those crows.

"Ben—"

"Tanner, Joe filled me in while you were resting. We spent a lot of time with Grace and James."

❧

Flock Together

"Well, what did you think?"

"Took old Chip a while to answer the door, but I could see why, same old seedy bunch."

"Desmond, that's a hilarious play on words, seedy bunch."

"Our feathered friends hadn't seen or heard anything out of line. In case you didn't notice, they all came back with me. I saw that kid Bryan there, too. He was on the couch playing a video game. You know, Roscoe, I hope you don't make any more mistakes like you did with that girl. That was so, how do I say it? Ugh, a stupid move."

"Desmond, you—"

"Don't try anything, Roscoe. I told you the crows all came back with me. They would tell the Boss. Now, wouldn't they? Don't go storming around all night. Things look pretty good. I like your set-up."

Hmm, stupid man. I've got a little party favor for him.

"Thanks for staying up with me. Here it comes, Carlton. It's Roscoe calling. What if I mess up?

"Bryan, answer that. You can do this."

"Yeah, what do you want?... I didn't get my phone back until a few hours ago... Well, you'd have to talk to Chip about that. I was in lockup... How should I know? The cops do what they want to. We all got hauled in for something about a theft... Are we playing twenty questions, or do you want something?... Okay, I can do that. You have to give me a clue where to go... Yeah, I can get that. What time do you want it delivered?... How come I can't tell Chip?... All right, all right, don't have a fit. I'll have the package there... Okay, I'll bring it to the side entrance to the place... Yeah, I know where the shed is... Oh, you want me to go through the tunnel under the wall?... I'll be there with that package. Tell me where and when to pick it up. Well, send out your message and then call me when you get a connection... I understand."

"Wow, Bryan, you sounded perfect. I've heard you guys on calls. Sort of robotic. You know, you were all drugged and given hypnotic suggestions. At least that's what I figured."

"Carlton, no, I didn't know that. That's why we couldn't remember the calls. We've got to tell Tanner."

"Ugh, it's not even close to daylight. We've got to get some sleep. This was a big test, and apparently, Desmond didn't pick up on anything when he was here. Good thing I was paranoiac enough to set up all those cameras outside on those poles. My paranoia bought us some time to get the stage set before he arrived at the door."

"Yep, I guess your paranoia saved us. Maybe God made a provision through you. He knows everything."

"Wow, he used me? Thanks, kid, I feel better. Maybe something I have done is right."

"Carlton, we have to tell the guys about the hypnosis thing. Toss me a pillow, and I'm over and out." Laughter.

"I haven't laughed in a long time, Bryan. Thanks." *Wait until Lieutenant Tanner hears this. Maybe I really can help. That first night of freedom. Sleep without nightmares. Thanks, God.*

❦

"Emily, sorry I left you while I was with the guys."

"Travis, I had a life-changing time with Grace. She's a very wise and dedicated lady. Her calmness has been a mystery to me. She explained so much to me. I want us to have the same sort of relationship that James and she have."

"Em, I know what you mean. I always feel humbled when I'm around them. They still have joy and peace, even through this horrible ordeal. I can see their concern for all of us. I would be furious and frantic if my child were in danger. They don't even know if Alyssa is alive."

"That's where you're wrong. They know she is. Grace explained all of that to me. I know she's right. I could feel it. There are others too."

"Okay, Em, I'll believe with you. You're always my positive girl."

"You'll see, Travis. Let's go to sleep. I'm glad Tanner didn't send you with Beanie."

"You're not afraid, are you? I'll always protect you."

"I know you will— you and God. I love you, Travis. Give me a kiss. Sleep tight. I'll see you in the morning. I'll holler if I need you."

I wonder what Grace said to her. Something is different and yet still super sweet. I never thought I'd have to compete with you, God.

❧

I wait until Leslie is asleep. I slip quietly downstairs into the den. Jan smiles at me and tosses me a pillow. "Jan, I'm sorry I woke you up."

"You didn't, Dee Dee. I was lying here thinking about everything that has happened. I liked your speech tonight. You know, I'm changed, too. Look at us now." She chuckles and tosses me a quilt. "Go to sleep, Dee Dee. It's great to be with you. The BMW would've been more fun, but this will have to do. After all, this loveseat is just my size."

"Okay, Goldilocks." *Ah, Jan. Still witty.*

38

STRATEGIC CONSORTIUM

The hope of a new day is peaking through the pink horizon. "Stuart, what are you doing?"

"Tanner, I woke up with the strangest thoughts. It was Rose's voice in my head. 'Stuart, be faithful. Please don't leave Jacob. Remember, I taught you that love is the greatest. Love never fails. Forgive him and tell him the truth.' Tanner, I could feel her presence."

"Stuart, I didn't tell you, but Irene wants you to be with them. By the way, thanks for cleaning up last night. I noticed you were really quiet after your presentation."

"Oh, I was thinking about Alyssa, and all of a sudden, I had a flash of Anne. Tanner, does evil come back for its prey? You know, mountain lions do. I had a flash of a mountain lion going after Anne. I didn't say anything because it sounded so crazy, and I didn't want to interrupt."

Ding, ding, ding. "Stuart, there was a mountain lion the night we found Anne! They're going after her again! Get dressed, Stuart! I'm taking you to Irene's. Take whatever you need for tonight."

"Tanner, a lot of my stuff is at my apartment."

"Okay, I'm sure Jamison or Art will take you over there later. I'm going to take Libby with us. Travis! I've got to call Travis!" *Oh, it's so early. Poor Travis.*

"Travis, sorry, buddy. I know it's early. This is really important. I need you and Emily to go to the hospital. Don't let Anne out of your sight. I'm on my way, but I've got to drop Stuart off... Yeah, we're already up. Something's getting ready to happen. Get on it, buddy... I'll fill you in at the hospital.

"Stuart, would you quietly make some coffee while I get dressed? Wake Libby up. Tell her to be quiet and to not wake up Jan."

"Do you want me to wake up Joe and Ben?"

"No, we need them here."

"Wow, Tanner, you said we."

"Yes, Stuart, it's a *we*. I guess Rose defined your assignment. Sounds like God has, too. By the way, Stuart, I think of you as a friend. I couldn't let you get off-track. Get that coffee and Libby. Hurry!"

"Aye, aye, Sir."

"Libby, Libby, wake up."

"Stuart, what?"

"Shh. Tanner needs you to go with us in a few minutes. Don't wake up Jan. I'm making some coffee. Do you want some?"

"Melinda... Who is this?... Where is Melinda?... How did that happen? Is she going to be okay?... Katherine, I need you to check on Beth Adams right now!... What do you mean she's not in her room?... Call security and lock the hospital down!... Find her, but keep that ward locked!... I've already got an officer on his way. Don't let anyone else in. Call security and tell them to clear my officer and another female for entrance. No one else gets in, and no one gets out!

"Travis, buddy... You're already driving? Thank God! Beth Adams is missing! Get there quick!... I'm on my way! I've cleared you and Emily to get in. Melinda's been hurt... I know. Pray.

"Libby, I'll explain in the car.

"Stuart, thanks for the coffee. Let's go. Stuart, you're in for the long haul. There's no time to drop you off at Irene's."

"What's happened?"

"Make sure the door is locked tight. I'll tell you in the car."

"Tanner, Emily and I are here. There's a white van parked by the dumpster near the emergency entrance."

"Travis, get in there and find Beth Adams! Go through the main entrance. Stay on the phone.

"Emily, you've got to pull it together. She'll remember you. Libby, Stuart, and I are on our way."

"There she is!" Emily is already running toward her. "Hey, Anne. Remember me?"

"Hi, Emily. What are you doing here so early?"

"Well, I have a good friend, and I had special permission to check on her. What are you doing up so early? Nice coincidence to see each other."

"Well, one of the nurses fell, and so an aid told me that we needed to evacuate the rooms on third. Some kind of an infection caused her to fall. He told me to go to the ER entrance, and a white van would take me to a hotel. He said they were keeping all the patients separated because of the infection. I tried to open the door and walk outside, but it was locked. I don't see any van, do you?"

"Nope, but you don't have to go to a hotel. We're here now. You can go with us. We have to wait for Libby to pick us up."

"I'll get to see Libby, too? It will feel good to get out of here. Could I see Erica?"

"Anne, meet Travis."

"You sure look familiar. Have we met before?"

"Oh, maybe. I've been to the Seaview Apartments before. I know Erica."

"This is like a reunion. Certainly better than a hotel. You could drop me off at my apartment if you want to."

"I think we'll take you home with us. Look, Libby's pulling up right now. We'll find somebody from security to let us out."

Travis flashes his badge to the security officer. "Tanner, where do we take her?"

"To Erica. Travis, go with the girls and stay put at Constance's house. I'll take care of the van. Buddy, you and Brett keep everyone safe.

"Stuart, it's you and me now. Yes, you're driving. I'm going to check out that van. Keep the engine running."

Tanner stuffs his gun into his waistband and walks around the corner and towards the van. The van lurches into reverse and tries to back over Tanner. Stuart intervenes by speeding forward and lays on the horn, trying to get between the van and Tanner. Stuart comes to a screeching halt as the van speeds away.

"Stuart, you saved me."

"I've always wanted to do something like that. Are you hurt?"

"No, I'm shook up! Follow that van!"

"Tanner, it's already out of sight."

"Drive. I'll give you directions. We're going to Mrs. Carter's house. Turn here. I think Travis would've traveled this route. I've got to call Brett.

"Brett, there's a bunch of us coming your way. Looks like the plan is really in motion. We rescued the first target. News travels fast, so be vigilant. Have Travis call me when he gets there.

"Stuart, a little detour, we're going to check out that van. We're going to see Carlton's buddy at the tattoo parlor... Look, there's the van.

"Carlton, I know this is early. Take a head count of the guys... Everyone's there? That's a relief. Where's your van?"

"I don't know."

Tanner calls Jack. "Jack, did you get that tattoo parlor guy busted last night?... That explains a lot. You couldn't find him? Well, Carlton's van is over behind his salon... No, don't worry about it. Leave him alone for a little while, and I'll get back to you.

"Stuart, drive past and let me out. Keep the engine running. Keep your eyes open." Tanner gets out and walks past the van. He feels the hood. *Uh-huh, the engine's hot.* He walks on down the block and motions to Stuart.

"He's our driver, Stuart. The engine was hot."

"This police stuff is terrific! That's why I like action movies. I loved figuring out how they did their stunts. Speed, velocity—"

"Stuart, you were always a brainiac, weren't you?"

"I confess."

"Well, that brain saved me. You're a great partner. Do you have any experience with guns?"

"Oh, I used to go to the gun club with my dad. He thought I should get my nose out of books and do some real guy stuff. I'm actually a pretty good shot."

"I bet you are. You'll have your own gun tonight."

"Ooh, James Bond stuff, a real tuxedo, and a gun."

"Let's pick up food for Carlton and the guys. I want you to meet them and Jack. We'll put your brain to work again."

"My brain and my stomach are at your command. I have to tell you, though, the drive-up will take too long. Call us in an order, and it will be ready when we get there."

"Good idea, Stuart." *This guy is terrific, and he seems as cool as a cucumber.* "I'm still a little bit rattled by the van experience."

"You might want to call that Jack guy and invite him too. Can't wait to meet him. A real undercover cop. You think he is in disguise?"

"Stop, Stuart. Don't get too far out there yet. Save some of your energy. I need your full mind.

"Libby, how's my girl?... You've all decided?... Put Erica on...

"Hey, kiddo. Lib tells me you think Anne should meet with James and Grace."

"Lieutenant, I know she needs to know what happened. She's been having flashes about Alyssa. I think she would be able to make a breakthrough. She needs to realize how important she is, how brave she's been. I believe there's information that will help all of us. We've already talked to Jamison, and he thinks she will be fine."

"Okay, if Doc approves. Make sure you're not followed over to Kaplan's apartment. Tell Travis. Erica, you're something special."

"Thanks. Will you be seeing Bryan?"

"He's going to be busy for a while. Erica, this is your case. Work it well. Gotta go. Bryan and the guys' food is almost ready."

❋

"Stuart, there's Jack. Pull over and park."

"Tanner, may I call Irene? I need to tell her where I'm at. You know, she's expecting me."

"Sure, take your time. Jack can help me carry all this food in.

"Jack, I want you to meet Stuart.

"It's such an honor. A real live undercover cop."

"Well, thanks, Stuart. It's great to meet you. You must be important if Tanner let you drive. I've been relegated to carrying take-out food."

"He's important, Jack. Wait until you see this guy unleash his brain. He's amazing at solving problems."

"Whoa, Stuart, that's a compliment. Come to apartment 77 right up there. Can't wait to see you in action."

❋

"Hey guys, you all look rested and human again. Chow down. We've got work to do.

"Bryan, Erica said to tell you hi, but I'm not giving you a kiss.

"Sir—"

"Bryan, it's okay. I think that's sweet. The rest of you guys quit snickering. That's an order. You all remember Jack, don't you? I brought him along as another set of eyes. There'll be someone else coming soon, so save him some coffee and food.

"Carlton, you're on. Pray over the food..."

"Someone get the door.

"Stuart, come on in. Eat fast. We've already blessed it. I've got to talk to Bryan and Carlton."

"Sir, I got a call. I'm supposed to pick up a special delivery item. Roscoe's going to let me know the details."

"What was he talking about? What was the delivery about? Why is it so special?"

"I don't know, but I don't think they have a clue about the changes in us. Lieutenant, Desmond was here, but I didn't think he was suspicious at all."

"I don't either."

"You don't? How did you know he was here?"

"I sent a guardian angel of sorts."

"Sir, I should've known."

"Yep, Bryan, you should have. Guys, we have a lot to share with you. Now that Stuart is finished eating. Let's get down to the plan."

"You'll be impressed, Lieutenant."

"Carlton, I hope so.

"Guys, Stuart is one of the best men you'll ever meet. Listen up. Tell him what you found out. Answer any of the questions he has.

"Stuart, you're on."

"People are being held hostage. We discovered certain names on the seminar lists that represent plants from Haiti and other parts of the world. As you know, Voodoo is involved; for instance, your lab work came back indicating that you ingested some of those plants. For lack of better terms, zombie drugs, mind-altering, memory loss."

"Stuart, I want Carlton to tell you what he told me."

"Stuart, not only were the guys drugged, but they also have been taken through some kind of hypnosis. That's why they struggle to remember."

"Okay, I'm going to go back to the list. Well, about that list... I'm going to say some of these names. See if they mean anything to you. Alyssa Kirschenbaum, Primrose, Cherry Tree, Gwen Madison, Gwo Medsiyen, Fay Lugano, Fey Lougawou, Anne Lacey King, Queen Anne's Lace."

"That's my sister! Anne Lacey King! I use King as my street name, but it's really my last name! I'm going to—"

"Stop, King! We have good news! She's safe."

"Where?"

"Calm down. She's in very good hands. There are others still in danger."

"That's right, we all know some kids that have disappeared. Be glad your sister's okay. I know someone on the list, too. Her name is Glow Madison. She said some girl that she used to know was trying to help her, and then she disappeared. I wonder who that girl was. How did you guys get all up in this mess to begin with?"

"Andrew, there was a murder of a college female student."

"You're talking about that Summers girl, aren't you?"

Haitian Style

"You're upset because they're not all native plants? I thought an assortment of seeds from around the world would add a little diversity to the planting. It makes it a little more interesting. The Boss might like the English link. He liked my work with Bloody Mary. We both enjoyed her. That's how I got a new rank." *Those were the good old days, very proper. Pretty maids all in a row, Haitian style. Clever, clever, clever. Desmond never even made the correlation. Walking past pure genius every day. That stupid man. You know you have to have a little extra fun sometimes.*

"Let's see these blueprints you guys drew of the property. What's this area by the big shed?... It's a tunnel under the wall to that area?"

"Yeah, that's where I'm supposed to make that special delivery."

"Bryan, what's in the package?"

"I don't know. Roscoe told me not to screw up. Someone else missed the delivery. He was threatening me with that."

"Explain the mounds. Why are there pipes sticking out of the ground?"

"We don't know. Stuart, we don't remember a lot about what we did there. Remember, we were drugged and hypnotized. We all talked about it. I don't think I even worked there. I guess I ran some errands. Lieutenant Tanner, you know about the phone calls."

"Bryan, what you're telling me is that we have to scratch using memories?

"Carlton, you weren't drugged, were you?"

"No, I didn't really understand much of what was going on. All I have is some things I overheard and observed. Usually, I'd be in the house watching TV and keeping an eye on the Professor. I was a fool, an obedient soldier. Sorry, Stuart."

"Okay, we have a possible first point of entry. I've been on that property many times with Rose. There was no tunnel. Did you guys dig it? What are the pipes sticking up? Who has information?"

"Stuart, looks like you got this. I have to go to the station.

"Jack, could you get somebody to check on that van driver? Make sure he's not out driving anymore."

"My pleasure. I'll call you when the loose end is tied up."

"Thanks.

"Stuart, I need the keys. By the way, guys, he drives like a crazy maniac in an action movie. Nerves of steel."

Tanner is still smiling as the phone rings. "Constance, you're right, it is a beautiful day. How were all your house guests? Or should I ask, how were you with all the house guests?"

"Tanner, you're so funny. Is Bryan—"

"Yes, your stray cat is fine. How's Erica?"

"Tanner, I thought they told you. They were going to see Grace and James."

"They did. I thought maybe you had heard from Erica."

"Nothing yet, but I did hear from Al Kaplan. He's on schedule."

"Do we still have a date?"

"Of course, we're still on."

"Call me, and I'll be there. Would you put Brett on?

"Brett, I don't like the idea of Constance and Mr. Kaplan walking into the bookstore. It's been empty for a while. One never knows what could happen. Plus, it sounds like Mr. Kaplan has something important to tell me. He doesn't know everything that's been going on. My bell has been lightly dinging. Something is off. Put Constance back on. Thanks.

"Constance, make sure you and Brett take some friendly company with you."

"I understand. We will. It makes me feel better to have Brett here. I know Aaron would appreciate you watching over me."

"I'm sure he would, but I would've watched over you because of who you are. The famous Constance Carter, detective of a supreme kind. Be safe."

"Oh, Tanner, how sweet."

"Call me when you get to the bookstore."

As Tanner arrives at the office, he sees Beanie. "Hi, Beanie, my favorite secretary. Feels so strange to actually be here. I see you're feeling better." Tanner winks at her.

"I know, Sir, it's amazing that I got healed up so soon. Everyone has been so glad to see me back. We have so many great people who work here. You'll be impressed to see how Jim has risen to the occasion. He is so loyal to you. Please give him some kudos."

"Yes, ma'am, I will. Everything is normal here? No bizarre events, I hope… No, nothing?…"

"Apparently, only mundane things. Sheryl said it's actually been really boring."

"Boring is good. Are you going to participate tonight?"

"I am. I haven't come this far not to finish this. I'll be with you to the end. By the way, Libby has a tux for you, and I'm dressing to the nines. I wish Art was going to be there, but he hasn't been briefed on all this. He's been a wonderful support to us. Never asks questions. I feel so deceitful."

"Well, Beanie, if you think you need an escort, invite him. He's a fast learner. Bring him up to speed. Would you call him and see what's going on with Jacob? Why are you grinning like a Cheshire Cat?"

"Well, I have a tux for him. I set that up, just in case."

"See, that's why you're the World's Best Secretary. Actually, Beanie, I would feel better if Art was there looking out for you. Is there something going on that I don't know about?"

"Art will tell you. He didn't want to burden you with anything else. Let's move on."

"All right, I'll leave it alone for now. Do you have any idea how to put this together for tonight?"

"We need to set things in motion when the caterers go there. We need to be in action way before this thing happens, but how do we do that?"

"Shut the door, and let me tell you what I learned from Bryan. He got a phone call."

"Oh, Sir! Let me divert the calls to Sheryl. I'll tell her I'm taking dictation. Jim is off today, so he won't be checking in."

"I'll call Libby while you do that.

"Libby, is everything going well? Beanie informed me that you have a tux for me. That was a piece I spaced out completely. How's it going with Anne?... She knows about Alyssa?"

"Erica and Anne have been with Grace and James. Anne is beginning to remember. It's miraculous. Dee Dee and I are so excited. You can feel peace everywhere in this apartment. Emily and Travis have been off by themselves talking. Looks like love is in full bloom all over the place. Ben and Joe have been holed up in their room praying. I've never felt such power before. Tanner, I know everything is going to be okay. You've got some great backup. Dee Dee got a call from her aunt, and they're experiencing the same thing in Meadow Brook. You don't have to carry all the responsibility this time. He's got everything under control. He'll show you what to do. I have been so worried, but it's all gone."

"Lib, that was quite the sermon. I needed encouragement. Beanie and I are meeting in a moment. She has some thoughts. I'll share your mini-sermon with her. Wait, don't hang up. What about Jan?"

"She's been sleeping. Jamison is coming over. She'll be fine. Dee Dee said to tell you not to worry... Yeah, we all know you so well— vigilant, nervous, paranoiac, and responsible."

"Okay, Lib, I'll let go and simply do my part. Tell Ben and Joe thanks. I'll call ya after I hear from Stuart and Bryan."

"Beanie, is everything set in motion?"

"Yes, I put a note on the door that you were in a conference and locked it."

"Well, lay it on me. What are you thinking?"

"Well, I don't know why, but I keep thinking about the Israelites and how the cloud covered them during the day, and a wall of fire was between them and the enemy. Can't explain that, but I know we're protected."

"Beanie, wait until I tell you what Libby just told me."

"Wait, I also keep hearing music every time I pray or even think about all that's happened. I hear the words, *'A divine cord is woven through the natural.'* You probably think I've lost a couple of marbles. Well, maybe not. We've all experienced so many unusual, unexplainable things. A curtain between the natural and supernatural has been pulled back. We've all been allowed to see and experience things that ordinarily we wouldn't have believed."

"Beanie, I don't understand a lot, but what I do know is that I would've blown off things that I no longer discount. That's the difference between someone telling you and living it for yourself. Libby told me that Anne is starting to remember. Lib sounded like she was on cloud nine. She said there was something so peaceful and powerful in the apartment. She told me she knows everything's going to be okay."

"Yes, it will, Sir. I know it will."

"I've been so filled with dread. It's like a giant relief to know that God's moving right now."

"One more thing, Sir. Dee Dee's right on with what she said last night. Her sister's death will not be in vain."

"Beanie, you talked to Al Kaplan several times. Would you like to meet him?"

"Yes, Constance told me he's arriving today. Is this an invitation?"

"Well, it's Constance's case, but you girls are partners, so it hit me that you should be involved. After I check in with Stuart, would you accompany me to lunch and then to the bookstore?"

"Sir, I'm so curious. It's a date. What's going on at Carlton's? You said we'd have a plan. Do we? I'm so unsure of what my part is."

"Beanie, you're going to be Art's informant and his date."

"Sir, don't joke about this. Let's call Stuart."

"Stuart, wait, wait, calm down... It's what?... The package is what?... Back up, slow down. Bryan just got another call?... He has an address?... It's our address? It's Mr. Kaplan's? How in the world?"

"I don't know, Tanner, but he's supposed to pick up a special package. He told Bryan to get someone to go with him. There might be two. I know it's Dee Dee, and the other one might be Anne."

"Stuart, that's pretty far out."

"Well, you asked me to unleash my brain. Why else would that have happened at the hospital this morning? Bryan was threatened by Roscoe. He was told not to screw up like the other guy did. Remember Madelyn's dream and Libby telling us about Dee Dee trying to leave the apartment the other night?"

Ding, ding, ding. "Stuart, call the station and leave a desperate message for me personally and give them Carlton's address. Beanie and I'll be right there.

"Come on, Beanie. It's war." Tanner brings Beanie up to speed as they drive to Carlton's apartment. "Beanie, how could they have figured out where Dee Dee is? I've always known that Anne was vulnerable. Carlton may be able to help us. He showed up at the hospital once. I've made a mistake somewhere. Who knew about Kaplan's apartment?"

"Sir, you have taken so many measures to protect everyone. You are human, so stop it. You're not God, but he's on your side. We'll figure it out. You are not alone anymore."

"Whoa, we're here, Beanie, Mistress of Details. Sorry I started going off." *The Chief would tell me to carry on. Constance, his words are still true.* "Let's see what they've come up with." *No crows. That's good.*

Tanner begins to knock! "Bryan, you startled me when you jerked the door open!"

"Sir, I was so excited to see you on the cameras. We have so many things to tell you.

"Miss Beanie, it's good to see you."

"Oh, Bryan, our favorite little stray cat. Please introduce me to all our new friends."

"See, guys, I told you what a great lady she is. Like a real mom to me. Beanie, meet our new team members and friends."

"Well, Bryan, we're all like the lost boys in *Peter Pan*."

"Miss Beanie, we need a Wendy. Don't we, guys?"

"How sweet. I guess we're all going after the evil Captain Hook. If I'm Wendy, is Lieutenant Tanner Peter Pan?... How nice to hear you all laugh. Let's see how good you are at putting it all together."

"Tanner, we've got a plan. We connected all the dots and filled in the holes. These guys are strategic thinkers."

"Stuart, they couldn't remember much when I was here earlier."

"Well, Jack took care of that. Turns out he knows a lot about breaking holds over people."

"Jack, what is he talking about?"

"Tanner, my grandfather was a pastor, and he taught me how to deal with things that go, well, bump in the night. I did what he taught me to do and prayed. We broke the hold of that hypnosis. Each one of the guys had a little piece of the puzzle, and we put them together. There was enough background to figure out why and how they were used."

"Jack, I had no idea—"

"Isn't that what we talked about the other day? Undercover Christianity?"

"Touché again, Jack.

"Okay, Stuart, lay it out."

"Well, Tanner, we were all sucked into this when Jacob had a breakdown. In his grief, he misunderstood what Rose and I were doing. Through insanity and brokenness, he thought Rose was working on a plan to resurrect the dead. She was working on addressing cancer through nature and creating a less damaging process of eradicating it. He couldn't believe Rose died and didn't believe in the true resurrection. Rose had books on Voodoo because she was researching the plants, not the practice, hence the trip to Haiti. Something diverted the researchers we were supposed to meet. We ended up with Desmond and the practice. Jacob was drugged and used by evil to start this bizarre project.

"There are two tunnels. One runs under the wall from the woods. Another one was dug full-length of the plot. They are big tunnels about eight feet wide and ten feet high. Some of the guys remember helping a contractor run the electrical and water in them. Jacob told the contractor that some plants needed to be grown underground. He said he was growing seeds that needed to be kept cool and out of direct sunlight. Remember when Dee Dee and I went through the lists?"

Beanie springs from her chair. "Oh, Dear Lord, Stuart! You're saying the seeds are people!"

"Yes, I am. We all agree there's more. The guys also helped install a huge ventilation system; hence the pipes sticking up. The mounds represent a person, and they grew Jimson Weed, known as Devil's Claw, over the mounds."

Oh, Lord, what a mix of the spiritual and natural. "I should have torn into that property without a warrant."

"Lieutenant Tanner, we would all still be like we were. We would've either been killed or hauled off to prison. If anyone died, you know we would've been blamed. Because you waited, we are free with a future. Carlton thinks we'd have been killed at the end of the project and dumped somewhere in Wilderness Walk. We think so, too, because a couple of the guys have already disappeared. If you had raided the property, all they had to do was shut off the air. The Professor and all of us would've been taking the blame."

"Andrew is right. I might even have been accused, and Carlton would've been charged or killed."

"Stuart, you're right. I wouldn't have realized what actually happened, and the whole thing would've been covered up by the University. I apologize for my comment. I'm grateful for every last one of you. What's the plan?"

"The guys have all gotten calls, and they understand their assignments. Carlton knows what he's supposed to do."

"By the way, Carlton, how would anyone know about Mr. Kaplan's apartment?"

"I'm not sure, but one of my recruits made a delivery there. He was bragging about a tip he got. Maybe he bragged to the wrong person. Plus, there were other things we can't totally explain, like the crows. There's always plenty of them on the walls. Remember the note you sent me—"Crows Everywhere. Be Careful." Well, at this point, I guess it doesn't matter how they know, but they do."

"So, Bryan, who are you taking to Kaplan's with you?"

"Sir, I'm taking King. If Anne is involved, who better?"

"King, you might be too close to this. Can you keep a cool head?"

"Yes, Sir, I know I can. I'm as concerned about everyone as I am about Anne. She would expect me to do that. If there are others, their families have been as frantic as I have been. My sister needs me. I want her to know I've changed and now am a new person. Please, I'm—"

"King, all right. I'm counting on you. In fact, many people will be."

"Yes, Sir."

"Jack, can you and Carlton orchestrate the ground operations?"

"Yes, we've got you covered. It will be a well-oiled machine. Do I need to have some of my officers at Wilderness Walk as a backup? I can line it up."

"Yeah, Jack, and have a couple of shooters lined up. Be choosy. No blabbers and no egomaniacs. You know how swat teams can be. We need cool heads and tight lips."

"I have the perfect team in mind, and we will run this off the record. Call it volunteer service. No questions asked."

"Always ready and off the record like you, Jack?"

"They're almost exact duplicates. Don't you ask questions either, then we'll all be fine."

"Tanner, it's Constance."

"Answer it, Beanie."

"Constance, thank goodness you called. Tanner is tied up. We're both coming to meet you... Mr. Kaplan's plane hasn't landed yet?... Oh, yeah. Tanner is bringing me, too. Partners again... It's been a productive morning. The plan is coming together. Tell Brett that he better take care of my partner... I know. He's a very nice young man. See you soon. Call us when you get to the bookstore."

"Stuart, let's get moving. We'll take you to your apartment to get your dress clothes before we drop you at Irene's.

"Beanie, call Art. Ask if Jamison is there.

"Guys, take care of Jack and Carlton. We'll work on getting acquainted when this is over. Thanks.

"Bryan, I'll talk to you later. Pray before you all go."

❧

"Tanner, I'm going to drive if it's okay. I'm still jazzed. Did I do well with my assignment?"

"Stuart, you are the driver of the day. I couldn't have managed that bunch like you did. You delivered for me and everyone. I had a few doubts."

"Really? Doubts about me?"

"Not doubts about you, but the guys. That was another issue. I'm glad Jack and Bryan were there."

"Me too, Tanner. I'd have to say, though, the guys were great. We all brainstormed. It wasn't just me with my unleashed mind. They're sort of free spirits in a good way." Laughter. "I've learned a lot."

"I'm sure you did. I know I have." *Jack, who is he inside? He's a complex man. I would've never known. I have to start looking at people through new eyes.*

"Beanie, I guess I dozed off. Poor Stuart."

"Sir, he's getting his clothes for tonight."

"Wake me up when we get to Irene's."

"I will. You need to rest. I'm going to call Art right now."

✽

"Beanie, does Irene know I'm coming?"

"Shh, Stuart. Yes, I spoke to Art, and I told him. Lieutenant needs to sleep. Are you going to tell Jacob what's been going on?"

"Yes, if he's in good shape. I had a dream about Rose. Did Tanner tell you?"

"No, I knew about Anne because they were all at the house before I left for work."

"Well, in this dream, Rose told me to forgive him and tell him the truth. Beanie, it was so real I could feel her presence when I woke up."

"You were really close to Rose, weren't you? Irene will know if Jacob's well enough to hear the truth."

"Beanie, you're right. Jacob and Rose were close to Irene long before I came. Thanks, she'll know what to do."

"Sir, we're here."

"Where's Stuart?"

"He's already gone in. Here comes Art."

Art has a puzzled look on his face. "Beanie, why are you in the front seat?"

"Well, Stuart was driving, and now I'm going to."

"When will you be back? Are you coming here?"

"Yes, and I've got a tuxedo for you. You're my date for tonight."

"Lieutenant, is that true? Am I supposed to go to whatever kind of celebration you're attending?"

"Art, you're invited unless you change your mind after what Beanie tells you. Will your wife be upset?"

"That's another issue. I guess Beanie didn't tell you. She won't be a problem. Turns out, she's gone. All that stuff about wanting me home was a spoof. She kept track of every minute so she'd know where I was. She was mixed up with another guy. She's gone for good. Cleaned out all the bank accounts, too."

"Art, I'm sorry."

"Oh, don't be. I feel stupid, but I'm free."

"Art, I'll be back, but I've got to get to a meeting with Constance. I'd leave Beanie, but she's going with me."

"Take care of her. I don't know what's going on, but it feels off to me."

"Thanks for the warning. I won't let anything happen to her. I know she's special."

"Tanner, that plane will be landing in a few minutes."

"Okay, Beanie.

"Art, our girl will be back." *I should have said your girl.*

A pat on the window as he shut the door. "Drive, Beanie. Let's eat close to the bookstore. Pick any place you want."

39
RECOMPENSE

"**M**y goodness, Al, it's good to see you. Lieutenant Tanner and Beanie will meet us at the bookstore."

"Constance, I can't tell you how good it feels to be here. I missed Oak City. All my best memories are here. You and Aaron are part of those memories. Thanks for picking me up. Lunch is on me."

"Al, this is Brett. Tanner thought we should have an official escort. There have been some very unusual things going on."

"It's a pleasure to meet you, Brett. I figured things were out of whack. That's what I wanted to talk to your boss about. Very odd."

"Mr. Kaplan, I'm sure he'll appreciate your insight. I'm aware of how generous you have been. I've never been to your store, and I love to read."

"Constance, it looked like the Lieutenant picked the perfect escort for us."

"Oh, indeed he did."

***

"Sir, will this suit you? We're only six blocks from Mr. Kaplan's store."

"Beanie, as always, it's perfect. Sorry I slept the whole way. I'm not very good company, am I?"

"You needed to relax. You've been hanging by a string ever since October of last year, before I even came. Thank you for letting me be more than just your secretary. You'll never know what a blessing working for and with you has been."

"Beanie, don't go all gooey on me. Let's go in and order." *I'm the one that's been blessed.*

"Oh, Tanner, Jamison hadn't gotten back yet, so Irene said she had no idea about Jan's condition. You're nervous about Jan being there tonight, aren't you?"

"You know me well. Jan seems so fragile, but Ben tells me it's hopeless to try to separate Dee Dee and Jan. Something about going clear to the end."

"Some people have to fulfill things in their lives. Apparently, Dee Dee and Jan have made up their minds. I think there's a special bond between those women. Jamison will be there if Jan has any medical issues. It's also neat to see how Ben and Jan connect with Dee Dee. Very special. You can't interfere with that. It's untouchable. Some things are simply the way they are."

"Beanie, you always see so clearly. You and Libby are my emotional eyes. I wonder what Al Kaplan is going to tell me. Hope it helps us and isn't a waste of time."

"Sir, Constance assures me that Al wouldn't dream something up. She says it must be important. Speaking of Constance, she's ringing in.

"Constance, we've been waiting for your call... You'll be at the bookstore in about thirty minutes?... Can't wait to meet Mr. Kaplan. See you shortly."

"Beanie, don't raise that eyebrow. I know, it's only partially true about Kaplan."

"I was just teasing. Sir, I know you hate half-truths."

"Let's talk about you and Art... Now, who has the arched eyebrow?" Laughter.

"Well, Mr. Kaplan, we finally meet. I want to thank you for your help. Your generosity kept me from going crazy."

"I told you before to call me Al. I'm intrigued about what is going on. Maybe there's a book to be written. I'm sure you know about my original intent— why I disappeared."

"Yes, Al. Beanie told me. I thought the case of the disappearing bookstore owner was a good idea. Initially, I thought of your situation as a distraction, an inconvenience. I had a murder case I was working on when you popped up. How could I have known you would've been such a vital part, a provision for all of us involved? Constance told me you have something to tell me.

"Brett, have you checked out the entire store?"

"Yes, Sir, I have. Looks like nothing has been disturbed, to my knowledge. What a great place it is. Mr. Kaplan, your store is every reader's dream. I saw your private collection. You must have spent years working on it."

"Brett, when whatever is going on is over, you remember to come, and I'll let you read every rare piece.

"Tanner, could I speak with you alone? We could go to my little apartment upstairs.

"Constance, you know where everything is. Please entertain our guests."

Oh, we're their guests. Wonder what the Chief would think of that— our guests.

As Tanner and Al travel up the third set of stairs, they arrive at a door. "Al, why do you have that number one on this door?"

"It's tender humor from a long time ago. My wife was number one, and this was our little hideaway."

"Al, this is outstanding and huge." *Not such a little hideaway.*

"She loved antiques. Some of these are over four hundred years old. Today is not a day for the grand tour, though. This is a day for recompense. Tanner, I think I may have done something that could've endangered your case. It has to do with Adlin Summers. There were so many holes. I got nosey while I was away. I made a phone call to one of the guys who helped me move. I sent him to spy on my apartment to see what was going on. Tanner, that's where it starts getting weird. He called me one night and was practically incoherent. He said he's been physically in the hallway by my door. How could he have gotten in? He was rambling on about picking up a delivery but couldn't get it. He was frightened."

"Who is this guy?"

"He's the one I had sold my car to when I disappeared. I liked him. He met your officer, Travis, once."

"When?"

"I guess you had a lot of groceries delivered to my apartment."

"Oh, Lord, Al!" *Ding, ding, ding.* "He's one of the guys Travis tipped. The delivery guy, the one with the tattoo."

"Yes, Tanner, I asked him about the tattoo, but he said he couldn't remember how he got it. Tanner, I'm so sorry. I can see the look on your face. Recompense is due."

"Al, can you contact him?"

"He told me he was required to make up for missing the first delivery by making another pick-up. I know he's in trouble. I haven't been able to contact him since. He was babbling about somebody praying for him and flashes of memories he was having. This has to be linked to you and this case. I told him to go to you. He tried, but you haven't been in. That's why I came. My curiosity may have killed the cat."

"What's his name?"

"Daniel, but I don't know his last name."

"Al, I've got to make a phone call.

"Jack, ask the guys if they know someone named Daniel. I'll wait... Do they?...No?... Call me back if you get some more information. That kid's really in trouble. He needs help now. He's the kid who missed the pick-up of Beth Adams. Send someone to that tattoo parlor ASAP.

"Al Kaplan, I could hug you. We'll talk about the recompense issue later. I've got to go, but I'm leaving Constance and Brett with you. No more snooping. They'll tell you the story of a lifetime. Let's quickly get downstairs.

"Beanie and I have to go. Constance, fill our curious friend in on everything."

"Tanner, everything?"

"Everything from the beginning. Then, Al will give you a dissertation on the meaning of recompense. Pray for Daniel."

"Daniel, who's Daniel?"

"Brett, Al will fill you in, and do not leave these people. Keep them safe."

"Sir, who is Daniel?"

"He's the link to the mystery of how they knew about Kaplan's apartment. Beanie, pray for that kid. He's in danger." *Daniel's in the lion's den. There's that word lion again. Lord, help that kid.*

❧

Uplifting?

"Roscoe, what are you sulking around about?"

"I'm not, I'm just thinking."

"That must be refreshing for you."

"Don't start, Desmond! You finally got up, and I've been putting the finishing touches on everything. Scheduling pick-ups… I have to do everything! Do you think you could waddle down and check on our little seeds, or do you have to eat breakfast first?"

"Just because you never eat."

He still doesn't get it what I feed on, what gives me strength. Stupid man. Stay calm, Roscoe. "Desmond, please check on the seeds. Be sure to log in on the progress chart and then eat all you want. I'm going for a walk in the woods. Can't be too careful."

"That's better, Roscoe. I can see why I had to come. Someone had to lift your spirits and keep you on schedule."

He has no idea how uplifting he will be. Lazy, lazy, lazy, and boring. That Paxton kid has been a fantastic informant. I would hate to have to terminate his connection.

40

THE LION'S DEN

"I almost forgot. Your car is still at the station."

"Look, Sir, there's a white van. Could it be the one that was at the hospital?"

"Let's find out. Call Jack and see if that van is still at the parlor or if they found that kid, Daniel."

"Jack, this is Beanie. Did you find anything out on the van or that kid, Daniel?... Okay, I'll tell him you didn't find either. Thanks."

"I'm going to pull him over. Do you have your friend on you?"

"Right here in my purse, Sir."

"If anything starts, use it."

Surprisingly, the van does not speed up as Tanner puts the flasher on the top of the car. "What, no high-speed chase? Beanie look. That young guy is getting out and putting his hands on the hood. Might be someone else in the van. Slide over to the driver's seat and be ready."

"Yes, Sir."

"Hey, driving a little fast, weren't you? Thanks for stopping, and thanks for not giving me a hard time. Let me see your license, and then put your hands back on the hood. Paxton D. Ross. Well, what does the D stand for?"

"Daniel, Sir."

"Well, Mr. Ross, could you show me your insurance? Is it in the glove compartment? Let's go and get it… Okay, let's see what you've got in here."

"Sir, there's no one else in the van if that's what you're wondering. Would you handcuff me and take me to your car?"

"What?"

"Please do it. I'm running from someone, but it isn't you. I'm the one who almost ran over you."

"Well, this is one story I've got to hear. Put your hands behind your back." Tanner puts his gun in his waste-band and escorts the kid to the car."

"Make it look good. Make it look like I'm struggling."

"Gotcha. Now, get in the back.

"Miss Sanders, meet Paxton Daniel Ross."

"Oh, my goodness! You're Daniel!"

"Yes, ma'am. Thank goodness I found you and Lieutenant Tanner."

"Were you tracking us?"

"Yep. I waited outside the station until I saw you come out. When you went to that restaurant, I got the van. I was hoping you'd see me."

"What in the world is going on? Do you know Mr. Kaplan?"

"Yeah, I followed you to the bookstore."

"Beanie, you and I are really starting to lose our instincts."

"I figured you'd leave at some point, and I'd give you a reason to arrest me. I need protection. I screwed up a couple of times. The consequences could be tough."

"Why did you try to run over me?"

"I got scared and didn't know who could be watching. I'm so sorry. That crazy driver was awesome. You must have some kind of partner. He came out of nowhere, but it snapped me to my senses, and I drove off."

"What were you doing at the hospital?"

"I was supposed to pick up a girl."

"Where were you going to take her?"

"I'm not sure. I didn't complete the pick-up. Well, you know that."

"How did you know me?"

"I was at Mr. Kaplan's when those gals had all that food delivered, and that guy sent us a really big tip. I had been there before to help Mr. Kaplan move in. He asked me to keep an eye on the apartment, and your picture had been in the paper. Big coincidence, isn't it?"

"Daniel, I've changed my thinking on that. I don't believe in coincidences anymore. Nothing is random."

"Like karma?"

"No, much more, well-planned and connected."

"Oh, you're talking about God. That's why I was trying to meet you. Had this friend. She would always tell me about Him. She said when we're in trouble, God always has someone praying for us. That's if they obey Him. You were working that murder case."

"Adlin Summers? You knew her?"

"Yeah, I used to deliver food to the University. So, I would eat in the park, and that's how I met her. I never met anyone like Adlin. She was special. I can't believe anyone would have hurt her."

"Daniel, did Adlin talk to you about evil?"

"She did. You know how it is. You keep on doing things you shouldn't. She thought that I might, as she put it, be led astray. I'm so insignificant. I didn't think the devil would be interested."

"Let me see your left wrist."

"I'm ashamed, Lieutenant. I don't know how I got it, but I didn't have the tattoo until after Adlin died. I think she would've been freaked out over it."

"I think she would've, too."

"What is going on? My memory loss was hacking me off. I started repeating what Adlin had said, 'Someone's praying,' and little bits started coming back. Those phone calls are connected to something weird. I started to think I was a zombie. I got completely away from all the crowd I hung with. I've been paranoid. Now, I've almost killed the person who might have helped me. Mr. Kaplan told me to talk to you, but you weren't in. That other officer, Prince, creeped me out, Carlton. I didn't know if I could trust him. I really didn't know if I could trust you. I'm really afraid. My memory is coming back. Am I going crazy, or did I—"

"Beanie and I are going to make sure you're protected. Daniel, you have no idea how many people are praying. I'm so glad you found us.

"Beanie, Jack is ringing me. Take my phone and tell him about Daniel. Daniel and I are going to pray."

"Sir, I'm going to give you both some private time. I'll take this one over by the van.

"Jack, it's Beanie. We found Daniel. Well, actually, he found us... Ask the guys if they know someone named Paxton...Tanner's motioning to me. I've got to go... I'll tell him. Thanks, Jack.

"Sir, Jack wants you to know they are ready. They're prayed up, and all have gotten calls with instructions."

"Daniel, who do you work for?"

"Some guy named Roscoe. I've never met him. I had gotten so weird I couldn't work for the deli anymore. One day, he called me. I pick up and deliver things for him. One night, I found myself in the hallway of your apartment building. I didn't know how I got there. Freaked me out. What have I gotten mixed up in? Did you find Adlin's murderer? There's been nothing in the papers."

"No, but we're about to. You may be able to help us. Share the memories that have come back.

"Beanie, you look like you know something. What is it?"

"Daniel, what do you have in the van?"

"Black robes with hoods, except for two of them. There are also two white ones with hoods."

"When are you supposed to deliver them?"

"Today, to creepy old, Carlton Prince. I'm driving his van. Makes me sick, and I'm afraid. I'm supposed to go to Wilderness Walk after that. I might not be coming back. It's just a feeling I have, but I'm afraid to *not* go."

"Kid, it's okay. We've got you covered. Some good news for you. Carlton knows the same Lord that Adlin was teaching you about. He's on the side of good. It's safe for you to make that delivery to him and you will be surprised. Bryan will help you, too. We'll figure out the Wilderness Walk issue. Nothing is going to happen to you."

"I have that mark, the tattoo. It's a mark of death; I know it is. Everyone that has it is going to die. It's a seal of some kind. Does what we prayed today change that?"

"Yes, Daniel, it does. He does. He's in control of you. In control of your future. He is life."

"Well, Adlin was the best person I've ever known, and she died."

"Well, I'll have her sister explain it to you."

"You know Dee Dee? Adlin told me all about her."

"Yes, you'll get to meet her soon. Adlin would be so pleased."

"Gosh, Miss Beanie, don't cry. I'll start, too. Sweet Adlin. Man, I miss her. I've got to get going. I need to get the van over to Carlton. I hope he's changed. Should I stay there until I hear from you?"

"Get going. I'm going to write you a ticket. You can put it in the glove box to prove why you were pulled over. It's your cover.

"Beanie, call Bryan. Tell him to watch for Daniel."

"Oh, Miss Beanie, thank you for the hug. You're bound and determined to make me cry, aren't you?"

"Godspeed and blessings on you, Daniel. There's a whole army of people traveling with you. Angels and believers."

As Daniel drives off, Tanner and Beanie sit quietly in the car. "Beanie, can you believe it? We're almost finished. There will be recompense and justice. It's Friday, and we are on our way to that celebration."

"Sir, when I was talking to Jack, Irene was calling in, but I knew Daniel was more important at that moment. Please call her. She's definitely not naggy or impatient. It must be important."

"Irene, I was in the middle of something when you called... Don't apologize... Heavenly Caterers called and asked if you needed a crew to clean?"

"Jacob's been ranting all morning about cleaning for tonight. I had him call Roscoe. Jacob wouldn't take no for an answer. They'll be there at 3:30 to clean. When I called Martina back, she said to tell you everything will come together nicely. Her tone of voice was so comforting. "Jacob had been coming unraveled until Stuart got here. They have been talking out on the back patio. Something big is going on. I peek out every once in a while. I can tell by Jacob's expressions and motions. I have never seen Stuart so...hmm, the word would be resolute. When he got here, it was like he was on a mission. Thanks for putting him here."

"You're right. He is on a mission. He got his marching orders directly from Rose. Stuart had a dream. Because of Stuart, we rescued Anne. Call Libby or Emily, and they'll explain all the details. Perfect Woman, keep your bunch together. Some other things have happened. Beanie would like to get dressed at your house. She can report all the news after she gets there."

"Send her over. I could use a female friend. I'm surrounded by guys. I know Jacob would love her, and Art already does. She can have her own room and a private bath. Tanner, Jamison and I will be with you to the end. It's been a joy to have you in my life. What a life we've had, World's Best Detective."

"Irene, we'll all be fine. Tell Stuart to watch for crows. He'll know what that means."

"I didn't tell you, but Martina said to tell you not to worry about the birds. I didn't know what she meant. I thought she had misspoken."

I hope the Heavenly Caterer does a good job of cleaning. Wonder what they'll find in that house?

The Rules

"How could you agree to a cleaning crew coming here?"

"Desmond, I guess you don't know the rules. The owner of something has to submit and give in. If they don't, we have no authority. After all, you know we have to be invited. Proper house guests, protocol. It's his house." *How rude. Desmond doesn't even know the basic protocol, the rules. Completely devoid of decorum.*

Tanner calls Travis. "Travis, I saw your car in the lot this morning, but Beanie and I got tied up. Where are you right now?... Great, I'm on my way to the station. Beanie's car is there... Okay, let's meet at the little area by the station... I knew you'd be checking up on everyone. Thanks for taking care of things for me. See you in about twenty minutes.

"Will it be okay if I take you to the station? Where are your clothes for tonight?"

"Sir, they're in my car."

"Always prepared, aren't you? The World's Best Secretary. I'm so thankful to have you on our side. You're a true partner."

"Sir, I'm going straight to Irene's. I won't go anywhere else. I'll be fine."

"You mean straight to Art? Close those beautiful eyes and rest while I drive."

As Tanner is pulling out of the lot after Beanie is safely tucked into her car, Travis is waiting. "Hey, Tanner, over here."

"Travis, buddy, I had to see you alone. We have been working on this from the beginning. There are so many people around it. It's hard to remember where it started— two lone officers and no clues."

"I've been hoping to hear directly from you, but I didn't want to bungle anything."

"You could never do that. I depend on you to take care of things. Travis, you're one of the finest officers I know. I treat you like my kid. If you were, I couldn't be prouder."

"Well, since you brought that up, Emily thinks of you like a dad. She's never had a man she respected more than you. I want to ask you for her hand in marriage. We agreed that we want your blessing."

"Buddy, I knew you were making plans. I'm honored and humbled. I give you my blessing and all of my support. You and Emily are a perfect match. I have to say, though, I wasn't expecting it, considering the timing is so unique."

"I know, Sir, but I couldn't hold it in. Especially when we're about to come to the end of this long ordeal."

"Travis, I've neglected both of you lately."

"That's not true. What you have done is beyond anyone else's abilities. I've learned so much about how to be a real man and a true leader. I came to get my orders directly from you. What is my part in this?"

"I want you to watch over Anne and Dee Dee."

"Sir, I thought you'd have Ben or Joe do that. They—"

"You're my star officer, and this is still our case. We started this together, and we still have the lead on this."

"What about Emily?"

"She'll be with Libby and the rest of us. I promise we'll take good care of her. You can turn the assignment down, but let me fill you in before you make that decision." The two sit quietly at the picnic table as Tanner brings Travis up to speed on the developments.

"Tanner, you want me to be with Bryan, don't you?"

"Travis, I need someone who can blend in with the guys. I have a copy of that tattoo in that drawer in my office. I want you to get a henna tattoo exactly like it. What do you think? I don't want anyone else with Anne and Dee Dee when King and Bryan pick them up. King doesn't have a tattoo, either."

"I'll pick him up, Sir. We can't take any chances."

"Talk to Emily and let her know if you're taking this assignment. I won't think less of you if you turn it down. You kids mean everything to me. We're in charge, so we make the decisions together."

"Sir, you know how I feel. Let's have a quick prayer." The scene in the park is a rare one. Two grown men with heads down and hands clasped. Tears shining and welling up in their eyes.

"Buddy, give me a hug."

"Sir, don't make me cry. Godspeed, Tanner. I'll see you at the apartment. I'll call Emily, and if it's a go, I'll get King and go to the tattoo parlor, but it won't be that salon connected to Carlton."

"Here's my office keys. That drawing is in the top metal drawer." Tanner grabs Travis and hugs him again. "That's for posterity and old times. Thanks for meeting me, and congratulations. Emily is a gift. You're a blessed man. Travis, make a good decision. Let me know what the two of you decide. We'll see you later."

Lord, did I make a mistake asking Travis to do this? I trust him so much. He's like a son. Thanks for bringing him here. Take care of him. Wonder if Libby will be angry with me over this.

"Libby, I'm on my way." *Why didn't she answer? Hope she hears my message. Fifteen more minutes, and I'll be there.*

It wasn't until Tanner got to the apartment that he realized his key was on the ring he gave Travis. The doorman laughed as Tanner asked to be let in. "Here, I'll use my elevator key, so you don't have to be buzzed up."

"Thanks." *This is strangely embarrassing. I wonder how many other details I'm forgetting. The tux, the keys, what else? Buck up, Tanner. You'll have to face Emily and Libby.*

Tanner barely taps on the door and it flies open. "Tanner, where have you been? I tried to call you back. You didn't answer. I'd have been frantic if the peace and power hadn't flowed through here all day."

"Oh, Lib."

"Oh, you thought Emily and I would be upset? I couldn't ever be, especially after the day we've had here. Remember, we have an agreement."

"Libby, let's get married. Shall we?" Tanner gently kisses Libby.

She whispers, "I told you I love you. I told you love was in bloom. The answer is yes. Let's not tell anyone yet, though. I know Travis asked you for Emily's hand today. This needs to be their special time."

"Some special time. We're about to deal with this horrible nightmare."

"Tanner, I have no idea what will happen, but all my fear is gone... That doesn't mean we are being casual. We are all just maintaining. Keeping close to God. Whatever we're dealing with is more than something in the natural. It's like we're all walking into the shadow of death. Remember the next line? That's where we all are."

"Libby, you know I would—"

"Shh, nothing is going to happen to me."

"Where is everyone?"

"Well, Emily and Erica and Leslie are all getting ready for tonight. We have a celebration to attend."

"Don't make light of this, Libby."

"I'm not, but we are going to play our parts. Ben and Joe went shopping. Joe called Jack, and we all have "friends" to take with us."

"I knew I loved those guys. Prayer and guns."

"Wait until you see my leg holster."

"Ooh, that sounds enticing."

"Everyone is carrying. Ben and Joe got the run-down from Bryan. Does that make you feel better? We took care of Stuart and Jamison, too. Jacob finally realizes the truth. He's got his part memorized. He's furious, but he will do whatever you want. Stuart will be with him. Jacob has a limo ordered so Art and all of them can travel together. See, all you have to do is get dressed and play your part... Yes, Irene called, and yes, they're getting ready. The cleaners were at the house and the caterers are on schedule. The caterer wanted to do an early run-through to see if Irene and Jacob approved the way everything is arranged."

Spotless

"That was awful. How could you tolerate all those people touching everything? Do you think they stole anything?"

"Roscoe, the place is spotless! You're the one who agreed that they could come. You could have come in."

"I couldn't. That fragrance was almost sickening."

"What fragrance? It was cleaning supplies, I guess."

"Help me hang this up against the garden wall. Hook it on those chains."

"What is it?"

"Oh, you'll see tonight. You'll be surprised." *I'm not going back in that house. Hmm. Cleaning supplies are sickening.*

❧

"Bryan, my phone is ringing. It's Roscoe."

"Answer it. I'll be right here. Don't be afraid."

"Yeah, I'm at Carlton's. I got pulled over... Just a ticket... It will take me a while to get there. Traffic's terrible... Carlton's apartment is jammed out with all these guys. He said he doesn't have room for 'em. He suggested I bring them to Wilderness Walk... Yes, I counted them. They're all there. Your costume party will be great. They're what you ordered. Carlton wants to know if the change of plans is okay... All right, I'll call you when I'm getting close... No, I'll be there. I won't mess up again... Okay.

"Bryan, what am I gonna do? That place is so creepy."

"Don't worry, Daniel, I'll call Tanner."

❋

"Tanner, Daniel got a call. He's got to make that delivery to Jacob's house. He can't go there by himself."

"Put Jack on.

"Jack, he can't go there. Period. How about a flat tire and another delivery guy helps him out? Two of them, in fact."

"I'll take care of it, Tanner. Don't worry.

"Daniel, you're going to drive towards Wilderness Walk, and there's going to be a big blowout on a tire. Conveniently, two guys are going to make the delivery for you."

Jack calls Tessa. "Tessa, I need a delivery van ASAP to the corner of Spruce and Sixth Street. Two undercovers... Yeah, some pins, so they have nametags and ballcaps too. There will be a white van waiting. They've got to make a delivery for me... About forty-five minutes?... Call me when they're on their way.

"Travis, are you and King about done? I need to make a trip with Daniel. I need you to wait here while I'm gone. I promised Tanner I'd keep an eye on everyone... See ya soon.

"Daniel, I'll be in the van with you. Nothing's going to happen to you.

"Tanner, Travis and King will be back, and they will stay with Carlton and the guys. It's all lined up. The delivery will get there. I told you; I've got you covered. You've got a whole army behind you now. We all know our parts. No time for a dress rehearsal, but we'll be ready. Did Joe and Ben enjoy "shopping?" I knew Tessa would treat them well. She's a great person. You have a Beanie, and I have a Tessa."

"Call me when the mission's complete."

"You know I will."

"I owe you, Jack."

"Tanner, I thrive on this stuff. I could never have a desk job. You can buy Tessa some flowers. A raise would be nice for her, too."

"You got it."

"See, Tanner, I told you everything would be okay."

"Libby, you're always right. Where's that tux? We'll all need to meet before we leave."

"Tanner, Grace and James want to talk to you. They're in the den with Ben and Joe."

"Tanner, thank goodness you're here. We have made some decisions, that is, if you approve. Anne and Erica are staying here tonight. Could Constance and Brett come here to be with them? Mr. Kaplan might enjoy being back in his apartment. I'm going to take Anne's place. I'm not allowing her to go. Alyssa needs me. We know Bryan is supposed to pick up Dee Dee and Anne."

"Grace, I can't let you do that."

"Well, pick one. Anne or me? You know the choice you have to make. Anne's been through enough. Erica wanted to go, but Alyssa is my daughter."

"Grace, no. I don't know how we'll pull it off. I don't want anyone to have to go. God will make a way. You'll see. The white robes. They have hoods."

"What are you talking about?"

"Well, black robes and white robes are being delivered to Jacob's house. There are hoods, too. Might be able to create an illusion if we keep everything moving in order.

"Libby, call Constance and have Brett bring his group over here. I'm going to call Beanie.

"Beanie, are you all set for tonight?... Good. We have to time everything down to the gnat. Daniel and I are out of here. Thanks."

"You're on, Travis. Let's see those tats. Come here, Bryan. Let's compare. Whoa, King! Travis, how did yours turn out? These are henna?"

"Yeah, what do you think?... That's a rave review. I guess these will get us in."

"Carlton, Tanner wants me to mix in and watch over Dee Dee and Anne."

"That's a great idea. I'm concerned. Look, there's the guys Tessa sent." Jack quickly gives them a thumbs-up and hops into the back of the van. "Drive, Daniel. We'll do it like the old switcharoo on those creeps at the Professor's."

"Will those officers know what we're doing?"

"Tessa texted their phone number to me.

"Thanks for helping, guys... Yeah, I know you really got the rush on. Right on time... I won't forget it... Nope... Okay, remind me in case I forget." Jack lays out the scenario of how to pull it off.

"See, Daniel, you're in good hands. We've been around a while. They are terrific men."

"What if they get hurt at the house?"

"If anyone pulls anything, they'll be sorry with these guys. We'll stop to help you with the blowout and semi-wreck. I'll give them more details. Just drive. When we get close, you'll call that Roscoe character, and then boom! We'll have this little booboo. My guys will stop to help. We'll transfer the robes to their van. They'll make the delivery. You won't have to go near that house."

"Thanks, Sir. Talk to me about fishing or anything to get my mind off this."

"I've got a great story. One time, I was night fishing."

"Night fishing? Why are you laughing?"

"Well, let me explain the night fishing..."

❦

More Than Luck

"When is that delivery arriving?"

"Paxton called. He'll be here in a few minutes."

"Make sure the count is right, and they better be what I wanted."

"Well, you could've gone with me when I ordered them."

"Desmond, you know I wouldn't leave Jacob."

"Well, then you can't gripe. I have good taste. They'll be perfect. Does that kid know what's in there?"

"Yes, of course. I had him count them. No room for mistakes."

He better not make any mistakes this time. I really wanted to have a lesson ready for him, but I need that van back to Carlton. Ugh, a little glitch. Those caterers. So, Desmond can't leave. The lesson will have to wait for another day. A slight reprieve for Paxton.

"Desmond, get the door. It's probably the delivery. Looks like Paxton's on time."

"Pull your van around the side and put them under the awning... Yes, I'll meet you there... Yes, over there."

"Sign here."

"You what?... What is going on?... Paxton, where are you? Who were those guys?... You've had another screw-up? A blowout?... How is the van?... I'm coming down there. Whose voices are those?... Oh, they came back to help you?

"I'm going to do a little aerial view of this. Desmond, I'll be back shortly..."

Well, it looks like he's not a liar. Maybe he's smarter than I thought. He wasn't about to miss that delivery. Some people are so kind to strangers. He's a lucky boy.

"I don't think he suspected anything."

"Kid, keep playing the part. You never know who's watching."

"Thanks, guys. I really appreciate everything."

"Sure, kid. Good thing that didn't blow out until you got here. You might have ended up in the canyon."

"Can I pay you?"

"Nah, I hope someone would help us out if we were in your shoes."

"Well, thanks. You saved me."

"We know. Here's the signed delivery receipt. You said you had to get the van back. We'll follow you down, just in case.

"Jack, are you good?"

"Yep, I'm going to use this little blanket for a nap. See, I told you not to worry. Daniel, that's a nice smile."

"Bryan and King, I'm supposed to drop you off to get that rental van. You know the plan, right? You're to pick up those two girls."

"Yeah, Carlton, we pick up flowers and go to the apartment. Roscoe said that's our cover."

"I can't travel with you guys. Remember, though, you don't know what's watching, but the Lord is riding with you. Godspeed."

"Jack, we know you'll be there, somewhere out there. If we're in trouble, you'll help."

"Carlton, get going. It's showtime. I'm traveling with you to make sure you're okay."

"Good deal, Travis. I'm a little nervous. I've met these entities before. You guys have no idea what kind of horrifying power they possess. I was never on the side of good, so this is the first time being decent. It's a new experience for me. Pray it up."

"Guys, we'll be back to get you."

"Listen, I didn't want to scare them, but I've seen what they can do. They're not mere mortals. I had never seen the power of God, though, until He changed me. I guess we all have to depend on Him and each other. This will be a battle. No slip-ups, King. Be wise."

Inside Out

"Well, the food people are still in there, shuffling around. They need to get out of here!"

"They have to wait for Jacob to approve their set-up. He might want to make last-minute changes."

"Really?"

"Remember, you said it's *his* house. They said it's *his* party."

"Don't start, Desmond. That fragrance in there makes me sick, weak, and upset. So, you better keep an eye on them. Why are you out here anyway? Did you put those outside locks on everything?" *No one is getting out of that house alive.*

"Roscoe, I've done my part, but I won't lock this up until the right moment. You know what the plan is. Follow it. You'll need me to work my magic. Now, won't you?"

He's so arrogant. Like I'm dependent on him. He forgets about the little group I recruited. Pride goes before his fall. "Yes, Desmond, you'll have to do your part."

"Oh, I forgot. Look at the caterer's card."

"Heavenly Planners and Catering? Thanks, Desmond. I needed a good laugh. What a ridiculous name. Makes this all the more pleasurable."

41

DRESSED TO KILL

"Irene, I must speak to Jan."

"Here, Jacob, it's ringing."

"Jan, is it you, my beloved friend? How good to hear that familiar, soft, little rasp... Oh, Jan, you make me laugh. Seriously though, you know you agreed to be my date for tonight. I have much to tell you... No, I didn't forget. You're a memorable person, most unique. Your kindness and humor helped me get back to myself. I hadn't laughed in years."

"Oh, Jacob, you sound so—"

"Young? Well, yes, I guess that's it."

"Did you find the fountain of youth or what?... Jacob, some horses can be led to water, and they actually do drink. I could use some rejuvenation, too."

"Jan, there are some other things I wanted to share with you. Are you going to be my date? You promised. Don't say no. Irene will have the limo pick you up."

"A limo? I'm not a princess."

"You are a princess. I would be so honored to have you in my home. Don't say no."

"Okay, I'll be ready. Thank you, Jacob."

"Libby, I need your help. Jacob wants me to be his date. He's sending a limo. Do you think it's possible to make me look human?"

"Oh, Jan, you'll look fabulous."

✳

"Jacob, Martina called. We are supposed to be at your house early and approve the caterer's layout and prepare for your other guests. Right now, we all have our assignments. Can you pull this off?"

"Irene, you mean our little army? Stuart explained all of it. I'm ready for war. Let's get the show on the road. I'm back! At least the new me is. I know I'm still supposed to pretend to be a dolt so they don't get a heads-up. I haven't acted since I was in drama class as a kid. I was quite good, though, and I will be tonight. Stuart's my bodyguard. Like Rose always said. The Good Shepherd sent Stuart to her. Now, he's assigned to me. When is the limo coming? Did you order one for Jan?"

"Yes, Jacob, it will pick her up later, and ours will be here in about twenty minutes. Jacob, what is that fragrance?"

"You're the one who ordered the tuxedo. I noticed it when I got dressed. I thought it was sprayed with something. By the way, Irene, thanks for making me look so good."

"Jacob, you look so—"

"Younger? Irene, I feel better than I have in years. What a doddering fool I have been. A weak and selfish man, the one with all the answers. The famous surgeon, Professor Jacob Warren, blinded by selfish grief. Rose would always sing the words to that hymn, 'I was blind but now I see.' Well, after all, Stuart was the one who truly continued Rose's legacy. Rose would be pleased. Finally, I see. Stuart is, as Rose believed, the son we never had. I realize now that I was jealous of his relationship with Rose, but all I had to do was join in. Well, I'm joined now. So yes, I look younger. Sin is an awful, aging burden, and I'm free. It's time for recompense, and I'm taking my property and my life back. The enemy cannot have it. Irene, forgive me. What do I say to Lieutenant Tanner? God bless him. Oh, Irene, how could I? That poor Miss Summers and everyone else."

"You'll have a chance to speak with Tanner later. We all owe him a lot. I believe he and the others will be very forgiving."

❧

"Well, Jacob, welcome home. Please introduce me to your guests."

"Desmond, this is Irene Carpenter and Jamison Lovett. You remember Stuart, don't you?"

"Of course. Stuart, I was hoping our paths would cross again someday."

"And this ladies and gentlemen, are old friends of Irene, Bernice Orr and Art Davis."

"Such a deep pleasure to meet you. This will be an exciting evening." *So that's Irene. Wait until Roscoe gets a hold of her.*

"The caterers are almost done. It's an adequate job."

"Adequate? Desmond, I would say they have done a spectacular job. What a magnificent homecoming for me.

"Where is our caterer, Irene?"

"Jacob, this is Martina."

"Martina, how beautiful! Everything is sparkling! I saw the vans outside. Whatever you have prepared smells so delicious."

"I'm honored to meet you, Professor Jacob. You have a wonderful house. It's a pleasure to serve you. Any changes needed?"

"The beautiful rainbow colors are... I'm speechless. It's perfect. Rose would love this. Don't you think, Irene?"

"Yes, Jacob, she would."

"Well, that's great, so you can finish up and be on your way as soon as you have put out the food."

"Excuse me, Desmond, Miss Martina's group will be serving tonight. Irene has it all arranged."

I can see why Roscoe hates this Irene woman.

"Actually, Professor Jacob, it's my company policy for this type of gathering. You understand— the crystal, silver, and all.

"Mr. Desmond, I'm sorry, you know the Professor is entertaining many important guests tonight. Oh, speaking of night, Desmond, we need to set up lighting. I promise to have the back area all brightened."

"Roscoe has the lighting prepared. The moon will be especially bright tonight and full. We'll have sufficient lighting." *This woman is getting on my last nerve.*

"Let's all go out, and I'll show you Rose's research plot."

"No!!! Well, I mean, it's a surprise for you, Jacob. Roscoe would be furious with me if I spoiled it."

"That's fine. We have some hot hors-d'oeuvres for you to sample. Desmond, would you like a taste?"

"No, thank you. I'll save my appetite for later. Jacob, do you need to rest?"

"See what good care he takes of me. Always concerned for my well-being. Desmond, that's thoughtful, but Jamison is a doctor."

"I'm sorry, I didn't know you were a guest. I apologize. When you were the only person here and let us in, I assumed you were the butler."

"Oh, no, Martina, Desmond and Roscoe are my house guests. I wasn't well, and they came to take care of me. Where is Roscoe?"

"He had some last-minute preparations to make. I'm sure he'll be back in time." *Good, he didn't hear the butler comment. He'd never let me live it down. I don't like this woman. Something's off about her.*

"Irene and Stuart, you'll finally get to meet Roscoe. Desmond and he are old friends. How long have you known each other, Desmond?"

"Umm, it's been at least a couple of decades. I don't remember when we first became acquainted. Ugh, it was a very long time ago. We've worked together on various interesting projects around the world."

"Well, then we'll be excited to meet Roscoe and learn about all the research. What is it that you research?"

"Miss Irene, I hope during the progression of the evening to present a personal glimpse of our recent project to you. I don't want to spoil the surprise. Well, I must excuse myself and get ready for this evening's presentation."

After Desmond disappears up the stairs, Beanie whispers to Irene, "That man makes the hair on the back of my neck stand up. Art kept squeezing my hand."

"Same with Jamison; he didn't like him either. Thank goodness Jacob is back in his mind. Can you even imagine what he's been exposed to? No wonder Stuart was so wary of Jacob when he was under that influence."

"What are you two whispering about?"

"Stuart, we now understand how creepy things must have been for you."

"Yeah, Jacob is sickened by all of it, and he started muttering. I don't know who the caterer is, but she began speaking to Jacob, and suddenly, he's smiling again. Catering and counseling. Good job, Irene, a great pick. I'm going to get back to Jacob. I told him I'd be like glue tonight. I was scared for a minute that Desmond had influenced him again. Where is everyone? Are they coming soon?"

"Stuart, you know Tanner will be here. Don't get nervous. Everything is in motion. He just called Art. Aren't we supposed to pretend to enjoy?"

"You're right, Beanie. Oh, look, here come the yummies. We have to pretend, so let's eat something."

"Irene, please call Lieutenant Tanner and tell him we're here and that there's a limo coming for Jan. Tell him I am so glad he is coming."

"Tanner, Professor Jacob and all of us are here, and a limo will pick up Jan... No, we met Desmond...Well, I'll fill you in. Roscoe hasn't appeared yet. Martina outdid herself. Wait until you see this. Jacob is so glad you're coming, and so am I... Has anyone called the Big 10?... Good, their prayers mean a lot to me... No, we're all fine. See you soon. Godspeed."

"Irene just called, and they're at Professor Jacob's. Everything is going well. Grace, are you still on this path? Please change your mind."

"Tanner, Dee Dee and I will be fine. After all, the guys and the Lord will be with us."

"Grace, you're right."

"Tanner, no, she's not. I heard everything you guys are saying. I'm going. She's not filling in for me. Those "whatevers" hurt me, almost killed me. Alyssa sent *me* to get help."

"No, Anne, I can't let you."

"Grace, you told me to pray, and I did. I know that I'm supposed to go. Grace, please don't cry, I've decided."

"Grace dear, go get dressed. We're going to be guests of Professor Jacob's."

"James, I can't let Anne do this."

"Grace, you're willing to go, but Anne is a free soul, so you don't have the right to interfere. We're going to be with Alyssa. Who knows what the Lord will do? Hurry, get dressed. We're going to get our daughter. Wear that gown that you and Libby bought. It's perfect. You're always beautiful, but tonight is special."

"Well, since we're all standing up for ourselves, I'm not staying, either. I'm going. All dressed up, and we have somewhere to go. We decided we would call a cab if we had to. Didn't we, Leslie?"

"Yes, Erica and I are going to be there. Tanner, I'm to blame for a lot, so this is my opportunity to stand up for once and not run."

"Well, since Leslie and Erica are going, I am too. Travis will be there, and so will I. I don't think Travis has ever seen me dressed up like this. It might be his one and only opportunity. This whole ordeal has tried to eat our lives."

"Emily, I know.

"Ben, did you know this mutiny was going on?"

"Yes, Joe and I suspected it, but we decided to let it play out. Tanner, you would've lost it. You have done a great job of taking care of everyone. You, my friend, are not God, though, and people must make their own decisions. If you can't trust Him and us, who can you trust?"

"Joe, Ben's right. Everyone in this room knows how dangerous this is. They also have been victimized by it. As I prayed, I became aware that He would make the assignments. Each person knows inside what He wants them to do. Man makes his plans, but the Lord directs his steps."

"Let's go, Tanner. Jack and Carlton, and the guys will know what to do, and they have all been equipped. You know Ben and I shopped for everyone today, so let's catch the bad guys and ruin their evening."

Libby's jolted out of the conversation by the buzzer. "I'll get it, Tanner… Brett's on his way up."

As Libby opens the door, everyone begins to laugh. There stands Brett in a tuxedo, and right behind him are Mr. Kaplan and Constance, dressed for a gala event.

"Sir, let me explain, I—"

"Brett, it's okay. More mutiny, I see."

"DJ Tanner, if you thought I was going to sit here while all the action was going on, plus I haven't had a chance to dress up in years."

"Constance, you look lovely."

"Thanks, Tanner. You all look so charming tonight. My Aaron would be proud of all of us. God's little army. Al knows everything, and he knows Jacob. Everyone, meet Albert Kaplan. He's our host and benefactor." Everyone claps. "Welcome home, Mr. Kaplan."

"I've had some honors in my life, but look at all of you. What a glamorous army you have, Tanner. Would someone take me on a tour?"

"Emily, since you picked everything out and coordinated this, please escort Mr. Kaplan through his home. First, let's have you meet everyone except for Grace and James. They've had a reassignment of sorts."

As Emily introduces everyone to Mr. Kaplan, Tanner takes Libby aside. "Well, Libby, I have something to tell you."

"Dereck James Tanner, do not start. It is going to be fine."

"Libby, I wanted to tell you that you're the most beautiful woman in the room, and that's saying something. What a group of people they are. Beautiful inside and out. Libby, where's Jan?"

"Well, Dee Dee and I have a big surprise. Jacob called Jan and is sending a limo to pick her up. He asked Jan to be his escort tonight. She accepted his invitation. She doesn't want anyone to see her until the limo comes."

"Libby, I've got to talk to Jan alone." As Tanner taps on the door to Leslie and Dee Dee's room, it is dead silent. "Jan, Jan, it's Tanner. Please, Jan, can I come in?"

"Tanner, I'm embarrassed to be seen."

"Open this door, Jan. That's an order... Jan, you look wonderful. I've been so concerned about you. I'm relieved at how well you look."

"I'm not used to being dressed up like this. I'm a jeans and tennis shoe person. Jacob called, and I found myself accepting his invitation. It shocked me, but it felt right. My assignment, I guess. Dee Dee said she felt it was right, and I made a promise to Jacob in the hospital."

"Jan, I—"

"Tanner, I want to be part of the action. I have a gun, and you know I know how to use it. Your Libby had bought this classy jacket and these flowing slacks for me. Tanner, keep that girl. She's picked the perfect outfit for me." Jan flashes her jacket open. Tanner laughs as he sees her shoulder holster. "Look at this too." She reaches down and pulls up the hem of her slacks. There, at the end of her short legs, Jan reveals an ankle holster and two glamorous glittering tennis shoes.

"Okay, Jan. Okay, I give up. You are prepared. Nice hairdo, too."

"Thanks, do you like it? Leslie did it. It was a team effort to get me fixed up. Truly, Tanner, I'm up for this."

"Jan, may I escort you downstairs?"

"Tanner, do you really think I look okay?"

"You look much more than okay. Stunning would be appropriate. The others will agree."

"How come you care about me so much?"

"Well, that's a story for another day. You have a limo to catch."

As Tanner and Jan descend the stairs, the whole room is floored. "Quick, someone take a picture. This is a once in a lifetime for me."

"Let's all take pictures. Jan's limo will be here in fifteen minutes."

As Grace and James enter the room, Jan asks them to ride with her.

"Jan, that's so thoughtful."

"Grace, of all the people, you should be riding in a limo after everything you've been through."

"I think that's a great idea. Jan, I was uncomfortable with you traveling alone. James will watch over you girls."

"Tanner, since you approve, Grace and I will go with Jan. I can't wait to get close to Alyssa."

"Quick, click some pictures before my carriage arrives. Get those phones out and get pictures of all of us. Dee Dee, come here. You too, Anne. I love you girls. I'm going clear to the end, Dee Dee."

After the last picture is taken, Tanner's phone rings. The doorman buzzes that the limo has arrived. "Come on, Grace and James, we're on. Tanner, will you go down with us?"

"Oh, we're all going out with you. The delivery guys will be here soon to kidnap Anne and Dee Dee. Before we go, Ben, will you pray?"

Jan runs over to Dee Dee and gives her a kiss. "Remember, all the way to the end."

"I know, Jan. I love you."

"Don't make me cry. I've got make-up on for the first time in years. The gals all worked too hard for me to ruin my face."

"Jan, let's do this."

Tanner turns his face towards Libby as the limo drives off. "DJ Tanner, don't start. We'll all be a mess."

"Okay, Ben and Joe are taking Leslie and Erica with them. Libby and Emily are with me. Brett is still assigned to Constance and Al.

"Ben, thank you for praying that the enemy is paralyzed by the blood of Jesus."

"Dee Dee, you also know that I'm with you until the end. Anne, that includes you. Our whole little army is with you. You girls go back into the apartment and keep the act going. Bryan and one of the other guys will be here shortly."

"Okay, Tanner, and by the way, thanks for everything you've done for both of us. Get that monster. Let's get Red October and save Alyssa and the others."

"I'll do my best. Dee Dee, have you talked to Linda?"

"Yes, I called her earlier. All the folks in Meadow Brook are together, praying for us. They've been interceding all day and will continue until this is over and we call."

"That's one phone call I can't wait to make."

Anne gently touches Tanner's cheek and goes into the building.

"Dee Dee, go with her."

"Tanner, she'll be okay. Anne has no family. I think she gets overwhelmed by the expressions of love. I used to be like that. Grace and James have taken her under their wings."

"I didn't know."

"No, I know you didn't. I can't tell you, Tanner, how much you have meant to me. Take care of Libby and Emily. Thanks for everything you've done for Adlin and me. God has a crown for you someday. Give me a hug. See ya later, Tanner."

As Dee Dee disappears through the doorway, Tanner stands motionless, almost frozen in time. When he finally gets in the car, he and Libby and Emily remain in reverent silence. The tiny caravan of cars launches forth to do battle.

❦

The goodbyes had seemed so casual. George, the doorman, had made comments about how elegant everyone had looked. He asked why I wasn't going. What a sweet man. I told him Anne and I had dates and were going later. I told him we were part of the entertainment.

Here I am on my way up the elevator. Once again, Dee Dee Summers, you're alone. Concentrate on Anne. Don't let your old self raise its ugly head. How do I reach out to Anne? Lord, give me the words.

"Anne, what are you doing?"

"Oh, I wanted to enjoy the warmth, the last rays of sun before the day passes to rest and is overcome by the night. Put your hand here, Dee Dee. Feel the glass."

As I press my hand against the warm pane, Anne reaches over and clasps my other hand.

"Dee Dee, don't worry. I'm okay. I had to leave. I could sense how fatigued and concerned Lieutenant Tanner was. I didn't want to cry. You know, this is the first time I've ever felt truly loved. Erica pried open the door of my heart. Our friendship was the beginning. Then, Alyssa set me free. James and Grace brought me to surrender in the completeness of God. I don't know how to explain how much Lieutenant Tanner has changed my view of the police. Considering my childhood, he's the first honorable man I have ever known."

"I know exactly what you mean. Jan squeaked my door open. This whole group of people is so unique and yet alike. Anne, you didn't know I was a police officer... Don't look so surprised. See, here we are in the same boat, many of the same thoughts. Ben, he's been the rock in my life. That's why I wanted to be an excellent police officer, and then there's my Aunt Linda. There are so many more that you haven't met. Some of the most powerful and loving women are in your fan club and praying for you, Anne."

"Dee Dee, are you afraid?"

"I've been shoving thoughts away for days. I know I have an assignment. I can't run away. I have to find Adlin's killer. Lieutenant Tanner wants you to know it's okay if you can't do this. He has a surprise for you. It will be arriving shortly. Make your decision, and we'll all be good with it."

"I know I have to go and rescue Alyssa. The shed was so cold and dark. I want her to feel the warmth of the sun again."

"Oh, Anne, give me a hug. We're stuck together like glue." *This kid reminds me of Adlin. I rebuke fear and ask for peace and protection. Lord, hold us in your love.*

"Thanks, Dee Dee, no tears tonight. Get the bad guys, Officer Summers."

"There's the buzzer. Let's get this show on the road."

"What in the world? Is that you, Bryan? All I can can see is your eyes."

"Where do you want these? The vases are really heavy. I guess the bad guys thought we needed a disguise."

"Is this the surprise Lieutenant Tanner sent me? They are beyond anything I've ever seen."

"No, Anne. I think they're cover for the real surprise."

"Bryan, let me help with that arrangement. Anne, would you help with the other one?"

"Here, let's put this one on the coffee table."

"Sure thing."

"What did you say?"

"Sure thing."

"Oh, it can't be... Dee Dee!"

As Anne begins to faint, King turns around. He catches her as she begins to fall. "You're still my little sister. Forgive me for abandoning you. I'm changed, though, and I promise I'll make it up to you."

"You're really here? How did this happen?"

"I guess you could say God sent me. A special delivery from Lieutenant Tanner."

"Dee Dee, I can't watch this. I'm getting teared up. Lieutenant Tanner said we could spend a few extra minutes."

"Me too, Bryan. Let's leave them alone."

42

ILLUMINATION

"Jacob, let's go outside. Jan will be arriving, and she has two guests with her."

"Irene, I wonder who she brought with her."

"Oh, Jacob, you'll be impressed."

"More army?"

"Absolutely."

❈

"Jan, welcome to my home. Who are our guests?"

"Jacob, this is Grace and James Kirschenbaum, my dear friends."

"Oh, Stuart told me about you and your daughter. I can't begin to ask for your forgiveness."

"You don't have to, Jacob, it's already given. We're here to reunite with her." Grace and James clasp Jacob's hands and quietly pray for Alyssa and blessings on him.

"Irene was right; I am impressed. You both have such a quiet strength in God. Thank you for your tender prayers.

"Jan, you look lovely. Take my arm. I'm so glad you came! I should've known you'd bring the very best guests."

"The others are right behind us. They're not bad either."

"Oh, Jacob, your home is radiant. Look at all this."

"Jan, I want you to meet Martina. Where is she?"

As Martina appears behind Jacob, she puts her fingers to her lips, signaling Jan to say nothing. "My, this is a pleasant surprise. Professor, Jan and I have met before. Haven't we, Jan?"

Jan can barely get it out but answers, "Yes, we have."

"Jan, you are full of unexpected surprises."

"Yes, Professor, she is.

"Jan, there are appetizers. You'll enjoy them."

So, this is where Marty and Oliver went when they said they were out of state. Jan's mind is still perseverating on Martina as the others begin to arrive. *Too bad Dee Dee doesn't know this.*

"Jan, thank you for all that you did to help Jacob. It's so wonderful to have him back."

"Irene, the time I spent with Jacob was my pleasure. I learned so much."

"Irene, Jan's a great listener. Where's Desmond? Is he still upstairs? I want him to be here to meet these people and to find Roscoe."

Tanner's phone interrupts the silence in the car.

"Sir, we made the pick-up. The special delivery items are on board. Estimated arrival time: thirty minutes… Yes, they are into their parts, blindfolded, drugged, and tied up. We are ready."

"Bryan, you and King… well, you know we'll be praying."

"We know, and Carlton's guys are already there. No contact with Desmond or Roscoe yet. We're following Roscoe's previous orders. See you soon."

"I'll call Jack.

"Jack, the cargo is on its way… Oh, you must have your guys in place if you know Carlton and Travis's groups have arrived… Good…

And Jack, I don't know how this is going to play out… I know… You, too."

"Okay, girls, we're almost there. Any last words?" Libby and Emily don't comment. Both are silently praying.

As Tanner pulls up to the house, he's surprised to see three very tall men motioning to stop. "Sir, we will park your car. We'll be watching over your vehicle. May I have your keys?"

"Who are you with?"

"We're part of Martina's staff." As the two other gentlemen escort Libby and Emily to the door, Tanner hands the keys over and follows behind.

Wow, Martina is something else. I never let go of my keys. What was I thinking? Is my bell broken? What's that guy saying to Libby and Emily?

"Tanner, they want us to wait here until the other two cars have arrived."

"Lib, how would they know there are other cars?"

"I don't know, but they gave us such a great sense of peace. They seemed so familiar."

"Weird, that's the same feeling I had about the guy that took my keys. That's why I asked him who he was with."

"Tanner, in all these months, I haven't seen you this calm."

"Libby, it's like everything is in slow motion."

"Tanner, that's the way it is for me too."

"Emily, two of us couldn't have the same illusion."

"Make that three." Libby grabs Tanner's hand.

The three attendants follow the same routine with Ben and Brett's groups as they pull up. While everyone is gathered on the massive porch, one of the escorts opens the door, steps in, and announces the arrival of Mr. Dereck Tanner and guests.

I never told him my name. Maybe Irene gave them a list. Did I hear him announce Mr. Garcia, Mr. Landry, and Mr. Kaplan? Irene didn't know about all the changes, nor did Beanie.

Tanner's thoughts are interrupted as Irene begins introducing everyone to

Jacob. No introduction for Al Kaplan. He's known Jacob for years, but Jacob hadn't seen him in a very long time.

"Thank you all for coming. This is a very, very important evening. Made even more special by our eloquent caterer, Martina, and Irene, and Lieutenant Tanner. Of course, my date for the evening is Jan Raskin. Welcome to my home. Please give them all a round of applause. This is an evening to be remembered, when the light removed the darkness. Please applaud for the Lord, who is The Light. Let's celebrate until our other guests arrive.

"Roscoe and Desmond originally arranged this whole evening, but I can't locate either one of them at the moment.

"Ben, would you bless the food? Enjoy this delicious trove. Sit at any table, my friends."

As Ben finishes his prayer, four of Martina's staff sing, "Our God is an Awesome God." The celebrants are engulfed by the resonance of their voices.

"Irene, it looks like we got more than we paid for with our caterer."

"And then some, Tanner. What a find she is."

"Jacob, where's Desmond? You've got to play the part of your life like you are still under their influence. I'll go upstairs and see if I can find him."

"No, Tanner, I'll go alone."

❊

"Desmond, are you still in here? It's me, Jacob. I've been waiting for you to make your appearance all evening. You made all this possible, and now you've abandoned me. So has Roscoe. Why? I can't think right around all those other people. You and I did so much together in Haiti. I want these old friends to see who you really are— a demonstration of your gifts so they will have their eyes open to the power of things that they know nothing about... Oh, you look, indescribable, like in Haiti. They will all stand powerless against this revelation."

"Jacob, you've been pretending?"

"Of course, isn't that the plan? Roscoe told me he would have new backing for the project— the corporate entities he raved about. Are they still coming?"

"Jacob, they're almost here. Roscoe's outside awaiting their arrival. I spoke to him from the balcony a few minutes ago. Are you ready to launch the plan?"

"You know I am. I know the other guests will be astonished. By the way, I had forgotten how impressive you are in your regalia. I can't wait for that narrow-minded bunch to become enlightened. I feel so empowered by seeing you. Let's go down and get the show moving. How nice to hear you laughing, old friend."

❋

"Ladies and gentlemen, meet my friend, Desmond. He has worn his native apparel, indicative of his status in Haiti. He's the head of a very select group of people around the world. You might call him the Big Man."

Desmond steps into the room in full Voodoo priest regalia. With sticks and all, face painted with white clay, and black circles around his eyes, he's an imposing and ominous figure. "Thank you, Professor. I'm here to reveal the unique project Jacob and I have implemented. This should be an evening of a true fusion of the ancient ways with knowledge and science of the current times. There are other guests who will be arriving. They will be enjoying our eventful evening with all of you. Your old friend, Professor Jacob Warren, has made this all possible. Please show him your gratitude." Everyone begins to applaud. Desmond lays his head back and laughs, more like a chortle. "I must excuse myself and prepare for the events that will be occurring in the research garden."

As Desmond approaches the double patio doors, they swing open without him even touching them. Jacob follows him out. Desmond speaks to Jacob in another language. The doors slam shut. The faint sound of bolts latching is overridden by Desmond's dark laughter.

"He was speaking in French, Tanner. He said, 'Welcome back to the embrace, Jacob.'"

"Stuart, one more surprise?"

"Well, languages were one of my interests. He also said what a bunch of fools we are. Tanner, do you think Jacob is under his power again?"

Jan interrupts, "I don't. As Jacob was going out, he winked at me and pointed upwards with his finger."

"Jan, you believe he's still on the good side?"

"Yes, Tanner, I can feel it. I have good instincts."

"I agree with Jan. I know Jacob is changed. I could hardly stand being around him before. It really creeped me out."

"But, Stuart, could he still be susceptible to that influence?"

"Well, maybe, but you sent him up there to get Desmond. What do you think?

"Joe, do you have any thoughts?"

"Yes, Jacob will be fine."

"Wait, Jack's calling."

"Tanner, there's some kind of dark cloud formation moving in. My guys have night-vision but can hardly see. The air is almost suffocating, and there is a whirring sound like wings. Tell everyone to get ready. We're moving in closer towards Travis and Carlton. Pray that whatever it is, doesn't see us. God, help us all."

"Lieutenant Tanner, may I speak with you alone?"

"Yes, Martina. Everyone, stay calm."

"It's important to be quiet and wait. Very important! The scripture says that the prudent man hides himself when he sees evil. Desmond is evil. I've already let my staff outside know what's going on. Have faith. God already knows what is about to happen."

I've been dreading this night, and yet, I'm like a horse at the gate. I'm ready to go and finish this and find justice for Adlin Summers. "Martina, you don't know everything that has transpired. We've all been trusting God through this."

"I know more than you think I do. God sent me here. Ask Jan.

"Jan, would you help me out? It's okay, you can tell Lieutenant Tanner where I'm from."

"At this point, I'm not sure. Marty and I met at the church in Meadow Brook. Dee Dee met her, too. She's one of the Big 10." Tanner's face is white.

"So, you see, Lieutenant, I do know a lot. God set this plan in motion a long time ago. He chose all of us to finish it." Simultaneously, the group all begin to praise God and sing. "See, he's preparing his troops for war. Prepare through praise. God inhabits the praise of His people. He's the one who delivers us from evil.

"Jan, all will be well with Dee Dee."

"Marty, I have made a promise to go to the end with her. I feel like I've broken that promise."

"You haven't come to the end yet. I'll be with you, Jan. Dee Dee is very much in the Lord's heart." Marty holds Jan and whispers something to her. The look on Jan's face is so tender, and her head is nodding.

"Marty, Ben has the same issues I do. Tell her, Ben."

"Miss Martina, I also promised Dee Dee I would be with her."

"She doesn't need you yet. At the exact moment she does, you'll be with her. That's a fact. Ben, you will fulfill your promises even as He has kept His promises to you."

"Marty, you are the super caterer and a primo counselor."

"Lieutenant, timing is crucial. Wait on the Lord. The last guest will arrive at 9:00. You must be patient."

"Lib, Tanner, is it my imagination, or are there more staff than before?"

Libby raises her eyebrow and glances at Tanner, "Yes, you noticed that too, Emily?"

As 9:00 approaches, the tension in the room increases until it's almost palpable. At the last strike of nine, silence pervades the room. The entire group is startled by the front door chimes. One of Martina's staffers opens the door.

"Are we on time? The invitation was extended for 9:00. Professor Warren, is he here? I had to ring the bell twice."

"Sir, I'm sorry. It was hard to hear. The clock was tolling the hour."

The handsome man dressed in a sleek, custom-made gray tuxedo and his two associates step into the entry. He hands the staffer a card and is announced as Mr. Dyab, the owner of R.O. Corporation & Associates. "Where is Professor Warren?"

"He's already gone into the back into the research plot."

"I had no idea he wouldn't be here to greet me. What a beautiful home. Oh, I see someone I recognize."

As the gentlemen cross the room, Brett whispers to Tanner, "Tanner, that's the guy from the tattoo salon, Salon Noir, and those two work there."

"Are you sure, Brett?"

"Absolutely."

Why is he here? Have we been duped?

"What an interesting gathering. Lieutenant Tanner, what a pleasure to finally meet you. It appears that Professor Warren has a whole army of friends. I've been trying to make corporate inroads in this area for quite a while. This project was the first serious opportunity that our company has had to seed itself in this area.

"The tragedy and mystery of the Summers case, for lack of a better word, intrigued me. I realized when I saw her pictures, I had met her once at the library. I've taken quite an interest in you because of that case. At one point, my curiosity got the better of me. I went to visit you at the station, but I missed you at the elevator. You seemed to be preoccupied, so I didn't introduce myself. Every time I went to meet you, some kind of interference occurred. Something always came up."

It was him behind me at the elevator the day I met with Bryan. Ugh, that ominous feeling.

"Isn't it always a relief when the pieces come together? This promises to be quite the eventful evening. I hope there's sufficient light."

"Oh, I'm sure there will be. It only takes a little to dispel the darkness."

"Indeed. It is a full moon. Perfect. I assume this could be... Well, your phone's about to ring. I'll visit with the other guests." As Mr. Dyab turns and walks away, he chuckles and says, "Perhaps, the lovely Irene."

Oh, Lord, how does he know Irene? This is so unreal. "Libby, something is getting ready to happen. My phone *is* ringing.

"What's going on, Jack?"

"It's like a science fiction movie, only it's in real-time. That dark cloud turned out to be creatures, entities. They were flying through the woods… Yes, all my guys are okay. I guess the eyes of the enemy were blinded. We could see them, but they apparently couldn't see us. We're all going to the tunnels to be with Travis and Carlton. There seems to be none of those demons there. Their stench is putrid. Can you see any of this? They're on the walls around the research plot. Tanner, we thought crows were bad."

"Jack, Martina told us not to move and to wait. I pulled back the patio drapes, but the glass was all blacked out. The Professor is out there alone with Desmond in the research plot. Jack, Jack, are you still there? Jack!" Dead silence.

Tanner calls Travis. It doesn't even ring. "Everyone, try your phones. Call each other. All the phones are dead. Something has drained the charge. The lights in the house flicker off. "No one move!"

Tricks of the Trade

"Roscoe, there you are. I wondered where you were. Why didn't you come and meet everyone?"

"I couldn't stand that smell."

"Good grief, what smell?"

"The same smell you have on you right now. It makes me feel sick and weak. Desmond said it's cleaning products. Wait a minute, you weren't here when they cleaned."

"Well, maybe I absorbed it when I was inside the house."

"Desmond doesn't smell like that, and he was with them all day." Roscoe's eyes are squinting as he asks, "Jacob, you haven't involved yourself in something displeasing, have you?"

Before he can answer, Desmond interrupts, "Stop it, Roscoe. Jacob is here with us, isn't he? He's doing exactly what we all worked on. The Boss will not be pleased. He's been waiting to meet the Professor who made all this possible. You better not mess this up. You better conserve your energy."

"I thought there was a full moon tonight. Why is it so dark?"

"Well, the clouds will clear off shortly, and the Boss and his guests will all land."

"Are they coming by helicopter?"

"Jacob, let's say they're flying in. They're scanning the woods and making sure we have privacy." As Desmond and Roscoe begin to laugh, Jacob pretends to be confused.

"Oh, I understand. We don't want any corporate espionage."

"Roscoe, what is that? That wasn't there when I helped you hang that rack thing up on the wall."

"Desmond, you thought you were the only one capable of magic, didn't you? You'll find out how relevant it is later on." *Oh, boy, will he find out. He thinks he's not disposable.*

❧

"Lieutenant, I told you I would have lighting."

The huge vases full of flowers around the room become illuminated. The light increases until the guests are immersed in transparent color, like a liquid rainbow filling the room.

"Search the house. Where did they go?"

"Lieutenant, that's not necessary. They're gone."

All the women are clustered around Irene. "Irene, what an imposing and creepy guy. How did you know him?

"Beanie, he came to the lab once inquiring about the research project. Jacob wasn't in, so I gave him a brochure. I had such an uneasy feeling. Fortunately, I had a meeting to go to, and I hustled out as fast as I could. It took me days to shake off that feeling. His face was embedded in my memory."

"I saw you jerk your hand back quickly."

"Yeah, Emily, he wanted me to touch his suit. It wasn't fabric. It felt like skin, but not animal. From my years in forensics, I knew what I was looking at."

"Oh, my goodness! You're saying it was human skin? I'm going to throw-up!"

"Oh, Irene, I can't imagine. I think he's pure evil."

"Me too, Beanie. I guess he's the one we've all been waiting for. Jacob's potential corporate partner."

Stuart pipes in with a frenzied voice, "Oh, that figures. By the way, everyone, the word Dyab means Devil in Haitian."

43

THE ARENA

&

Who's the Boss?

Desmond and Jacob are startled by a soft, drawling voice behind them. "Professor Warren, at last. Your home is beautiful. I've been visiting with your guests. A fascinating group. I've heard so much about you, a brilliant man. What an opportunity to expand my corporate kingdom. Thank you for being so open."

Smiling, he continues, "Desmond, how refreshing to see you again. Haiti has always held my attention. This new concept is intriguing. I can't wait to see your presentation.

"Professor, I must excuse myself. This tuxedo makes me feel like I'm in someone else's skin. I've got to change into something else. Those clouds should break up shortly. The moon will be magnificent, and we'll be able to clearly see the project."

"I'm speechless that you came. Roscoe told me that you rarely attend corporate meetings personally. He said that you're usually indirectly involved in the research."

"Oh, this one's been given my full attention. It's been one of personal interest. The sort of thing I've been looking for a long time.

"Roscoe, it looks like you overheard the conversation. Please give the Professor a closer look at your handiwork."

Dark figures with drums seat themselves on large stones arranged around the massive slab.

"Oh, Desmond, the musicians are here. Now, we wait for the Boss and his officers to be seated."

A fortress of fog has now completely encapsulated the property at 322 Wilderness Walk Road. The giant walls shield from prying eyes and sound-proof the air. Nothing can be seen or heard from the outside world. Hanging over the research plot is a whirling globe, like a three-dimensional puzzle of shining obsidian armor. Pieces of it drop into the research plot. Others land on the stone walls and fold their ancient wings onto their sides.

"Are you impressed, Desmond? These are warriors and generals of the most elite guard. Isn't their scaled armor beautiful?

"Desmond, you're on. Bring Jacob closer to the Boss."

❧

Several of Marty's staff move to the men in the group and motion for them to follow. As they near the side door in the kitchen, it swings open.

Joe nudges Ben to get his attention. The staff seems to have little flecks of rainbow light marking the outlines of their bodies. The air is thick. The men follow their outlines as it is impossible to see into the inky abyss.

"Ben, there's no light from the moon. It's as though we have been cast into utter darkness."

Still whispering, Joe touches Ben's shoulder. "Look behind us. There are hundreds of these guys."

"Joe, it looks like the Lord's army showed up. I hope Tanner notices."

❀

The drummers begin to beat in a slow rhythmic cadence, different from before. The troop moving towards the tunnel shudders. Suddenly, Jack appears at the entrance. His men are crouched in darkness with him. "Tanner, how did you get here? We can't see anything."

"Well, the staff guys led us here."

"Who? Where are they?"

"They were here, but they're gone."

"What do we do now?"

"I guess we have to feel our way down the sides of the tunnel." It flashes through Tanner's mind that this is how it all began. *Me feeling my way through Adlin's murder.*

The Meadow Brook group is praying. They can feel the suffocating darkness that has descended in Oak City. They begin to sing and worship the Lord as the Father of Lights. Dot softly prays, "Bring your light to those in darkness. Send your light to your army in Oak City. Prevent the enemy from fulfilling his plan. Lord, we bind the enemy and his minions. Bring forth the beauty of your glory."

The tunnel is entirely empty. Travis, Carlton, and the rest are gone. "We have to find the upper tunnel to the shed to get out onto the research plot. There has to be a door somewhere. Lord, help us find it."

"Tanner, I found it, at least it feels like a door!"

"Stuart, you saved me again. How did you... Never mind, you can tell me later."

"Tanner, let me and my guys go first. We've got the big guns."

"Okay, Jack, go for it."

Quickly, the group ascends the tunnel to the shed. Now, they can maneuver into the research plot. Yellow-orange wicked light flickers from giant torches around the walls of the plot. The scene is ghastly. Black-robed figures are spaced between the mounds. Upright on the mounds, there appears to be wooden crates. Desmond is kneeling in front of the glittering figure on the stone slab. Beside him is Professor Jacob. Desmond has his hand on Jacob's neck and appears to be forcing him to kneel. A tiny figure in an ancient red cloak is being dragged towards the stone by two of the robed figures.

James realizes it's Alyssa. "Lord, help us."

Tanner places his hand over James's mouth. "Don't."

The drumbeats intensify. The inhuman screeches coming from the tops of the walls are almost deafening. Desmond rises and grabs the girl. She goes limp. He lays her on the slab. As he turns again, he levitates about three feet off the ground. "Let the celebration begin!"

Jacob crumples to the ground. The drums stop, and Jacob is jerked upright by Roscoe. "Professor, behold the project, the resurrection." The hooded figures between the mounds undo the straps and open the crates. In slow, labored steps, the contents of the crates begin to move off the mounds. Indiscernible— what used to be humans are now creatures covered in oily, white clay with vines and thorns growing out of them. A fearsome sight. At the same time, a whirling black mist is twisting around them.

The stench of death is increasing the enthusiasm of the crowd perched on the walls. Desmond is laughing and commanding the creatures to come forward. They begin to shuffle towards the stone slab. Desmond begins an incantation, and the earth in front of the slab pushes upward until a red coffin with markings exactly like the tattoos appears. The beings start to scream and moan as if in horrible pain. Once they all reach the front, they begin clawing at Alyssa and finally cast her body into the coffin.

James is frantic, "Where are you, Lord?"

As Desmond scoops dirt and throws it on Alyssa, she begins to scream, and the creatures throw more and more upon her. Desmond slams the lid and stands over it. Her screams can no longer be heard.

"For you, Master, a gift, wrapped in the cloak of Madame Delphine LaLaurie."

The audience is in a frenzy. The drums are frantic in their beat. The coffin begins to descend. Two white-robed figures are brought from the opposite wall and placed in the middle of the plot. Their hoods are removed— Anne and Dee Dee. "The traitors have been found! A special additional gift for you! My surprise that I promised. The failures of the past will be erased."

The wicked, glittering, green figure lifts off the slab and moves toward the young woman. "So, you're the one!" A long-clawed hand moves out of the glimmer and runs its talons down Dee Dee's cheek. "This face, after all these years. You look exactly like your mother. Give me the stone!" The talons dig into Dee Dee's face, but she doesn't make a sound.

It moves to Anne. "You defiant, foolish girl! You almost ruined the project, but as you can see, there is no escaping! A big price to pay!

"Release the seeds, Desmond!" The creatures move towards Anne and Dee Dee. The evil figure speaks a name, unintelligible.

The swirling black mist spirals upwards to reveal a gigantic, monstrous figure with red eyes and long fangs. The fear in Desmond's eyes is evident. It's Roscoe in his true form.

"You lost the master's stone in Haiti, and now you pay the price for failure." With that, Roscoe leaps and grabs Desmond. He hangs him on the rack that Desmond had helped him mount on the western wall behind the slab. Desmond is screaming as the hooks and nails rip through his flesh. The smell of blood fills the air.

The creatures have reached Anne and Dee Dee and are clawing and gnawing at them. The group of men is paralyzed momentarily. The scene is so surreal.

Tanner realizes Stuart and James are missing. Joe and Ben pull out their weapons and are running towards Anne and Dee Dee. Kicking at the thorny plant creatures, they realize they are humans. The black robes are dropped, and the recruits are screaming the name of Jesus and running into the fray.

❖

The women from inside the house are beating on the French doors. Marty walks to the doors, and they fly open. Marty leads the women out onto the patio. She pulls Jan aside and kisses her on the forehead. "Remember what I told you, and remember that He loves you. It has been a joy to be assigned to you. See you soon. Go now. Help Dee Dee to the end!"

The women are all running to take their place in the battle. They don't see what Jan sees as Marty is transformed into a beautiful, masculine angel revealing her true identity. "Marty, don't go!"

"I'm going to confront the enemy. I'll be there with you. Never be afraid. The battle belongs to the Lord."

Jan wipes away the tears and runs into the research plot. *I haven't been able to run like this in years. Thanks, Lord... plus, Libby, for getting me tennis shoes.*

Oh, I like the feeling of this gun. It's comforting, too. Where's Dee Dee?... There she is. These are the plant people Anne talked about! "Dee Dee, I'm coming!"

While Roscoe marches back and forth, the glimmering green figure emits an angry, massive snarl... "Mere mortals, they look like ants! Get them! This is ruining my evening!"

Dee Dee hears Jan and joins in yelling. "Anne, they're coming!"

King is coming from the other direction. One of the attendees drops off the wall and tries to grab King's leg. An unseen hand slings the attendee up against the southern wall of the plot. Others begin to attack and are met with the same violent flings.

"Tanner, I guess we're not alone!"

"Joe, I think you're right! Look, Jack and his guys are taking control over the creatures, the plant people."

Black-winged entities are being slung across the plot, and some are being dragged off the walls. Jan and Ben finally reach Anne and Dee Dee. "Oh, Dee Dee, you're all scratched and bleeding! I'm finally here!"

"What about Anne? Ben, help Anne!"

Ben cradles Anne in his arms and is praying as King slides to his sister's side. Ben wraps his arm around King, and all three sob together.

"Boss, they're getting your prize!" The green evil moves until it's standing over Dee Dee. Jan stands up and shoots for his head. Startled and angered by such a short human taking a brave step, he pauses long enough for Dee Dee to get up and run.

"Run, Dee Dee! Run! Run to the west end!"

This makes no sense! I'm running right towards that monster and Desmond!

Jan hollers, "Dee Dee, look! Look who's there!"

She sees a man holding something out towards her. Dee Dee keeps falling and is torn and scratched by the rose bushes. As she nears the slab, she realizes it's a stone pendant on a silver chain. Immediately, flashes of lightning hit her memory. *Oh, Lord, he was at the canyon in the rain that night!*

The Boss drops Jan before he can kill her and tries to reach Dee Dee, but an invisible wall of force separates him from her.

Dee Dee flings herself to the ground, and she reaches upward. The man drops the heavy silver chain and stone into her palm.

"You did it, Dee Dee! You did it! Dee Dee, he's Oliver!" Jan is kneeling in the dirt, crying.

Standing beside Oliver is Jacob, fearlessly declaring the Devil has no right to be on his property. The shrieking hordes of winged spectators lift up and take flight into the night. The women still standing and singing in a circle are firing scriptures at the demons. Emily starts screaming, "Tanner, where's Travis?"

"I don't know! We were back-to-back shooting, and then he was gone! Look, Jack's got him, and the other guys have Bryan."

"Oh, Lord Jesus! Travis, you're bleeding badly!"

"Don't look, Emily!"

Jamison is yelling at everyone to get in the house. "The lights are working! Ben, bring Anne, too!"

"Tanner, where is Jan?"

"Ben, she's over there with Dee Dee and some guy. Maybe he's one of Carlton's recruits. Where is Carlton?"

"Last I saw, he was going after that monster, Roscoe. He was screaming, 'I'm free! You failed! You have no power over me!' Pretty brave in my book... There he is. Leslie is with him. It looks like he can still walk.

"Carlton, are you guys still okay?"

"I'm not sure. Tanner, I have no breath left. Roscoe almost did me in until Satan grabbed him, and they flew off. That was so satisfying. He failed. Wouldn't want to be him. Professor Jacob was unbelievable. He never moved. He stood there firmly planted, making declarations about his property and speaking protection over all of us. I thought Roscoe was going to eat him, but he showed no sign of fear."

"Jamison, what about Marty and her staff?"

"Martina told me to look in the catering vans. She said she had something special for us to find at the end of the evening. Tanner, they weren't filled with food. There were all kinds of medical supplies. They are fully equipped emergency vehicles. Jack's guys and I have already started working on, as Anne calls them, the plant people. They're sedated and calm. Let's get busy on everyone else. Irene, can you help me?"

"Jamison, of course. I'm always in it with you."

"Bryan, Bryan! Jamison, is he dead?"

"No, Erica, he's been knocked unconscious. His breathing is good, and his pulse is fine."

Al is consoling Constance as they enter the house. They had been frantically searching for Bryan. They spot Erica and run to her.

"Erica, I had the best dream."

"Shh, you can tell me later, Bryan."

"Joe, are you talking to Peaches?"

"Yes, I told her it was over. She's with the women, and Tim and Clay are with them, too. Peachie, I will call you back. We are trying to account for everyone and take care of needs... I miss you too... I'm still your best man?... I'll be home as soon as I can."

"Lin, I need to help Jan and Dee Dee right now. It's over. I'll have Dee Dee call you as soon as we can... She's fine... No, Lin, I wouldn't cover anything up. I love you more than you know. Can't wait to see all of you. I can feel your prayers."

"Tanner, all my guys are accounted for. No major injuries, but where is Stuart?"

"Carlton, they're now *our* guys. They were so brave."

"Libby, have you seen James or Grace? I lost track of James and Stuart."

"Tanner, I haven't seen Grace since we all went outside. Alyssa... they went after Alyssa!"

"King, would you and Anne come with me?"

"You're not getting my sister without me coming along."

"Anne, we may need your help with Alyssa."

"It was so horrible what Desmond did. Alyssa saved me. She can't be dead."

Tanner begins to yell as they enter the tunnel. The light system is working, so they don't have to feel their way.

"Is it over? Is it safe to bring Alyssa up?"

"Yes, do you need help? Anne is here."

"Oh, Anne is here? She made it."

"Alyssa, is that you? I came to rescue you."

"These guys made it to me first, but no one may have ever found me without you. You did rescue me, Anne."

Stuart emerges, embracing Alyssa. James and Grace are right behind. "Hey, Tanner, I followed James when he dipped out. I knew that he was going after Alyssa."

Desmond's screams have faded into dying whispers and moans. "Andrew, get some guys. Lift him down and take him into the house."

"Lieutenant, you've got to be kidding. After everything he's done?"

"He's still a human being. He'll suffer the consequences, but we are not judge and jury. He'll be in the hands of God, and we're not God."

❉

"Jan, don't go, please."

"Dee Dee, Marty told me it was my time. She has always been assigned to me. She'll be with me, and I will see you again. Don't be sad. I understand everything now. It's been a wonderful time, and I wish we could have met years before."

Jacob interrupts, "Jan, let me take your pulse."

"Jacob, thank you. That was so impressive of you, how you stood there and made declarations. I'm free now, Jacob. I need to sit down after all that running. These guys will help if we need anything. I finally made it.

"Linda has my will, and everything I have is yours, Dee Dee. Friendship is the gift he gave you and me. The Father knew I didn't want to be withering away with cancer. I haven't run like that in years, and I'm going to be free. Running made me feel that sense of freedom, running to you, Dee Dee.

"Marty, there you are. Are we going now? Can you see him, Dee Dee?" With that, Oliver places his hands on Dee Dee.

"Jan, I do see him. He's glorious."

"I've got to go. Hold me until I'm gone. Tell everyone how much I love them, but I love Him more. Isn't it perfect that I'm all dressed up? Tell Libby thanks. Tell Tanner goodbye and to carry on the great work."

"Oh, Jan, you look beautiful, and it is perfect. Thanks for being with me to the end."

"Just think, I'll be with Adlin. It turned out to be the last thing I did, Dee Dee."

"Jan, don't go!"

"Dee Dee, don't hold her back. Adlin's waiting for her. Peace, the Lord gives to you."

"Take care of her, Marty. Usher her to heaven." *Oh, the smile on Jan's face at the touch of Marty's hands tells me everything's okay.*

"Oliver, you were with Adlin and me at the lake."

"Yes, I was, and I was with Anne. I get assigned to rescue people. It has been such a privilege to see you grow in faith and love. You will go forth and fulfill many plans of the Lord. Always remember that you are not alone. Angels travel with you. Many will be diverted from the hands of the enemy. Keep a tender heart and walk in wisdom. We'll meet many more times. Goodbye for now, Dee Dee."

"Wait, what about the necklace?"

"Weren't you going to lay it at Adlin's feet?"

"Can I hug you, Oliver? I so appreciate what you did for Adlin and me. I want to touch you one more time. I will never forget the feel of your arms and the smell of rain."

❧

With Anne and King safely in the house, Ben realizes Dee Dee isn't inside. In all the confusion of the battle, Ben had lost sight of her.

Rushing into the plot, he sees her in the distance. There seems to be someone else with her. Ben hurries to Dee Dee's side, kneels in the dirt, and wraps his arms around her.

Dee Dee is still holding Jan. "She's gone, Ben."

"Why Jan? No one else was killed."

"Neither was she, Ben. Angels were here. She left with a special escort. It was so sweet. Jan is free, and she wanted to go. I have so much to tell you, but I need a favor."

"Anything, baby."

"Take this chain. Don't let anyone other than Joe or Tanner see it. Look, Ben."

"Dee Dee, how did you—"

"It was like Madelyn's dream. The pendant was dropped into my hand by Oliver. I know you are really strong spiritually. Only you and Joe will understand what the real meaning of this is. I want you to show it to Tanner, but later."

"Lord, we render this pendant and chain powerless, and we bind any evil that is attached to it in Jesus' name."

"This robe has no pockets. Quick, Ben, put it in your pocket."

"Thank you for trusting me, especially after I let you down. I broke my promise to go to the end with you. In my heart, Jan was in that promise."

"Ben, you are here, exactly when I needed you. Jan has passed, but I'm still here. We haven't come to the end. Have we?"

"No, we haven't."

"Is Anne okay?"

"Yes, she is."

"Ben, you always have been there for me, and I expect you to keep on. When we get to the house, please pray over everyone."

"Dee Dee, the Lord has already spoken to me about it. What a wonderful Savior He is."

"Ben Garcia, how I love you. What a guiding light you have been in my life."

✽

"Where's Jan? Libby, I've got to find Jan." Tanner and Libby are running towards Dee Dee and Ben. Breathless, Tanner sees Jan on the ground. Kneeling, he picks up the tiny figure and cradles her in his arms. "Oh, Dee Dee, what happened? Who hurt her?"

"Tanner, Libby, we made it! Tanner, Marty came and escorted her out with great love. It was tender and peaceful, but she told me to tell you to keep up the great work. It was quite an experience. We'll talk later."

Ben calls Joe. "Please prepare everyone for the news... No, she wasn't killed, she went home. Dee Dee said she had a special escort."

"Look, Tanner, everyone is lined up on each side. Jan would've loved this grand entrance. It looks like she's sleeping. She's with Adlin." *Adlin, are you pleased? Lord, did we fulfill your plan?* "You know, we didn't really catch Red October."

"No, but we saved a lot of others from him, including the victims from the project. I guess you could say we confounded the enemy."

Irene gently touches Tanner's shoulder. "You've been crying. I'm so sorry. I loved Jan, too. We all did. Jacob is distraught. He feels like he abandoned her. Jamison has already called for an ambulance to make it look official. Lay her on the couch. We're moving all the others into the den so the paramedics don't see the dinner guests. Carlton's group has been wonderful. They've gotten so much cleaned up. We'll all be playing our parts again like dinner guests. Jan will be taken to a funeral home, old friends of Al Kaplan's. Beanie has it all set in motion. She and Constance and Art will drive to take care of the paperwork until Jamison does the death certificate. They'll stay with Jan. Ben has called everyone in Meadow Brook. The tears are flowing there, too. Jan wants to be buried there. She had covered it with Linda."

"Thanks.

"Libby, I'm going with Jan."

"No, Tanner, not this time. Others need your help. Emily, Travis, and I need you here in case anything else happens."

"Joe, Jamison checked out Alyssa. He said she needed to be with James and Grace. Jamison's only a phone call away. Will you go with Stuart and them? Ben will take King and Anne to the apartment, too. You and Ben keep watch over everyone."

"Tanner, you know I will.

"Stuart, let's get going before the ambulance gets here."

"Dee Dee, I'm so sorry. Jan was the best."

"Stuart, you are so sweet. I have much to tell you. Take care of everyone. I'll see you tomorrow. Don't look so worried. I'll be all right."

"Jacob, I told you I'd be by your side, but I have to go."

"Stuart, thank you for all you did. I'm fine. I'll see you later. We have a lot of plans to make for the future."

As Stuart, Joe, and the others drive away, the sound of the ambulance siren is faint in the distance.

"Beanie, you're still on it. The World's Best Secretary. Thanks."

"Sir, don't worry about Jan. Art and I will be with her. We will be sure she is treated with great care."

"Don't cry, Beanie. You're in good hands with Art. Watch over Al and Constance."

"Sir, could you—"

"Art, don't even say it. I'll take good care of Erica and Bryan. Sounds like Jan's ride is here.

"Constance, thanks. I'll see you tomorrow.

"Al, I can't express how much you have done for all of us. Take care of Constance. She's special."

"Believe me, Tanner, I know that."

"Sir, do I need to go with them?"

"No, Brett, change of assignment. I need you here. We can't let our guard down. Not yet. Coordinate between Jack and Carlton's guys. Start compiling evidence and document it. I don't have any idea how we can explain this. Some plausible explanations will be demanded. There's no way we can let all this come to light."

"I know, Sir. It's unexplainable. I'll do my best. Thanks for trusting me."

"Brett, you really do know me."

"Yes, and it's an honor."

As the ambulance drives away, the group left at the house feels the void.

"That was some kind of person. Jan helped me so much. She made me feel like a real person again. I had hoped to have a long friendship with her. She was so much fun. She made me laugh in the hospital. I told her more about Rose than anyone else ever knew."

"Well, Jacob, she has met Rose by now."

"You know what, she has. Thanks, Irene. I needed to be reminded that this is not the end."

"No, Jacob, it's not.

"Jamison, what will we do with the girls that have been so traumatized?"

"Well, Jacob and I have a plan. They're in very bad shape. I know what the toxins are. Remember, Anne was my practice case. Carlton and Leslie are going to stay here. All of Carlton's guys have been really helpful. They want to stay because Bryan and Erica are here, too. I guess you could say Jacob and I are creating our own little triage unit. Jacob's special assignment is Desmond."

❧

Desmond, in all his agony, tries to grasp Jacob's hand. "Jacob, save me! All my power is gone!"

"Desmond, you really never had any power of your own. It was Satan's power through demons. There's nothing I can do to save you physically or spiritually. You used me to bring forth great evil. Repentance is your only hope. Forgiveness from the Lord. Use your last breath to repent."

'Jacob, he's a human being.' Rose... 'Jacob, the scripture says, that whosoever believes in Him...' Okay, Rose, okay.

"Desmond, acknowledge Jesus as your Savior and ask Him to forgive you of all your sins. Receive eternal life. Do you agree?" Jacob follows the words that Stuart spoke concerning receiving the Lord. *I hope this is okay with you, Lord.*

"I see Him. Forgive me, Jacob."

"I forgive you, Desmond."

Desmond, though he can barely speak, has rivulets of tears splashing down his face. He's speaking in French. The last words that Jacob hears are spoken in English with a strong voice.

"Lord, erase the horrible things of my life by making the end of it a provision and a blessing to many. I take all the blame. Leave something good for Jacob and the others. I surrender to you and to your care, Jesus."

"Jamison, did you see what I saw?"

"Yes, I did. Jacob, he was transformed."

"Jamison, that was so hard to have mercy. All I could hear was Rose's words in my head."

"Oh, Jacob, we never know who the whosoever wills are. His perfect will is for all to repent and believe. It looks like Desmond made it. He was far too weak to have raised his hands like that and make that beautiful smile. I know his repentance was answered. It's over."

"Could you believe what he prayed at the end? I wonder what it means."

"Me, too. This was quite an experience. You and I both will sign the death certificate."

"Oh, Jamison! I know what the provision and the blessing are. Adlin's murder! We have the person responsible. He said he would take the blame. The end of his life is a provision and a blessing to me and all of us. We can give a plausible answer to the newspapers. Tanner will be free, and Dee Dee will have peace. We all can! Rose would be so pleased."

"Jacob, everyone will be. What a journey this has been. What a gift Desmond left us. Thank you, Lord. Rest in peace, Desmond."

"I've got to call Stuart. If he hadn't led me to the Lord, I wouldn't have known what to do."

"While you do that, I'll tell Tanner and the girls what Desmond left us. The Great Physician is here with us."

"Tanner, I have some good news. Desmond has passed away."

"Jamison, that's good news? How do we explain all of this?"

"It was a complete transformation. Jacob led Desmond to repentance and forgiveness. With his last breath, Desmond asked the Lord to make his life a provision for all of us. I want you to see him."

Irene pops up and says, "We also want to see him. Dee Dee, Irene, and Libby let's go."

"Girls, wait until you feel the presence in the study. Desmond left us a gift. I wish everyone could experience what Jacob and I were witness to."

As the group enters the room, Jacob is quietly cleaning Desmond's body. The room is filled with a beautiful fragrance and peace.

"Oh, Jamison—"

"I know, Irene. This is about life and not death. The Great Physician is here."

"Dee Dee, are you okay?"

So, Lord, this is proof of your forgiveness. I want to be free. Adlin, is this a glimpse of what you became part of when you went to God? All this beauty?

"Dee Dee—"

"Libby, I'm okay, I'm free.

"Thank you, Jamison, for bringing us in here. I really needed to see and feel this."

Jacob tells them what Desmond's last words were.

"Oh, Tanner, everything you were talking about, so worried about. It's been taken care of."

"Libby, my love, Desmond has set us free. We could've never believed or envisioned this. We have a plausible explanation. Thank you, Lord.

"Jamison, I want everyone else who is still here to experience this. They will never be the same. You can see the light of God on Desmond's face."

As they open the doors to the study, Erica and Bryan, and all the other recruits are gathered.

"Bryan, my favorite stray cat.

"Erica, where's Daniel and Andrew?"

"They volunteered to stay and watch over the girls, the seeds."

"Tanner, Jacob and I will go and let Andrew and Daniel come in."

"Thanks, I know it's important that they are here. I'll call Jack and his group." Tanner steps into the hallway.

"Jack, you and your guys need to come in... No, right now. It's very important. Gotta go, Ben's calling.

"Hey, Ben... You and Joe are right on again. It's over. It's so peaceful... Stuart was right, too. Desmond became a blessing for all of us. We don't have to lie. Call the Meadow Brook group. This is a glorious day. I can't begin to tell you and Joe how thankful I am for your friendship and help. You guys are the brothers I never had. Talk to you later.

"Travis, should you be up?"

Travis answers with, "The whole house is filled with the most awesome presence and fragrance. Did you think Emily and I would miss out on anything?"

"Buddy, let me help you. Don't put pressure on that leg. We did it, Travis... I should have—"

"Don't, Tanner, it's been a real trip. Thanks for taking me under your wing. You're a great mentor and a great man.

"Emily, you were right. I've never felt anything like this. We need Him in the center of our lives."

After everyone has left the room, Jack and his guys arrive. Only Tanner goes in with them.

"Jack, how can I ever thank you for your loyalty and your knowledge of God?

"Guys, I will never forget you for showing up and watching over us."

"Lieutenant, we all have been talking about what a mind-blower this has been. We would follow Jack anywhere, and now we feel the same about you."

"Whew, that's humbling."

"Well, it's true. We all know something will happen in the future, and we're in."

"Okay, guys, we still have to scour the property. It's almost daylight."

"Thanks for including us in this peace and His presence. God is a mighty fortress and a safety for His people who surrender to Him."

Jack and all his guys bow their heads and stand silently for a moment.

"Let's get moving, guys. I'll update you on what we find out there, Tanner."

"Libby, we need to have one more meeting at Al Kaplan's. I'll call Beanie."

"Well, at least wait until Beanie has gotten some rest. We all need rest. Jack and his guys are doing surveillance."

Carlton and Leslie are the last to see Desmond. "Leslie, isn't it perfect that you and I are the last two? I never thought I could show my respects to Desmond. Dee Dee's sister was murdered because of her resemblance to you. I was the connection to Roscoe, the catalyst for evil. Praise God we've been forgiven. God showed mercy on us and Desmond. I love you, Leslie. I never had the capacity to say something like that before."

"Neither did I, Carlton. I love you, too, but I love God more. This all began because of us. Here we are, standing in the victory. Rest in peace, Desmond. Thanks for setting us free from having to live in fear and lies."

44

UNTIL WE MEET AGAIN

The headlines read:

The young college student's murder has been solved. After long months of no leads, finally, information slowly leaked in. The assailant was located and identified. He apparently had been stalking Miss Adlin Summers, her older sister, and perhaps others.

According to Lieutenant Tanner, a massive plan was developed through the efforts of individuals across three states to trap the assailant. During the pursuit and confrontation at Wilderness Walk, the man was critically injured. He made a full confession to Dr. Jamison Lovett and Professor Jacob Warren during a futile attempt to save his life. The motive and the reasoning behind this tragic death and attempted murder remain undisclosed.

The department will issue official letters to all who participated in bringing justice to this case. The commendations for all the officers and staff involved at the Oak City Department will be scheduled at a later date. A special commemoration will be given posthumously for Jan Raskin. She passed away from an unrelated illness during the events at Professor Warren's residence, where the trap had been staged. Jan was part of an informal group known as The Meadow Brook Investigation Foundation. Meadow Brook was Miss Adlin Summers's hometown. The residents and the University of Oak City

can now return to normalcy. The dark cloud has been removed. The case is closed. At this time, no further information will be given.

Tanner laughs as he sees the shocked looks on the faces of everyone gathered at Kaplan's. "Guys, you look like you've seen ghosts."

"Tanner, well, you all look wonderful. You look so rested."

"Irene gave me the keys to her house, and we've all been there sleeping. We have showered and rested, and now we're ready for what might be our last meeting. Let's get started.

"Well, here we are once again, safe at Mr. Kaplan's. We are standing in his generosity. Thanks, Al.

"Beanie, thanks for putting all this together— one last gathering. You really are the World's Best Secretary and one of the best friends I have.

"I love and appreciate each one of you. God's little army. What a privilege to know you all. I hope the press release suits everyone. No one would ever believe what we know to be the whole truth. God bless you. It's Sunday, and I would like Ben to pray."

Every head and heart are bowed in humble gratitude. "Father God, merciful and mighty, deliverer, you are the one who came to set the captives free, bind up the broken-hearted, redeem the lost, and declare the acceptable day of the Lord. Though we do not understand everything about the death of precious Adlin Summers, we do understand that you always take what the enemy means for evil and turn it for good to those who love you.

"As Adlin went home to you, a seed was planted. Her death was not in vain. The seed... as it died, it sprung up, and growth began in our lives, a harvest of deliverance and salvation. Her life of faith flooded into all of our lives. I pray for everyone in our army that we will continue to multiply and bring others to His love. Amen."

"Oh, Ben, you said everything I wanted to say. So I'll just say thank you to everyone. Let's celebrate!"

While the others are chatting away, Anne and Dee Dee slip into the study. "Dee Dee, I felt I was abandoning you when I left with James and Grace. Forgive me."

"You had your own assignment. Alyssa and her parents needed you, and so did your brother. How brave you were, Anne. We confronted the evil one together. Are you okay?"

"It's really special. I have never felt so loved. You know, Oliver came to see me last night. He was the one who saved me. He's the one that kept coming in my dreams. I recognized him at the research plot talking to you, but then King and Ben took me into the house. He's an angel, but you know that, don't you? He told me that he used the name Oliver."

"Yes, he rescued Adlin and me when we were little girls. He told me he's often sent to rescue people. Anne, we both have been rescued by the same angel! He told me I would see him again many times."

"Oh, Dee Dee, he told me that, too! What a bond we have! A forever bond. All the others are waiting to see you. I wanted you to know that. I'll talk to you later. I love you, Dee Dee."

"I love you, Anne."

❧

As the last morsels of food disappear, and all the memories are recorded with photos, Dee Dee rises and taps the side of her glass. "I want to thank all of you. As I look at our little army, I see a room full of brilliant minds and deep hearts. Thank you for helping Adlin and me. It's sad that we might never be together like this again. Please don't forget me. You've changed my life forever.

"I'm going to Meadow Brook. All the arrangements have been made for Jan's service. It's so sad to leave all of you. On the other hand, it's exciting because it's the first time since I was a child that I feel like I'm going home. Here's to all of us brave and loyal friends." Everyone toasts.

"We have a surprise for you, Miss Deidre Summers. This is not the final goodbye. All of us are planning a trip to Meadow Brook as soon as Jamison gives an okay on our little seeds that we rescued."

"Tanner, even the guys, like Jack and his group? All the street recruits, too?"

"Definitely, but they'll be coming later! They're all a provision. Without them, I'm not sure how things would've turned out. I didn't realize how weary I was. From the moment Jack was included, I felt the load lift because I knew I could trust him. Without Jack, the guys, and the recruits, I would never be comfortable about going to Meadow Brook. They have it all under control. Leslie and Libby will be working on it. We'll have the commendations here for Jim and the others, including the gals from the library. The real awards ceremony will be in Meadow Brook. Ben's already told Linda. The group, or should I say family, are all excited. I *have* to meet the investigators who launched this plan."

"Oh, Tanner."

"Dee Dee, no credit towards me. This is a group plan, and Grace and James have come up with the perfect topper."

"The last time we were in Meadow Brook, it was a sad and dark time. So, well, there will be a beautiful double wedding at the same church if you agree."

"Grace, who's getting married?"

Before Grace can answer, Libby blurts out, "Travis and Emily, and Tanner and I are."

"No wonder everyone's been whispering around. Thanks for being so sneaky." *Wow, I don't feel that left-out feeling.* "Congrats, I see everyone else is as teared up as I am. Grace and James, what a wonderful idea. The church will be filled with joy. I wonder if Oliver and Marty will show up."

"James and I are pretty sure they'll be there. You never know what God will do. Look at all of us. It will be quite a reunion. We felt we needed to wait long enough for the press to quiet down and to see if our little seeds, the girls, are okay."

"Oh, and there's one more thing."

"What, Tanner?"

"Well, Libby and I would like to go with you. I want to be there to officially honor Jan. Someday, I'll tell you why she was so special to me."

"Dee Dee, Lin knows. She thinks it's wonderful."

"Ben, are you and Aunt Linda conspiring again? Just kidding! I love it! Let me guess... Oh, never mind.

"Tanner, Libby, I know Jan would be so honored if you came, and so would I."

"Well, there's one more surprise. Stuart is flying with us. The folks were so curious to meet Leon."

"Oh, Gloria must be beside herself. She really honed in on you, Stuart."

"So, it's okay with you if I come?"

"Absolutely!

"Joe, didn't you invite Brett?"

"As a matter of fact, I did."

"Boy, you have all been busy."

"Well, Jan and the gals worked so hard on finding out who was in that car at the funeral that I thought they should meet him."

"It's perfect! I was so sad to leave everyone. I felt like things were still undone. Joe, everybody must be so excited!"

"Well, now, you have a secret to keep. Only Peaches knows that Stuart and Brett are coming. The guys will stay at the ranch until Jan's service. I'll be flying with them tomorrow."

"Oh, my gosh! You're too much!" *Adlin and Jan must be laughing.*

"Ben, who are we flying with?"

"Libby and Tanner. We're going later in the day tomorrow. Tanner wants to take you for a drive. He has some things he wants to talk to you about privately. So, Libby and I'll wait until you get back."

"Okay. Where are we going, Tanner?"

"I thought it was important, Dee Dee, that you see Oak City the way it was before all these things happened. That you saw it perhaps through Adlin's eyes as a college student."

"Oh, Tanner, I would love to see Oak City and all the places Adlin went."

"See, here's Irene's forensic lab. Professor Warren and Stuart also have their labs and offices in this building."

"Tanner, there's the library. It's Madelyn's dream. It looks exactly like Madelyn's dream. Even the parking lot. Oh, goodness. Tanner, this is traveling the path."

"Yes, it is."

"I want to see Adlin's apartment."

"Do you think you should?"

"Yes, I want to see it. I think it will bring some closure."

"Well, first, I'm going to take you to the park where Adlin used to study."

"Tanner, it's so beautiful. It's exactly like Adlin described it. So this is where she met Daniel."

"Dee Dee, this place has brought me so much peace and clarity over the years. It really is special, isn't it?"

"Yes, it is."

"Do you want to get out?"

"No, that's okay. Let's drive on to Adlin's apartment."

"It's a short distance from here."

As they slowly drive through the gates, Tanner blanks out the flash of his last memory of Adlin. *Lord, don't let Dee Dee pick up on anything.*

"Are you okay? Tanner, it was horrible, wasn't it?"

"Dee Dee, you don't want to know. You saw the pictures."

"I didn't mean that. I meant how you felt. Pull over. Let's sit here for a moment."

Lord, I guess you let her pick up on it.

"We're going to pray for that horror to be simply a picture in a case file.

"Lord, we ask that Tanner, Travis, and anyone else who was affected by this be released from the enemy's hold over that picture in their mind. Adlin is no longer a victim. She's victorious. She's whole again. Amen."

"Thanks, Dee Dee. That brings up something I hadn't touched on before."

"I know what you're going to say. I wondered about the girl who found her. I've been praying for her. I don't even know her name."

"Well, I'm not allowed to release that yet. I've been wondering if she's the one Adlin was trying to help. The hospital said she was much better, and I gave orders that she not be released until I talk to her. Jamison's spoken with her doctors, too, so they know not to let her go before we find out the truth."

"That missing piece, or in this case, person, has been nagging at me."

"Do you want to go in?"

"No, this has been a wonderful ride. Let's leave it at that. Where did all of Adlin's belongings go?"

"Your Aunt Linda had them shipped to Meadow Brook. Didn't she tell you?"

"No, I never asked. I guess Aunt Linda knew I would've dug through those things. The person that I was, it could've been, well, horrible. There's a season for everything. Linda is very wise."

"I can't wait to meet the person who raised you, Deidre Summers. She did a great job. Closure?"

"Yes, let's go on... Oh, Tanner, Wilderness Walk is rugged in its beauty. It gives me a perspective to see where so many events were happening."

"Yes, I wanted you to see it, but not from a van and that nightmare. Here's Jacob's house."

"Ooh, I thought Irene's house was beautiful, but this is a true mansion. It all looks so different in the sunlight. I hope someone brings Alyssa and Anne on a drive, too."

"Well, here we are..."

Wow, there sure are a lot of cars here. "Aah, this time, I get to go through the front door."

"Yes, you do. That's the point."

"Tanner, the door is open. Do you think everything's okay?"

"Oh, I think so. I think it will be all right."

Did he just wink at me?

"Let's go in."

"Professor Warren, where is everyone?"

"Well, I wanted to spend some time with you, Miss Summers. I have a few things I wanted to speak with you about.

"Tanner, why don't you go and see if you can find the others."

"Professor Warren, call me Dee Dee."

"Please call me Jacob. I don't even know what to say. Your sister and you, well, all the misery I caused."

"Jacob, all is forgiven and over. I want to thank you for everything you did by letting us all come to your home, bringing this to a close."

"Oh, Dee Dee, I have something I want to ask you. Would you honor me by walking into the research plot? I feel you really need to see what the young guys have been working on this whole time."

"Oh, I don't know, Jacob."

"Please don't say no. They've worked so hard."

Oh, Lord, he's got tears in his eyes. "Okay."

"Here, take my arm. I didn't want your last memory of my home and Rose's research plot to be revolting to you. I felt it was important that you see what it looks like in the sunlight."

"I'd be honored, Jacob... Oh, Jacob, it's breath-taking. How did they get all this done?"

"Well, it's only the initial clean-up and restoration. Isn't it lovely in the sunlight?"

"Yes, and the fragrance of these roses is intoxicating."

"The young men are all going to work under Stuart. We'll be expanding the plantings using Rose's research on healing. They call it The Silver Shovel Project. Silver represents salvation in the scripture. It will be dedicated to Adlin and Jan. Herbs, plants, and flowers blooming everywhere again. Stuart will be in charge of it all. The young guys all respect him. They'll all be able to earn college credit. Imagine how that will help them. You know, Rose and I had no children, but now we have many."

Dee Dee softly touches Jacob's cheek and clasps his hands. "Well done, Professor Warren. I will have sweet memories. Aah, Jan and Adlin, together. It's wonderful. Jacob, thank you. Thank you for sharing this with me. What a kind and thoughtful man you are."

As they walk back into the house, the entire room bursts into applause and joyous laughter.

"Do I look better than the last time you saw me?"

They all shout, "Do We?"

"Yes, but you looked mighty good to me on Friday night. You guys are another regiment of our little army. Look at this food! Who catered this?"

Dead silence until Professor Warren says, "Well, it seems Martina stocked the fridge and the freezer, too. One more splendid touch.

"Dee Dee, I discovered I could still master a kitchen, at least with some help from the guys."

"Irene, you're so sweet to do this."

"Emily, were you in on this? By the way, congratulations. I heard about your wedding plans."

"Thanks. I worked hard on the food. I've actually enjoyed being with everyone here. Professor Warren is so gracious."

"Where's Travis and Jamison?"

"They told us to go ahead and eat. Dee Dee, they thought you'd understand. They're checking on the girls, the little seeds. They're doing so well.

"Leslie, sit by me."

"Is it okay if Carlton sits with us?"

"Of course! Leslie has told me so much about you."

"Please don't hold it against me. I'm a brand-new person."

"So am I, Carlton. Aren't we all?"

Jacob says grace. The group happily chats, and Jamison comes in and out, making appearances.

"Well, Bryan, the guys are certainly joyous. It looks like you and Erica have been good examples."

"Were you pleased with the work we did? They've been waiting to see your reaction."

"Oh, my gosh, you guys! It's wonderful!"

"So, you like The Silver Shovel Project?"

"Oh, absolutely! I am so honored. Thank you so much for dedicating it to Adlin and Jan."

As they finish eating, Carlton says, "There's one person who wants to speak to you privately. I'll get him, Dee Dee. He'll meet you in the study."

"Okay." *I wonder what this is all about. Stop it, Dee Dee. You know everything's good here.*

❋

"Miss Dee Dee, could I speak with you?"

"Of course." *That voice.* "And you are?"

As Dee Dee turns around, she's frozen. The owner of the voice so resembles Oliver. His eyes have the same gentle gaze, those deep blue pure, sparkling pools. "Are you an angel?"

"No, but your sister Adlin was my angel and best friend. I'm Daniel. I want you to have this. Adlin gave it to me."

As he pulls the little book from his jacket, he kisses it and begins to cry. "Here, take it. I loved your sister."

I'm crying for the first time. The dam has broken. I'm actually letting it go.

Clinging to each other sobbing, Daniel whispers, "It should've been me."

"Daniel, don't say that. Adlin wouldn't think that way."

"Well, I was bad, and she was almost perfect. God let her die. Why? Her life was beautiful, and she loved Jesus so much. Why?"

"Daniel, evil killed Adlin, and she wasn't even the target. I was so angry for so long, but I know the truth now. Did Adlin tell you about Jesus telling his most beloved friends he was going to die? He gave the parable of the grain of wheat, a seed. What's the matter, Daniel?"

He's shaking as he's fumbling through the pages of his little Bible. "She underlined that. See… 'When a grain of wheat, a seed, falls into the ground and dies, it becomes many and bears much fruit.' She used this verse to explain the way He made for us to live forever. She wanted me to have eternal life, bloom, and tell the others while I was here on earth."

"Did you receive Him?"

"Yes, Miss Dee Dee, I've been changed."

"We both need to bloom, Daniel."

"Adlin said God had big plans for my life. I always laughed because I was such a loser."

"If Adlin thought you'd be great, I believe you will be."

"Can we pray? You're the closest I've been to Adlin. I can feel her in you."

"Daniel, a seed has been planted through all of this, the seed of God—Adlin's seed.

"Heavenly Father, Daniel and I are humbled in your presence. We praise you for your faithfulness and your sacrifice. You are the Living Word. May we be faithful to bear much fruit to honor you and Adlin's memory."

"Amen. Miss Dee Dee, can we stay in touch?"

"Always and forever, Daniel."

"Can I give you a kiss for remembrance?"

Did he just kiss my forehead? "Oh, Daniel, how precious you are. We'll always be friends. I want you to keep your Bible, though. Adlin gave it to you. Stay close to Lieutenant Tanner and Doctor Lovett. They'll help you bloom and bear fruit. I see Tanner is ready to go. Promise me you'll stay on track."

"I will, Miss Dee Dee. I'm sorry about your friend Jan. She must've been a great lady."

"Thank you. Don't make me cry again. You've got work to do. Help those girls, the seeds that the enemy tried to plant. Are they improving?"

"Yes, Doctor Jamison and Jesus are working on them."

"Daniel, I love you."

"Back atchya, Miss Dee Dee. I've got work to do. Remember me."

"You're unforgettable, Adlin's friend, wow."

✽

"Did it go well?"

"Oh, Tanner, it was healing, a blessing. You and Jamison must help Daniel. He loved Adlin. I told him he could count on you guys."

"He can, I promise. That stands for all the street guys who helped us, too. What a flock! Adlin's Project will go on."

"Adlin's Project? Did you say Adlin's Project?"

"Yes, isn't that what we all have been part of?"

Adlin's Project. "Oh, my goodness, yes!" *Oh, Adlin, how beautiful. Your faith lives on— Adlin's Project.*

Continued To P.S. ....

P.S.

A good police officer is trained in following the leads to uncover the truth. We also are supposed to consider nothing as being random or mere coincidence. Ben had trained me well. The quest for truth should be noble and pure.

As you know, my journey to find Adlin's killer was fueled by no measure of the pure or the noble. Rage, anger, selfishness, self-protection, resentment, and murder. The list was long. What you may not have considered is that underneath all of that, I was trying to rid myself of blame, overwhelming guilt, and shame. I had rejected Adlin's loving invitations to participate in her life. This, I justified by telling myself that "someday," when I wasn't so busy, we would spend more time together.

The other serious problem was my cynicism of the spiritual, anything beyond my natural understanding. Maybe the second flaw in my thinking is the reason I rejected Adlin's invitations. By destroying Adlin, Red October had collapsed all my "somedays." Implanted on my heart was a stone, the weight of that guilt. It was chained with murder and revenge. I believed this was a journey to find a killer. How wrong I was! This wasn't singularly about Adlin's death. It was about the significance of Adlin's life of faith, trust, and dedication to spiritual truth.

I was surrounded by those who were making a pure and noble effort to find the truth. They were motivated by genuine love. The light in their lives and their true characters made me see the shabbiness of my soul.

The truth that nothing is random or mere coincidence was revealed in the fact that all these amazing people were divinely connected.

Tragedy is always pivotal. This tragedy has caused many of us to change. We were all connected by love from One much greater than ourselves. We had been brought together to advert the plan of darkness.

As I think about Adlin now, all I see is her in the place she always wanted to be, in the loving presence of her Savior.

It has been such a privilege to share the journey with you and all my forever friends. Their constant resolute faithfulness and dedication to truth is beyond anything I could've ever imagined. They are gifts. The Word says that we are to be salt and light in the earth, cleansing and preserving. I believe that our little army did exactly that and will continue to do so. Our lives are entwined together, forever. I know this is not the end. I can feel it.

About the Author

Deborah Hoffman is an award-winning author who utilizes her talents to instill eternal good and compassion into the lives of her readers. Her debut book, *The Last Christmas Tree,* has earned various prestigious gold and silver awards along with numerous five-star editorial reviews.

Growing up on a Nebraskan ranch in the Wildcat Range, Deborah spent her childhood amidst the vast plains, deep canyons, and towering bluffs lined with juniper trees. As a result, her appreciation for nature and God's countless treasures began at an early age. Her devotion to God translates into her friendships and has paved the way for an array of wonderful, unexpected connections.

Before her career as an author, Deborah managed a school district-funded coffee shop, where she facilitated the training of life skills with Special Education placement students and adults from the mental health community. Ultimately, through this unique initiative, she played a key role in preparing these individuals for the "real world" and entering the workforce.

Deborah's affinity for the written word started far before the release of her first book. However, after years of helping her kids with their school assignments and technical writing for inventors, patents, and business plans, she lost touch with her creativity. But as God's plan would have it, a move to a tranquil house in the South breathed fresh air back into the creative corridors of her mind. From that point, poems and stories flowed as if by divine guidance.

Residing in a 121-year-old house with her husband, Deborah reconnected with her creative touches. She vividly recalled countless hours as a child spent in quietude flipping through pages of *Reader's Digest* and *National Geographic*. From age four until the present day, reading has been very near and dear to her heart.

Throughout her life, Deborah has found purpose from her consistent search for knowledge and exhibiting a caring heart towards people. As an author, she is able to encompass this inspiration into her gift of writing and create books that vividly show the importance of foundational truths.

Deborah has a large family with five children, numerous grandchildren, and greats. She and her husband, Virl, have been married for fifty-five years.

She writes children's books, novels, novellas, and short stories. In all of her books, she includes a P.S. at the end. This is her unique signature stamp.

She and her daughter, Abigail, co-founded PipStones LLC, an author services, marketing, and publishing company.

facebook.com/pipstonespublishing

x.com/pip_stones

instagram.com/pipstones

tiktok.com/@pipstonespublishing

ALSO BY DEBORAH HOFFMAN

THE LAST CHRISTMAS TREE

The Last Christmas Tree is a treasured family gift book about a little tree named Twig, a farmer named Mr. B., and the One who is the maker of ALL things. This beautifully illustrated book imparts a lasting message for all ages and seasons.

The Last Christmas Tree Awards:

- *Gold— Christian Book Awards (Picture Book)*
- *Gold— Royal Dragonfly Book Awards (Children's Picture Book)*
- *Silver— Royal Dragonfly Book Awards (Best Illustrations)*
- *Gold— Illumination Awards (Holiday Book)*
- *Bronze— Moonbeam Book Awards (Children's Picture Book)*
- *Honorable Mention— Readers' Favorite Awards (Picture Book)*

The Last Christmas Tree also received Five-Star Editorial Reviews from Kirkus, Readers' Favorite, and Christian Book Award.

Go To: www.pipstones.com for more information.

RESOURCES

PIPSTONES PUBLISHING:

To discover more about Deborah Hoffman's publishing company and the
authors they work with, go to:
https://www.pipstones.com

To seek information about the services that
PipStones offers, go to:
https://www.pipstonesmarketing.com

DEBORAH HOFFMAN - SOCIAL MEDIA:

https://www.Facebook.com/pipstonespublishing
https://www.Instagram.com/pipstones
https://www.Twitter.com/pip_stones
https://www.tiktok.com/@pipstonespublishing